Rail Against Injustice

PENINSULA MYSTERIES SERIES

John Marks

Black Rose Writing | Texas

The author grants the final approval for this literary material.

First printing

This is a work of fiction. Names, characters, businesses, places, events, and incidents are either the products of the author's imagination or used in a fictitious manner. Any resemblance to actual persons, living or dead, or actual events is purely coincidental.

ISBN: 978-1-68513-037-4
PUBLISHED BY BLACK ROSE WRITING
www.blackrosewriting.com

Printed in the United States of America
Suggested Retail Price (SRP) $23.95

Rail Against Injustice is printed in Plantagenet Cherokee

*As a planet-friendly publisher, Black Rose Writing does its best to eliminate unnecessary waste to reduce paper usage and energy costs, while never compromising the reading experience. As a result, the final word count vs. page count may not meet common expectations.

For friends and coworkers at
Michigan's Legislative Service Bureau.

Rail

Against

Injustice

Chapter 1

The western region of Michigan's Upper Peninsula, April 15.

A late-season polar vortex had slipped beneath Canada and into the region like a stealth bomber flying under the radar. Its arctic winds blew open his hoodie and stung his face and neck with frigid gusts of snow. Other than an occasional shiver, however, Stuart Lamar stood unphased, peering over a guardrail barrier at the end of Robbins Pond Road. Extending north from the road's dead end, for as far as he could see, a power line right-of-way carved a narrow path into the dense forest ahead. Where the path disappeared, trees to each side formed a distant notch on the twilit horizon.

The storm was beginning to calm when finally the awaited thing appeared... a shiny orb... hovering out there in the notch as if uncertain of where to go next. Moments later the apparition set its course and began a slow, undulating trek along the path, toward him, growing larger and brighter as it approached.

Soon there came another light, this one from behind. A visitor he was expecting had turned her snowmobile onto Robbins Pond Road and was heading his way. The vehicle's beam cut through the dark woods and, as it neared, revealed a message that had been unceremoniously spray-painted on the guardrail's surface... a name for the shiny phenomenon still floating toward him...

"The Paulding Light."

A few days ago, a shopkeeper in the nearby town of Paulding had referred to it also as the "Mystery Light" when she caught Stuart browsing some souvenir T-shirts trading on its mystique. She went on to share some local lore about the orb with an enthusiasm so palpable that Stuart dared not say he had already heard the story many times before. It was an old tale, set in these remote woods of Michigan's western UP, where once upon a time a railroad brakeman tried to warn an incoming train of rail cars stopped on the tracks by standing in front of the obstacle and waving a lantern. As fate would have it, the train failed to stop, and the brakeman failed to clear the tracks. "And therein lies the mystery," the shopkeeper had said, "whether the shiny orb is the brakeman's lantern, still carried to this day by his wandering ghost, or the light of the train that crushed him, also a ghost, still in search of the station."

The theory of it being the brakeman's lantern seemed to be favored, though tongue in cheek, by a sign posted near the guardrail barrier, which bore the logo of the United States Forest Service and an imprint of an old cartoon character, Casper the Friendly Ghost, beneath the warning: *"Beware—for where you stand, many have encountered the ghost of a railroad brakeman returning to the site of his untimely death."*

Stuart, to be sure, never did believe in ghosts, friendly or otherwise. In fact, he and a crew of fellow students from Michigan Tech University—the school's Society of Photo-Optical Instrumentation Engineers—had twice visited these remote woods on missions to debunk the Mystery Light. The first visit was one year ago, and it was thought then that SPIE would never have to come back given their scientific finding of the orb's true essence.

It was merely the headlights of a motor vehicle traveling along a stretch of highway so far away as to look like a single ball of light floating in the distance.

Simple truths, however, do not always hold sway in a world where, it would seem, an alarming rise in media gaslighting has duped the masses into increasing acceptance of alternative realities. And *this reality*, in SPIE's case one year ago, had joined forces with another— bad timing. Just days after the group released their first study, the SyFy channel happened to release one of its own during a nationally televised episode of *Fact or Faked: Paranormal Files*. SyFy's study, of course, was based not on photo-optical experimentation, as SPIE's was, but instead on something they called "parapsychological testing for electronic voice phenomena." In other words, the SyFy folks applied a ghost voice-finding gadget to the orb, and, to SPIE's chagrin, the gadget yielded results conducive to alternative realities.

According to SyFy, the phenomenon defied explanation.

So, a year later, in response to a ghost-confirmation bias gone viral, SPIE had returned. But this time, to ensure success, they had brought along a big gun, tenured faculty member Professor Lorna Rybicki, whose expertise in the fields of optics and photonics was renowned in scientific circles. And this time, there was no alternative version of reality on the horizon, which meant that SPIE now had the floor and with it was poised to tell the world the simple truth without distraction, once and for all.

There is no Paulding ghost. Period. End of story.

Or so it seemed until earlier this evening.

The snowmobile slid to a stop and Professor Rybicki quickly rose from it, pulled off her helmet, and shook into place her long, straight black hair. She looked first at the path ahead before turning her stare to Stuart. Her emerald-green eyes reflected the only thing glowing in the evening's overcast sky—the orb.

"It's the same damn light we've been looking at all week, Stuart."

"Hello to you too, Lorna."

"For this conversation, maybe you should call me *Professor Rybicki*."

Stuart hadn't called her that since his first day of grad school at MTU. "Professor... Rybicki?" he nervously stammered that day when he walked into her classroom. The two happened to have met the prior evening at a frat party, where he proceeded on the assumption that she was an impressionable undergrad, smitten with a graduate student, and he hit on her all night. Though to no avail. He never got more than her first name. At the time, he thought his paunchy gut and receding hairline had turned off a young coed who failed to appreciate the sophistication of an elder classmate. As it would turn out, he was mistaken not only about who had seniority in age and status but also about who had designs on robbing the other's cradle.

"Oh c'mon, Lorna, lighten up," Stuart replied, his thoughts digressing to the warmth of her body inside her snowsuit and how it would feel pressed against his if he could somehow get in there with her.

She picked up on the sentiment. "No way, Stuart. You'll have no more luck with me than you did on that blackjack table tonight. Is that why you left the casino without saying goodbye?"

He nodded sheepishly at the reminder of his prior misadventure. Earlier that evening the professor had taken her students on a special field trip to the nearby Lac Vieux Desert Casino. It was supposed to be an evening of fun and diversion after their weeklong study of the Paulding Light. But Stuart—the professor's most promising graduate assistant and protégé—decided to use the event for further scientific inquiry. Taking a turn playing teacher, he offered his classmates a lesson in statistics by attempting to demonstrate how he could manipulate probabilities on a blackjack table with a card-counting technique he had learned in Vegas. It was a form of cheating, of course, but Stuart assured his classmates that he would stop once he was up a hundred dollars on the ten-dollar table.

He was down two hundred when he stepped outside for some fresh air, and he never returned.

"Serves you right," Lorna said. "So why'd you come here? And where's your coat?"

"I went for a drive, not a hike. But then when I saw how hard it was snowing, it made me wonder what the orb might look like in these conditions."

She glanced in the direction of the orb's location a few seconds ago, where it had disappeared. "It didn't look any different to me. Why'd you make a big fuss about it when you called?"

"Because the one I saw then *was* different—in fact, *very* different."

She stepped close and gave him a long, reprimanding stare. "Be careful about what you say next, Stuart, if you really want to be a scientist someday. I can dismiss your prior rant over the phone about Paulding ghosts and goblins as being a poor attempt at humor after having spent five consecutive days out here in this wilderness, staring at the horizon. But right now I can clearly see that you're serious—that you know you're talking to the prof who will make or break your chances of getting into MTU's doctoral program next fall. So, with that in mind, tell me what you saw out here this evening."

He took a deep breath. "Well, like I was trying to say when I called, it started out as a red ember floating on the horizon, like a big spark from burning wood or coal. And then it came at me and—"

"Oh please, Stuart, knock off the *bullshit* and just tell me what you really saw."

"I'm trying to. Why won't you hear me out?"

"Because I've heard this nonsense before, and so have you, during scores of interviews with wide-eyed Paulding Light groupies. We never saw anything to corroborate their stories about red embers floating toward this viewing area."

"If you let me, maybe I can corroborate it right now."

"You can't. Because it's not possible. You know damn well what's out there. You've seen it all week."

What he had seen over the past week, no doubt, was an optical illusion—the effects of distance and diffraction on human perception of a motor vehicle's twin lights some five miles away, where the degree of angular separation between them was so miniscule that it couldn't be resolved by the naked eye. As a result, the taillights of a northbound vehicle converged into what seemed to be a single light, a red orb, drifting away from the viewer into the distance; conversely, the headlights of a southbound vehicle converged into what seemed to be a single white orb that floated toward the viewer, like the one they had just seen.

"I'm telling you Lorna, what I saw was red, *and it was coming at me*, the way only white lights did this week."

"Was it flashing?"

"No, it wasn't an emergency vehicle."

"How do you know? Did you put a telescope on it?"

He shook his head. "I didn't bring one."

"Do you remember what you saw this week, as clear as day, when you did?"

Of course I do, he thought, nodding slowly. The very first test SPIE had done that week was a simple viewing of the orb with a high-powered, night-vision telescope. He was the first to look, and at the time an atmospheric inversion layer provided a line of sight so clear that he could make out not only the features of the passing cars five miles off but also an "Adopt a Highway" road sign that they were passing. With this find and an assist from Google Maps, SPIE was able to ascertain the orb's specific location and replicate and record various versions of it with their own vehicles, sometimes messing with their headlights in predetermined patterns—flashing them or alternating between high and low beams—to corroborate the orb's worldly source.

"And I suppose it goes without saying," Lorna continued, "that you have no spectrographic analysis of your strangely behaving red orb."

"It was *not* an orb," Stuart replied defensively. "Like I said before, it was an ember, you know, from a fire. And I didn't need a spectrograph to tell me that its characteristics were *not* like those of an artificial light. It was something burning."

"Okay, maybe it was an ember—from somebody's campfire."

"No, it couldn't have been. It came straight at me, never deviating from the path. And then when it got about halfway, all of a sudden it switched to a white light, something that, at that point, *did* look artificial... but kept coming, without missing a beat."

"Sounds like two cars to me," Lorna said, "the taillights of one heading north, followed by the headlights of one going south, optically distorted by the hallucinating effects of hypothermia, seeing as how you were less than half dressed for the blizzard that passed through here."

"I was fine. Heck, I even had the presence of mind to try recording it with the video camera on my cellphone... but..."

"But what?"

He unlocked his phone and showed her the recording, which turned out to be nothing but a black screen. "That's how it recorded."

"How *what* recorded?" Lorna snapped. "There's nothing there—because you never saw these lights you're talking about now."

"Where's the forest, Lorna? It wasn't fully dark yet. Even if nothing was floating around out there, I should have at least gotten a recording of the trees."

"What are you saying, Stuart? That this ghost commandeered your cellphone's camera and wouldn't let itself be recorded?"

"And look at this," he continued, ignoring her comment. "At the bottom of the screen, there's a timer going. It gives accurate reads on the duration of my sighting—which I'm telling you happened—and shows it was close to ten minutes. I estimate that the red ember showed itself for about half that time, and the white light for the other half. That's way too long for passing cars on that short stretch of highway."

She shrugged. "Maybe they were slowed down by all the snow we got tonight."

"I doubt it, Lorna. We're in the heart of the UP, and you know how diligent Yoopers are about clearing their roads of snow. Tonight's no exception. I'll bet you had to ride your snowmobile on the shoulder to get here."

Lorna did not disagree, he knew, because she couldn't.

"And the white light," Stuart added, "started out at least twice as big as any of the orbs we've seen out here, and it had grown at least two times bigger when it..."

Lorna leaned forward to prevent him from avoiding eye contact during a pause in his account. "When it what?" she asked.

Stuart was making a conscious effort to slow his breathing. He did not want to sound as panicked as he had felt when it happened. "When... it communicated with me."

"What?" Lorna shrieked. "Are you telling me you talked with this brakeman's ghost?"

Stuart stared off, still grappling with his realization of what had happened and the prospect of saying it out loud for the first time. "It… wasn't the brakeman," he said haltingly. "It was… the train. And the communication wasn't verbal… it was telepathic."

"Oh, now I understand," Lorna replied, her eyes rolling and her words dripping with sarcasm. "That explains why the paranormal freak show on the SyFy channel struck out last year. They were trying to detect the electronic *voice* phenomena of a ghost that doesn't talk—it *mind melds*."

"Please, Lorna, try to be objective for a moment, and think about it. Most trains back in those days used coal to operate. That explains the initial appearance of the red ember. It came from the burning coal. And what I saw next—the oversized white orb—that was the headlight on the engine."

"And the mind-melding thing," Lorna pressed, "what was that all about?"

"I dunno. I guess trains from back then—or for that matter, trains nowadays—can't, you know… talk."

"Oh my God, Stuart! You sound insane!"

Although he nodded in agreement, he had no intention of retracting a word he had said. Lorna seemed to understand his resolve. "Okay," she said, her lips pursed as she strained for composure. "Let's pretend that I'm taking you seriously for a moment, and that I'm willing to entertain a belief in ghost trains visiting Michigan's northern woods. It still makes no sense that you would have seen one here, given the history of this part of the woods."

"What are you talking about?" Stuart objected. "This was logging country a century ago. There were all kinds of railroads running through these woods that are now buried in the underbrush."

She raised her eyebrows and shook her head. "Not here, sweetheart. Not along the path used by the orb. Didn't you read the analysis done by SPIE's historical unit?"

In fact he had. It explained how the path was actually the remains of a military road authorized by Abraham Lincoln during the Civil War in anticipation of a British attack through Canada. It was never the site of any railroad facilities.

"It's not trying to follow its old tracks," Stuart replied. "It has some other reason for coming here. It always has."

"Is that what it told you, Stuart—when your minds became one?"

He didn't respond.

"Well, why does it come here rather than where its old tracks once were?"

"I don't know. It didn't elaborate on that. It had something more important to tell me."

"And what would that be?"

After a long pause, Stuart asked, "Did you bring the flashlight?"

"Sure. Why did you ask for it?"

Stuart gazed into the now black forest. "It wants me to go out there."

"The train?"

He nodded.

"It wants you to go down the path, into the woods?"

He nodded again and added, "To look for something."

"For what?"

"I'm not sure. I just know it has to be found before the spring melt."

"Spring melt? Why would that be an issue for whatever's out there?"

Stuart shrugged and then, after another long pause, he watched her retrieve a large flashlight buried deep in her snowsuit. She held it out for him to take, but he didn't. He instead looked at her longingly.

"Oh no, Stuart, don't even think for one second about me joining you."

He smiled, thinking about just that.

"Are you serious? Do you really want me to go with you, despite my utter disbelief?"

"No, I want you to go with me *because* of your utter disbelief."

"Oh really, and why is that?" she asked, stifling a laugh. "So you can have a skeptic confirm some premonition that you believe was telepathically planted in your head by a ghost train?"

"Exactly."

She sighed deeply as she handed him the flashlight. "All right, Mr. Train Whisperer, lead the way."

Chapter 2

Watersmeet, Michigan, two weeks later.

Harlan Holmes and his life partner, Roz Cortez, were nearing the end of a journey across the Upper Peninsula, westbound on Highway 2, when an isolated public square—the Watersmeet Plaza—appeared ahead. A neon sign in the parking lot welcomed them to the town and described it as the "Home of the Nimrods™".

Harlan looked up at the sign after stepping out of their vehicle. "Why would they call themselves that? And what's up with the trademark? You'd have to *be* a Nimrod to steal that name."

"It's actually an honorable title," Roz replied.

"Since when?"

"Since ancient times."

This insight only confused him more.

"You obviously haven't read your Bible," Roz said. "The Book of Genesis gave Noah's great-grandson that title when describing him as a mighty hunter before the Lord."

Roz would know, Harlan thought, but not due to any expertise she had about the Bible. She would know because she had lived in this town until age ten, when her parents divorced; and although she and her mother then moved three hundred miles south to Milwaukee, she frequently visited throughout much of the rest of her childhood to see her father, who remained behind for his job.

"That title underscores the rugged lifestyle of many people from around here," Roz added, "folks barely on the grid who hunt, fish, and live off the land to a degree that you would never even consider trying."

The couple shared a look at their fully equipped, thirty-foot Winnebago coach, which he had insisted on renting for an upcoming week of camping deep in the Ottawa National Forest. In tow was another creature comfort, his Jeep Rubicon, which he had also insisted they bring along.

"What can I say, Roz? I'm no Nimrod."

"Don't underestimate yourself, dear," she said as she turned toward the other road that formed the intersection where they stood, Highway 45, and looked north. Five miles in that direction was the turnoff for their campground, Robbins Pond Road. But he knew that her focus was much closer, just a few blocks away, where there once stood the Peterson Lumber Mill, her father's place of employment until he lost his job in the mid-seventies. That was about the time her visits to Watersmeet ended. She was a young teen then. Now she was pushing sixty, though not quite as imminently as he was.

For Harlan, the upcoming milestone birthday would not be just a number. It would be yet another of many metrics conspiring against him and his hope that, after thirty-eight years in law enforcement and private investigation, he might last for at least a few more. The other metrics pertained mostly to physical fitness—measures of speed, strength, and endurance—that he had seen fall off in recent years like the Dow Jones upon the first reports of a Coronavirus pandemic. The rapid decline was due mostly to old sports injuries and early-onset osteoarthritis, which these days had left him bone-on-bone in both knees and one shoulder.

"What makes you so sure about my capacity for wilderness survival—*dear*?" Harlan replied in a tone Roz didn't deserve. He caught himself blaming her for his career ending ahead of schedule, when in fact she was merely responsible for suggesting that they clear their calendars and visit the distant woods of the western UP for a quiet week alone to think and talk about the possibility of retirement. "Sorry," he added.

Her look back suggested that she knew exactly what was going on with him. She always did, beginning the moment they first met a few years ago. Both were private eyes at the time and happened to be working the same case, though from different angles. He had broken into the house of a person of interest to conduct a search, surreptitiously he thought, until he found himself at the point of her gun and learned that she was working for the homeowner. Under the circumstances, she could have put a bullet in his head with impunity. But she heard him out, and fortunately, their clients' interests were aligned. The two of them went on to deepen that alliance both professionally and personally. On the professional side, they eventually brought justice to a gang of drug dealers who had murdered several associates of their respective clients.

Roz returned to surveying her old stomping grounds, as Harlan continued to survey her, comparing the effects of time on her person with its effects on his. Everything beneath her graying hair was the new forty when they met, and still was—her soft face only gently seasoned by years her body would not concede. But her greatest resilience came from within. She held firm to ideals of professional integrity that he had long ago let slip away, beginning the day he began taking on some old-school Chicago mobsters as clients. The wiseguys whom he served in the case the couple first worked together, however, had to be his last; that was the one condition she had placed on their partnership going forward.

"Well, what's the verdict?" Harlan asked as Roz completed a full turn.

"It's just what I expected, but only because I checked it out online before we left. Nothing matches up with my childhood memories. There used to be railway facilities down the street there," she said, pointing north. "They served the lumber mill, which was where that Polaris dealer is now. And on the corner across from us was Minnie's Diner, where that Citgo station is now."

"What about this place right here?" Harlan asked, turning back to the row of businesses before them in the plaza. "Did it look this way when you were a kid?"

"Some of it. The gas and propane pumps were here as I recall. And so was the convenience store, Nordine's Foodland, but I remember it being smaller."

"That's odd. Usually when you go back to someplace where you were a kid, you remember things being bigger. You think they remodeled the store and added some square footage?"

"I don't know," Roz replied as her gaze drifted to the adjacent businesses in the plaza... the Roadhouse Grill and, adjoining it, the Roadhouse Tavern. "Now, those places were built since I was last here. Either that, or my memory is seriously losing its battle with time. You think I'm getting old, Harlan?"

"I'm the one getting old," he quipped. "And hungry. Let's check out the Grill."

Chapter 3

The mouthwatering aroma of that day's dinner special—broasted chicken—welcomed them to the Roadhouse Grill and one of its few available tables, which they snagged ahead of others entering behind them. It was a small table for two along a paneled wall decorated with the head of a deer wearing a Green Bay Packers baseball cap, a reminder that Michiganders this far north and west lived much closer to Wisconsin's big cities than Michigan's. Harlan took the seat facing the deer so that Roz would have a view of their fellow diners. She was curious, he knew, about whether she might recognize any of them from her past connection to the area.

He studied the deer and its surrounding wall décor, an eclectic blend of highway-related artifacts—old license plates, hubcaps, street signs, and the like—in keeping with the establishment's roadhouse theme. The artifacts steered his thoughts in reverse along the roads they had traveled that day, back home to Traverse City and his uncertainty about life's next chapter upon their return there next week.

"Can I get you something to drink?" a table server asked.

Harlan's attention snapped back to the moment. "Decaf and a water, please," he answered.

"Same here," Roz added as she continued scanning the room.

"Would you folks also like to put in your dinner order now? If you're having the chicken, you don't want to wait. It goes fast."

"Sounds good," Harlan said. Roz simply nodded. Her distant gaze was now fixed.

"You're staring, Roz," Harlan said after the table server left. He glanced over his shoulder and spotted an elderly man waiting in line at the cash register, looking back at her. "Do you know him?"

"I'm not sure. He doesn't look familiar. But he's been staring at me since he came out of the men's room."

Harlan continued sneaking peaks at the man at the cash register, who paid his bill and then began a slow trek across the restaurant toward them, his progress impeded by his use of a walker that had to be manipulated between tables and chairs along the way. Even absent the obstructions, Harlan thought, he would have taken a while, given his age and physical limitations. He finally arrived at their table, right behind their drink order.

"I'm sorry if I'm intruding, ma'am," he said to Roz, "but you look a lot like someone I think I've seen before."

Roz's eyes widened. "Well, I used to live in Watersmeet when I was a child, and then after moving away, I continued visiting until I was a teen. My name is Roz Cortez."

The man repeated the name, "Roz Cortez…" and then shook his head. "I must be mistaken. It doesn't ring a bell."

"Maybe you're recalling my mother, Joanna Cortez. People used to say I took after her."

The man continued shaking his head and then abruptly jerked his walker around to leave.

"Hold on," Roz said. "Do you have a name?"

"Oh my, I've completely forgotten my manners," the man said, turning back. "The name's Ed Charlevoix, but people around here call me Doc, because I used to be one before I retired."

Roz stuck out her hand. "Nice to meet you, Doc. Like I said, I'm Roz Cortez. And my partner here is—"

"That's it!" Doc exclaimed as he stopped his hand short of hers.

Almost every patron in the Roadhouse Grill turned to look at them.

"That's what?" Roz asked.

"I know who you are. You and your partner." Doc turned to Harlan and continued to speak excitedly. "You were in the photo, too, along with her on the front page of the Iron Mountain Daily Globe. It was the headline story, about how you two busted those drug smugglers in the eastern UP, on Drummond Island as I recall."

"You're right, Doc!" shouted a patron seated halfway across the room. "I recognize him too. The dude has the same name as that British PI from those old novels. You know, Inspector Sherlock—"

Harlan cleared his throat. "The name's *Harlan* Holmes," he said, glimpsing at Roz as she rolled her eyes. This was not the first time they had been outed in a northern Michigan setting for their highly publicized work on their first case together. The last time, however, was well over a year ago, and they had come to think that their fifteen minutes of fame had finally ended. Apparently, they were wrong.

"You folks must have a slow news cycle way out here in the western UP," Harlan said.

Doc laughed. "Truth is, we do, Mr. Holmes. We just don't get very many of those kinds of crimes here."

"What are you talking about, Doc?" came the other patron again, piping in like a bystander shouting from the gallery. "We got us the Mystery Light murder just a couple weeks ago."

"That's true," Doc said, nodding at the bystander. "We did get that one."

"What murder?" Harlan asked Doc.

"You don't know?"

"I'm not from here. How would I know?"

"Well, do you live in Michigan?"

"Sure, downstate, just under the Bridge."

"Seems close enough for a big story like our Mystery Light murder to make your news."

Harlan thought for a moment. "I don't think it did. I would remember something with a name like that. What's the Mystery Light?"

"You don't know that either? Seriously?"

"Careful, Doc," interjected the bystander again. "If memory serves, Inspector Holmes can play some wily tricks when he's on a case."

Doc grinned at the couple. "I get it," he said, his voice now soft and accusatory. "You two don't just *know* about the Mystery Light murder; you're here to *investigate* it, undercover, aren't you?"

"Wait… what?" Harlan replied. "You can't be serious."

When Doc's expression showed that he was, Harlan added, "Listen, Doc, you're way off base. My partner and I came up here for a vacation. For crying out loud, man, look out the window. What PIs in their right mind go undercover driving a monster Winnebago?"

Several patrons leaned toward windows and looked out, including the vocal bystander. "So that's your ride, Inspector?" he said. "Where're you going with that contraption?"

"Robbins Pond Campground, if it's any concern to you."

"Aha!" the bystander blurted. "I knew it. Out there by the Light."

Perplexed, Harlan turned to his partner. "What the hell, Roz, did you know about any of this when you picked the campground?"

"About the Mystery Light? Sure. Saw it myself when I was a kid. But I know nothing about any murder out there. I'm beginning to have second thoughts about coming here, Harlan. The place has changed, and I don't know the people anymore. Maybe we should just pick up and push on to the Porcupine Mountains. There's some good camping there too."

"Not so fast, you two," Doc said. He reached into a handbag hanging on the front of his walker and pulled out a newspaper. "The front-page story is all about the murder," he said, sliding the paper across the table to Harlan. "If it's not a bother, Mr. Holmes, I'd be interested in your professional perspective on some of the underlying facts." Then Doc turned to face the crowded dining room and said, voice raised, "My new friend here—Ms. Roz Cortez—has roots in Watersmeet. But it's been a long time. Anybody know the name?"

Seconds later the faint voice of a woman answered from across the room. "I knew a Joanna Cortez some forty-plus years ago. We sang in the church choir together."

Roz sprang to her feet. "You knew my mother?"

"I guess I did, if she's the same Joanna. You must be her little one. I think I see the resemblance."

Roz hurried across the room to chat with the old family acquaintance as Harlan turned his attention to the newspaper article about the Mystery Light murder. It began with an account of the legendary brakeman's ghost that was cryptic at best for an outsider unfamiliar with the story. Curious, Harlan decided to accept Doc's invitation and explore it.

"Do folks around here really believe there's a ghost traipsing around the woods near Robbins Pond Road?" he asked, looking up from the paper.

The outspoken bystander had joined them and was helping himself to Roz's empty chair, his slender right hand extended. "I'm Lanny Lynchowski. Glad to make your acquaintance."

After shaking Harlan's hand, Lanny added, "What we believe, Mr. Holmes, is that a lot of interested tourists are willing to entertain the possibility. And those tourists are important to our local economy."

"So then, what is it that people really see out there?"

"Headlights," Lanny answered, "from cars traveling along a stretch of Highway 45. It's no coincidence that the sightings of those lights started in the mid-sixties, when they put in that part of the road."

"That road doesn't explain what I've seen out there," remarked a young patron from the next table, "not the red light that floats right up to the guardrail and changes color to white when it gets close. Those lights sure as heck aren't made by cars. They're coming from—"

Doc raised a hand up from his walker and shook his head. "Not now, Sandra." Returning to Harlan, he said, "Most folks see it the way Lanny does, myself included, but there are some who insist on supernatural explanations."

"Like one of the hikers out there a couple weeks ago, from MTU," Harlan said. "According to this article, they were on a mission to debunk all the supernatural theories, until one of them had a change of heart when they walked the Light's path and found a dead body."

"It was just a misunderstanding," Doc countered quickly, his tone defensive. "After stumbling upon that corpse, one of them jumped to an irrational conclusion about the ghost somehow being involved. That's all."

Harlan noticed for the first time a college graduation ring on Doc's right hand. Perhaps it explained the man's reaction. "Did you go to MTU, Doc?"

"That's where I did my undergraduate studies a long time ago. It's the western UP's premier university. And I can assure you that the scientists who work there don't believe in ghosts."

Harlan reread a couple paragraphs about the hikers from MTU and then looked back at his guests. "One of them apparently believes—the leader of the investigation no less, this Professor Lorna Rybicki. She's quoted as saying that the dead guy had been run over by the ghost of some train—the same train, she says, that ran over a brakeman caught on the tracks a hundred years ago."

"For Pete's sake, Holmes—that's fake news!" Lanny argued, chiming back in. "They're taking what she said about the train out of context. Ranger K told me and Doc that himself."

"Ranger who?" Harlan asked.

"Ranger Kole Koerber. He's a regular here at the Grill. Works for the Forest Service. Kole was the first responder. He told us that when he got to the scene, some MTU professor was beside herself after finding a body and was spouting off all kinds of stuff that made no sense."

"Like she just flipped out?" Harlan asked.

"Exactly," Doc said. "She and her grad assistant were out there hiking the path that night, and she came across a scarf sticking out of the snow. She pulled on it, and wouldn't you know, it was still attached to the dead guy. His frozen head popped out of the snowbank and freaked her out. Took her two days to recant her story about the ghost train being involved. In the meantime, her grad assistant did all he could to straighten the story out with all the cops and reporters who were hounding them for interviews. He told Ranger K that she'd been working long days for the past week. Exhaustion, he said, coupled with the shock of finding that body, triggered a temporary break in her sanity."

"Of course, when the grad assistant's account of things finally got some press," Lanny added, "it was too late. The retraction can't seem to undo public perception of the professor's initial hysteria, which makes her and the rest of us folks up here in the western UP look like a bunch of superstitious Yoopers."

Harlan looked back at the paper for the name of the levelheaded graduate assistant, Stuart Lamar, and then continued reading. The initial theory attributed to the professor was indeed misguided. The victim was not hit by a train, let alone the ghost of one. He was murdered by a being of this world, a man who thought his victim was having an affair with his wife. At least that was the theory the prosecutor had offered to the media.

Harlan paused over the names of those involved, wondering whether Roz might recognize them. "Are these guys from around here," he asked, "the dead lover, Zach Romanelli, and the jealous husband who they say killed him, George Viola?"

Doc and Lanny both nodded.

"Well, what do you know about them?" Harlan pressed. "Did this Viola guy have any history of—"

Doc jerked his hand up from his walker to silence Harlan, so hurriedly he almost fell over. "What's wrong?" Harlan asked.

"Well... uh," Doc stammered, "your food's here."

A table server had just arrived, balancing a large tray full of food in one hand while carrying a pot of decaf coffee in the other. She was not the table server who had taken the order, however.

"Stevie?" Doc said to her, his voice filled with surprise. "I didn't know you were working tonight."

"I wasn't scheduled to," she said. "They called me in to help with the dinner rush."

"Well... uh... how long have you been here?"

"Long enough," she answered, staring sternly at Doc and then at Lanny.

"Excuse me, Miss," Harlan said, unsure of what was happening. "One of those plates is for the woman over there, sitting at the big table by the counter."

"I know," Stevie said. She glanced over at Roz, who was now surrounded by talkative locals. "I'll make sure she gets it." Stevie refilled Harlan's coffee and shot another stern look at his dinner guests before heading for Roz's table.

"Way to go boys," said the woman at the next table, the one whom Doc had silenced earlier for speaking of ghosts.

"Give us a break, Sandra," Lanny replied. "How were we supposed to know that Stevie was here?"

Harlan watched as the unexpected waitress served Roz her dinner. "Does she have something to do with this?" he asked, tapping his finger on the newspaper as it lay on the table.

Doc cleared his throat, leaned over his walker, and whispered, "Her name is Stevie Viola."

Harlan looked down at the paper to confirm his recollection of the alleged killer's name. "Is she George Viola's wife? The woman who had the affair with the victim?"

Doc nodded. "But it wasn't the usual kind of affair, like the kind you're thinking of, or that George imagined when he killed him."

Harlan dove back into the article.

"You won't learn about it there, Mr. Holmes," Lanny said.

Harlan set the paper aside as Lanny continued, "The victim, Mr. Romanelli, was Stevie's long-lost brother."

"Her brother?" Harlan remarked. "She was sleeping with her—"

"Not so loud," Doc admonished, looking at the kitchen door that Stevie had just used to exit the dining area. "That's a misunderstanding too. She and her brother weren't really lovers. It just kind of looked that way for a while, until..." Doc paused as the kitchen door opened, for the return of a different table server, it turned out.

"Until when?" Harlan asked.

"Until it was too damn late for retractions to undo that one too," Doc said. "Talk about misguided stereotypes—that's the last kind we want outsiders to have about us Yoopers."

At that moment, Stevie returned to the dining area.

Doc again leaned over his walker and lowered his tone to a whisper. "Maybe we should continue this conversation some other time, Mr. Holmes, assuming you and your partner are still planning on camping at Robbins Pond."

***

His dinner guests had left shortly after their social faux pas, and Harlan was now picking at the bones of his chicken for the last few morsels. He considered wandering over to Roz's table to help finish hers, but he preferred people watching for the time being, especially those whom Roz continued to meet across the room during the meal.

"Can I get you anything else, sir? Perhaps dessert?"

Harlan looked up at his table server, Stevie Viola, and noticed now some features he had overlooked before—a tiny gap in her front teeth, a small crook in her nose, and a slight asymmetry to her thin face. These imperfections, however, managed not to detract from his initial impression of her as an attractive woman in her early thirties.

"No thanks," he replied. "I think I'm ready for the check."

She placed the check on the table, extended her hand toward his plate, and paused. "Would you like me to get this out of your way?"

"Actually, no. I think I'll keep picking at it until my partner is ready to leave."

She pulled back her hand and then paused it again, over the check. "Your customer copy is underneath the one you pay at the cash register," she said, pointing down at it.

"Okay."

"Right here," she added, pressing down with her finger and sliding the merchant copy off the customer copy. "This one underneath. It's for *you.*"

"O… kay," Harlan replied as he watched her press her finger again, this time onto the customer copy, and slide it closer to him before turning to leave.

Of course he had to look. He could see her watching as he did. She had stopped by the cash register and was staring back at him. And then, after he flipped the customer copy over, she turned away and headed for the kitchen door.

Chapter 4

The events at the Roadhouse Grill delayed Harlan and Roz's arrival to the Ottawa National Forest, which they now accessed via Robbins Pond Road. A half mile ahead the road would come to a dead end at the guardrail viewing area for the Mystery Light. Stopping there, however, would have to wait for another time if they were going to set up camp before nightfall.

They veered off the dead-end road onto a narrow dirt drive that cut deep into the forest, their Winnebago scraping through the undergrowth on both sides as it sloshed through the spring melt. After five miles of slipping and sliding through the woods, they came upon a tiny sign indicating their arrival to Robbins Pond Campground.

It had been advertised online as a limited-services, deep-woods campground. Harlan stepped out of the Winnebago and did a slow three-sixty to assess just what that meant in person, on the ground: three campsites, an outhouse, and nothing else. No running water, no electrical hookups, no trash or recycling pickup, and, no wonder, no other campers.

The couple, nevertheless, did not intend to rough it in the wild during the week ahead. After detaching the Jeep, they set up their Winnebago on one campsite and, on another, pitched a six-person tent to use as an enclosed space for storing trash, dirty laundry, and anything else they didn't want to live with but had to keep because of the rule that whatever dispersed campers pack into the woods, they must pack out. To supplement the Winnebago's many amenities, they had also brought along a portable filtration system to sanitize the nearby creek water, a battery-powered generator for various electrical appliances, and several solar-ready charging banks capable of storing the sun's energy for powering up cell phones, iPads, and the like.

Roz had been doing most of the talking during the drive to the campground and, after their arrival, while they set things up. She was excited to have connected with some people at the Grill who remembered her family back when they lived in Watersmeet. Most exciting was the prospect of reconnecting with a close childhood friend, Patty Rock, the daughter of the woman who had sung with Roz's mother in the church choir. Patty now lived in Land O' Lakes, Wisconsin, which was just eight miles south of Watersmeet. The two old friends had already talked by phone and had made plans to visit the next day.

Harlan was content to listen. It postponed breaking the news about an upcoming visit of his own that was still in the making—a meeting with a prospective client, Stevie Viola. Her handwritten note on the back of his dinner tab had provided a phone number and asked him to text or call later that evening to arrange a meeting if he might be interested in taking her husband's case. He was, but he was also quite sure that Roz would feel differently about it.

It was after dark, and he still had not scheduled the meeting or said anything about it to Roz. At this point, he figured he would be better off begging for forgiveness than asking for permission. "I'll be right back, Roz. I have a couple things to take care of in the camper."

Roz had been assembling materials to build a huge campfire and would soon have it blazing. He sensed her intentions. It really was—or should have been—a perfect evening for what she seemed to have in mind for the two of them, now alone in this secluded setting. The sky was clear, the moon was nearly full, and the air was a crisp but comfortable forty-four degrees.

"Be sure to grab a bottle of wine, sweetheart," Roz said. "Something nice."

"Sure thing, Roz. I'll try to surprise you."

Once inside the camper, Harlan seated himself at a small dinner table and composed a text to Stevie Viola. It said, "My partner and I would like to discuss the case with you in person. When can you meet?"

He then added Roz's name to the recipient list. And then, looking out the window at her, he waited until she struck a match before clicking "send."

While Roz was occupied with creating the campfire, Harlan pulled up the settings on his cellphone and turned to the task of creating a Wi-Fi hotspot to get his laptop computer online. He could use that device much faster than his phone to surf the web for information about the Mystery Light murder—but only if he could somehow get a good internet connection out here in the middle of nowhere.

About the time Harlan was reading the second item produced by his Google search, Roz entered the camper. He glanced over the top of the computer screen. She, too, must have had five bars' worth of reception on her cellphone, which she held in her left hand, screen lit. Her expression was stern. Of her intentions now, he had no doubts.

"How are we getting such a good connection out here?" Harlan asked, trying to deflect for a bit longer the impending confrontation.

"There's a cell tower nearby," she replied matter-of-factly, "centrally located out here to service Watersmeet and Paulding. That was one of the reasons I chose this campground."

"Good thinking."

"What I was thinking, Harlan, was that we could use it for *Netflix*— not the stunt you're pulling right now, behind my back."

"Actually, Roz, the whole thing came about right in front of you, at the Roadhouse Grill."

"Do you mean to say that while I was on one side of the Grill reconnecting with old friends, you were on the other side pitching our PI services to Mrs. Viola?"

Harlan slid the note from Stevie Viola across the table for Roz to see. "She's the one who did the soliciting," he replied.

Roz looked up from the note, her expression unchanged. "I don't give a damn how it happened. Why didn't you say something before you volunteered me for a meeting?"

"No offense, Roz, but you've been a little chatty ever since we left the Grill, you know, about all the catching up you did with the folks there. I didn't quite know how to interject this development."

She did not have to tell him how weak that excuse was. He would have to do better, but that could get him into his real reason, an elephant in the room that he sensed she wanted him to acknowledge first. He fidgeted in his seat before doing so.

"Okay, look, I know that this is the first vacation we've ever taken together. And I know that the reason for taking it in these woods, where it's just the two of us, is so we can reflect and talk seriously without distraction. But this thing we're supposed to talk about... it... how do I say..."

"It scares you," Roz offered, "because retirement reminds you of your mortality."

"No—because it pronounces *dead* who I've been for forty years."

He looked away as she sat down beside him at the table. "It doesn't have to be a complete break, Harlan. I mean, lots of cops and PIs find law-related things to do in retirement. You know, part-time jobs with less risk."

"Like what? Being a *fucking* mall cop?"

She didn't flinch at the comment but instead took one of his hands in hers.

He looked up, into her dark, penetrating eyes. "I'm sorry I said that, Roz."

"It's okay."

"No, not the way I said it. You didn't deserve that just because you're willing to speak the truth. I get it. Better than you know. I live in this arthritic body, and fight with what it tells me every day."

They continued staring at each other until the simultaneous pings of their cellphones alerted them to incoming texts. Harlan pulled his hand from hers and reached for his cellphone as she brought hers up from under the table. It was a response from Stevie Viola, saying, "I'd like to meet tonight."

"I'll call her back," Harlan said, "to cancel."

He was serious. He was about to tap the callback button, when—

"Hold on," Roz said. She took a deep breath before adding, "I guess I don't see the harm in having a simple conversation with this woman. Besides, from what I heard during dinner, it doesn't sound like her husband has much of a case anyway."

"You learned something about it?"

"Of course I did. It's a small town, and I met a bunch of its people tonight."

"What did they tell you?"

"I'll let you hear it from Mrs. Viola herself."

"You will?"

"Don't get too excited, Harlan. I have some conditions."

He leaned forward and stared at her intently.

"For starters, no matter where this little diversion takes us, when it's over, you and I are going to take our vacation, and we're going to continue this conversation."

He nodded, as she continued. "And the case will end before it gets started—tonight—if we learn that the Violas can't pay the usual rate for our services."

"Is there some reason to think they can't, Roz?"

"Are you kidding? She slings grub in a roadside diner for a living, and he's in jail."

"Maybe he was doing something a little more productive before the arrest."

"And maybe you need to read further into your Google search, Harlan. The man's battling alcoholism and hasn't held a steady job since the birth of their child two years ago."

"Well, even if they're struggling, it wouldn't be the first time that we've—"

"No way, Harlan. No friends-and-family discount on this one. We came here for a vacation, and until it begins, we get paid for any work we might do."

Harlan thought better of pointing out that half of the services would be his, and that perhaps he should be entitled to waive his share if he chose to. "Okay, Roz. I'm on board with all that. Anything else?"

"Just one other thing." She stood up and looked out the window, her face reflecting the orange glow of her campfire roaring outside. "You get to build the next one."

Chapter 5

"We'll be there in thirty minutes," Harlan said at the conclusion his phone conversation with Stevie Viola. He and Roz then went outside and put out the campfire before getting in the Jeep and on the road.

Roz drove while Harlan used his phone to resume the internet search he had begun earlier on his laptop computer. He had previously paused the search just as he learned where the murder victim, Zach Romanelli, worked before his death—the law firm of Lesko & Craine, P.C. The name of the firm was familiar, given its location in Harlan's hometown of Traverse City and its employment of a couple criminal defense attorneys whom he had met in the past. Romanelli had practiced tax law, however, so it was no surprise that he and Harlan had never crossed paths.

Lesko & Craine's website included a section with links to bios of the firm's attorneys. Harlan scrolled through them until he reached and clicked on the name "Zachary Romanelli." The bio that popped up was impressive. Romanelli had graduated second in his class from Harvard Law ten years ago and had since developed an extensive client list of mostly corporate-owned big-box stores and home improvement centers.

"Dammit," Harlan complained as his screen froze on the client list. He had been thrown offline, ironically, when they got *out* of the woods. "I lost the cell tower."

"It'll come back," Roz said. "It's supposed to provide service all the way through town. What were you looking at?"

"Background information on the murder victim."

"Ahh, the dark-store attorney," Roz said. "I heard about him today at the Roadhouse Grill."

Harlan glanced down at his frozen screen and the list of Romanelli's retail clients still there, as he repeated the phrase, "Dark-store attorney?"

"It's what some of the locals called him when the subject came up at dinner tonight. It has to do with a property tax write-off that he invented. They called it the dark-store loophole."

"Never heard of it," Harlan said. "Is it something we should know about for our own purposes? You know how much I dislike paying property taxes."

"I don't think it applies to homeowners and small businesses. From what I heard, it only works for major retailers, you know, big-box stores."

"Figures," Harlan said.

They were getting close to downtown Watersmeet, heading south on Highway 45, when Harlan's cellphone reception returned to two bars. He decided to run a search for "dark-store loophole" and reviewed a few items in the list that elaborated on its underlying theory. The idea seemed counterintuitive. According to the theory, no matter how big and prosperous any given big-box store might be, its value for property tax purposes should be assessed as if the store were shut down after going out of business—in other words, as if it were a *dark store*.

Harlan read further into his search results. Proponents of the dark-store theory explained that big-box stores are effectively worthless at the point of closure and sale, and that this prospective obsolescence should offset their current property tax bills—no matter how much money they currently make. Opponents of the theory, mostly tax assessors, countered that the theory defies common sense and pointed out some suspect examples of its application, including the first case to reach the courts.

That test case, it turned out, was what had earned Zach Romanelli his "dark-store attorney" moniker. He was the lead attorney who litigated it before the Michigan Tax Tribunal and, in the process, managed to convince the tribunal that a ten-million-dollar megastore built two years ago in nearby Bessemer, Michigan, should be valued, for tax purposes, at less than the one-million-dollar cost of the parcel of land on which it was built. The judgment slashed the store's tax bill by 90 percent and inspired an avalanche of tax-averse retailers to follow suit.

"What did folks at the Grill say about Romanelli and his tax loophole?" Harlan asked.

"Nothing nice," Roz replied.

"What do you mean?"

"From what I gather, it sounds like big retailers and home-improvement centers used to account for a huge chunk of the local tax base—but not anymore. That loophole has blown holes in municipal budgets all over the region, putting the burden of financing local services on homeowners and small businesses who can't pay enough taxes to keep up."

"And they blame Romanelli for that?"

"They sure do," Roz replied. "The way they described him, you'd think he was a heartless villain who took pleasure in causing their municipal cutbacks."

"Cutbacks? What kind?"

"The closure of their public library and the crumbling condition of their roads, to name just a couple." The Jeep slammed through a deep pothole in the road before Roz added, "They don't' even have a police force anymore."

"What? The town's lawless?"

"Basically, yes. They used to have two Gogebic County deputies stationed remotely in Watersmeet. But due to revenue losses, the county had to downsize its branch offices, leaving the town to rely on deputies stationed fifty miles away in the county seat."

A few miles south of town, Roz turned left onto Allen Lake Road. Stevie Viola's house soon came up on the right. They paused outside the Jeep to take it all in—a two-level contemporary home with an attached garage on a large, wooded lot bounded by a sharp bend in the road. This placement and surrounding woods obscured neighboring houses located around each side of the bend.

"Isolated," Harlan said.

Looking at the house, Roz added, "And a lot more than I expected for a waitress at a roadside café, even if she's only renting."

Chapter 6

Stevie Viola's house was even more impressive inside, Harlan thought, after she greeted them at the door and escorted them through a spacious family room and then down a plush-carpeted hallway lined with enlarged family photos, each illuminated with its own recessed light. Harlan slowed to look at one of Stevie Viola and her husband George, whom Harlan recognized from other photos he had seen earlier in the newspaper and online. This one obviously had been taken on their wedding day. Stevie wore a white gown, George a black tuxedo, and both the kind of smiles a couple has when imagining their happily ever after. The occasion notwithstanding, George looked much like the formidable arrestee depicted in his recently publicized mug shots. He towered over his wife, like a linebacker over a cheerleader, and in this photo, as in his mug shots, sported a thick mustache on a stubbled face that stared back with piercing eyes set beneath bushy eyebrows and a mussed-up crop of dark brown hair.

Many of the other photos included an infant, presumably the couple's child whom Roz had mentioned hearing about earlier at the Grill. In one of these there was another man—not George—posing with the infant and his mother. It was an amateurish selfie, blown up to fit a large, ornate frame. Harlan also recognized this guy from photos he had seen earlier. He was the man whom George Viola had allegedly murdered, Zach Romanelli, a.k.a. the dark-store attorney. The ominous-sounding label, Harlan thought, did not fit Romanelli's thin, wholesome face, especially juxtaposed as it was with another photo of his alleged killer.

"The little one's my son, Bobby," Stevie said as she smiled awkwardly at the selfie. "It was taken a few months ago, on the day my brother moved us into this house."

"Your brother?" Harlan remarked. He leaned close to the selfie and studied the beaming face of an apparently proud uncle cuddling his young nephew. "Zach Romanelli? He gave you this house?"

Stevie averted her eyes as she nodded. "And pretty much everything in it, for Christmas." Her tone sounded apologetic. "I imagine you were wondering how I could afford a place like this for little Bobby and me."

"Just you and Bobby?" Harlan asked.

She continued looking away. "George and I have been separated for some time."

Stevie then turned from the selfie and led them through the remainder of the hall and into a dining room furnished with a long, mahogany-wood table and matching chairs centered beneath a wide pendent chandelier. The table was set with coffee mugs, spoons, cream, and sugar.

"Sit wherever you'd like," Stevie said as she turned to a buffet that sat beneath a window overlooking an expanse of densely wooded forest outside. On top of the buffet, next to a baby monitor, there waited a Keurig single-serve coffee, latte, and cappuccino maker, its power light on, ready to be loaded with an assortment of coffee pods. "Are you two still drinking decaf?"

Harlan declined the invitation to sit down and instead joined Stevie by the buffet. "Why don't you have a seat, Mrs. Viola," he suggested, "and let me take a turn being your table server." He did this more in deference to Roz, however. Given the way he had manipulated her participation in this meeting, he thought it best to occupy himself with a task like this while she took the first crack at their prospective client.

"Okay," Stevie said. She then sat across the table from Roz, who got started after Harlan took their coffee orders.

"Let me just clarify up front, Mrs. Viola, that you are not yet our client. We want to hear your story first, and then decide whether to get involved. But even if we decline the case, you should know that everything you tell us here tonight will remain strictly confidential because of a legal privilege that applies when private investigators talk to prospective clients. So, you can speak freely and not be concerned about Mr. Holmes or me ever telling anyone else what you say to us. Do you understand?"

Stevie nodded as she poured some cream into a steaming cup of coffee. "I was already planning to tell you everything."

"Good," Roz said. "Why don't you go ahead, then, and start at whatever point you consider to be the beginning of the story."

"Which story?" Stevie asked.

The question struck Harlan as odd and seemed to have the same impact on Roz, who paused over it.

"I had relationships with both of them," Stevie explained, "George and Zach. Which one do you want me to start with?"

Roz leaned forward. "Let's start with *their* relationship. How did these two men in your life get along with each other?"

Stevie shrugged. "To my knowledge, they never met."

"Your brother and your husband never met?"

"Ms. Cortez, I didn't even meet my brother Zach until last summer, about a month after George and I separated. Zach and I were twins, adopted at birth by different families. Growing up, all I ever knew was that I had a twin brother. I didn't know who he was until that day."

"Do you recall the date of that meeting?"

Harlan leaned over the buffet and began using its surface to take notes on the legal pad he had been using during his online research. He turned to a clean page and brought his pen to the first line, where he would insert, he expected, an estimate of the date Stevie Viola first met Zach Romanelli.

"It was last June 15," she answered without hesitation, "right at the start of my morning shift at the Grill. We had no customers yet, so I was in the kitchen helping the cook with some prep work. Then I heard the door chime and I looked up, through the service window, to see if I got a customer, and there he was, standing up front like he was waiting to be seated, right by the sign saying, 'Seat yourself.' It was Kimmy, the manager, who went over and talked to him first.

"I went to wash my hands, thinking I might be needed up front, and next thing I know Kimmy comes into the kitchen and tells me that the guy wants to see me. He asked for me by name, she says. I didn't know what to make of it. I knew who he was from his picture being in the paper and reading about him being some downstate tax lawyer who was causing problems in the UP, but I'd never met him before. In fact, I think that was the first time anyone ever saw him in the Grill. Anyway, I told Kimmy I'd take his order as soon as I was cleaned up. But then she says he wasn't there to eat. He just came to see me, she said.

"So then I go up front to see what he wants, and I can tell as soon as our eyes meet that this guy is happy to see me—I mean, *real* happy. And he seems to think I should know why. 'Don't you know who I am?' he asks right off. And all I can think is, *Of course I do. You're the big-city lawyer everyone in town despises.* But I can tell he means something else by his question.

"Then he pulls out his cellphone to show me something... a photo already on the screen. It was of him and a woman. I looked down at it and darn near fainted on the spot, cuz the woman staring back from that phone looked just like me, plus a few years. Same color eyes and hair. Same crooked teeth and bent nose. And the same thin face, like this guy had too. And that's when I knew who he was... because I knew who *she* was."

"Your mother?" Roz asked.

"*Birth* mother," Stevie amended. "Zach wanted to talk about her, but he knew it wasn't a good time or place, there in the restaurant in front of people. I told him it was just as well. That I had no interest in talking about *her*, or anything to do with *her*. But he pushed the issue. Practically begged me to meet up with him later. Said he'd been searching for me all his adult life. I ended up giving in."

"Where did you meet?"

"The Bel-Air Motel, in Land O' Lakes, where he was staying."

"How'd that go?"

"Not as I expected."

"What do you mean?"

Stevie shrugged. "I fell in love."

"Excuse me?"

Stevie smiled. "Not like that." She looked off as her expression returned to serious. "It was like he really *was* my brother. And not just by birth. My *big* brother. That's what I started calling him that day when he told me he was born first, ahead of me by a whole seven minutes. And that's what he became to me. A big brother who wanted to make up for lost time and start looking out for me, the kid sister who got the short end of the deal when it came to adoptive families."

Stevie's eyes had been welling up with tears, and at this point one broke free. Harlan scanned the room for tissues. Finding none, he grabbed a napkin from a stack on the buffet and gave it her. "Thank you," she said as she took it and patted her face.

"Sounds like you saw some more of your brother Zach after that first meeting," Roz continued.

"A lot more. He started making a point of visiting regularly—sometimes when he came up north to see clients, but most of the time just to see me and Bobby. Those two really took to each other too."

"But you never introduced him to George and never told George about him."

"No. I never told anybody."

"Why?"

"Because Zach thought it best for me—and my tip income at the Grill—if people didn't know I was related to... you know..."

"The dark-store attorney."

Stevie cringed. "I always hated that label. The way people said it, you'd think he worked for Darth Vader. Same people who shop in those big-box stores for all the discounts they can give—because they got smart lawyers like Zach."

"But those people found out anyway," Roz said.

Stevie turned to face Harlan, who stood at the end of the table, still ready with more napkins, like a dutiful manservant doing his best to be seen but not heard. "You know what they found out, Mr. Holmes. You heard it yourself tonight at the Grill—the ugly rumor that people were spreading about me and Zach."

Harlan cleared his throat. "What my partner's driving at, I think, is that if people in town had that misperception, your husband George may have had it as well."

With that, Roz pulled out her notebook and pen. It was now Harlan's turn.

"Did he?" Harlan asked.

"I don't know."

Harlan sat in a chair next to Roz, rested his elbows on the table, and leaned toward Stevie. "You said you met Zach last June—a month after you and George broke up."

"*Separated* was what I said, Mr. Holmes. George and I separated last May, coming up on a year ago."

"Why?"

Stevie nervously stirred her coffee before responding, "Because of George's problem with drinking."

"What kind of problem?"

"A bad one. Real bad, especially after Bobby was born. Like it was George who was suffering postpartum depression. Come to find out he probably was. His doctor said so—that it can happen to men. PPD, he called it—*paternal* postpartum depression. But hearing that only made it worse for George. He couldn't admit it. Heck, it took him forever to admit that he was an alcoholic."

"Have you seen George since the separation?"

"Just occasionally. He moved to Iron River, about thirty miles east, but he still has friends in town, guys he used to work with before he lost his job driving a log truck. Some of them were also his drinking buddies. They liked to meet up at the Roadhouse Tavern. I'm sure you noticed it earlier tonight."

"Next door to the Roadhouse Grill," Harlan said. "They share the same parking lot."

"They also share restrooms inside, in a hallway that connects the two. That's where I sometimes see George, stumbling in and out of the men's room."

"What about his visitation rights?" Harlan asked. "Don't you see George when he comes to see Bobby?"

Stevie shook her head. "They've never had that kind of relationship, on account of the PPD I was telling you about. Bobby was a colicky baby during the first few months, and George took it personally, like he felt rejected by him. It was one of George's symptoms, the doctor said, along with irritability and depression. George drank to avoid all that, which only made it worse. Not once did he ever ask to see our son... until the last time I saw him."

"When was that?"

"A couple days ago at the jail. I thought seeing him there in handcuffs and inmate clothes might be difficult, but for once he was stone-cold sober, and he went on and on about how much he missed Bobby and me."

"How'd that meeting come about?"

Stevie reached into her purse. "He arranged it," she said, pulling out a business card and setting it on the table between Harlan and Roz. It was for an attorney named Kerry Jammer.

"George's attorney?" Harlan asked.

Stevie nodded. "I appreciated him doing that. It ended up being the best time I've spent with George since long before we separated."

"Did George talk about the case?"

"No. Mr. Jammer never left the room, and he wouldn't allow it. But to hear George talk about how much he loves Bobby and me—it made me think he couldn't possibly have done to Zach what they say he did."

What they say he did, Harlan thought, *probably wasn't done while he was stone-cold sober.* He decided to change the subject. "When was the last time you saw Zach?"

Again, Stevie's recollection of a date was quick and specific. "The second Monday of March, the night before he went missing. He came here to the house for a visit."

Harlan watched Roz scroll a calendar on her cellphone for that Monday's date and jot it into her notes—March 12.

"Why do you remember the date of his last visit that way?" Harlan asked. "As the second Monday of the month."

"Because that's how Zach talked about that date when it was coming up—the way it's written into the law. Every year, the second Monday of March is the day the local Board of Review starts hearing property tax appeals, Zach said. And this time around, they were starting with his appeals for his big-box store clients, every single one of them in the whole UP. They did 'em all here in Watersmeet. Took all day and into the night, and they still didn't finish, Zach said, because he and our local assessor got into a serious argument. Almost turned into a fistfight, he said. He came here after because he thought seeing me and Bobby would help calm him down."

"He almost got into a fistfight?" Harlan said. "At an official meeting of the Board of Review?"

"That's what Zach told me. The assessor either bumped into him or shoved him—he wasn't sure which—when he was up at the whiteboard working through the numbers for one of the stores. Either way, when he pushed back, she completely lost it, Zach said."

"She?"

"That's right, Jackie Diebolt, the local assessor. Zach said that the township supervisor had to jump in and physically restrain her. That's when they stopped the meeting and said they'd resume it the next day. But Zach didn't show up the next day, and he wasn't seen again until five weeks later, when those hikers found his body in the forest."

"Did you and Zach discuss anything else that evening?"

Stevie fidgeted in her seat. "We talked a little about money," she said. "Zach used to give me cash every so often, you know, to help out with bills and stuff. He was very generous."

"Did he offer you some that evening?"

"Yeah. He had a big wad of it for me, rolled up in a rubber band. But I told him that I was still good with what he gave me the last time. He went ahead and peeled off a few bills anyway, hundreds, and left them on the kitchen counter for me."

"Was anything else said?"

"Not really. Just small talk. Zach didn't stay long. I offered to make him dinner, but it was running late, and he wanted to get in a cross-country ski to work off some steam. Last thing I said to him was that I'd leave the light on."

"What did you mean by that?"

"Just what I said—that I'd leave the porch light on, the way I always did when he went cross-country skiing. Zach used to stay at the Bel-Air Motel, in Land O' Lakes, when he came up north. There's a trail that picks up near there, called the Agonikak Trail. It runs clear through to Watersmeet and along the way connects with other trails that go all over the place. Zach used to ski those trails all the time."

Stevie glanced at the dining room window. "The Agonikak Trail goes right by my house, out back, about halfway between the Land O' Lakes trailhead and Watersmeet. Sometimes on his way there or back, Zach would let himself in for a rest; and if he was real tired, he might stay the night. So I'd leave the light on for him, you know, if he wanted to stop."

"Did he have his own key to your house?"

"Sure. He bought the place. And he was a night owl. Sometimes he went skiing at the craziest hours, and he didn't want to wake me up."

"Did he stop by that night?"

"He might have, while I was sleeping, but I don't know for sure."

"So, the next day, you didn't find any sign of him having visited—dishes he might have used, an unmade bed, or pillows or blankets left on a couch."

"No, there was nothing like that."

"Do you know for sure whether he went skiing that night?"

"I'm pretty sure he did. He was really into that sport. And like I said, he felt the need to blow off some steam."

"Why did he stay in Land O' Lakes? Why not Watersmeet?"

Stevie shrugged. "Because Land O' Lakes is on the Wisconsin side of the border, and the motels on the Michigan side stopped having vacancies for him a long time ago."

"Around the time people learned he was the dark-store attorney?" Harlan asked.

Stevie responded with a long sigh. It was followed by a pause in the conversation that ended when Harlan leaned back in his chair to yield the floor again.

"Is that it?" Roz asked. "Is that all you can tell us about these two men in your life and the recent events involving them?"

"I think so," Stevie said. "It's the same as I told the police."

"When?"

"A couple weeks ago, after they found Zach's body. The next day a state trooper came by the Grill to see me, along with Ranger K."

"Ranger Kole Koerber, from the Forest Service," Harlan clarified in response to Roz's questioning look. "He was the first responder."

Roz turned back to Stevie. "What'd you tell them?"

"Basically everything I just told you about George and Zach."

"Have you spoken with anyone else about any of this?"

"Not in any detail. People I know tend to talk about it behind my back, not to my face."

"How do you think folks caught on to you having some kind of relationship with Zach?"

"I don't know. Maybe it was because of what happened in front of Kimmy and the cook that day at the Grill. All I can tell you for sure is that they weren't the only ones who knew there was something between us. In fact, the day after the Board of Review meeting broke down, when they were going to try meeting again, I got a call from someone over at Township Hall saying Zach didn't show and asking if I knew where he was. So other people already knew, even before this thing became a murder case."

"What did you tell that caller?"

"The truth. That I had no idea where Zach was. Then I called Ava to see if she knew."

"Ava?"

"Ava Romanelli, Zach's wife. He'd told her about me in the past, and we'd talked on the phone a couple times before all this happened. But she didn't know where he was either."

"Have you talked any further with Mrs. Romanelli?"

"Sure, just last week, when I went down to Traverse City for Zach's funeral."

"After George's arrest?"

Stevie nodded.

"How did she react to you?"

"As far as I could tell, she didn't hold it against me that George is my husband, if that's what you mean. She was very understanding. She even let me and Bobby stay the night at her house while we were there. But we didn't really talk about what might have happened to Zach or the charges against George."

"Do you know anything about the charges?"

"Just what they say in the papers, you know, about him being arrested and the prosecutor saying he killed Zach because of an affair he thought Zach was having with me. I guess there's supposed to be some hearing about it soon."

"The preliminary hearing," Harlan added, recalling what he had also read in the paper and confirming it in a page of his notes where he had created a timeline of key events he knew of so far. He shared the timeline with Roz; she scrolled her finger down it and stopped on the last item, the preliminary hearing, scheduled in ten days. Then, as she looked up, he caught her eye and gently nodded his head to signal his feelings about taking the case. She gently shook her head in disagreement.

The nonverbal exchange ended with Roz unzipping her backpack and dropping her notebook and pen inside. "I'm sorry, Mrs. Viola, but I don't think we can take this case."

Harlan held back an urge to disagree. There would be a better chance of getting Roz onboard if Stevie Viola pressed the issue, he thought.

"Why?" Stevie asked.

"Well, for starters," Roz replied, "we'd probably be wasting our time and your money for the next ten days trying to figure out the case that the police and prosecution are going to disclose at the preliminary hearing anyway."

This might be true, Harlan thought, if the case was in fact as open and shut as the news media had made it seem. But if there was any complexity to the case—any evidence that might cast doubt on the accused's guilt—the prosecutor would more likely play it close to the vest in order to limit defense counsel's ability to use the preliminary hearing as an early discovery tool.

"And even if there is some helpful evidence for us to uncover here," Roz continued, "the client would have to be your husband, George. That's the only way we'd have access to his defense attorney, this Kerry Jammer fellow, and the prosecution's case as it gets revealed to him through a discovery process overseen by the court. You said yourself that Mr. Jammer didn't want to let you in on the case. And that's exactly how he'll respond to us if we're working for you, because we wouldn't be part of *his* team."

"But I think he would welcome your help," Stevie said.

"What makes you say that?"

"Because I know he needs it."

"How do you know?"

"He told me, in so many words."

"What did he say, specifically?"

"The other day when I met him at the jail, after I saw George, he asked if I could contribute to George's defense. He said he's a court-appointed attorney and the budget they give him doesn't go far. I got the feeling that he's handling the case all on his own—that he *has no team*—and I'll bet he'd be thrilled to have two high-profile detectives like you and Mr. Holmes join up with him."

Stevie reached for Jammer's business card, which was still on the table between Roz and Harlan. "Here, let me have that back," she said. "I'll call him right now and get this worked out."

"Hold on," Roz said as she snatched up the card. She glanced at Harlan, caught him stifling a smile, and then rolled her eyes before returning to Stevie. "Do you have any idea how much Mr. Holmes and I charge for our services?"

"I… guess not."

Roz reached into her backpack and retrieved a two-page, standard contract that she and Harlan used with most of their clients. "This is what you, George, and Mr. Jammer would have to sign before we would take this case," Roz said as she slid the document across the table. "Our daily fee is listed on the second page."

Stevie turned the page. Her eyebrows rose. "I've heard that you two do PI work for people in Chicago… the Mafia, according to what was said after you left the Grill tonight. Is this what you charge them?"

"We *used* to do some work for people who might be described that way," Roz said, shooting a glance at Harlan. "And, yes, that's the kind of rate they paid."

"I think I can manage it," Stevie said.

"You can? May I ask, how?"

Stevie reached into her purse, pulled out a checkbook, and slid it across the table to Roz and Harlan. It was opened to a page in the register listing a recent transaction that practically jumped out at them—a deposit of $200,000. Beneath it were a two small debits for a water bill and groceries.

"Didn't you say that Zach helped with the bills by giving you allotments of cash every so often?" Roz asked.

"That didn't come from him," Stevie replied. "It came from Ava, his wife, last week when I visited with her. She said Zach would've wanted me to have it."

Harlan again caught Roz's eye, only this time he was not stifling a smile—he was staring intently, thinking, *Let's do this.* At that moment, a gurgling sound came through the baby monitor. Both women turned their attention to it as Harlan's returned to the checkbook and second thoughts about Stevie Viola's financial situation as a single mother of a young child. The big chunk of money in her checking account certainly would help, but it would not, by itself, see little Bobby through from this day to completion of the college education that his Uncle Zach probably would have wanted for him.

"Let me have your pen," Roz said to Harlan. After taking it, she retrieved the contract, crossed out the amount listed as their daily fee, and inserted an amount equal to one half of it. "I neglected to mention," she said, "that I won't be able to work full-time on this case, Mrs. Viola. I'll be spending some of my time with friends I have in this area, and it wouldn't be appropriate to charge you all of this."

Roz paused over the document after discounting the daily fee, and then crossed out a retainer provision that would have required Stevie Viola to pay much of the fee up front. Then she slid both the contract and Mr. Jammer's business card back across the table to Stevie.

Chapter 7

Pop! Pop! Pop!

The sound of the blasts roused Harlan from a deep sleep and launched him to the edge of the bed, where Roz was already perched. He froze beside her and listened to the sound, now, of nothing but the low hum of the generator they had placed as far from the camper as a lengthy extension cord would allow. No birds, no bugs, and no more blasts. The clock on the nightstand said it was 4:28 the next morning, an hour before sunrise.

"I counted three," Harlan whispered.

"That means you slept through at least half of them," Roz whispered back. "I heard six or seven."

"Steady cadence? Like the last ones?"

"Yeah."

"Probably a gun then. Not fireworks."

"Uh huh. West of us, I think. Not far off."

Harlan slipped on some clothes and armed himself before going outside. After two laps around the campground scanning his flashlight in every direction and finding nothing unusual, he returned to find Roz seated at the kitchen table, still in her pajamas, poking at her cellphone.

"What are you looking at?"

"Hunting regs."

Harlan mulled over the possibility of a shooter doing something other than hunting… maybe target shooting. But that didn't square well with an isolated series of gunshots. "What's in season?"

"Small game mostly. Nothing you'd have to shoot that many times. And nothing that can be taken by firearm before sunrise."

Chapter 8

A few hours later, Harlan and Roz drove fifty miles west to the combined residence and office of George Viola's attorney, Kerry Jammer, in downtown Bessemer, the seat of Gogebic County. They were greeted at the front door not by a receptionist but by Jammer himself, who led them down a dimly lit hallway and into a small room cluttered with books and files that had to be cleared out of the way before he could offer them seats opposite his behind an old wooden desk, where he sat down to review the contract signed by Stevie Viola the night before.

According to a diploma on the wall behind him, Jammer had graduated cum laud from Detroit College of Law forty-seven years ago. That put him in his early seventies, Harlan estimated, which in turn explained his full head of shaggy gray hair, styled as though he was still a 1970s college kid. A few strands of it fell into his face as he shifted in his seat while turning to the second page of the contract. He drew his finger down the page and stopped it on the paragraph where Roz had crossed out the retainer provision. Eventually he looked up, across the desk at his guests, his brow furrowed as he slowly shook his round, wrinkly face. "Given your reputations, I thought you two would charge a lot more than this."

"We've changed our business model," Harlan replied, "now that we're semi-retired."

"You don't say. That's what I've been for the past few years—semi-retired. But you two seem too young for that sort of thing."

Only by comparison to an old has-been like you, Harlan thought as he imagined Jammer's financial struggles if he was working from home on court-appointed cases like this one.

"Why, thank you, Mr. Jammer," Roz said. "It's nice to be considered youthful for a change. Isn't that right, Harlan?" She nudged Harlan's foot with hers and shot him a glance that told him to mind his manners.

"Yes… uh… real nice," Harlan said.

Jammer's attention turned to Roz, the furrow in his brow deepening. "Cortez… Roz Cortez," he murmured. "I remember once reading about you and Mr. Holmes in the paper, how you two busted those drug dealers on Drummond Island. But seeing you now, in person, makes me think I've heard your name somewhere else, and have maybe even seen you, or someone you resemble, a long time ago."

"I grew up not far from here, in Watersmeet," Roz said. "Maybe you knew my parents."

Jammer reflected further before asking, "Did your father work at the mill?"

"In fact he did, for a long time, until—"

"September 9, 1976," Jammer said. "The day he got laid off, along with over half of the other mill workers there at the time. Frederic Cortez. If memory serves, he went by 'Fred.'"

Roz dropped her gaze and tensed slightly, a reaction Harlan understood from her past accounts of that day and how it marked not only the end of her visits to Watersmeet but also the last time she knew the whereabouts of her father. And then, just as abruptly, her focus returned to Jammer, as if she had suddenly realized what he just said. "How did you know about my father losing his job at the mill?"

"Because I was there when it happened—the day he and the others got let go. It was a last-ditch restructure of the mill, trying to avoid bankruptcy. My law firm was handling the downsizing, and one of us had to be there for the exit interviews, you know, to make sure the mill foreman handled the job terminations in a way that didn't spur any lawsuits."

"So, you saw my father get fired."

"I'm afraid I did. I was the attorney for the ones doing the hatchet job. It went on all day, one at a time. I still remember every one of those men—their names, faces, and reactions to it."

"Sounds like it was a significant experience for you too," Roz said.

"It was. The foreman and I sat at a table in the conference room as each one came in, alone, and sat opposite us, some of them angry, but most just plain scared, worrying, I could tell, about how they were going to support their families. As we were working our way through the carnage, I got to thinking, more and more, how much I wanted to be on the other side of that table—representing the mill workers rather than the corporation that had wrought this change on their lives."

Roz leaned forward. "How much longer did you work for the firm?"

"I put in my notice the next day. Two weeks later I was on my own as a solo practitioner, struggling to make ends meet doing work for regular folks, mostly criminal defense and probate matters."

Harlan studied Jammer as he shared this piece of his past and found his initial assessment of the aging attorney evolving. Despite his years, he was no has-been, at least insofar as his convictions were concerned. His whole demeanor evinced a continuing passion for his work and those he long ago set out to serve—so-called *regular folks.*

"Is that what George Viola is?" Harlan asked. "A regular guy who's up against something he can't take on alone?"

Jammer signed the contract before responding. "That's right, Mr. Holmes. And I'll tell you about it after you've added your signature to this piece of paper." With that, Jammer slid the contract and his pen across the desk.

Harlan, however, ignored the items before him and instead held his stare on Jammer. Good intentions or not, the man should answer some direct questions first, Harlan thought.

"Tell me, is George Viola guilty? Did he kill Zach Romanelli?"

"I don't know."

"You expect me to believe that?" Harlan pressed. "You just said you've been practicing criminal defense for over forty years. Your livelihood has depended on your ability to read clients and witnesses. Obviously, you've met the guy. You must have at least an impression."

Jammer's gaze remained on the items in front of Harlan, who continued to ignore them. "Well, what does George Viola say about the charge?"

"He doesn't know either," Jammer said. "George says he was pretty drunk the night they say Romanelli went missing. He doesn't remember much."

"What?" Harlan remarked, voice raised. "How could he not know something like that—whether or not he killed a man and ditched his body in the woods?"

Jammer looked up, into Harlan's eyes. "Are you going to sign that, Mr. Holmes?"

"What about the county sheriff and prosecutor? What have they told you about their case?"

"Nothing. I submitted my discovery requests a week ago when I took the case, and as I'm sure you know, the law gives them twenty-one days from then to respond. Knowing the prosecutor, she'll take every one of those days."

"So, tell me if I'm seeing the big picture here," Harlan said. "The prosecutor's playing hardball with you on a murder case that she's telling the media is a slam dunk. She says your client, the jealous husband, killed the man who he thought was sleeping with his wife, plain and simple. And the defense I'm hearing from you, the jealous husband's attorney, is that he was too shit-faced to remember if he did it."

"Look, Mr. Holmes, I'll tell you what I can, once you…"

"I know," Harlan said as he snatched up the pen. He paused again, however, before signing the contract. "You okay with this, Roz?"

"I'm not sure. It'd be nice to know if his attorney thought there was at least a shred of hope for the guy before we go off half-cocked, spinning wheels and spending Mrs. Viola's money."

"Well, what do you say, Counselor?" Harlan said. "Is there a shred of hope?"

"I think so."

"Based on what?"

Jammer glanced back and forth between his guests before responding, "Based on a statement George gave on the night of his arrest."

Harlan cocked his head. "What statement?"

"A videotaped statement that George gave to the arresting officers."

"You've seen this video?"

"Sure. One of the officers gave me a copy of it himself."

"But didn't you just say that the sheriff's office hasn't given you anything?"

"The sheriff's deputies didn't make the arrest."

"Who did?"

"The LVD Police."

"What police?"

"I think he's referring to tribal police," Roz said. "We passed a couple of them patrolling the casino when we left Watersmeet this morning. You were busy looking at your phone, Harlan. Their squad car had those letters on the side, LVD. I think they were Chippewa."

"The Lac Vieux Desert Band of Lake Superior Chippewa, to be precise," Jammer said. "I doubt you knew anything about them before today, Ms. Cortez. The feds didn't officially recognize their band until 1988."

Roz's eyes showed recognition, nonetheless. "But I've heard of the place, the Lac Vieux Desert. I just can't remember what I was told about it."

"It's near the casino," Jammer said, "where the watersheds for Lakes Superior and Michigan join up with the watershed for the Mississippi River—where the waters meet, as they say."

"That's it, the name of the town," Roz said, a smile animating her face. "That's how Watersmeet got its name when it first became a village."

"Why did the tribal cops make the arrest?" Harlan asked, trying to return the conversation to the matter at hand. "Was Viola on reservation property?"

Jammer shook his head. "No, they arrested him at the Roadhouse Tavern, about a week after Zach Romanelli's body was found. George strolled into the place just before closing time, completely clueless about the fact that he was the prime suspect in the case. But the bartender knew, given how it was all over the local news. He called 911, but apparently it was going to take a while to get deputies from here in Bessemer all the way out to Watersmeet. So they called on the LVD Police for assistance."

Harlan recalled what Roz had said the night before about Watersmeet's loss of its own law enforcement officers after the decline in tax revenues. "Is that who handles law enforcement in Watersmeet since the town's deputies got laid off?" he asked. "The LVD Police?"

"Oh, you've heard about that," Jammer said. "No, the LVD hasn't really filled the void—not in an official capacity anyway. Early on there was talk about cross-deputizing them, but the county couldn't even pay for that limited service. So the LVD has been left with the choice of either letting the neighboring town go lawless, or stepping in without a formal arrangement, free of charge. Fortunately for the town, they've chosen to intervene in at least the more serious cases. That's why they made the arrest that night. They had George in custody for a couple hours."

"If they were pitching in unofficially," Harlan said, "why did they interrogate him?"

"It wasn't their idea."

"Did the county sheriff ask them to do that too?"

"No, it was George's idea."

"What did you just say? That George Viola wanted to be interrogated?"

"Basically, yes, he wanted to talk. The LVD officers told him he didn't have to; in fact, they objected to the idea. They told George that they didn't have jurisdiction, and that if he wanted to talk, he should wait for the deputies to get there. But George insisted."

Harlan and Roz both sighed in sync. The willingness of so many arrestees to talk to their adversaries—whose abuses every day fill the media—never ceased to amaze.

"George was confused," Jammer tried to explain. "He seemed to have no knowledge of Zach Romanelli's disappearance and death, let alone that he was suspected of murdering the guy. He wanted to talk. So the tribal police obliged him."

"How thoughtful of them," Harlan said, his sarcasm unfettered. "And how did you get a videotape of this debacle if the tribe was cooperating with the sheriff?"

"Like I said, from one of their officers directly."

"On the sly?"

Jammer nodded as he retrieved a framed photo from his credenza. It was an action photo from what appeared to be a high school basketball game. "I got the video from him," Jammer said, pointing at the kid with the ball, who was airborne in the photo, about to launch a shot from well beyond the three-point line. "His name's Frank Wolcott. And the one here," Jammer added as he pointed at a tall, beefy kid under the net, "is my grandson, Lucas Jammer. Those two boys led Watersmeet High to the UP championship that year and, from there, just two rounds shy of the state finals. Along the way, they showed some downstate hoopsters how the game is played in *Nimrod Nation*— Franky shooting the lights out from downtown, and my boy Luke pounding the boards down low."

"So that photo was taken some time ago," Harlan said, "and Frank Wolcott is now Officer Wolcott of the Lac Vieux Desert Police Department."

"That's right. Franky now serves another nation—a sovereign nation not beholden to the county prosecutor's office."

Chapter 9

Kerry Jammer waited until Harlan and Roz had signed and dated the contract before turning the computer monitor on his desktop so that they all could watch the video together. It began with two uniformed LVD police officers leading a shackled George Viola into a room that looked carefully constructed for interrogation. At approximately eight-by-ten feet, the room was large enough for the three to sit comfortably around a table in its center, but not so large that the suspect could psychologically escape into the void. Walls free of windows or distracting artwork were painted a light pastel color, creating an office-like appearance that would play better to a jury than would cold gray or sterile white. Built into one wall was a one-way mirror that would allow unseen outsiders to study the suspect's every move, while its placement about five feet from the floor would prevent the suspect from seeing his own reflection when seated.

The camera, no doubt, was hidden, probably disguised as an ordinary accessory—a thermostat, clock, light switch, or the like—along the room's unseen, fourth wall. It captured Viola's entire body as he was seated in a chair that faced another chair on the same side of the table, which was taken by the officer whom Harlan recognized as Frank Wolcott from the photo on Jammer's credenza. The other officer sat opposite them, on the other side of the table.

To Harlan, this seating arrangement, like everything about the room, was purposeful. The other officer would merely observe from across the table as Wolcott would conduct the interview in full view of his subject, the table sitting beside them rather than interposed as a barrier in between. From behind such a barrier a guilty suspect may feel more confident and protected when lying to the interrogator. In addition, a barrier would conceal the suspect's lower body movements, which could be critical for interpreting nonverbal behavior.

George Viola, an unemployed log-truck driver, probably understood none of this. He also probably had no clue that the way he appeared on camera only added to his problems. The man's athletic frame outsized the larger of his captors by about six inches in height and fifty pounds in weight. But what really made him look like the beast he was portrayed as being in recent media was the hair on his head and face. It was thick and wild, like that of the old actor Lon Chaney well into his theatrical transformation from human to wolfman. Adding to the effect was Viola's juxtaposition with the clean-cut cop seated beside him, whose smooth face looked almost as youthful as it did on the day he was photographed shooting the three-pointer from way downtown.

Wolcott cleared his throat. "It bears repeating, Mr. Viola, that you don't have to give us this statement. We're LVD cops—tribal police—and the tribe has no jurisdiction of this matter."

"I understand," George said, barely above a whisper. The audio output, however, was perfectly clear. The microphone must have been nearby, Harlan thought, perhaps under the table.

"Do you also understand, sir, that when we turn you over to those who do have jurisdiction—the county sheriff—you'll have some important rights, like the right to remain silent and to have a lawyer present if you do choose to speak?"

"I know," George said. "You already told me all this."

"Then I'll tell you something I haven't said yet. Something important, so listen carefully." George straightened up in his seat as Wolcott continued, "Right now, we're making a video recording of this interview, and we're going to give a copy of it to the sheriff's deputies when they come for you. That means everything you say to us, you're saying to them."

George looked blankly around the room.

"The camera and mic are hidden," Wolcott said. "We don't always tell people that when we're in charge of a case. Since we're not this time, I thought I'd tell you; that way, you can make an informed choice. So, I'm going to ask you one last time, Mr. Viola—Do you really want to go forward with this?"

"What I want," George said, voice raised, "is to know why you guys are saying I'm a murderer."

Wolcott shook his head. "That's not coming from us, Mr. Viola. It's the Gogebic County sheriff and prosecutor who suspect you of that. And all I know about their reasons is what I've picked up from the local news, same as you I imagine."

"What local news, man?"

"The papers, TV, social media, you name it. Bits and pieces of the story have been surfacing everywhere."

"Not where I've been."

"Where's that?"

"Off the grid, man. Just look at me—my hair and beard growing out all over the place. I've been out in the woods for a long spell."

"How long?"

"About six weeks."

Wolcott looked down at his cellphone and began tapping and scrolling. "Hmm… you don't say," he mused after pausing the search. "According to what it says here, Zach Romanelli went missing about six weeks ago."

George tried leaning over to see the phone but was impeded by his shackles. "What are you looking at?"

"One of those newspapers I was telling you about. Says here that Romanelli went missing sometime between a big property tax meeting on March 12, which he attended, and another meeting that he missed the next morning, on March 13. Where were you in that time frame, Mr. Viola?"

"March 12?"

"Yeah, starting around 8:00 p.m., when the first meeting ended."

The room went silent as George Viola looked away, to his left. According to some of his interrogation training, Harlan recalled, a right-handed person's look in that direction usually meant he was accessing his actual memory and was thus more likely to be followed with a truthful statement than if he had looked to the right. Eventually George's head began shaking as he said, "But I didn't shoot him."

"What are you saying, Mr. Viola? You skipped something. You didn't shoot... who?"

"Romanelli... when I went there that night."

"When you went where?"

"To Township Hall, where they were having the big property tax meeting. I parked across the street, by the pavilion over there, around six o'clock, thinking he'd be coming out soon. Had my gun... and was drinking whiskey. Ended up being lots of whiskey, cuz they went into the night. But even with all the juice, I still didn't have the nerve to do it. I know I didn't, cuz I only had the one mag—in the gun—and it was still fully loaded the next morning. I never shot it."

Wolcott glanced at his partner before tapping and scrolling on his phone some more. "Cops haven't said much about cause of death. But what they do say doesn't suggest anything about him dying by gunshot." Wolcott scrolled further. "Looks like they think he got hit by a motor vehicle, a car or truck maybe. Were you in a motor vehicle that night while you were waiting for him?"

George nodded. "My pickup."

"Why did you want to shoot him?"

George's eyes narrowed. "Because the son of a bitch was sleeping with my wife."

"Is that what you *really* think?" Walcott asked, his tone genuinely curious.

George slammed himself back into his chair and clenched his teeth as his stare intensified. "It's not what I *think*, man. It's what I *know*. That rich bastard put her in a house in the woods—like some kept woman— thinking nobody would catch on. But I did."

"Did you follow him to that house on the night we're talking about?"

"I dunno. I might have. Just not sure if what I'm remembering is from some other night when I saw him go there. Sneaky little son of a bitch would sometimes ski through the woods to get there. And then spend the whole damn night."

"You saw this for yourself?"

"Are you even listening to me, man? That's what I just said."

"Look, Mr. Viola, you seem to be getting agitated. And like I said before, you don't have to talk to me. Would you like to stop?"

"Just tell me what the hell else it says on that damn phone of yours."

Wolcott shrugged as he returned his attention to his phone. "Well, the hikers who found the body say it was wearing skis, and you say that you recall seeing him skiing. Do you think it might have been that night?"

"I told you already—I don't know. I was fucking hammered, dude."

"Whenever it was you saw him skiing, where was it?"

"On the trail out there, where it crosses her road."

"What road?"

"The one she lives on... Allen Lake Road."

Wolcott leaned back in his chair and stared off briefly. "The Agonikak Trail?"

George shrugged. "I guess you would know. It goes right by where some of your people come from... the Indian village out that way."

"You know, Mr. Viola, that trail also crosses a few other roads north and south of Allen Lake Road. Do you remember driving any of those other roads that night?"

"I don't remember much of anything else from that night. Think I had one of my blackouts. I'm an alcoholic, you know, and when I'm active, I can get those. After that one, all I really remember is waking up the next morning, and not being at the pavilion anymore."

"Where were you?"

"That sporting goods and rental place west of town, Sylvania Sports. Gal opening the shop knocked on my window and woke me up. Wanted to know what I was doing there. I told her I wanted to buy some supplies for a long hike."

"What hike?"

"The one that took me off the grid for the last six weeks, like I already said."

Wolcott leaned forward, holding his stare on the suspect. "Tell me why you went into the woods for six weeks, Mr. Viola."

There was a long pause during which Harlan noticed for the first time a low, incessant buzz, the kind that fluorescent lights sometimes make. He glanced around Jammer's office to find the source of the distraction, and then realized it was coming through the computer speaker. Something in the interrogation room was making the irritating sound, perhaps the bright light hanging directly over George Viola's head.

"What is it, Mr. Viola?" Wolcott asked. He leaned in further. "Are you remembering something? Something that might explain why you disappeared into the woods after that night?"

George nodded his head slowly. "I thought it was my idea, the whole time I was out there. But it wasn't. It was *his* idea... *he* told me to do it."

"Who?"

"A guy I think I met that night, after I left the pavilion... and went to a meeting."

"What meeting?"

"A support-group meeting—that's where I went."

"Like a Twelve-Step meeting?"

"Yeah, for recovering alcoholics. I've been to some of those before. I think I went to one that night... when I realized..."

Wolcott waited through another long pause as George stared into space. "When you realized what, Mr. Viola?"

"W-When I realized... I hit rock bottom... that night... like the end of a nosedive off a skyscraper."

"Tell me what you mean by rock bottom, Mr. Viola. What exactly was that for you?"

"It was what all the drinking had brought me to. I set out to kill a man that night. And the reality of that hit me hard. That's why I went to the support-group meeting. And there was a guy there who gave me the idea."

"What idea?"

"To do a recovery hike, the way he once did, he said."

"What's a recovery hike?"

"I don't think it's a thing people generally know about. It was just something he came up with by himself. A way to get clean and sober by getting lost in the woods and taking your time finding a way out. It seemed like a good idea to me at the time. So I gave it a try."

"How so?"

"After buying supplies at Sylvania Sports, I drove my truck west, through the national forest, clear into the Porcupine Mountains. Then I siphoned the gas from the truck and camped there for a week, detoxing. And then I made my way back on foot, like he told me to."

"You walked from the Porcupine Mountains to Watersmeet?"

"That's right."

"And how long did it take?"

"Five weeks, like I said. After the week in the mountains."

"But the mountains are only ninety miles from here. Why did it take you so long?"

"I didn't exactly walk a straight line."

Holding his stare on the suspect, Wolcott removed a piece of paper from his shirt pocket, unfolded it, and placed it between them. "We found this among your effects. It's a map of the western UP, drawn up by hand with what appear to be directions on it."

George looked perplexed as he examined the map.

"What's the matter, Mr. Viola? Don't you recognize it?"

"No, it's not that. I've seen it before. Hell, I've been using it as my guide for the past five weeks. But all along I was mistaken about where it came from. Just like I've been mistaken about the idea to do the recovery hike in the first place. He drew this up for me too."

"The guy from the meeting? He created this map for you?"

George nodded as he moved his shackled hands to the map and began tracing his finger over it. "From here in the mountains, I went due east about sixty miles to the southern tip of the Keweenaw Bay. Then I followed this trail, here, south about a hundred miles, into Wisconsin. From there, I looped back northwest another forty or so miles to Watersmeet."

Wolcott looked up from the map at his fellow officer, whose eyes had been glued to the map and remained so until Wolcott turned back to George and asked, "What do you know about the middle, hundred-mile segment of your journey through the interior UP and into Wisconsin?"

George struggled with the question. "I think he had a name for it."

"The guy you met at the meeting?"

"Yeah, but I can't remember what he called it. I just remember him saying something about it being a trail used a long time ago by Natives. Forget what he called them."

"The Ojibwe," Wolcott said, "ancient ancestors of the Chippewa. The trail this guy marked out by hand matches up perfectly with one they used for hunting and trade in prehistoric times. These days my people call it the L'Anse-Lac Vieux Desert Trail—what's left of it. I've never known it to be on any of the maps of your people."

George nodded his head slowly. "Maybe so, but... I think that's what he called it. He said it would keep me in the woods, away from towns and bars and liquor stores. And he told me to take it slow—to set up camps for a few days at a time along the way—and stay out there for as long as my supplies could keep me alive."

"What's this guy's name?"

"I don't know. I don't remember him saying."

"Was he Native American?"

George paused. "Not sure. Maybe a little."

"So, what race might he have been more of?"

"White, I think."

"What color hair and eyes?"

"Don't recall. Hell, he might not have had any hair at all."

"You saying he's bald?"

"No, I'm saying I don't remember one way or the other what was on top of his head, or what color his eyes were, or anything like that."

"How about his overall size? His height and weight?"

George shook his head. "Sorry, I just don't know. Like I said before, I was loaded that night. Don't recall many details."

"What about the location of this meeting? Do you remember that?"

George shook his head again but then stopped abruptly, looking to his left. "I remember where I *used* to go for those meetings. It might've been the same place."

Walcott waited as George reflected further. Eventually he turned back to his interrogator. "You ever see the nondenominational church up there in Paulding?"

"Sure. The church across the street from the General Store."

"Yeah, that's the one. Pastor Ed holds support-group meetings there, down in the basement where his office is."

"Is that where you met this guy that night? The one who put you on an ancient Ojibwe trail for a recovery hike?"

"Like I said, maybe. I feel like I'm remembering that office... the desk... the computer... the..." George's eyes showed realization.

"The what?" Walcott asked. "What else are you recalling right now?"

"The cats," George answered.

"Cats?"

"Yeah. The pastor is a cat lover. He has two or three living down in the basement where his office is. I remember one hopping into my lap while I was talking to the guy about the recovery hike."

"What did it look like?"

"The cat?"

"Yes, Mr. Viola. Can you describe it?"

George's stare returned to his left. "It was black... but not all black. I remember scratching it under the chin and seeing a patch of white fur… a small patch at the base of the neck… shaped like a triangle… kind of like Superman's patch."

"Superman's patch? The one with the 'S' on it?"

"Yeah, right there on the cat's chest. Course there was no 'S' on the cat's patch."

Wolcott glanced at his partner before leaning back in his chair to resume his study of the suspect. "That's a lot of detail to remember about a cat, Mr. Viola. Are you sure you don't recall anything more about the guy you and the cat were with?"

George's expression went blank. "I think that's all I got, Officer…" He paused and leaned over to examine his interrogator's name plate. "Can I ask you a question, Officer Wolcott?"

"Sure."

"Do you believe me? I swear I'm telling the truth."

Wolcott's manner remained as it had been throughout the interrogation, businesslike, revealing no hint of his thoughts or feelings. "It doesn't really matter what I think, Mr. Viola. What matters is what the prosecutor is going to think after she sees this video."

"She? I'm dealing with a chick prosecutor?"

"Don't let that put you off guard. From what I've heard, she's plenty capable. And after she sees this video, she's likely to have a field day filling in all of your blanks about this rock bottom of yours."

"Do you think she'll say it was something more than just me setting out to kill him?"

"What I think, Mr. Viola, is that you need a good attorney."

"Don't think I can afford one. I'm not exactly well off."

"The court will appoint one for you in that case," Wolcott said as he again looked across the table at his partner. The other officer responded with a subtle nod that seemed to mean something to Wolcott, who then turned back to Viola and said, "It so happens we know a good attorney who takes court-appointed clients. If you'd like,

I can get you his cell number and let him know you'll be calling him when the deputies give you your one phone call."

**

"I don't get it," Harlan said after the video ended. "Where's the shred of hope you promised before we signed onto this case, Jammer? All I saw was your Chippewa friend tee up George Viola for an easy prosecution, and then refer him to you—for what? A defense?"

"That's all you saw?" Jammer complained.

"Well, what else did you see?"

"That he was telling the truth. He really doesn't remember killing Romanelli. And it's like you said yourself, Holmes—a man would remember something like that if he did it, no matter how drunk he was."

"Really," Harlan remarked. "Is that what you're going to argue in court after the jury watches this video? He couldn't have done it, because he says he can't remember doing it? And what, the jury is just supposed to take him at his word—an angry drunk with a gun who was stalking his wife's apparent lover on the very night the guy goes missing?"

"Officer Frank Wolcott believes him," Jammer replied. "He told me so, and he was right there during the interview in a position to study George Viola's demeanor. And Franky's willing to say so in court, too."

Harlan glanced at Wolcott's high school basketball photo on the credenza. "The young man has many talents; I'll give you that, Jammer. But unless you can convince the jury that he can read minds, that's no defense."

"What about the support-group meeting at the church?" Roz asked. "Did you follow up on that, Mr. Jammer?"

"Sure, I talked to Pastor Ed, but... uh... apparently there was no meeting at the church that night."

"Terrific," Harlan remarked, rolling his eyes.

"But he does have cats," Jammer added quickly, "three of them in fact, just like George said."

"So what?" Harlan said. "George Viola could have seen those cats and met his recovery buddy on any prior occasion."

"Maybe he went to a meeting somewhere else that night," Roz said, "and he's just got his wires crossed about the location. Have you checked for other meetings that night, Mr. Jammer?"

"I did, with Pastor Ed himself. He had a list, and it showed one scheduled that night up in Marquette... but... truth is, it might have been difficult for George to have been there for it."

Jammer looked away.

"All right, out with it," Harlan pressed. "What else do you know about his whereabouts that night?"

Jammer took a deep breath before looking back. "Okay. Couple days ago, Franky ran into one of the deputies who picked up George at LVD headquarters on the night of the arrest. The deputy was an old high-school buddy of Franky's, and he got a little chatty about some evidence they uncovered regarding George's activities on the night in question... security-camera footage of him at a liquor store in Land O' Lakes, buying a bottle of whisky."

"At what time?" Roz asked.

"According to the deputy, 9:15 p.m."

"He was that specific," Roz remarked as she began turning pages in her notebook. "Where is this store in relation to the Bel-Air Motel?"

"Same street. Two doors down."

Roz stopped turning pages and looked at Harlan. Neither of them had to say out loud what they were thinking.

"I know," Jammer said. "Romanelli was staying at that motel. And that's about the time he would have returned there after visiting with Stevie Viola that night."

Chapter 10

"Whose old bones are making all the racket—yours or mine?" Jammer asked as they entered Bessemer's downtown district on foot, walking west on Iron Street. Harlan's arthritic right knee was the culprit. It had been clicking and grinding since about halfway into the short hike from Jammer's house. The sounds and accompanying pain were reminders of a need for knee replacement surgery that Harlan's orthopedist had recommended over a year ago when corticosteroid- and gel-injection therapies had stopped making any difference.

"It's definitely me," Harlan answered. "Where's *your* arthritis?"

"Hell, it'd be easier to tell you where it isn't," Jammer replied. "That's why I need exercise like this. To keep moving the old body, so all the joints don't freeze up."

"Do you want to stop for a minute?" Roz asked Harlan.

"No need for that," Jammer chimed in. "County lockup is coming up ahead, just past the courthouse there on the right."

Harlan decided to stop anyway, but more so to take in the sight of the impressive courthouse—a sprawling Romanesque-style building with a four-story tower on the façade. According to a nearby historical marker, it was built in 1888 and enlarged in 1915, on both occasions using hand-carved sandstone blocks, red in color due to iron oxides common to the soil in the Lake Superior region. During that time frame, the marker said, the prosperity of the region's copper and iron mining, lumbering, and shipping industries resulted in the proliferation of similarly constructed courthouses, city halls, and other government facilities throughout the western UP.

The architecture of that era, however, did not find its way next door to the Gogebic County Jail, which was a more modern facility consisting of four brick-and-mortared walls, a black-tarred roof, and a fenced-in yard out back topped off with coiled razor wire. As unsightly as it first appeared, the caged yard, to Harlan, was a welcome sight, for it might provide a solution to a problem that had arisen before they left for the jail. When Jammer had called ahead to schedule their visit, he was reminded of the sheriff's strict rule limiting nonfamily inmate visitors to the inmate's attorney plus not more than one other person at a time.

"Why don't you two go inside," Harlan said, "and see if they'll let you visit with George Viola in the yard, while I stand outside the fence."

"I suppose there's no harm in asking," Jammer said.

As Harlan made his way to the yard it became apparent that within the approximately fourteen-foot-tall chain-link fence there was another, inner fence about twelve feet high that was also topped off with coiled razor wire. Inside the inner fence, a basketball hoop mounted on a pole stood over a concrete slab that had been painted with lines marking off the sides and top of the key, the free-throw line, and the three-point arc.

Harlan stopped near the outer fence in front of a sign that prohibited loitering anywhere near the jail and threatened that violators would be prosecuted. He then turned from the sign to scan his surroundings. Of all the things that could be located behind the jail, in plain view of its double-caged yard, were the grounds of a public high school. He wondered whether this placement was intentional, perhaps a way of telling the kids next door where they could end up if they dropped out of school.

Another sign caught his eye. It was on the scoreboard for the high school's football field. "Home of the Bessemer Speedboys," it said. Harlan thought for a moment about where he might have seen or heard the name before—the "Speedboys"—and then recalled it was on the jerseys of the kids on the opposing team in the basketball photo on Jammer's credenza.

"Harlan Holmes?" someone called out from behind him.

Harlan turned back toward the jail and saw two uniformed officers coming, one carrying a rifle. "Yes, I am," he replied.

The officer with the rifle split off and took up a position some distance away as the other one came over and stopped, Harlan thought, way too close, in Harlan's space. And then the guy leaned in even closer and eyed Harlan up and down. Between the graying hair sticking out from under his hat and the lines in his face, he appeared to be about Harlan's age, maybe a few years older.

Harlan looked down at the officer's badge. On it was an inscription notable for what it did *not* say. Beneath his name, Jake Mills, it read, "Gogebic County Sheriff"—not *Deputy* Sheriff.

Also notable—indeed, impossible not to notice—was the huge wad of gum crammed into Sheriff Mills' mouth and the way he parsed out his words between rapid chomps. "I must say… Holmes… what you're asking for… well… uh… it's… you know… a bit unorthodox."

After deciphering the complaint, Harlan glanced at the double-caged yard and shrugged. "Doesn't look to me like there'd be any security risk."

"Just the same, Detective… I'm gonna… you know… have to pat you down."

Harlan took this as good news and promptly assumed the position, spreading his feet and placing his hands on the fence, one to each side of the no-loitering sign. Sheriff Mills' incessant gum-chewing was interrupted now by grunts and bursts of heavy breathing, as though at any moment he might inhale the wad of gum and choke to death before completing the pat down.

"All right," Mills said as he stopped the search. "Where the hell is it… you know… your piece… Holmes?"

"Not carrying one right now. Thought it wouldn't be a good idea… *you know*… to bring a gun here to the county jail."

"Appreciate that," Mills said. He then turned toward a camera mounted on the back of the jailhouse and waved for someone to come out before joining the officer with the rifle.

A few minutes later, Jammer, Roz, and George Viola, again in shackles, emerged from a back door of the jailhouse, entered the yard, and stopped at the top of the key. Viola faced Harlan directly, flanked by the other two, who were dwarfed by the man's towering frame.

"Harlan Holmes?" Viola asked.

Harlan responded with a nod as he stared at Viola. The man seemed unphased by the forty-degree chill in the air despite wearing only a jumpsuit with short sleeves wrapped high and tight around his thick, tattoo-covered arms. At least he had trimmed down his wild hair and beard, Harlan thought before nodding again, this time at Roz.

"How are they treating you, Mr. Viola?" she asked.

Viola looked confused as his gaze darted back and forth between Harlan and Roz. He was surprised, it seemed, either by the nature of the question or by which of the two was asking it. Or perhaps both.

"You mean, here at the jail, ma'am?" he asked, settling his attention on Roz.

"Yes, the deputies who have you in custody. Are they treating you well?"

"I... guess so."

"Good," Roz said. "And how are you feeling today, sir?"

Viola gave Harlan one more perplexed look before answering, "Okay, I guess."

"You're not too cold out here without a jacket, are you? Because if you are, we'd be glad to get you one."

"I'm fine. I'm used to being cold, from back in my lumbering days, working outside in the woods in a lot worse weather than this."

"Tell me about that, Mr. Viola. Your lumbering days, that is. Where did you use to do that?"

Harlan studied George Viola as Roz continued with the small talk, asking him simple questions that he presumably could answer honestly without difficulty. She was trying to establish a baseline perspective on the man's nonverbal cues when he was being truthful. The movement of his eyes and his patterns of breathing when he spoke, the frequency of his eye blinks, the direction his head might turn when searching his memory of past events, and so on. It was the same technique used by those who administer polygraph tests. They start with simple questions that can be answered yes or no, with no stress, to get a baseline on the subject when he is telling the truth.

Once he was satisfied with his perspective on George Viola's tendencies, Harlan gave Roz another nod, and she segued into a line of more pertinent questions, aimed primarily at Viola's whereabouts and activities on the day Zach Romanelli was last seen alive.

Of course, this was the same subject of inquiry that Viola had already been through with the tribal cop and then again with his attorney, Kerry Jammer. Roz was thus purposefully disorganized in her line of questions, coming at the subject out of chronological order, rehashing questions asked and answered after lengthy discussions of other matters, and occasionally, in response to perfectly clear answers, following up with questions like, "What? Come again?"—just to watch the man struggle to restate the same thing he had just said, differently.

Throughout, George Viola's nonverbal cues remained true to his baseline, and his story remained identical to the videotaped statement he had previously given to the tribal cop.

"You're not saying you didn't do it," Harlan pointed out after the interview ended. "You're just saying you don't remember, one way or the other."

Viola stepped out of the key, beyond the three-point line, as close to Harlan as the inner fence would allow. "That's because I *don't* remember—*one way or the other*—Mr. Holmes."

Harlan took note of Viola's stern tone and expression and, despite the presence of a loved one inside the double cage, decided it was time to poke the bear locked in there with her.

"So, you can't deny anything suggested by a mountain of evidence—that you stalked and killed the man you thought was fucking your wife; stashed his body in the woods; and then fled deeper into those same woods yourself, ashamed of your alcohol-induced rock bottom, until your survival depended on coming out of hiding."

Starring into Viola's glaring eyes, Harlan added: "And the jury— you know what they're going to think? That your claim of a blackout is *bullshit.* That you're *lying,* Viola."

"I'm not fucking lying, man!"

That outburst had to get Sheriff Mills' attention, Harlan thought, as he held his focus on the angry bear.

"Looks like you're easily provoked," Harlan said.

"Just don't like being called a liar."

"How about being called a killer? You have a problem with that?"

"Maybe I am one," Viola said, returning to his baseline.

"In that case, do you really want a couple PIs looking into this? Because we *will* figure out who did it. And by the looks of things, there'll be no *maybe* about it being you. Wouldn't you rather go through the rest of your life with at least a shred of doubt about your guilt?"

"I gotta know, man."

"Even if we prove you did it?"

"Especially if you do."

"Why?"

"So I can mean it," Viola said, tears welling in his eyes, "when I beg my wife to forgive me for killing her brother."

***

The conversation during the walk back to Jammer's house began with the topic of George Viola's memory loss.

"Have you considered hypnosis or psychoanalysis?" Roz asked.

"We've already begun the process," Jammer said, "with a shrink who specializes in unlocking repressed memories. She's met with George a couple times but says it can take a while. And she says that if the amnesia was alcohol-induced, George might never remember."

"Why?" Roz asked.

"Apparently binge drinking can shut down neurological pathways between short- and long-term memory. If that's what happened to George, whatever occurred that night would've never gotten into his long-term memory."

"So there'd be no repressed memory to unlock," Harlan said.

"Exactly."

"But he claims to have some memory—fragmented recollections— of the support-group meeting," Harlan added. "If there's any truth to that, then something from that night got into his long-term memory."

"Very good, Mr. Holmes. That's what the shrink said too. Which raises another possible source of his amnesia, she says."

"What?" Roz asked.

"Trauma."

"You mean like the trauma of committing murder?" Harlan asked.

"Or maybe something else," Jammer was quick to respond.

"Like what?" said both Harlan and Roz simultaneously.

"I don't know, but the shrink says that a way to get George to remember it might be to confront him with some physical reminder of the place and circumstances surrounding it."

"You mean like a photo or video of the murder scene?" Roz asked.

"If committing murder was the traumatic event, yes. But I can tell you before you even ask your next question, I already took video footage of the area where they discovered Zach Romanelli's body, and everywhere else I could imagine George might have been that night if he did it. And nothing happened for him when the shrink confronted him with the video during their last session."

"Nothing he would admit to you or her," Harlan said skeptically.

"You've now seen the man for yourself, Holmes. You tell me—do you think he's lying about not remembering?"

Harlan chose not to answer, though his glance at Jammer as they walked probably revealed his impression of Viola as being completely truthful. "Okay, let's assume for the moment he's being honest. And let's even assume that his nonreaction to your video means that he didn't do it. Then that would mean someone else did. Do you have any candidates, Counselor?"

"Just one. Someone Stevie Viola told you about, I'm sure."

Harlan did not have to think about it too long. "You can't be serious," he said. "The local assessor who got in Romanelli's face at the property tax meeting that night? You think she was so pissed off by his dark-store tax loophole that she whacked the guy?"

"What can I say? It's all we have right now. But there may be more to it than you think."

"Says who?"

"Says her boss, the Watersmeet Township supervisor who had to break up the fight and put her on administrative leave because of it, without pay, and still hasn't hired her back."

"How would you know?"

"Because he told me himself."

"I thought nobody from local government was talking to you—that they're playing hardball with you, as Viola's defense attorney."

"I said that about the *county* cops and *county* prosecutor. This guy's with the township, not the county. He's also a client of mine. I help him with his estate planning."

"Besides saying he fired her, what else did he tell you?"

"We only talked briefly on the phone and haven't yet had the chance to meet and get into the details. And to be honest, I would just as soon let you and your partner do that without me."

"Why?"

"Because I can't stand being around the guy unless I'm billing him for my time. He's a first-rate asshole. You'll see. I texted him while you two were talking with George Viola. You're scheduled to meet him in an hour."

Chapter 11

Roz stood waiting, arms folded, at the entrance to Watersmeet Township Hall. "Are you coming, Harlan?"

He had paused at the curb to check out the pavilion across the street, the place where George Viola had admitted to having remained parked in his pickup truck on the night in question, sipping on a pint of bourbon, straight from the bottle, while lying in wait to gun down Zach Romanelli after his meeting with the Board of Review.

But that was all George had clearly admitted.

Harlan pondered the man's alleged memory lapse as to subsequent events, his claimed inability to recall whether in fact he did—or did not—later see Romanelli exit Township Hall, or track him to Stevie's house, or follow him to his motel in Land O' Lakes. Even more troubling than the gaps in the story, Harlan thought, was the one George tried to fill in with a vague recollection of attending an alcoholics' support-group meeting, at a venue where none was held and at a time when in fact he had been recorded on video purchasing a bottle of bourbon at a liquor store two doors down from Romanelli's motel.

Roz opened the door. "Let's go, Harlan. You got us into this case."

Inside Township Hall they followed a sign directing them to the supervisor's office, where they were greeted by a petite, blonde-haired receptionist who could have passed for a ninth grader.

"Hi, I'm Julie," she said, her big, blue eyes beaming with excitement. "You two must be the PIs everyone in town is talking about."

"I suppose we are," Harlan replied. "We're here to see the township supervisor, Mr. Tafani."

"Of course," Julie said, "but just some friendly advice, Detective, don't ever call him that. He prefers to be called Mr. T. And whatever you do, don't call him by his first name."

"Archibald?" Harlan said, catching the name on the door behind Julie.

She wagged a disapproving finger. "Shush. Our walls are paper thin. I'll let him know you're here, assuming he doesn't know already."

Julie pressed the intercom button on her desk phone. "The detectives are here, Mr. T. Would you like me to send them in?"

The gruff response that came through the phone's speaker could be heard just as clearly through the walls. "Gimme a minute, would ya?"

"You two are welcome to have a seat," Julie whispered. "He can sometimes take a while."

Roz accepted the invitation as Harlan chose instead to browse the surrounding décor. The walls were packed with framed photos, all of them featuring a balding man whose beady eyes and sloping nose rivaled caricatures of former President Richard Nixon. "Is that your boss, Mr. *Tee*?" Harlan asked, his tone judgmental as he stood before a photo of the man posing in front of the state flag while shaking hands with Michigan's governor.

"That's him all right. It was taken last fall when the governor stopped here during a tour of the UP."

"Her apology tour?" Harlan asked, recalling the political climate of that time. The hot-button issue was the state's budget, from which the governor had line-item vetoed a "bonus" half-billion-dollar appropriation for restoration of the state's crumbling roads. The governor claimed that the so-called bonus, though sizable on its face, was much less than what was needed for the job, and that her veto was intended to bring adversaries in the state legislature back to the table to talk about spending five times more, in keeping with her campaign pledge that they *"fix the damn roads."* But the strategy backfired. House and Senate leadership instead seized the opportunity *to do nothing*, hoping she would take the rap for rendering even more anemic a roads package that would continue to leave local municipalities, like Watersmeet, twisting in the wind.

"I guess that's what some people called the tour," Julie said. "The governor held one of her town halls right here in this building, in our meeting room downstairs."

"Is that where the Board of Review meets too?"

As Julie nodded, the door behind her opened and there stood the man in the photo, Archibald Tafani. "Let's get on with this, detectives," he grumbled.

The shrine to himself that was Tafani's work environment continued with a vengeance in his private office space. Walls plastered with more photos, honorary degrees, and acknowledgments—all focused on him—surrounded a solid wood executive desk that remained uncluttered, it seemed, so as not to distract from its hand-crafted contours and antique brass hardware. Tafani seated himself in a tilt-swivel chair behind the desk and gestured for his guests to do the same on a couch upholstered with matching plush leather.

Again, Roz accepted the invitation as Harlan opted instead to remain on his feet and browse the surroundings, taking in probably the only public property in all of Watersmeet Township to escape budgetary restraint.

"Nice office," Harlan said. "What do you think, Roz? Should we get the name of Mr. *Tee's* interior decorator before we leave?"

Roz responded with a look that said, *Behave, Harlan.*

"Julie has it in the Rolodex up front," Tafani said. "She can get it for you on your way out."

"We appreciate that," Harlan replied. "We also appreciate you making the time to meet with us. You mind telling us why you're willing to help with George Viola's case?"

Tafani shrugged. "Can't say as I know the man. It's his attorney, my friend Kerry Jammer, who I'm willing to help. Jammer's a good man."

"He says the same about you," Harlan said, holding a straight face. Roz held the same expression, though visibly pressing her lips together as she no doubt recalled Jammer's actual description of the man.

"So, Mr. *Tee*," Harlan continued, "Jammer tells us that you have a theory about who may have killed Zach Romanelli—a theory that differs from the one held by the county sheriff and prosecutor. Can you elaborate?"

"Sure. But let's get something straight first. I'm not saying she did it. I'm just saying it seems entirely possible that she did—maybe just as possible as that Viola fella being responsible."

"Who's *she*?"

"You know, our local assessor, Jackie Diebolt. Or former assessor, I should say."

"And why would Ms. Diebolt do such a thing? Because Zach Romanelli simply got the better of her at some meeting of your Board of Review?"

"There's more to it than you're making it sound like, Holmes. A lot more."

"Okay, tell us about it."

"That meeting was the culmination of all kinds of things, a real shit storm that had been brewing since over a year ago when I was pressured into hiring Diebolt to be our township assessor."

"Who pressured you into hiring her?"

"Practically every municipal official in the western UP, including the boards of commissioners for both Gogebic and Ontonagon Counties and the chief execs of damn near every city, township, and village in those counties. Watersmeet had an opening for the job, and they all saw it as an opportunity to bring in an MMAO-4 assessor if all the municipalities chipped in to cover her salary."

"What's an MMAO-4 assessor?"

"A level-four Michigan Master Assessing Officer. It's the highest level of assessor certification you can get in Michigan. Only a half dozen assessors in the whole state have it."

"And Jackie Diebolt is one of them?"

"That's right. And the only one in the UP. She was working on the east side of the peninsula, in Sault Ste. Marie, at the time, when Romanelli and his fancy downstate law firm set their sights on the western peninsula to test out and their dark-store property tax loophole. They saw us as easy pickings because our towns are staffed with lower-level assessors."

"So, you went along with the other municipalities and agreed to hire Ms. Diebolt to even the playing field against these downstate lawyers."

"Yes, I did, and it turned out to be the worst hiring decision I've ever made for our town."

"Why?"

"Oh, man, I'll tell you what, Holmes. She was a head case right from the get-go—the damn *dyke*."

Roz shot to the edge of the couch and scowled. "What did you just call her? A dyke?"

"Damn straight it's what I called her—or *it*—whatever the hell she is. From day one she could make a big fuss about something as simple as her name, of all things, some days being okay with what it actually is, Jacqueline, but other days insisting she be called *Jackie* or *Jack*, like she can't make up her mind if she's a man or a woman."

"Sounds like she might be gender fluid," Roz offered.

"Gender what?" Tafani asked.

"Gender fluid. Also known as nonbinary. Someone who doesn't identify as being strictly one gender or the other and can feel more female on some occasions, more male on others, and sometimes something in between—or neither at all. You know, *fluid*."

"No, I don't know. All I can tell you is there was nothing fluid about the way she acted and dressed. Always wearing suits and ties and keeping her hair cut short—like a *man*, for crying out loud."

"That's gender expression," Roz said, "something altogether separate from gender identity. One can express oneself outwardly as one gender, while identifying psychologically as another. It's really no big deal."

"It is if you work for me. I won't have it. It's disruptive."

Roz cocked her head. "Is that how she was acting during the meeting of the Board of Review last March? Like a man?"

"You bet she was. Dropping f-bombs like a sailor and getting into Romanelli's face when he was up at the whiteboard running his numbers on one of the stores."

"Well, would you have fired a *man* for acting that way?"

Roz's question hung in the air as she turned to Harlan and gave him a long look. He could feel her reading his mind and ascertaining where it had suddenly been transported by the question—to his final days as a detective with the Michigan State Police. They were downsizing the department in those days, and he was let go and replaced by a younger, female detective. Initially, it seemed to his attorney that age and sex must have been factors in the decision, which would have meant that Harlan had been the victim of civil rights violations. Although he later learned that his attorney was wrong, the indignation Harlan experienced at the mere prospect of being so victimized would never be forgotten.

"I didn't fire her," Tafani objected when Roz turned back to him. "I put her on administrative leave."

The denial fueled the sting of Harlan's recollection of his own near experience with workplace discrimination. "You put her on leave *without pay*, which is the same damn thing as firing her, Mr. *Tee.*"

"Why are you calling me that, Holmes?"

"Calling you what? Mr. *Tee?*"

"Yeah."

"Because that's what your receptionist told me to call you."

"No she didn't. Not the way you're saying it. I heard her when you got here, clear as day through the walls. You're not saying it the way she told you to. Like maybe you gotta problem with me."

"Maybe? You think?"

"Harlan, just chill," Roz said. "Please accept my apologies, Mr. T. We've gotten way off track here, and that's my fault, for getting us into your dealings with Ms. Diebolt. And it's also my fault that my partner is behaving the way he is. Being a woman myself, I can get defensive about how women are sometimes treated in the workplace. And now, it seems, he's coming to my defense."

"No he's not," Tafani argued. "He's been saying my name that way since you two first set foot in my office. I don't like it. And I think he knows it."

"I'll tell you what I know, Mr.—"

"Harlan! That's enough!" Roz admonished. "We came here looking for help with our case, and Mr. T's been kind enough to take time out of his busy schedule to try to provide it. So let's just stick to the point of our being here and finish up with our questions, shall we?"

"What other questions do you have?" Tafani asked.

"Well, due entirely to my own digression, sir, you still haven't had a chance to explain your answer to our first question—Why would Jacqueline Diebolt kill a man over a mere property tax dispute?"

"That's what I've been explaining all along. She was some big-shot MMAO-4 assessor who was supposed to take Romanelli down. But *he* ended up whipping *her* ass, right in front of the Board of Review and government reps from practically every municipality in the UP. He humiliated her. And she had a meltdown—went batshit crazy in front of all of us, screaming at the man and shoving him into the whiteboard. Hell, it took three of us to physically remove her from the room."

"I see," Roz said, her tone less than sincere. "She killed him because he embarrassed her."

Harlan had to pretend to be distracted by his cellphone after Roz's comment, lest he smile at her with approval for making the subtle jab.

"You're still making it sound like nothing happened," Tafani complained. "I'm telling you, there's more to it than you're seeing."

"There must be, sir. Please, tell us more about what may have made her homicidal."

"Well, you know, there's me firing her—with the approval of all the municipalities, I might add."

"You mean, putting her on administrative leave, don't you?"

"Yes, of course, that's what I meant to say. On leave… uh… without pay… which is, you know, a pretty hard pill to swallow."

"Uh huh."

"And then there's the future consequences for her now that she has this blemish on her employment record. It'll be harder for her to find work."

"Assuming that another of only five other MMAO-4 assessors in the entire state is available to the next employer who needs one," Roz countered. She let Tafani mull over the point before adding, "Speaking of hiring decisions, Mr. T, before you decided to hire Ms. Diebolt, did you do a criminal background check on her?"

"Of course. We always do."

"What did you find?"

"Well… nothing."

"No criminal history whatsoever?"

"No, but she sure as hell committed a crime that night at the meeting when she assaulted Romanelli. And I'm not the only person who suspects her of being capable of taking it further."

"Are you saying that others there at the meeting share your suspicions?"

"No. I'm saying that the sheriff did, for a while anyway, until that guy Viola went and put the noose around his own neck."

"You've spoken with Sheriff Mills about this? When?"

"A couple days after Romanelli was reported missing, the sheriff came asking specifically about Jackie Diebolt and what she did at the Board of Review meeting. I told him exactly what happened, and it obviously got him to thinking, especially when I told him what I saw of her the next day, just before the follow-up meeting that Romanelli missed."

"You saw Jackie Diebolt the next day?"

"That's right. She came in first thing that morning, like I told her to the night before, to clear her stuff out of the office. And get this—she shows up wearing the same clothes she had on the night before, looking like she hadn't slept a wink. And guess what she claims she was up doing all night?"

"I have no idea."

"Driving her fucking car is what she told me."

"Driving her car? Where?"

"Nowhere in particular. 'Just went for a drive,' is what she said when I told her she looked like hell and asked what she'd been doing all night. 'A drive across the UP and back,' she said. And I'm like, 'You went for a drive across the whole fucking UP—and back—after all the snow we got yesterday?' And she says, 'Yeah, to visit my ex-boyfriend—someone I could talk to about losing my job—but then I changed my mind and turned back.' And I'm thinking like, *You? A boyfriend? That's fucking impossible, freak*."

"Why would that be impossible?" Roz objected. "A person designated female at birth could go on to be gender fluid, express themselves as male, and still be sexually attracted to men. Gender identity and expression don't dictate one's sexual orientation."

"What the fuck are you talking about, Detective?"

"What are *you* talking about, Mr. T? Why does any of this matter?"

"Because like I said, when I told Sheriff Mills about it, he got real suspicious. 'So, she's got no alibi for that night,' were his exact words."

Harlan had been messing with his phone but, at this point, he stopped and looked up.

"Ahh, so now you're interested in what I have to say," Tafani said, returning Harlan's stare.

"I'm interested in what else the sheriff had to say."

Tafani offered a gotcha smile. "I dunno, Holmes. I like having connections with important people like the sheriff. It keeps me in the know, and knowledge is power. Maybe I shouldn't betray his confidence."

"You already have, Mr. *Tee*."

"There you go again, Holmes, saying my name that way."

"Would you rather I call you Archibal—"

"Both of you!" Roz shouted, "Knock it off!"

Harlan went back to messing with his phone as Roz continued. "My partner does make a point, Mr. T. You've already told us some of what the sheriff has said about the case."

"But I haven't told you the best part—the part I know he wouldn't want me telling anyone, especially Viola's defense team."

Harlan could feel the man's stare but did not look up from the email he had opened on his phone. He was not reading it, however. He was pretending to, as though he had something more important to attend to than this witness, whose ego no doubt could not tolerate for long being second to anything or anyone else.

"Why aren't you listening to me, Holmes? I know you want to hear this."

Harlan stuck the phone in his pocket and started for the door without so much as even glancing at Tafani.

"You're leaving?" Tafani complained. "Without hearing me out?"

"You're wasting our time," Harlan said, pausing at the door. "Let's go, Roz."

Roz rose from the couch and started for the door.

"Jackie Diebolt was a suspect!" Tafani blurted. "That's what Sheriff Mills called her the next time we spoke. A *suspect*—that was his word. And cops don't use that word unless they're real suspicious, like they think they got their perp. Until then, they call someone a person of interest. I've been around. I know these things."

Roz stopped and turned back as Harlan continued to wait at the door. "When did you have this subsequent conversation with the sheriff?" she asked.

"Right after they found Romanelli's body. Before Viola showed up and got her off the hook."

"What hook? What'd the sheriff have on her?"

"After they found the body, he called me into the station to give a formal statement—a video-recorded statement—about everything I saw, you know, her going nuts the way she did at the meeting and assaulting Romanelli, and her looking like something the cat dragged in the next day, and telling me some cockamamie story about driving across the UP right after a blizzard to see an ex-boyfriend. It was after he shut off the video when the sheriff told me that she wasn't cooperating with him or the prosecutor when they tried to question her about that night."

"Well, she can't be too happy with anyone from local government after they joined you in firing her. And she does have a right to remain silent."

"Is that what she was doing—remaining silent—when she told the sheriff and the prosecutor, right to their faces, *arrest me or fuck off* during her interrogation? I'm telling you, their sights were set as much on her as they were on George Viola until he practically confessed to the whole thing."

Chapter 12

After they finished at Township Hall, Harlan dropped Roz off at the Roadhouse Grill for a lunch date she had previously scheduled with her old childhood friend, Patty Rock. While there, he grabbed a takeout sandwich and soda before continuing in the Jeep by himself to the nearby Ottawa National Forest Visitor Center.

Among the vehicles in the center's parking lot when he arrived was a pickup truck with government plates and logos on each side for the United States Forest Service. Harlan passed the vehicle on foot and then followed a paved walkway marked with painted bear tracks that led along the center's fieldstone facade to its entrance.

On display inside were many interpretive exhibits and animal mounts, including a wild-eyed wolf who stood guard over a children's reading area and an enormous black bear on its hind legs who welcomed visitors to the "Bear's Den" souvenir shop.

Next to the wolf was a brochure stand. Harlan paused by it, pretending to browse some promotional materials while waiting for a few tourists to finish their conversations with a helpdesk employee who worked inside a circular information counter in the middle of the room. The employee fit the description of Ranger Kole Koerber provided earlier by some locals at the Grill—a man so youthful looking in his olive drab uniform that, but for his badge and gun, he could have passed for a Boy Scout.

"Ranger K?" Harlan asked upon reaching the counter.

"Yes, I am. And you must be Detective Holmes."

"How did you know?"

Koerber set a laptop computer on the counter. "Because everybody in town knows," he answered as he turned the screen toward Harlan. "And because I was advised to check you out before you tracked me down."

Harlan looked at the screen. Downloaded on it was a photo of him and Roz alongside an article about their drug bust on Drummond Island a few years ago.

"Who advised you to run a search on me?"

"Sheriff Mills did, right after you left county lockup this morning."

"I suppose he also advised you not to speak with me."

"He did."

"Even if all I want from you is background information about the discovery of Zach Romanelli's body in the forest? You were the first responder that night, right?"

"Look, Mr. Holmes, this is nothing personal. I'm sure you've done some other background research already—on me—and you know why I can't help you."

Harlan had in fact learned beforehand what he could about Kole Koerber online and from some of the locals at the Grill. Koerber, it turned out, had been one of the two sheriff's deputies previously stationed in Watersmeet who were laid off over a year ago as part of the municipal downsizing caused by tax revenue shortfalls. According to Harlan's sources, the sheriff's termination decisions inexplicably disregarded the seniority of Koerber and his partner over some other deputies who were retained back at headquarters in Bessemer.

"I can relate," Harlan said.

"To what?"

"To being laid off. It happened to me too, years ago, when I was a state trooper. There was a time when I would have done anything for my former boss to get that job back."

Koerber glanced at him sideways. "Yeah, right, Mr. Holmes."

"What? You don't believe me?"

"Of course I don't."

"Why?"

"Because of what I've been reading online. Hell, this article right here says that after you left the Michigan State Police, you took up with mobsters. Even when you made the big drug bust on Drummond, they say, you were working for a Chicago underboss, some bad guy named Shotgun Gino Cruzano. That doesn't sound like an ex-cop who wanted his job back."

"By then I no longer did. I'm talking about before that case, during a time when I couldn't stop thinking of myself as being anything but a state trooper."

"If that's true, then maybe you can explain how you got past the feeling of wanting to go back," Koerber said with less skepticism in his tone.

Maybe he really wants to know, Harlan thought, *because maybe he's lost hope of ever returning to his old job and is dealing with the reality of being stranded behind this information counter indefinitely.*

"I didn't get over not being a cop until I met her," Harlan said, pointing at Roz's image in the photo. "She helped me get my shit together, both professionally and personally. Ironically, when the Drummond case was over, MSP wanted me back. But I didn't want to stop working with her. I'd finally moved on."

"You mean to say that they offered you your job back—as a detective—and you turned it down?"

"That's right."

Ranger K looked down at the computer screen and began shaking his head. "Says here you're a con man, Mr. Holmes. That you messed with the heads of those drug dealers to get them to talk. Is that what you're doing with me right now? Messing with my head—bullshitting me about how you can relate to me—trying to get me to talk?"

"Well, if I thought it would work, I most definitely *would* lie to you. But it just so happens I'm *not* on this occasion. I really did lose my job, I really did miss it, and I really did get over it—enough to turn it down when they offered it back to me. If you had proof of all that, would it make a difference to you? Would it make you more willing to talk to me?"

Ranger K continued looking down at the computer screen. "Obviously you know," Harlan added, "that as a federal officer, you don't answer to the county sheriff on this case. It's *your* call—not his—as to whether you have any objection to helping a PI who's simply looking for the truth on behalf of the accused. What do you say, Ranger? Do you object to me knowing the truth?"

"How would you prove what you're saying about your good standing with the Michigan State Police?" Ranger K asked.

"I wouldn't. I'd only suggest that you call their Traverse City Post and check for yourself. If you ask about me, I can pretty much guarantee that they'll put you through to a Detective Riley Summers, my former partner. She'll confirm what I'm saying. And if you're still not satisfied, tell her you want to hear it from the captain. He never liked my mobster clients, by the way. But he knows I never lost sight of right from wrong. He's the one who offered me my old job back."

They paused their conversation and watched the last of a few tourists leave the visitor center. "Looks like a good time for you to make a phone call," Harlan said. "I'll step outside and give you some privacy."

Harlan had meandered about halfway back to his Jeep when his cellphone rang. The caller ID said, "Riley Summers." He let it bounce into voicemail and waited until he reached his vehicle to play back the message. "Harlan, it's Riley Summers. I hear you're in the UP communing with Mother Nature, among others. Call me as soon as you get this message."

He instead waited a while longer by the Jeep, watching the visitor center entrance. A few minutes later Ranger K showed up at the glass door and manipulated the hands on a cardboard clock hanging inside to inform visitors that the center would be closed until 1:30 p.m.

Ranger K did not join Harlan, however. He got in his truck and had backed it out of his parking spot by the time Harlan sprinted over, his right knee objecting to every step. "Ranger K, where are you going?"

The truck's driver-side window dropped down. "To the Grill, for something to eat on the road."

"On the road? Where to?"

"The Mystery Light viewing area."

"Alone?"

"I doubt you would allow that."

Chapter 13

"Hey Google, call Roz," Harlan said as he drove north on Highway 45.

The Jeep's hands-free system followed the prompt, and Roz answered on the third ring. "Harlan? You're not coming to get me already, are you?"

"Not yet. I'm heading to the Mystery Light viewing area for a meeting with Ranger K. Just wanted to let you know I'll be running late."

"No problem," Roz said. "You won't have to pick me up anyway. Patty and I are extending the visit to tool around town and see some of our old stomping grounds. She's offered to drop me off at the campground later, after dinner."

"Glad it's going well."

"Sounds like it is for you, too. How did you talk the ranger into a meeting at the crime scene?"

Harlan's phone alerted him to an incoming call from Detective Riley Summers of the Michigan State Police—her second attempt to reach him since he told the ranger to call her. "I'll have to tell you later, Roz. I just got a call that I have to take."

He switched over to the incoming call. "How's it going, Riley?"

"I guess that depends on whether you plan to involve me again in whatever mischief you're up to this time, Harlan."

Twice in the past Harlan had pulled Detective Summers into one of his cases, the last time to assist with the drug bust on Drummond Island. Although she received ample credit for being the arresting officer on the scene, she functioned more like a pawn in a scam he was running on the perps. In fact, to this day, she still did not know the whole story.

"Don't worry, Riley, I have no plans for you. Heck, I didn't even call you today. One of my witnesses did."

"Uh huh. At your suggestion. So, tell me, what have you managed to get into in the remote hinterlands of the western UP?"

"Have you heard of the Mystery Light murder?"

"I have."

"Well, that's the case. My client is the suspect, George Viola."

"Is he innocent?"

"That's what he hired me to find out."

"What do you mean, *to find out?*"

"I mean, he doesn't know whether or not he did it. So, I'm going to find out for him."

"What? How the hell could he not know something like that?"

"It's a long story, Riley. And much of it is confidential information."

"Confidential? Which part? The man has already spilled his guts to the police about everything but the lethal blow itself."

"Well, that's the part he doesn't remember. And like you said, a man would remember something like that if he did it."

"Good grief, Harlan. You sound ridiculous."

"And you sound like you're familiar with this case, Riley. Is MSP involved?"

"Not as the lead agency."

"But MSP is involved," Harlan pressed.

"It's just a support role. We're providing some resources that Gogebic County lacks."

"Are you one of those resources?"

"I am now."

"Why?"

"Because of you, Harlan. Why else? As soon as the captain learned that you're working for the defense, he offered me up to Gogebic County for whatever help they may need to deal with *you.*"

"To deal with me? Why would they need help with that?"

"Just don't make me come up there, Harlan."

***

Harlan turned from Highway 45 onto Robbins Pond Road but stopped well short of the viewing area. He had traveled this short stretch of road several times in the last twenty hours but now noticed for the first time something near the turnoff—a rusted metal post about a foot in diameter and five feet high, just off the right side of the road, partially obscured in the brush. He looked to his left and, just off the other side of the road, saw another, identical post, also in the brush. Each post had a thick eye bolt protruding from the top.

As Harlan contemplated the purpose for the posts, Ranger K turned onto the road, slowed while glancing at him, and then proceeded to the Mystery Light viewing area. By the time Harlan caught up, Ranger K was already standing at the guardrail.

This was Harlan's first visit to the viewing area, though he knew what to expect based on Roz's description and his online research. Spray painted on the guardrail was the phrase, "The Paulding Light," which a nearby Forest Service sign described as the light of a lantern carried by the ghost of a railroad brakeman who a century ago had been crushed by a train while trying to warn its engineer of an obstruction on the tracks. The alleged ghost, however, was reportedly a creature of the night and would not likely make an appearance at this hour.

"It was April 15, around 9:00 p.m., when I got the call from county dispatch," Ranger K said after Harlan had finished reading the sign.

"About the discovery of the body?"

"Well, yeah. That's what we came here to talk about, right? I mean, we could discuss the fact that you and your partner are camping out here three weeks before our forest campgrounds are officially open to the public. But then I'd have to kick you two out of here."

"Think I'd rather talk about the night of April 15."

"Okay then. After getting the call at nine, I came here as quick as I could. Got here inside twenty minutes." Ranger K pointed to a spot near the Forest Service sign describing the site. "A car was parked there. A Subaru. And alongside it a snowmobile. I checked them out for a minute and then ran down the path and got to the hikers in another three, maybe four, minutes. They were still out there with the dead guy, a little less than a half mile into the woods, I estimate. You want to see where I found them?"

"Sure, but a quick question, first," Harlan said, pointing back at the highway. "Those two metal posts I saw at the turnoff—what are they for? A gate to control access to this road?"

"A chain," Ranger K replied, "in the back of my truck. I hook it to the posts when Robbins Pond Road needs to be blocked off due to heavy rain or snow. Otherwise, we can get visitors coming to see the Mystery Light who get stuck in mud or snow and end up calling on me to get them out."

"What qualifies as heavy snow?"

"Eight or more inches within a twenty-four-hour period," Ranger K answered. "That day we had only six, though I gave some thought to blocking the road anyway because it came fast, with high winds and drifting conditions. But I ended up deciding not to."

They forged ahead on foot along the path that extended beyond the guardrail and into the forest, plodding through mud and remnants of melting snow beneath a tunnel of trees that had not yet begun sprouting leaves. Along the way a rickety bridge gave them passage over a creek so swelled by the melt-off that their final steps to the other bank were through frigid water about an inch higher than Harlan's ankle-high hiking boots.

Ranger K stopped abruptly after they crossed the bridge.

"Is this the spot?" Harlan asked.

The ranger looked ahead. "No, it's up there, about thirty yards beyond that bear."

Harlan scanned the woods to both sides of the path ahead until he saw, on the left, a black bear staring back at him. It wasn't much bigger than the German shepherds he recalled seeing in the K-9 unit back when he was a state trooper. "Probably a female," he guessed given the size.

"Definitely female," Ranger K responded. "Her cubs are on the other side of the path."

Harlan looked right and squinted into the forest until he located them. "I take it you don't want to walk the path in between."

"She's not *that* small. Besides, she won't leave her little ones alone over there much longer now that we've shown up."

No sooner had the ranger said this than mother bear began lumbering her way toward the cubs. Soon after, the family of three disappeared into the woods and the two men were able to continue their hike.

"Right here," Ranger K announced as he veered a few paces off the path and stopped. "This is where those hikers found the scarf sticking out of a snowbank. The woman—Professor Lorna Rybicki—was the one who spotted it and discovered that it was still tied around Romanelli's neck."

"When she pulled his head out of the snow," Harlan said.

"And the rest of him by the time I got here. The guy was still fully outfitted for cross-country skiing and looked to be in good enough condition to still do it, except for the fact he wasn't breathing."

"He was wearing skis?"

"Yep, and still had poles strapped to his wrists." Ranger K stared down at the spot. "The medical examiner said it was the snow he was buried in that kept his body fresh, despite being dead for probably a month. And that helped establish cause of death—vehicular homicide by something bigger than any ATV that could've fit on this trail."

"So, the nature of his injuries suggested he was killed somewhere else, by a motor vehicle, and then was moved here."

"The injuries, and the beet juice that was all over his snowsuit."

"Beet juice?"

"Yeah. A few of the UP's cash-strapped counties, including Gogebic County, have been experimenting with a new de-icing agent for the roads in the winter—beet juice. It's cheaper but supposedly just as good as road salt at melting snow and ice. Downside is, it's messy. And it stinks. Believe it or not, Romanelli's body still had the stench of it, though the professor didn't realize it was just beet juice all over him. She thought it was blood. Man, she was carrying on when I got here."

"About the ghost train running him down?"

Ranger K laughed. "Sounds like you've read some of the local papers. Trust me, they've grossly embellished her story."

"She told you something else?"

"Oh, she told me about the ghost train all right, but not about it running Romanelli down."

"What'd she say?"

"That her grad student—the guy with her, Stuart Lamar—had actually seen the train earlier that night. He even had a conversation with it, she said."

"Lamar talked to the ghost train?"

"Not like you and I are talking. Telepathically, she said, earlier in the evening before she joined him. She said the train told Lamar to walk the path and look for something—something important that needed to be found before the spring melt."

"Like it knew there was a body out here that law enforcement needed to discover soon?"

"That was my take on what this train supposedly said. And that much of it was true. We had a warm spell and lots of rain the following week. Had those hikers not found the body when they did, it would have been exposed to all kinds of wildlife in these woods—wolves, coyotes, bobcats, you name it—and may never have been found in the condition needed to determine cause, time, and location of death."

"Time and location, too?"

Ranger K nodded. "Gogebic County is the only county in the western UP using beet juice to de-ice the roads, and it only uses it for major snow events. The last one of those before the night they found the body was the blizzard that dumped over a foot of snow on our roads on March 12—the day Romanelli was last seen alive."

"So, you and local law enforcement think Romanelli was hit that night by a motor vehicle on a road in Gogebic County that had been sprayed with beet juice?"

"Yes, and if he was skiing the Agonikak Trail, like some witnesses say he probably was, that narrows the possible murder scene to one of the roads that intersect with the stretch of trail he used between Land O' Lakes and Watersmeet." The ranger paused before adding, "That's why the Forest Service lost jurisdiction over the case to the Gogebic County Sheriff."

"Because the murder *might* have happened at one of those intersections?" Harlan asked, his tone skeptical. "On some unspecified county road?"

"I suspect that the county sheriff found a way to narrow the possible crime scene down further, to just a few of those roads, or maybe even pinpointed the specific one."

"How?"

"Well, before I lost the lead on the case, I had a call in to someone over at the County Road Commission. I was planning to ask CRC about the road crew's schedule for snow removal and de-icing that night, you know, to get a handle on the exact sequence that those roads intersecting the Agonikak Trail got sprayed with beet juice. But we never had the conversation."

"Who at CRC did you try to contact?"

"An old friend of mine, and former partner. The deputy I served with back when we worked for the sheriff's department together, until the layoffs."

"Your former partner now works for CRC?"

"It's where he landed after we were canned. He heads up the road crew for the eastern half of Gogebic County these days. Thing is, Mr. Holmes, I don't think he'll talk to you. He wouldn't talk to me about it after I lost the case."

"Why?"

"Because unlike me, he still works for the county, and he's following Sheriff Mills' gag order on this."

"What's his name?"

"Rayden Jude."

"Do you think you could try again? See if he might talk to me?"

Ranger K smiled. "I suppose I could tell him about the former state trooper who got canned the same way we did and is now an earnest PI in search of truth, justice, and all that bullshit you laid on me. Can't make any guarantees, of course. He and I haven't had much contact since the layoffs. As you probably know, it's hard to hang out with folks who remind you of something like that."

"I understand," Harlan said, "but just the same, I'd appreciate anything you can do to try to connect me with him."

Harlan's attention returned to the other crime scene, the one in front of them, and the peculiar circumstances surrounding its discovery. "What do you think about this claim that a ghost train is to thank for finding the body here?"

"I can only tell you what the professor said."

"But, what do you think of what she said about this ghost train's alleged concern—like mine—for truth, justice, and all that bullshit?"

"I think she believed everything she told me. And I think Stuart Lamar was hiding something when he denied her story."

"Lamar didn't back her up?"

"Not a word of it. He took me aside and told me that the professor was suffering a break from reality due to the shock of discovering the body."

"So he claims to have never told her about an encounter he had with a ghost train."

"That's right. He said the two of them just went for a hike, like a stroll in the woods. Which still made no sense to me."

"Why?"

"Because we had freezing temps and blowing snow that night, and he was wearing nothing but a hoodie, khakis, and tennis shoes. So I asked him, where's your coat? Your boots? Your gloves and hat?'"

"And what did he say?"

"Nothing. He got evasive with me. Wouldn't even give me a straight answer when I simply asked whether he came here first, ahead of her, and then called her to join him, which was what she said happened—and which was obviously true."

"How do you know?"

"Because his Subaru's tire tracks were completely covered over with snow when I got here, while her snowmobile tracks were fresh, barely affected by any falling or blowing snow. That means he was here before the storm ended—and she wasn't. It wasn't a planned excursion together. He was out here alone, and for some reason called her to join him—just like she said."

"What do you think was his reason?"

"Well, I don't believe in ghosts, and I don't get the impression that Lamar does either. Which leaves only one other reason that I can think of."

"Do you think he already knew about the body and conjured up a ghost story, so he'd have someone else out here with him when he found it?"

The question went unanswered as Harlan snapped a few photos of the scene and imagined Lamar's more innocent explanation—the couple out for an evening hike happening upon a half-buried scarf and deciding, out of simple curiosity, to pull the rest of it out of the snow. *It was close to the trail, after all*, Harlan thought, *and the body attached to it was buried only under snow, not underground.* The train of thought led to another. *Why didn't the gravedigger take it further into the woods and bury it deeper?* An answer came to mind as he recalled George Viola's enraged and drunken condition on the night of March 12. *Maybe he just forgot to bring along a shovel.*

"I imagine you don't see many crimes like this out here in the national forest," Harlan said after snapping the last photo.

Ranger K shook his head. "No, and like I said, this one didn't even happen here. Not the murder anyway. All we got was the body."

Harlan sensed the ranger's disappointment over the Forest Service having lost its role as the agency in charge of the case. Heading up a murder investigation probably would have been a welcome diversion from his usual duties behind the visitor center's helpdesk. "What crimes do you generally get in these woods?" Harlan asked, curious about what else the ranger did besides chat with tourists.

Ranger K stifled a laugh. "Well, on a regular basis, I get to roust the kids who come to Robbins Pond Road to drink booze, smoke weed, and have sex between sightings of the Light. Next most common crimes are hunting and fishing violations. Some of those are committed by real felons, but they're hard to catch."

"You mean, poachers?" Harlan asked, recalling the gunshots that woke him and Roz before sunrise that day. Maybe they should have reported the incident, he was beginning to think.

"Oh yeah, we definitely get poachers in these woods. Lots. And the bigger the game—bears, wolves, moose—the better the perps are at dodging me."

"Dodging *you*?" Harlan remarked. "What law enforcement resources do you have out here?"

"You're looking at all of it, right in front of you, for the entire Watersmeet District—which covers about a third of the million-acre Ottawa National Forest."

"Seriously? How do they expect you to be the least bit effective covering all that ground by yourself?"

"They don't. They just expect me to be as visible as possible, you know, to keep the honest hunters honest."

"What about the tribal police?" Harlan asked. "I'm sure the Chippewa don't take kindly to poachers cutting into their wildlife harvests."

"They have the same problems I do trying to police this much forest. There are never witnesses. Just animal carcasses stripped of parts of value that you randomly come across now and then. You might even hear the gunshots but not find the scene of the crime for weeks."

"I think I may have," Harlan said.

"May have what?"

"Heard gunshots this morning… an isolated burst of shots more consistent with someone hunting than target shooting. Whatever it was, they woke us up, my partner and me, about an hour before sunrise."

"You sure it was gunfire?"

"My partner was. She woke before me and heard more of the blasts, six or seven of them. Steady cadence, she said. Not erratic like fireworks or a car backfiring. She thinks they came from west of the campground, deep in the woods."

"Did you investigate?"

"Sure. But it was like you said. There was no sign of anything."

"That's how it always is, Mr. Holmes. Truth is, the only poacher I ever bust is the weekend warrior fishing on an expired license or whose kid catches a turtle and makes the mistake of showing it off to me before trying to take it home."

Chapter 14

After meeting with the ranger, Harlan returned to the campsite for a for a quick snack before continuing in his Jeep along ORV trails heading generally west through the forest. His aim was to do the kind of investigation he probably should have done earlier that day when he and Roz heard gunshots from that direction. The search, however, got him nowhere, except almost lost.

It was getting dark by the time Harlan found his way back to his campsite. Roz had texted during his journey and was herself due back in another hour. That would be enough time, he thought, to create the same romantic, fireside setting that she had tried to create the night before, until he blew it up with news of a meeting with a prospective client.

Harlan had two guys on his mind as he built the fire and prepared appetizers. One of them was Stuart Lamar, the guy who was so instrumental to finding Zach Romanelli's body that, according to Ranger K, he might have known where to look for it all along. The other was the unidentified guy whom George Viola claimed he befriended at a support-group meeting on the night Romanelli was killed and his body ditched.

Could Lamar and George's new friend be the same guy? Harlan wondered. That might explain how Lamar could have known the location of the body all along; he could have learned of it from George. And it might also explain why Lamar, whose conscience may have become troubled, would later tell his colleague, the professor, that a ghost directed him to search the Mystery Light's trail. It was an excuse, albeit a bizarre one, that would allow discovery of the body without incriminating his friend George. Of course, that bizarre excuse would become even more unbelievable if Harlan proved the two were indeed friends or otherwise acquainted.

The campfire was blazing and the appetizers—an assortment of fresh fruit, cheeses, and crackers—looked sumptuous in the orange glow of flames dancing beneath a star-studded sky on this clear, cool night deep in Michigan's northern woods. All that remained to be done was to uncork the wine and let it breathe for the appropriate length of time. Harlan checked his watch. Roz was due in twenty minutes. *Perfect,* he thought as he popped the cork and then eased himself into a canvas chair facing the fire.

Ten minutes had passed when the hypnotic effect of the fire was disrupted by the headlights of a vehicle turning into the campsite. *Must be Roz's ride,* Harlan assumed. But due to the glare of the headlights, which remained on after the engine stopped, he could not confirm the assumption. All he could see was an outline of the vehicle—a massive SUV—and even less of the person who stepped out of it.

Then the headlights went off, and he could see that the approaching person was far too tall to be Roz. *Might not even be a woman,* Harlan realized as the visitor neared.

She… or he… stepped into the glow of the fire and stared at him from the other side of it, through the smoke and sparks it spewed.

"I'm Jacqueline Diebolt."

Harlan rose slowly from his chair, his mind turning over what he had learned that day about the local assessor who assaulted Zach Romanelli at the meeting of the Board of Review on the eve of his disappearance—the ballistic, gender-fluid assessor, who this evening identified *not* as Jackie or Jack, but as Jacqueline. *That means more woman than man,* Harlan thought, *at least for the moment.* In his binary mindset, that assumption somehow eased his nerves and made fleeting a thought he had of the direction he might bolt into the woods if necessary. Still, he found himself sizing her up ahead of a possible confrontation: her bleached-blonde crew-cut hair, chiseled facial features, and deeply set blue eyes that stared into his, straight on due to their similarity in height, about six feet even. Their builds were also similar, though hers was slightly broader and thicker than his 180-pound frame, as revealed by her tight-fitting leather jacket and jeans.

"Harlan Holmes," he finally replied as he stepped around the fire and extended a hand.

"I know."

"How so?"

"Because everyone in town knows you're at this campground, including my best friend—Julie."

"Julie?" Harlan replied, again searching through memories of his earlier activities that day. "The receptionist at Township Hall?"

"That's right," Diebolt said, "the one whose desk sits right outside the supervisor's office."

Harlan recalled their adjacent workspaces. "Separated by only a paper-thin wall," he said.

Diebolt nodded.

"Did Julie hear what we discussed with your former boss, Mr. *Tee*?"

Diebolt smiled with apparent approval of his judgmental tone as he uttered the moniker. "Julie heard every word of your meeting with that jerk—as did I."

"You too? How? You weren't there."

"I didn't have to be. Julie was, and she knows what Mr. *Tee* has been saying about me to anyone who'll listen—his bullshit theory about me being a murderer. Julie's heard it all. She called me as soon as you and your partner went inside his office, and she put the phone up against the wall so I could listen in."

"So, I take it you came here to correct his story," Harlan said, "to dispute his version of what happened at the March meeting of the Board of Review."

Diebolt shrugged. "Well… what he said about the meeting actually was true."

Harlan experienced a resurgence of his previous thoughts of an escape route into the woods. He glanced in that direction before asking, "You mean to say that Tafani is right about what happened at the meeting? That you flipped out and attacked Romanelli?"

"I did."

"And that it took three men to pull you off him?"

"It did."

Harlan continued studying her—this Caucasian version of the savage warrior Zula played by Grace Jones in the 1980s movie *Conan the Destroyer*—until an alternative emergency plan came to mind. Although he was unarmed, he did not have to remain so... not if he could get ahold of the wine bottle that rested on a log between them.

"May I?" Diebolt asked as Harlan looked at the bottle. It took a moment for him to realize that she was asking if she could pour herself a glass. "Allow me," he replied, grabbing the bottle ahead of her.

She helped herself to some grapes and a canvas chair as Harlan poured each of them a glass of red wine. Choosing to stay on his feet, holding the bottle, he asked, "If you didn't come here to dispute Tafani's statement, then why'd you come?"

"I wanted to say thanks to you and your partner."

"Thanks? For what?"

"The way you two stood up to him and took my side of things."

Harlan tried to imagine where this view of the meeting with Tafani was coming from.

"It meant a lot to me," Diebolt added, "the way your partner called him out for his bias against me because of my gender identity, and how you told him he shouldn't have fired me for it. A lot of straight people wouldn't do a thing like that for someone like me."

Harlan set down the wine bottle and seated himself in the chair next to his guest. "But you must realize why my partner and I went to see Tafani in the first place, don't you?"

"Sure, I understand. You're working for George Viola, who stands accused of murdering Zach Romanelli. And you were hoping that there was something to Tafani's murder theory involving the angry *dyke* who went *batshit crazy* on Romanelli before he disappeared."

She really did hear every word of our meeting, Harlan thought. "And yet you're here to say thanks?"

"And to drink your wine," Diebolt said, smiling, before gulping down what remained in her glass. She helped herself to another, pouring twice what he had poured into her first glass, and then she topped off his first glass to equal the level of her second. "You're falling behind, Mr. Holmes."

Harlan took a long drink before asking, "But you do dispute the murder theory itself, correct? I mean, a moment ago you called it bullshit."

"Because that's what it is."

"How about your lack of an alibi later that night, when Zach Romanelli likely was killed? Is Tafani right about that?"

"I'm afraid he is."

Harlan took another long drink. "So, it's your story that on the night in question, after you whipped Romanelli's ass, you went for a long drive across the entire UP, alone, for an unannounced visit with your ex-boyfriend, but then when you got there you changed your mind, turned around, and drove all the way back—and nobody saw you at any point until Tafani himself did upon your return the next morning, when you came to clear out your desk, looking like something the cat dragged in."

Diebolt swallowed the last of her wine. "That pretty much sums it up."

"Maybe you should eat something more substantial than those grapes," Harlan said as he again grabbed the bottle ahead of her and waited for her to load a plate with cheese and crackers. He then poured her third glass, glanced at her monster SUV, and asked, "Is that what you drove across the UP that night?"

She nodded while chomping on a mouthful of cheddar.

He looked again at the SUV, which now, under the lights of the night sky, he could make out. It was a GMC Yukon Denali. "How many miles do you get on a full tank of gas in that beast?"

"Around four-fifty."

"Was it full when you left that night?"

She shrugged.

"No matter," Harlan said, "the roundtrip to and from Sault Ste Marie is well over four hundred and fifty miles, which means you had to refill it at least once somewhere along the way. Do you remember where?"

"I don't... but I always pay at the pump with my credit card." Her face lit up. "There should be a record of it." She set down her drink, pulled out her cellphone, and began poking at it.

Harlan leaned over and watched as she made her way to a Capital One website and entered her password information. "Didn't Sheriff Mills already cover this ground with you?" he asked.

She looked up from her phone. "It's like Tafani told you earlier. When the sheriff came to interrogate me and poke holes in my lame alibi, I told him to arrest me or fuck off."

"Why were you so uncooperative with him?"

"Because I was fed up with all the local officials by that point. The spineless bastards."

"What do you mean by that?"

"I'm talking about the way all the locals just sat there at that Board of Review meeting, saying nothing while Romanelli ran over us—they were spineless."

"What were they supposed to do? You were their hired gun—the level-four master assessing officer. Weren't you supposed to take on Romanelli?"

"Yes, I was. But he and his slick downstate law firm were pulling a stunt, and I needed the locals to stand by me when I called them on it."

"What stunt?"

"Their comps on the big-box stores were rigged."

"Their what?"

"The comps that they were using to calculate true cash value of the big-box stores—they were rigged."

"Slow down. I still don't follow. These terms you're using—*comps* and *true cash value*—what do they mean?"

Diebolt paused, apparently thinking about how to explain. "Okay, look," she began, "let's say you've just become the proud owner of a brand-new house, and you're about to start paying property taxes on it. In order to figure out how much taxes you owe, we need to know the value of the house—its market value or, as tax experts say, its *true cash value*. The bigger that value, the more property taxes you owe. You with me so far, Mr. Holmes?"

"Sure. I pay property taxes. I get that much of it—all too well."

"Okay. So, you understand how critical it is to figure out the true cash value of your new home. Now, if the house had been listed on the open market and you just bought it, the sales price you paid would be good evidence of that value. But let's say you didn't buy it—you built it brand new. So there's no recent sales price paid for your new house. How do you suppose we figure out its value then?"

Harlan shrugged, "I dunno. Maybe you find sales prices for similar homes."

"Very good, Mr. Holmes. You've just defined what I mean by the other term I'm using—*comps.* It means sales of comparable properties. And that, in fact, is the number-one method for figuring out the true cash value of property for tax purposes. You look at sales of comparable properties and make adjustments to those sales prices as needed because no other property is going to be exactly the same as yours. There can be differences in size, age, state of repair, that sort of thing. Are you still with me, Mr. Holmes?"

Harlan nodded. "Sure. If you want to know the value of a house that was built brand new, you can look at the price someone paid for a similar house, and maybe adjust that price up or down depending on differences between the two."

"That's right, but it's not always so easy. Suppose, for example, that this new house you just built is a mansion, and you built it in a place where nobody's ever built a mansion—say, out in the country somewhere where the only nearby properties that have sold recently are old farmhouses. That means we have no comps to look at—no sale of a similar house in a neighborhood that's even remotely like yours. In that case, how do you think we figure out the true cash value of your new house?"

Harlan shook his head. "I don't know."

"Well," Diebolt pressed, "what was it worth to you—the person who built it?"

He still had no answer.

"Think about it, Mr. Holmes. What was it worth to you to have a mansion in the middle of nowhere?"

"I... guess... whatever I was willing to pay to build it."

"Yes!" Diebolt exclaimed. "And now what we're talking about is an alternative method for determining true cash value—the cost of construction. We use it for odd structures, like your mansion in the middle of nowhere, when we can't find comps. We take the value of the land it's sitting on, add the historical cost to construct the building, and adjust that construction cost for depreciation as the building ages."

Harlan tried his best to appear to share in his guest's obvious enthusiasm for this technical subject matter, but it wasn't easy. "Okay, Ms. Diebolt, this is all very... uh... interesting, but what does it have to do with—"

"Don't you see?" she said. "Which of these two property assessment methods—comparable sales or cost of construction—do you think makes the most sense for a big-box store built somewhere where there are no other mammoth retail facilities?"

"Uh... the... cost of construction?"

"Yes!" Diebolt replied, still riveted. "And that's the method I wanted to use—cost of construction—for all the big-box stores that have been popping up in recent years in the UP. Of course, Romanelli wanted to use the usual method—an analysis of comparable sales."

"Of... course," Harlan responded, clueless.

Diebolt sighed. "Romanelli thought there were comps, for crying out loud, even though big-box stores throughout the country are almost never sold until they go out of business... when they're vacant, worthless, and *dark*."

"Ahh," Harlan said. "The dark-store theory."

"Yes. Romanelli thought he could assess the true cash value of a fully operating big-box store by looking at prices paid for big-box stores that have gone out of business. His comps were dark stores. And the adjustments he made for the difference between them and a fully operating big-box store were negligible."

Harlan began to grasp it. "The dark-store loophole," he said, "you're explaining how it works... how it lowers the true cash value of currently operating big-box stores... and in turn lowers the taxes they pay."

"That's right. And now maybe you can see what I was dealing with at the March meeting of the Board of Review. I saw it as a fight over assessment methodology—comparable sales versus cost of construction. And I wanted to take that fight over methodology all the way to the Michigan Supreme Court if I had to. But the local officials—including Mr. *Tee*—didn't want that. The spineless bastards. They were afraid of litigation and, against my advice, went and negotiated a settlement with Romanelli."

"What kind of settlement?"

"One that had the local officials agreeing to use Romanelli's dark-store methodology if the locals got to pick a neutral real estate appraiser—an outside expert with no stake in the matter—to adjust Romanelli's so-called comps. Romanelli's law firm countered with a proposal that let the locals create a list of five neutral appraisers—five outside experts—from which the law firm would get to pick the one who'd adjust the comps."

In response to Harlan's confused reaction, Diebolt explained, "It's the same kind of agreement you and I might reach if the two of us both wanted the last of the wine in our bottle here. I might put two clean glasses in front of you and suggest that you pour, and I'll pick the one I want."

"Okay, I get it," Harlan said. "The deal was for your municipal clients to identify five expert appraisers who were acceptable to them, and Romanelli's firm would pick the one who'd adjust the comps."

"Exactly."

"Who'd they pick?"

"Some high-profile real estate appraiser from Vestaburg, Michigan. Dave Trumane. He looked good on paper—strong resume, good references, et cetera—but he did not turn out to be the neutral referee that he was supposed to be."

"What do you mean?" Harlan asked.

"You know—what I said before about the comps."

"You said they were rigged."

"They were."

"By Trumane?"

"Had to be. He faxed in his final analyses for all the comps on the day of the Board of Review meeting."

"March 12?"

"Yes, right before the meeting started, which gave me no time to deal with the bomb he'd dropped on me."

"The bomb meaning…"

"Trumane's adjustments on Romanelli's comps were worse for us than Romanelli's were before the settlement. For some of the properties, far worse. That's why I lost my shit at the meeting. Romanelli was running Trumane's numbers on the whiteboard, and they were driving down my estimates of true cash values on every parcel of big-box property by fifty percent or more. And the whole time, the local officials—including Mr. *Tee*—were looking at me like I was supposed to do something about it. Those cowards caved on assessment methodology and let Romanelli's law firm pick the expert to apply it. And then they're scowling at me, like it's somehow my fault."

"So that's why you're not fond of the local officials around here."

"You got that right, Mr. Holmes. Fuck 'em all."

The two then turned to Diebolt's cellphone, but by this point the screen had gone dark. She powered it back up and returned to her credit-card account information. Harlan scooted close and asked, "Does it show any transactions on that night?"

Before Diebolt answered, however, another vehicle pulled into the campsite alongside the Yukon. Again, the glare of the headlights made it difficult to see anything more than an outline of who exited the vehicle. But the outline was all Harlan needed to identify his next visitor.

Chapter 15

Roz stepped into the glow of the campfire, on the side opposite her partner and his guest, who remained huddled close together over the cellphone, the near-empty bottle of wine beside them. The look on Roz's face made clear that Harlan had some explaining to do. He turned to his guest. "This is my partner, Roz Cortez. Roz, this is—"

"Let me guess," Roz said. "Jackie Diebolt."

Harlan cleared his throat. "Tonight, Roz, I think she's *Jacqueline.*"

"It's okay," Diebolt said. She stood up and looked over the fire at Roz. "You can call me any version of my name you like, Ms. Cortez. I'm not as sensitive about that sort of thing as Tafani made it seem."

"How would you know how he made it seem?"

"It's like I told your partner, because I heard everything that was said during your meeting with him today."

"Courtesy of her best friend Julie, the receptionist," Harlan said. "Julie looped her in by telephone, through the wall."

Roz paused over this news. "The paper-thin wall?"

Harlan nodded. "Ms. Diebolt heard everything and came here—unannounced—to thank us for confronting her bigoted ex-boss. We've since been chatting about his accusations."

Roz smiled. "And drinking a little wine, I see. Don't let me interrupt. I'm also interested in hearing Ms. Diebolt's side of the story."

"We were just talking about my alibi for the night they say Mr. Romanelli was killed," Diebolt said.

"What alibi?" Roz asked. "According to Mr. T, you don't have one."

Diebolt held up her phone. "I have this. It's a record of a credit-card transaction just before midnight on March 12, when I filled up my Denali at a gas station in Rudyard."

Roz stepped around the fire and looked at the phone. "Rudyard Township? How far is that from Watersmeet?"

Harlan had already begun a search on his phone. As an online map popped onto his screen, he held his phone up next to Diebolt's. The map highlighted a 250-mile journey along winding roads that Diebolt would have had to navigate on a night when most of the UP had been slammed with over a foot of snow.

"Is that where you turned around that night, Ms. Diebolt?" Roz asked.

"No. As I recall, I was still outbound when I made the stop in Rudyard and continued on from there to Sault Ste. Marie, another twenty miles or so east, to my ex's place, and then turned around."

"Without visiting him?"

"There was a car in the drive that I didn't recognize. I thought it might belong to a new girlfriend, so I turned around."

"And you hadn't called ahead to save yourself the 270-mile trip if he couldn't see you?"

"Look, I wasn't even sure where I was going when I first set out. The way I blew up at the board meeting, I just wanted to get the hell out of town for a while. At some point I thought of heading downstate. But when I got close to the Mackinac Bridge, I heard on the radio how it was closed due to all the snow. That's when I decided to continue east to see Drew, my ex. I only had a little way to go at that point and decided to push on without calling ahead."

Roz gave Harlan a look that asked, *Do you believe her?* He nodded and then asked Diebolt, "Did you happen to notice if this gas station had an outdoor security camera?"

"I'm afraid not. I didn't know then that I needed proof of where I was."

"Apparently you don't," Harlan said, "not as far as the prosecutor is concerned, thanks to George Viola."

After their guest departed, Harlan and Roz remained by the campfire, and he gave an account of his day since the two had parted ways earlier. He concluded with his thoughts about Stuart Lamar, the hiker who Ranger K suggested may have known the whereabouts of Zach Romanelli's body before reportedly discovering it.

"If that's true," Harlan said, "the most logical explanation is that Lamar was himself involved in the crime, or that he learned the location of the body from someone else who was."

"And the only *someone else* you can think of," Roz said, "is our client, George Viola."

"Based on what little we know to this point, yes."

"You mean, what little we know about Viola's alleged encounter with an unidentified guy at a support-group meeting that night—who you think might also turn out be Stuart Lamar."

"I know it's not much, Roz, but still, I think it's worth following up."

"Why don't you let me do that?"

"Thought we'd to it together."

"No, you're going to want to follow up on the lead I got today—a much better one if you ask me."

"What lead? Weren't you hanging out with your friend Patty all day?"

"I was, but it turns out that Patty is also good friends with Stevie Viola. Stevie's son, Bobby, and Patty's grandson go to the same daycare, a co-op where Stevie and Patty both do volunteer work and have gotten to know each other. We saw Stevie at the Grill during lunch and invited her to join us later for drinks."

"What'd she tell you?"

"That things weren't so good between Zach Romanelli and his wife Ava before he died. It sounds like Mrs. Romanelli may have had an extramarital lover."

"Who?"

"Stevie doesn't know. It's something she surmised as she observed Zach spend more and more time in the UP and eventually make himself a new home up here, living and working out of a room at the Bel-Air Motel in Land 'O Lakes. Do you remember Stevie telling us about her visit with Ava in Traverse City for Zach's funeral?"

"Sure."

"The subject came up then with Ava. Stevie confessed to feeling guilty about the way Zach had essentially relocated to the UP, like she and Bobby might have come between them. And Ava responded, 'It wasn't *you two* who came between us.'"

An inference of adultery on these facts struck Harlan as uncertain. "Even if Stevie Viola is onto something, how does she know it wasn't *Mister* Romanelli who was having the affair, maybe with someone up here in the UP?"

"I asked Stevie that very question, Harlan, and the truth is she doesn't know. She said Zach never talked about his marriage, and her conversation with Ava went no further than what I just told you. But either way, if one of them was cheating on the other, it's a better lead than the one you got today on this Stuart Lamar fellow, if for no other reason than it suggests someone other than our client may have had a motive to kill Zach Romanelli."

Chapter 16

Early the next morning, Harlan and Roz drove eight miles south of Watersmeet on Highway 45 to the small border town of Land O' Lakes, Wisconsin. In town they took a right on County Road B and then the first left onto a long drive that led to Wisconsin's most heralded northern resort—the Gateway Lodge.

Waiting for them at the lodge's gated entrance was a stretch limo golf cart whose taciturn driver quickly hoisted Harlan's suitcase from the rear seat of his Jeep and onto one of the rear seats of the cart. The driver then whisked the couple across the lodge's golf course to a private airstrip reserved for use by a select few lodge VIPs, one of whom had arranged all this for Harlan the prior evening.

The driver slowed down when they reached a long row of airfield floodlights running between the airstrip—a well-groomed grass-covered runway—and the adjacent fairway for the fifteenth hole. Up ahead was an aluminum-sided hanger. According to Harlan's contact, the facility also served as a caddy shack for the golf course and a rental center for a fleet of off-road vehicles parked in front.

Harlan and Roz remained in the golf cart along with their driver after he parked among the ATV rentals. It was still too early for there to be any activity on the airfield or the adjacent golf course.

"Shouldn't be long," Harlan said.

Roz did not respond because she was still upset, he assumed, about the identity of his VIP contact, a former client from Chicago, Angelo Surocco, who had also arranged a flight Harlan would soon board on one of several prop planes owned by Surocco's import-export business. Surocco was not just a former client, however. And he was not just an import-export mogul. He was also an old-school mobster whom Harlan had long ago served well when he solved the murder of Surocco's son and brought the killer to justice.

"He's just doing me a favor, Roz."

"You of all people, Harlan, should know that favors like this from a man like him don't come without expectations."

"This occasion is not like old times, I'm telling you. The man knows I'm done working for him and his... uh... associates."

"For Pete's sake, just listen to you. His *associates*. You say that like they're not the morally bankrupt racketeers you know them to be."

He let it go as he knew she would, eventually. The fact remained, he needed quick transport to two locations hundreds of miles away from this remote airstrip, which itself did not offer anything resembling a commercial flight departing to anywhere for another month.

***

Harlan had caught his flight, and Roz was now back on the Michigan side of the border, driving north of Watersmeet on Highway 45 into the neighboring town of Paulding. Her destination, the Paulding Community Church, came up on her left at the only intersection in town with a traffic light. On the other three corners were the Paulding General Store, a gas station, and a vacant lot for sale. According to her online map, this was downtown Paulding, in its entirety.

She cut through the church's parking lot and around the tiny, steepled building to a back door sheltered beneath a wide overhang. As soon as she stopped, the door opened and there appeared a young man dressed in a black tab-collar clergy shirt who excitedly waved for her to join him inside.

"Pastor Spiteri?" Roz asked as he escorted her in.

"Please, call me Ed, or Pastor Ed if you must. And you must be the one and only Detective Rosalina Cortez who's created so much excitement among my senior congregants."

"Me?" Roz replied. "What did I do?"

"Well, maybe it's not so much what you did as what I did. After you called to arrange your visit, I mentioned it to some church members here today making sack lunches for the homeless shelter. And when I told them about your family once attending this church, a few of the older ones remembered your mother, Joanna. They say she was a dynamic contributor to the church choir back in their day, and they're hoping that her daughter has returned to follow in her footsteps—like the second coming of Joanna."

"They obviously haven't heard me sing," Roz replied.

The pastor smiled broadly. "Just the same, I expect to see you at service this Sunday—8:00 a.m. sharp. No excuses."

"I'll try, Pastor Ed, but I'm in the middle of a murder investigation, and I doubt it'll be wrapped up by then."

"Well, let's see if I can help speed it along."

He took her directly to his basement office. "This is it," he said, "the weekly meeting place of our support group for individuals battling alcohol addiction. Participation is supposed to be kept confidential, but I guess there's no harm in me confirming for you that George Viola has attended, seeing as how he already told you himself. Now, this other guy you're asking about—Stuart Lamar—I really can't say one way or the other because, like I said, it's an anonymous group and it needs to stay that way. I hope you understand."

"I get it," Roz replied as she went ahead anyway and pulled up a photo of Lamar on her cellphone. "This is him. Maybe you've seen him somewhere else, possibly at a Sunday service."

Pastor Ed took a long look before responding. "Oh yeah, I've seen him before. In fact, I think I've seen this very photo of him. Isn't it from the newspaper, after he and his friend found the body of the dead attorney?"

"Look, Pastor Ed, I need to know whether there's any connection between this guy and George Viola. Can you help me with that?"

"I'm afraid not."

"Are you sure? I mean, if Stuart Lamar has *never* attended your church or a meeting of your support group, it wouldn't hurt to tell me *that*, would it?"

"Sorry, Detective, but I can't say either way. I probably shouldn't have even confirmed what George told you about his own support-group attendance. I'm a recovering alcoholic myself. I know how important it is that I keep my group's trust."

"Okay, fair enough. Maybe instead you can tell me something in general about the treatment of the illness, given your expertise in the area."

"I can try. What's your question?"

"It's about the method Mr. Viola used to overcome his addiction. He called it a recovery hike. It involved him hiking and camping in the woods for a prolonged period—long enough to detox and break the habit. Are you familiar with this technique?"

"Only based on what I heard from George's attorney, Kerry Jammer, when he asked me the same question. Before then, I'd never heard of such a thing. It struck me as crazy—detoxing in the mountains in the winter cold and then hiking all those miles on an ancient Indian trail. If anyone ever asked me what I thought about pulling a stunt like that, I'd do everything in my power to talk them out of it. Excuse my choice of words, Detective, but the damn fool is lucky to be alive."

Roz glanced around the room after switching her phone over to its camera function. "Do you mind if I take some photos of your meeting area?"

"No, take all you want. Is there anything else you'd like to ask me?"

As she formulated the question, something relevant to it appeared in her camera view. It was a cat, though not one fitting the description of the black cat reportedly seen by George Viola at a meeting here on the night Zach Romanelli went missing. The cat before her now was calico—mostly white with large orange and black patches.

"George mentioned that you're a cat lover," Roz said.

"Oh, yes, I most certainly am. They are truly one of God's greatest creations."

Roz then noticed a large litter box on the other side of the basement and, within the office area itself, several food and water bowls on the floor. "How many cats do you have?"

"Three right now, but over the years I've had as many as five."

"Do you let them roam free when you hold meetings down here?"

"Sure, as long as nobody is allergic. The friendlier ones can be very therapeutic for some group members."

"By friendly ones, do you mean cats that will hop into the laps of strangers?"

"That's right. Would you like to see what I mean?" He picked up the calico cat. "Take a seat, Detective, and spend a minute holding this one. His name's Marty."

"Thanks, but, if I could, I'd like to hold one of your others."

He looked confused by the request as he set Marty down. "I guess I could go find another."

"Perhaps your black one?"

"My... black cat?"

"Yes, the one with the patch of white fur on its chest."

"A white patch... on its chest?"

"Yes, you know, in a triangular shape, like the patch Superman wears on his chest, except without the 'S,' of course."

"Is this some kind of joke, Detective?"

"No. Do you not have a cat fitting that description?"

The pastor shook his head.

"George Viola says you do. He says he met your black cat here at a meeting on the same night that Zach Romanelli went missing."

"But there was no meeting here that night. Didn't Mr. Jammer already tell you that?"

"Yes, he did," Roz said. "And I'm sure you're right about George having his nights confused. But George didn't seem at all confused about the black cat he says he saw here. My specific description of it was provided by him, verbatim. May I see that cat, or whatever one you have that best fits George's description?"

"That would be this one here, Marty," Pastor Ed said. "He's the only cat I own who has any black coloring at all. In fact, the last predominantly black cat I ever owned died years ago, long before George ever started attending meetings here."

***

"Hurry up, man. My boss could be here any minute."

The plea came from a cashier who was working alone at an EZ Mart and its affiliated Sunoco gas station located near the eastern end of Michigan's Upper Peninsula in Rudyard Township. Harlan had paid the cashier fifty dollars for access to video recordings from the gas station's outdoor security camera and, while seated at a computer in the boss's office, was taking his time reviewing a segment of one particularly interesting recording.

It was from the night of March 12. He rewound it, played it again, and confirmed it was her, Jackie Diebolt, caught on camera refilling her gas-guzzling GMC Yukon Denali. The time, according to a footer on the video, was 11:55 p.m., which coincided with the time her credit card had registered the transaction from the same location. Harlan tried to imagine Diebolt driving her monster SUV from Watersmeet to a gas pump in Rudyard—two hundred fifty miles east—on that snowy evening in the few hours since Zach Romanelli's sister had seen him alive, minus the time it would have taken to kill him during his subsequent ski outing and hide his body in the woods.

She didn't do it, he decided. *She couldn't have.*

Harlan thanked the cashier on his way out to a rental car he had picked up at the airport in Sault Ste. Marie an hour ago. The plan now was to drive back to the same airport, reboard the same plane that had flown him there, and begin the next leg of this day's journey.

He checked his cellphone before starting the car. Roz had sent an email reporting the results of her meeting with Pastor Ed and attaching photos she took of the church and the basement office where he held meetings for his support group. After explaining that their questions about Stuart Lamar remained unanswered, the email concluded, "I'll see what I can find out at Sylvania Sports."

Chapter 17

Roz had driven deep into the woods, west of Watersmeet, when she spotted Sylvania Sports coming up ahead on the left. After pulling into the establishment's grassy parking lot and cutting the Jeep's engine, she remained in the vehicle for a minute to take it in. It was one of the few places around here that had not changed since her childhood. By outward appearance it was still the area's biggest provider of sporting goods and equipment for outdoor enthusiasts gearing up for camping, fishing, hunting, hiking, and other such adventures in the Sylvania Wilderness and surrounding Ottawa National Forest.

It was also the place, she recalled, where some of *her* best childhood adventures began, including several family canoe trips on a branch of the Ontonagon River that passed through the woods behind the store, continued south into the Sylvania Wilderness, and eventually took them as far as the Lac Vieux Desert headwaters of the Wisconsin River, a tributary of the mighty Mississippi.

A sudden rap on the passenger window startled her. Outside the Jeep stood a young, freckle-faced woman with red curly hair sticking out from beneath a Detroit Tigers baseball cap. "Can I have a word, ma'am?" the woman shouted.

The Jeep's touch-screen display was still powered up, and Roz was able to lower the passenger window with the press of a button. "Sorry if I scared you, lady," the redhead said, "but are you with the Bollman group?"

"Who?" Roz replied.

"Some folks takin' out a bunch of our kayaks. The Bollmans. They're puttin' into the river right now. Are you with 'em?"

"No, I'm not here for anything like that."

"Then, what can I do for you?"

"You work here?"

"I do."

"Perfect. My name's Roz Cortez. I'm here to see if I might speak to—"

"Roz Cortez, you say? Are you the PI lady?"

"Uh... yes... I suppose I am. You've heard of me?"

"Damn straight I have, lady. And I got nothing to say to you, or that partner of yours—Herbert Holmes."

"You mean, *Harlan* Holmes."

"Whatever. Point is, Sheriff said you two might come snoopin' around here with questions for me. And he told me to pay you no mind."

The woman's remark got Roz to thinking about the woman whom George Viola had once encountered in this very parking lot. "Wait. Are you her? The store clerk who found George Viola parked here in his pickup truck on the morning of March 13, sleeping off a night of heavy drinking?"

"Well *la-di-da*, aren't you a clever one, *Inspector* Cortez. Now, why don't you get your smart ass the hell outta here before I have to call on my boss to boot you out."

"What's the problem out here?" someone shouted from behind the Jeep. Roz turned to see a wiry, middle-aged man coming from that direction.

"It's okay, Uncle Bob," the redhead replied. "It's one of those PIs the sheriff warned us about, come here to stick her nose in our business. But I got it under control. She'll be gettin' outta here momentarily. Ain't that so, *Inspector*?"

Roz had already gotten out of the Jeep and stood motionless, staring at the man. The more she blocked out his wrinkles and gray-stubbled beard and focused instead on the overall shape and appearance of his face, the more familiar he looked. "Do I know you?" she asked as he came to a halt in front of her, his eyes widening in sync with his mouth.

"As I live and breathe," he replied. "Roz Cortez? Is that you? Damn, I should've made the connection when the sheriff told us about you and your partner."

"What connection?" Roz asked. "Who are you?"

"You don't remember? I'm Bob Lewandowski. Class president when we were in middle school. You were in my administration. Class treasurer, as I recall."

Roz pressed her memory but came up with only a vague recollection of her childhood involvement in student government. "You mean forty-five years ago, when I was in sixth grade?"

"There ya' go. Had me worried there for a moment, Roz. Thought maybe you were having one of those scary senior moments. So, now do you remember me?"

She still did not. "Oh yes, I definitely do," she claimed anyway. "My old classmate, Bob Lewandowski! My gosh, how could I not have known right away?"

"No worries, Roz. I had the advantage. Everyone in town's been talking about you and your partner being here, investigating the Mystery Light murder. All I had to do was connect your face to a name I already heard."

"From Sheriff Mills, you say."

"That's right. But don't worry about that. How might I help you?"

"Are you sure you're willing to?"

"For an old friend? You betcha. Just fire away with whatever questions you have."

During this exchange, the redhead had shot Roz a frustrated eye roll, turned from the old school chums, and headed back toward the store.

"I appreciate that, Bob," Roz said, "but the truth is, my questions are more for your employee—the fiery redhead who just stormed off."

"Ah, my niece Rachel—the eyewitness to George Viola's escape into the mountains. Sure, I get it."

The two former schoolmates turned toward the store and saw Rachel climbing the stairs to its main entrance. She did not proceed through the door, however. She instead stopped and stuck her face in front of a young man who stood outside the door holding a clipboard.

"Ya' no-good tree hugger!" Rachel shouted. "What's the matter with you? You got beans in your ears? Didn't I tell you to never come back again? Now get the hell outta here before I throw you off this porch!"

"Whoa, hold on, Rachel," Bob said as he climbed the stairs ahead of Roz. "First you're yelling at my old friend. Now this guy. What's going on?"

"I'll tell you what's going on, Uncle Bob. This here low-life tree hugger's been pestering our customers with some lame petition he wants them to sign."

"Petition?" Bob asked, turning to the young man. "About what?"

"The cell tower, sir," he answered as he held out the clipboard, "the one they're planning to build in the woods out back behind your store. This petition is for signatures from folks who oppose it because of the trees that'll have to be cleared to build it. Would you like to sign on?"

"Hell no," Bob answered. "We need that cell tower. Can't keep a decent phone connection between here and Land O' Lakes with just the one out by Robbins Pond. Besides, they're not taking that many trees."

"You tell him, Uncle Bob," Rachel added.

The young man started for the stairs.

"Where you going?" Bob asked.

"Well, I'm leaving. Like you want, right?"

"I never said that."

"Then… what are you saying?"

"All I'm saying is that I disagree with your petition. It's a free country, young man. People are entitled to disagree about things like this."

"So… I can stay?"

"Sure, as long as you don't block the door."

"Uncle Bob, what are you doing?" Rachel objected.

"The man has rights, child. Just like you have rights."

"Me?"

"Uh huh, like the right to talk to my friend, Detective Cortez, about the day you met George Viola—no matter what the sheriff says."

Chapter 18

Harlan's flight out of Sault Ste. Marie had landed in an airfield in Pellston, just south of the Mackinac Bridge, in Michigan's northern Lower Peninsula, and he was now traveling further south by rental car to Traverse City. On his way, he called Ranger K to see if any progress had been made on arranging a meeting with former Deputy Rayden Jude, who these days headed up the county road crew responsible for plowing and de-icing roads in the Watersmeet area, including roads that Zach Romanelli had regularly crossed when skiing the Agonikac Trail.

"Sorry, Detective," Ranger K said. "It's like I told you before, Jude still has hopes of getting his old job back. He's not willing to talk about the case with anyone except Sheriff Mills."

"Not even for you, his former partner? You're sure?"

"Yes, I am. Anyway, I'd be surprised if he knew anything more than what I figured when the sheriff took over the case."

"And by that you mean what you said yesterday about the beet-juice de-icing agent the county uses, and how its stain on Romanelli's body may have helped Sheriff Mills narrow down which of the roads Romanelli was crossing when he was run over."

"That's right."

"But you don't think the sheriff would have told Jude which roads."

"No."

"Why?"

"Because I don't think Sheriff Mills is as brokenhearted as Jude is about the severance of their prior working relationship."

After ending the call, Harlan made another, this one to his client's defense attorney, Kerry Jammer.

"Jammer, it's Holmes. Tell me you got something for me."

"Wish I could, but sorry, I've made no progress."

Anticipating the problem he would have getting Rayden Jude's cooperation, Harlan had previously contacted Jammer to see if he might have any connections with local government that could give him access to Gogebic County's road crew records on the night of March 12.

"What about your good friend and client, Mr. *Tee*, the township supervisor? Did you ask him?"

"Sure, but what you're looking for are *county* records. He's with the *township*. And besides, after the way your meeting with him yesterday went, he's not inclined to do us any more favors."

"What about your own county connections? You've been practicing law in Gogebic County forever, and your office is right there in Bessemer, the county seat. You must know people."

"I do, but they all know that George Viola is my client, and nobody wants to help me defend him. Sorry, Holmes, it's an interesting lead, but you're going to have to find another way to flesh it out."

Chapter 19

Roz followed Bob Lewandowski and his niece Rachel into Sylvania Sports. Like its exterior, the store's interior had not changed much since Roz had last seen it forty-some years ago. It was still the same huge retail outlet—aisle after aisle of outdoor sporting goods and supplies—bustling with customers and employees.

"It's like this place is frozen in time," Roz said.

"Just the way my mom and dad built it," Bob replied as he turned to Rachel and sternly added, "and just the way it'll stay because every generation of this family respects the decisions of their elders."

No longer the fiery redhead, Rachel stared down at her feet, looking humbled. "I came in early that morning, at six o'clock," she said, slowly looking up at Roz.

"On March 13?"

"Yes, and he was in the parking lot sleeping in his pickup. George Viola. Though I didn't learn his name until later. He was all outta sorts when I knocked on his window and woke him. Eyes red and sleepy. Hair all messed up. After he came to, he told me he wanted to buy some stuff for a camping trip. I told him we didn't open for another two hours. But he said he couldn't wait and opened the door. That's when I smelled it."

"Smelled what?" Roz asked.

"The liquor on his breath. It was faint, but I could smell it, the way I used to on my ex-boyfriend's breath after he'd been on one of his binges. Viola kind of reminded me of my ex. Big dude. Serious eyes.

Which scared me, to be honest. I told him he should come back later and tried to walk away. He asked me to hold on and grabbed a piece of paper off the dashboard. It was a shopping list. 'This is what I need,' he said. I took the list and looked it over. It was long, like the guy had never camped before and was starting from scratch. 'This'll cost a fortune,' I told him. He said he could cover it. I asked him how, cash or credit? He answered by showing me a big wad of cash."

Roz imagined where George Viola, an unemployed log-truck driver, got that kind of money as she recalled the wad of cash that Stevie Viola had said Zach Romanelli tried to give her the night before he went missing. Stevie had accepted only a few bills; presumably, Romanelli kept the rest on his person.

"Do you remember whether the wad of bills was bound together in some fashion?"

"Bound together?"

"Yes, bound or fastened together in some way, with a money clip or a..."

"It was a rubber band," Rachel answered.

Which was how Romanelli's cash had been bound together, Roz recalled. "Were you able to get an idea of how much money was in the wad?"

"I can tell you it was well over a thousand bucks, cuz that's what the bill for the goods came to—one thousand two hundred and some-odd dollars—and he still had a chunk of cash left over after paying it in full."

"So, you let him into the store?"

"No, I didn't want to be in here alone with him. So I took his list inside and got the stuff myself. Brought it all out to him with a cart and told him what he owed. He gave me thirteen hundred, so I went back to the store for his change. But he drove off before I could get it. Just like that. West on the road out front."

The same direction George Viola had said he went after getting his supplies, Roz recalled—west to the Porcupine Mountains where he would detox for a week before beginning his survival hike.

Rachel left to assist a customer, and Bob offered to show Roz something in his office that he thought might be of interest—two computer monitors displaying activities currently happening inside the store. These were real-time images captured by security cameras on the premises, Roz realized.

"Do you have a video of the transaction that Rachel just described?" she asked.

"Kind of," Bob answered. "Our surveillance cameras only record what's going on inside the store. We don't have a camera in the parking lot."

Roz thought about Rachel's account of the transaction as Bob pulled up the recording. It showed only Rachel inside the store collecting up the goods on George's shopping list.

"Did you give Sheriff Mills a copy of this?" Roz asked.

"Yeah, along with a copy of another video I thought he'd want— taken on the one occasion when Zach Romanelli visited my store."

"Romanelli came to your store? When?"

"About a month before, in mid-February. He stopped in to see if we could repair a busted binding on one of his skis. Said he had an accident a couple days before. I fixed it myself while he waited. And when I was done, he tried to sell me on that dark-store loophole of his—you know, his property tax write-off for big-box stores. He said my store was ideal for it and that his law firm could set it up for me. But I told him no thanks. I have no issue paying my fair share of property taxes for things like the schools that my kids and grandkids have attended. Besides, it's a small town; might not be good for business if people learned about me dodging the taxes they're all paying."

Roz could not imagine the relevance of this to the sheriff's investigation.

"The sheriff reacted the same way you are," Bob said, "when I told him about how I met the infamous dark-store attorney. But he ended up taking a copy of the video just the same."

"Can you get me copies of these videos?"

"Of course, that's why I'm telling you about them."

Rachel appeared in the office doorway as Bob was downloading copies of the videos to an email addressed to Roz. "Uncle Bob, some kayakers asked me for a ride over to Bond Falls. Did you or the detective need me for anything else?"

Bob looked up from the computer at Roz, who retrieved a photo of Stuart Lamar and held it out. "Just one other thing," she said. "By any chance, have you ever seen this guy before, perhaps making a camping-supply purchase similar to the one George Viola made?"

Rachel studied the picture. "I think I *have* seen that guy, but not around here. In the news, maybe. Isn't he one of the hikers who found the dead attorney?"

Roz nodded. "But you haven't seen him around here?"

"I have," Bob said as he, too, looked at the photo. "Little less than a month ago."

"Here at your store?"

"Yeah, him and those college kids—you know, the science majors from Michigan Tech who came to the area to investigate the Mystery Light ghost legends. They were looking for information about the trails and waterways out there by Robbins Pond. The clerk helping them was new to the store and wasn't sure how to handle their questions. So he directed them to me, and I ended up giving them a bunch of maps, free of charge, and some advice about navigating the trails during the late spell of winter we were getting."

"Would those maps have included the power line right-of-way, where this fellow, Stuart Lamar, found the body?" Roz asked.

"Sure, that's a main corridor through those woods."

"Do you happen to know if Lamar hiked that corridor on any occasion before the night he reported discovering the body?"

"No, but why don't you ask him directly?"

"How might I do that?"

"I've got his phone number right here in my Rolodex," Bob said as he reached for it on his desktop. "He gave me his card after I helped him with those maps, and he said that if I was ever up his way at Michigan Tech, I should give him a call and he'd show me around. If you'd like, I can call him right now and ask him to extend the same courtesy to one of my old school chums."

Chapter 20

Harlan arrived in downtown Traverse City fifteen minutes before his 2:00 p.m. appointment with Ava Romanelli. He spent ten of those minutes in his car, parked on Front Street, reviewing some background information on her.

She worked a few doors down the street at the law firm of Lesko & Craine, P.C., as had her deceased husband, Zach Romanelli. Also like him, she had an impressive bio on the firm's website. It touted her academic performance at Michigan Law, where she had graduated third in her class eight years ago with a dual concentration in intellectual property and internet law. Since then, she had specialized in the development and protection of client copyrights, trademarks, internet domain names, trade secrets, and patents. Hobbies also listed in her bio demonstrated similar interests outside the workplace, including electronic gadgets, coding, web development, gaming, and robotics.

A regular geek girl, Harlan thought as he glanced at an accompanying photo of her chalk-white face sporting a pair of horn-rimmed glasses with lenses so thick it was nearly impossible to find her eyes.

He arrived at the office on time and was directed to a seat in the lobby. A few minutes later, Ava Romanelli came out and greeted him.

"Thank you for meeting with me," Harlan said. "My client is grateful."

"If by *client*, Mr. Holmes, you mean George Viola, you should know that I'm not doing this for him. I'm doing it for his wife, Stevie Viola—my sister-in-law. Poor girl. She's suffered so much loss."

Wonder if she knows that the poor girl suspects her of adultery, and possibly worse, Harlan thought. "Understood, Mrs. Romanelli."

She escorted him to her office, offered him a chair in front of her desk, and then sat herself in another chair beside him rather than the one behind the desk. "I don't have much time, Mr. Holmes. What would you like to know?"

"For starters, when was the last time you heard from your husband?"

"The night the police think it happened... the night of the murder. Though I didn't hear from him directly. He called Bernie that night and left him a voicemail."

"Bernie?"

"Yes, Bernie Dufflemire, another attorney here at Lesko & Craine. Bernie and Zach worked together for our large retail clients. They were a team."

"That would have been the night of March 12, correct?"

"Yes."

"Before or after the meeting of the Board of Review?"

Ava hesitated before responding, "After."

Harlan sensed some discomfort coming from her, though he was not sure why. "Do you know what he said to Bernie in the voicemail?"

"It was work-related."

"Something related to the meeting of the Board of Review?"

"That's how it sounded to me."

"To you? You heard the message yourself? On Bernie Dufflemire's phone?"

"I was with Bernie when he got the call."

"Here in the office?"

"No, at his place." Her expression went completely deadpan. "We were in bed, making love when Zach called. We listened to his voicemail later… when we were done."

But of course, Harlan thought, *first things first.* He, too, put on a deadpan expression, opting to ignore for the moment the remarkable admission. "What specifically did Zach say in his voicemail?"

"It was a confidential attorney communication regarding a client matter, Mr. Holmes. I can't tell you any details."

Odd that she'd get evasive about the phone message but not about what she was doing before listening to it, Harlan thought. The reaction made him even more interested in the content of the message. He decided to press harder for it. "Are you saying that you *can't* tell me about the voicemail, or that you *won't* unless you're compelled to do so?"

"What's that supposed to mean?"

"Look, that voicemail may contain the last words your husband spoke before he was murdered. You're a lawyer. You know that the attorneys in George Viola's case will find a way to have it subpoenaed—assuming the prosecution hasn't obtained it already."

"They haven't. Their investigation hasn't gone down the path you're on right now."

What path? Harlan thought. *I'm totally fishing.* "Well, maybe this path can be avoided at trial if you'll tell me now, just between us, what Mr. Romanelli said. I mean, it probably won't amount to anything, or you would have told the police about it already—right?"

Ava opened her purse and retrieved a cigarette. She lit it and took a deep drag before responding. "What I remember best about Zach's voicemail was not so much what he said but how he said it—yelling and cursing and carrying on. I'd never heard such filth come out of his mouth. And I never imagined I would, not after how he'd previously taken the news of my relationship with Bernie. Zach made no scene or fuss about *that.* He just moved out, into a motel up north. Like, so what?

But this occasion involving the big-box stores was different. It was like he wanted to tear Bernie's head off."

Her admission to adultery was still curious, Harlan thought, but even more so was her continuing effort to avoid disclosing the specific content of the voicemail. "What had Bernie done to make Zach so angry with him?"

"As I said, Mr. Holmes, it was a work-related message intended for his colleague. And when those two were in their property-tax wheelhouse, it's like they spoke a foreign language. If you heard Zach's voicemail, you wouldn't understand what he was complaining about. There was so much technical mumbo jumbo between the f-bombs, I barely understood."

"That's okay, I'll do my best to follow along," Harlan replied as he recalled some of the mumbo jumbo Jackie Diebolt had taught him during her tutorial on the dark-store loophole. "Why don't you start by telling me why Zach was angry in the first place. I mean, from what I heard, things went very well for him and his big-box-store clients at the meeting."

Ava's deadpan expression began to falter. "What did you hear, Mr. Holmes?"

He paused before responding, "Oh, you know, that Zach was able to lowball the true cash value of his clients' megastores because the appraiser came in so favorably on the comps."

Ava stopped her hand and the cigarette in it short of her mouth as a look of concern replaced what had remained of her deadpan expression. Harlan could see he was onto something. He decided to take a shot. "I mean, the only thing I can imagine is that Zach wasn't expecting such favorable treatment from an appraiser who was supposed to be a neutral third party." After letting it sink in, he added, "Tell me, Mrs. Romanelli, what else was Bernie Dufflemire doing to mess up your husband's life besides having an affair with you?"

"Wh-what are you suggesting, Mr. Holmes?"

"Oh c'mon, just say it—Bernie got the appraiser to rig the comps, behind your husband's back."

Ava snatched up her cellphone. "Get down here now... Because he knows... No, not about us. Well, on second thought, yes; I kind of told him about that. But I'm talking about the other thing... Yes, that... Okay, I'll come see you first."

Chapter 21

Roz had almost completed an eighty-mile drive north to Michigan Tech University by the time she received a phone call she was expecting from George Viola's attorney, Kerry Jammer.

"I take it you got my email," she said after they exchanged greetings.

"Yes, I did."

"Well?" she pressed, hoping for news of a break in the case. Attached to the email she had sent was a copy of one of the security videos provided by Bob Lewandowski that morning. In the video Bob's niece Rachel could be seen inside Sylvania Sports using George Viola's extensive shopping list to collect various camping and hiking supplies for him while he waited outside. If paused in the right place, the video offered a clear view of the shopping list.

"I showed it to George, like you asked," Jammer said.

"And?"

"It helped him recall one thing—that the guy who recommended the recovery hike also wrote down the list of supplies he'd need. But it prompted no specific recollection of the guy himself, or anything else about the night they met."

"Did you show him a zoomed-in image of the list?"

"Sure. I also had George provide a writing sample of his own before I showed it to him to see if *he* was the author. But it's clear he wasn't."

"What about the money he used for the purchase?" Roz asked. "Where did he get all that cash?"

"He doesn't remember."

The directions that Stuart Lamar had previously provided by phone led Roz to MTU's Grover C. Dillman Hall, Department of Engineering Fundamentals. Inside the building she hiked up three flights of stairs and found the office of "Professor Lorna Rybicki." The door was open, and inside sat a young man behind a desk taking notes while reading a book—the same young man whose photo she had been showing to witnesses that day. He looked up at her standing in the doorway.

"Oh, you're here. Detective Cortez, right?" His cheerful tone did not match the expression on his face. He was *not* happy to see her, Roz thought.

"Yes, I'm Roz Cortez. And you must be Stuart Lamar, the scientist who studied the Paulding Light and discovered... well... a dead tax attorney."

"I guess that's one way of putting it. Please, come in. Can I get you something to drink, a bottle of water maybe?"

"No thanks. I won't be here long. I really have only one question for you."

"Just one question? After coming all this way?" Again, his tone did not match his expression. He sounded surprised, but he looked relieved. He all but told her why: "And here I was expecting you to grill me about finding that dead guy."

Roz stared at him. "No, I just want to know why you *lied* to the ranger about how that happened."

"W-Why I... lied?"

Roz had been standing in the doorway but now stepped into the office. She stopped in front of the desk, where he remained seated, his face flushing red from his cheeks all the way up his large forehead to his receding hairline. She waited for him to respond. When he did not, she unlocked her cellphone and retrieved Harlan's notes from his meeting with Ranger K.

"According to the ranger, you went out for a leisurely hike that night—after dark in freezing temps and blowing snow—wearing nothing but a hoodie, khakis, and tennis shoes. No coat. No boots. No gloves or hat."

She paused. He remained silent, staring into space.

"But before you set out on your hike," Roz continued, "you called the professor and asked her to join you, which she did, and later she told the ranger quite a story about how you got her to go along. Do you remember how you persuaded her with a story about the Paulding Ghost? The professor told the ranger what you said, but you told him she was mistaken—that she was suffering a break from reality due to the shock of finding the body."

Roz paused again before adding, "That was your lie."

Lamar slowly nodded his head.

"Why did you take that hike, Mr. Lamar?"

His head dropped as he turned his stare to the desktop. "For the reason you just described," he whispered.

"Because a ghost told you to do it?"

He nodded again, still looking down at the desk.

"Telepathically?" Roz asked, her tone even more sarcastic than it had been for her prior question.

Lamar jerked his head up. "You see? You *still* think I'm lying. That's why I denied what the professor said to the ranger."

"So, tell me if I have this right. You went to the Mystery Light viewing area that night, in the middle of a snowstorm, and had an encounter with the ghost of a train that killed a brakeman a century ago, and this ghost train told you, telepathically, to take a hike down the power line right-of-way and look for something that needed to be found before the spring melt, but it didn't tell you what this thing was and you didn't know what it was until you found it—the body of the dead tax attorney."

Lamar nodded again, but this time too slowly to satisfy Roz that he was in full agreement with her take on what had happened that night.

"Well?" she pressed.

"All right, yes!" Lamar shouted. "That's exactly what happened. And it's a damn good thing I listened to that ghost, or the sheriff might never have solved the murder."

"Is that so? Tell me something, Mr. Lamar, had you been drinking that night?"

"Uh… yes… some… at the casino earlier. But I wasn't drunk."

"Do you ever get drunk?"

"Well, I do enjoy wine, and occasionally might have a little too much. But what does that have to do with—"

"Have you ever attended a support-group meeting for persons suffering alcohol addiction?"

"I'm telling you, I wasn't drunk that night. And no, I don't go to any meetings with recovering alcoholics."

"Are you sure? How about a meeting with George Viola and a black cat?"

"George Viola? And what?" Lamar replied, his tone now matching the look on his face—genuine confusion.

"Do you know George Viola?"

"The guy they say killed the tax attorney? No, I don't… I mean, other than what I've read in the news."

"How about the black cat?"

"What black cat?"

"You know, the one with the patch of white hair on its chest—like Superman's patch."

"A black cat with a Superman patch? Are you really a detective? What the hell kind of question is that?"

"I just have one more, Mr. Lamar." Roz pointed at the pad of paper that Lamar had been using to take notes while reading his book. "May I see your notes?"

"What for? Do you have an interest in photonics, too?"

Roz helped herself to the notepad as she switched her phone over to a screen that displayed the shopping list that might have been prepared for George Viola by a mystery acquaintance on the night of the alleged murder.

The handwriting did not match up.

Chapter 22

"Stuart Lamar believes in ghosts," was all Roz's email said. Attached to it, however, were pages of notes explaining what she had learned that day from several witnesses. Harlan would have to read the attachment later. Right now, he needed to focus on two other witnesses who would soon return to Ava Romanelli's office, where he had been waiting by himself, still seated in front of the desk.

A man who Harlan assumed was Bernie Dufflemire entered the office first, his eyes hidden somewhere beneath an enormous pair of thick horned-rimmed glasses that covered much of his chubby, chalk-white face. Ava followed. And that's when it hit Harlan like a thunderbolt—*Holy crap, they're twins... a couple of geeks*. On the theory that likes attract, he could only imagine how the sparks must have flown between the spectacled duo in this secluded, law-office setting while her husband was on the road attending to clients. *Poor guy never had a chance.*

"Mr. Holmes," Ava said, "this is Bernie Duffle—"

"How the hell did you know?" Dufflemire interjected as he stepped in front of Harlan, stood over him, and slipped his hands on his hips.

Harlan rose from his chair, his face passing close to Dufflemire's; once upright, he stared down at him until he located the man's tiny eyes beneath his coke-bottle lenses. "You mean, how did I know you committed tax evasion, *Bernie?*"

Dufflemire stepped back, though not as far as Ava, who retreated to the chair behind her desk.

"I guessed," Harlan said.

"Good for you," Dufflemire snapped. "But it doesn't matter. Going down this rabbit hole won't help George Viola one bit."

"Maybe if you can convince me of that, I'll back off."

Dufflemire hesitated. "Just tell him," Ava said.

Dufflemire slowly turned back to Harlan. "From what Ava told me, it sounds like you already know a thing or two about the dark-store loophole."

"I know it's a way for big-box retailers to avoid paying property taxes," Harlan replied, "and that Zach Romanelli masterminded it."

"What Zach Romanelli masterminded, Detective, was the *legal theory* underlying the dark-store loophole." Dufflemire's tone was dismissive as he continued. "He wrote a scholarly article about it—for academics—that got published and made it look like *he* was the expert. And because of that, every big-box retailer in the state wanted him to handle their property taxes. But what they never knew—hell, what nobody ever knew—was who actually made the theory work in the *real world.*"

Harlan could have guessed who Dufflemire believed was the real force behind the dark-store loophole, but he let the man say it himself.

"That was my job," Dufflemire said. "I'm the firm's real-estate expert who operated behind the scenes on every application of Zach's theory to make it work in the trenches. And let me tell you, in many cases, that wasn't easy."

"What wasn't easy?" Harlan asked.

"Pulling together the hard data—like the analyses of comparable sales—in a way that lowballs the true cash value for many of the stores. And for the retail clients in the UP, the challenge was made even more difficult by the deal we'd reached with the local officials who wanted all the numbers to be crunched by an independent appraiser."

"Do you mean the deal that permitted your law firm to select an appraiser from a list of five outside experts offered by the locals?"

"You heard about that too?"

"I did, and that your firm picked Dave Trumane, an appraiser from Vestaburg."

Dufflemire nodded.

"Because he was the appraiser you were able to compromise," Harlan added, "the one who was willing to crunch the numbers the way you liked."

"That's right, Holmes. I got to Trumane. And I worked directly with him on massaging the comps as needed to make the dark-store loophole work for every damn big-box store in Michigan's Upper Peninsula."

"But Zach Romanelli didn't know you were doing that," Harlan said.

"No, he didn't. I couldn't let him know. He would've been too squeamish to go along with what had to be done in many cases. Besides, it was easy to keep him from knowing, given how entrenched he'd become in his dark-store theory. The man had come to believe it should work for every big-box store—across the board—no matter the local market conditions."

"Then how did he find out?"

"I guess that was my fault. I got greedy and took it too far. And I played it wrong. I told Trumane to hold back the most controversial sales studies until right before the March meeting of the Board of Review, so that Zach and the local assessor wouldn't have time to digest the data beforehand. But I guess the numbers were so stark, both Zach and the assessor were stunned when they were disclosed at the meeting. Thankfully, the assessor was so stunned she flipped out and assaulted Zach. That distracted everyone there from her complaints about the comps being rigged."

"Which they were," Harlan said.

Dufflemire nodded almost imperceptibly. "And now you know why Zach left me a hostile voicemail that night. He was pissed because, as he put it, I played him for a fool and used him to perpetrate tax evasion."

"How'd you get Trumane to go along? Did you pay him off?"

"In a manner of speaking, yes."

"What's that supposed to mean?"

"It means you've heard enough, Holmes. The rest of what I did is none of your damn business."

"It may be none of my business, but it sure as hell is the business of honest taxpayers in the UP—homeowners and small businesses—who are footing the bill for your tax fraud."

"Maybe they need to get themselves their own attorneys."

Asshole, Harlan thought. "You ever been up there, Dufflemire?"

"Can't say as I have."

"So you've never seen for yourself the results of your handiwork—police, fire, and emergency services hanging by a thread, local parks and libraries closed, roads in shambles, and tax foreclosures happening to little guys all over the place."

"You're breaking my heart, Holmes. But the answer's still no. How I got Trumane to go along is none of your concern."

"Are you sure about that? Because the way I see it, Zach Romanelli got himself killed on the very night he figured out what you were doing."

"I wasn't anywhere near Watersmeet that night, and you know it."

"Oh, yeah, that's right, how could I forget? You were here in Traverse City—fucking his wife."

"That's enough, Mr. Holmes," Ava chimed in. "Bernie's right. You're off base, as I knew you would be when Stevie Viola asked me to meet with you. I just didn't know you'd be off in this direction."

"Let me guess," Harlan replied. "You were expecting me to be interested in your adulterous affair, and the obvious motive that it gave you and your boyfriend to be rid of your husband."

"In fact, I was," Ava replied.

"Well, I'm still interested in that, just as I'm still interested in your boyfriend's added incentive to be rid of a reputable attorney who probably wasn't going to let him get away with tax fraud. Now, if you've got something that'll make me less interested in all this, let's have it."

Ava remained calmly seated at her desk as she opened one of its drawers and pulled out a manila folder. She reached across the desk and gave it to Harlan. He opened it and removed two documents. One was a list of items inventoried by the Gogebic County Sheriff's Office informing Ava of certain personal effects belonging to Zach that the sheriff was holding as possible evidence in the case.

The other document contained another list—of what, however, was unclear. Harlan held it up. "What's this?"

"A list of password information for all of Zach's online activities," Ava said. "It'll get you into everything he did on the internet—banking, shopping, social media, et cetera. I gave it to the sheriff's deputies. And later I tracked everything they did with it, and I learned what I imagine they're not telling you about their case against your client."

Harlan was more than a little impressed. "You mean to say that you tracked the cops, while they tracked your husband's past online activities?"

"Sure. All I had to do was follow the metadata they left behind everywhere they went—like footprints."

Harlan only vaguely understood what she was claiming to have done. Recalling *her* past online experience, however, he understood how she could have done it. She was, after all, an intellectual property and internet law attorney who, in her spare time, was into everything digital. A regular geek girl.

One item on the password list was marked with yellow highlighter. "Map My Ski," Harlan said, reading it out loud. "Why is that one highlighted?"

"Because you'll want to look at it closely," Ava answered. "It's a fitness app that Zach always used when he went cross-country skiing. It tracks a skier's distance, pace, and calorie burn. And it has a GPS mapping feature that also tracks the route and elevation changes throughout the ski trip—every second of the trip, in fact."

Harlan took a few moments to process what Ava was saying. She seemed to know what he was wondering most. "Yes, Mr. Holmes—Zach was using the fitness app on the night of March 12. And the data it recorded not only corroborates your client's guilt but also vindicates the innocence of Bernie and me."

"How so?" Harlan asked.

"You'll see. And when you do, be sure to go back through the GPS data for some of Zach's prior ski trips, as the deputies did. That will make things even clearer."

"When did you provide the sheriff's office with this evidence?"

"Two days after they arrested George Viola."

"Did they ask for it?"

"No, they didn't know it existed. I offered it to them after looking at the fitness app's GPS data myself, the day after the arrest."

"Why didn't you look at it sooner? Your husband had gone missing six weeks before the arrest."

"Because until they found his body, I thought for sure that Zach had decided to desert his wife and his law firm."

"Did you tell the sheriff that theory early on in the case?"

She nodded.

"And your reason for it—because of your affair with Bernie?"

She continued nodding.

"And did you tell them about your professional fallout with Zach?" Harlan asked, looking at Dufflemire.

"In so many words," he answered.

"You mean, without getting into any details about your tax evasion," Harlan said.

"Obviously."

"Why did you two tell them anything?"

"Because they asked about marital and work issues," Ava answered, "and because, like we just acknowledged, we suspected those were the reasons Zach went missing. We never imagined that he could have been murdered."

"How about after his body was found? Did you imagine it then?"

"Actually no," Ava said, "because the sheriff didn't tell us anything about the evidence at the scene. At that point, we just thought it was an accident. Not until they arrested George did we suspect foul play. And that's why I looked at the GPS data when I did and turned it over to the sheriff."

Harlan again scanned the list of Zach Romanelli's passwords. "Did the sheriff's deputies show interest in anything else on here?"

"Well, they went through everything else on the list but in very cursory fashion, except for one other thing—Zach's photo library."

"His Google Photos?" Harlan asked, locating the item.

"Yes. Apparently, Zach took a lot of photos and videos of things—mostly wildlife—when he went cross-country skiing. He didn't take any on the night of the murder, though. But the deputies still searched his library back for a few weeks, focusing on those wildlife photos and videos. My guess is they were hoping to find a photo of George Viola or his vehicle, maybe in the background of one, stalking Zach. But they didn't. There were no people in any of the ones he took while skiing."

Harlan turned to the first document he had removed from the folder, the deputies' evidence inventory. After scanning the list again, he held it up and asked, "Why are you giving me this?"

"Because of something that's *not* on it," Ava said.

"And what would that be?"

"Zach's cellphone. It's not listed, yet I'm certain that's the device he used for his fitness app."

"And you're certain he was using the fitness app on the night he was murdered?"

"He was, and it recorded his movements until it went dead."

"Zach's phone died that night? Before or after his body reached the burial site?"

"Before," Ava said. "You'll see exactly where, when you look for yourself."

Chapter 23

The next morning Harlan caught a flight back to Land O' Lakes, again courtesy of his well-connected former client, Angelo Surocco, though at an inconvenient time due to the pilot's tight schedule. It was 4:50 a.m. when the prop plane touched down on the grassy airstrip adjacent to the Gateway Lodge's golf course.

Rather than ask Roz to pick him up at that hour, Harlan had called ahead to the Lodge's ORV rental center and reserved a vehicle for the drive back to the Robbins Pond Campground. He had specifically requested something basic—a utility task vehicle—but what was waiting outside the hangar for him—a side-by-side four-seater tucked inside a roll cage—had more suspension, more engine, and more tire tread than any vehicle designed for "utility" as he had intended the word. A note taped to the steering wheel explained the discrepancy: "Compliments of Angelo Surocco."

No doubt this Baja-style UTV could go anywhere the rugged trails of the UP wilderness might take him, and it could do so, if he desired, in high-adrenaline fashion. But he instead proceeded with caution on the dark, unfamiliar trails, relying heavily on an overhead rack of LED lights and a hand-held map to find his way back to camp.

During easier segments of the drive, Harlan's thoughts returned to what he had learned the prior evening after leaving his meeting with Ava Romanelli and Bernie Dufflemire. He had spent the evening in the comfort of his own home in Traverse City, mostly in front of a desktop computer, studying various recordings from Zach Romanelli's fitness app. As Ava Romanelli had promised, the app's GPS mapping data was revealing, especially the data from the night of March 12.

According to the GPS signal, the last physical exercise Zach would ever get in his life began that night at a time consistent with Stevie Viola's description of him as a night owl who went skiing at all hours. At exactly 10:32 p.m., the GPS signal left his motel room in Land O' Lakes, heading north toward Watersmeet, and soon merged onto the Agonikak Trail. It continued north on the trail a short distance, averaging 9.77 miles per hour, until it reached the trail's first intersection with a surface street—Indian Village Road. At that point, just ten minutes into the trip, the GPS signal, which appeared on the map as a bright green dot, stopped moving and just sat there, blinking. Five minutes later, at 10:47 p.m., the blinking dot finally resumed its journey, though no longer on the trail and no longer at its prior average speed of 9.77 miles per hour. It in fact turned west *onto* Indian Village Road, accelerated to 30 miles per hour, and continued traveling at an average speed of 25.4 miles per hour up and down numerous back roads in what appeared to be a random manner.

Romanelli must have been run down at the Indian Village Road intersection, Harlan imagined, and then transported by motor vehicle on the back roads by someone looking for a place to ditch his body.

After meandering the back roads for a while, the driver of the motor vehicle apparently got an idea. Rather than cross over Highway 45 as the GPS signal previously had done several times, it turned onto the highway and sped twelve miles due north, averaging 74.2 miles per hour, until it reached a point four miles past Watersmeet. There, it turned left onto Robbins Pond Road, headed west for a half mile, and then stopped at the end of the road—precisely at the Mystery Light's guardrail viewing area. Five minutes later, the GPS signal stopped transmitting. Its time of death was March 13, 12:52 a.m., two hours and five minutes after it had begun its haphazard motorized journey up and down the back roads.

Harlan thought about the GPS data and the harm it did to any theory of the adulterous lovers—Bernie Dufflemire and Ava

Romanelli—organizing a hit on Zach Romanelli. Harlan's leading theory along these lines had the lovers killing Zach because of his discovery of Bernie's tax fraud. But the timing was all wrong. According to the GPS data, Zach's fateful ski trip occurred on the same evening that he left his angry voicemail message about the discovery, which Harlan had heard for himself at the conclusion of his meeting with Ava and Bernie. The message made clear the recentness of Zach's discovery—indeed, how he had been blind-sided by it that very evening at the meeting of the Board of Review. As a result, Bernie and Ava would have had little time to arrange for Zach's execution even if they did not wait until after making love to listen to the message, as they had claimed.

Of course, there was also the theory of the adulterous lovers organizing the hit just to be rid of Ava's lawfully wedded husband. And this theory did not suffer from a lack of time between the onset of the motive and the time of the murder; by Ava's own account, the extramarital affair was in full swing long before the night of the murder. But Ava also seemed to think that the fitness app's GPS recordings cleared them of suspicion on this basis, or any other basis, for that matter, because of the case the recordings so clearly made against someone else—namely, George Viola.

And she might be right. The recording on the night of March 12 established a time frame for the abduction of Zach Romanelli's dead or disabled body that aligned with the timing of George's appearance on a security video at a liquor store two doors down from Zach's motel—which happened at 9:15 p.m., just one hour and seventeen minutes before Zach's fateful ski trip began. George thus had opportunity, in addition to motive. And he had means—his pickup truck.

Further evidence was added by the GPS recordings of Zach's prior ski trips. Zach, it seemed, always began his trips as he did on the night he was killed—heading north on the Agonikak Trail until he reached his sister Stevie's house. At that point, if he did not stop there, his routes varied along the network of trails in the northern woods. No matter where he went, however, he always returned along the same segment of the Agonikak Trail that passed his sister's house. It was a way of staying close to her, Harlan imagined, as he recalled Stevie's tradition of leaving a light on for Zach if he wanted to stop by to rest or spend the night.

It was also a way for a stalker, like George, to know exactly where Zach would be for the first and last few miles of every ski trip he took—on a segment of the Agonikak Trail that crossed only a few roads. One of them, Indian Village Road.

Harlan thought through the rest of the narrative that would soon be laid out in court against George Viola. The prosecutor would say his prolonged back-road journey with Romanelli's body resulted from his inebriation and panicked state of mind. He had not thought past killing the man, and in his condition, it took a while to figure out what to do next. He probably didn't even think to search his victim for something like a cellphone that might provide evidence of his whereabouts, at least not until he reached the Mystery Light viewing area. That's likely when he discovered Zach's cellphone and destroyed it. And then he dragged the body down the power line right-of-way, pulled it a few feet off the trail, and buried it in the snow. And why not beneath some soil too? Because he forgot to bring along a shovel needed to dig up the frozen ground. And why would he forget to bring that? Because he was an enraged, drunken, jealous husband who had planned an execution, not the cover-up.

Morning twilight had arrived by the time Harlan neared the campground. He decided to stop short of the entrance so that the roar of his UTV would not wake Roz. While hiking into the campsite on foot, however, he found her already wide awake—when she popped out from behind a tree, in her bathrobe, and stuck a pistol in his face.

"Move and you're dead, Motherfu—"

She stopped herself. "Harlan? Was that *you* driving here?"

"Yeah, in a UTV I picked up at the airstrip. Looks like I scared the hell out of you. Sorry to wake you."

"You didn't," she said, lowering the gun. She looked away and nodded at something large on the ground near the firepit. "What happened to him woke me." She clicked on a flashlight and led Harlan to the object—a dead moose laying in a pool of blood.

"What the hell, Roz? You shot a moose?"

"I did no such thing." She pointed the flashlight at a spot in the woods. "*They* did."

Harlan peered into the woods but saw no one. He remained still and listened, but all he heard was a breeze stirring tree branches and underbrush.

"Who did?"

"It happened just like the other day," Roz said, staring into the woods.

"What happened?"

"A burst of gunshots woke me up, just like a couple days ago. I got my gun and came out here. Next thing I know, this moose shows up and drops dead right in front of me." She clicked the light off and looked back at Harlan. "They were practically on top of me."

"The poachers? Did you see them?"

"No, but I heard them, several men talking among themselves. They must've been tracking the moose. But then the talking stopped. I thought maybe they saw the light of the camper. Then I heard your UTV coming this way; they must have too."

"How long ago?"

"A few minutes. Maybe five."

Harlan drew his gun.

"I'm sure they're gone," Roz said. "Your vehicle was loud. When I heard it coming, I thought it must be one of their crew, coming to help haul this moose out of here. That's why I drew down on you. I think you scared them off, Harlan."

He was not convinced. Even a skilled hunter in northern Michigan might go days without seeing any sign of a moose, let alone get a clear shot at one like this, a thousand-pound bull in the prime of his life, though he would have been a better prize in a few months after completing the annual regrowth of his antlers.

"We should call the ranger," Roz said.

Chapter 24

Harlan had already investigated the area by the time he heard Ranger K's pickup truck pull into the campsite. He stepped out of the camper and directed the ranger to the slain moose, near the firepit. "Sorry about the delay," the ranger said as he got out of the vehicle.

"No problem. Whoever did this didn't stick around very long."

"According to dispatch, they left when you arrived in the Polaris side-by-side parked down by the entrance."

"That's right. About an hour ago."

Ranger K tossed him a set of keys over the carnage, which lay between them. "Next time you park it, make sure to take those with you. Not everyone in these woods can be trusted."

"Obviously," Harlan said, struck by his guest's casual attitude about the situation.

The ranger snapped a few photos of the crime scene while asking Harlan questions about the incident. "Suppose you want him hauled out of here," he said after taking his last photo.

"That'd be nice. You need a hand?"

"No thanks. I got this."

The ranger opened the cargo gate and turned on an electric winch mounted in the bed of his truck. He then slid out a sheet of plywood and extended it from the cargo gate to the ground. After strapping the winch's synthetic line around the belly of the moose, all he had to do was flip a switch and let the machine drag the animal up the ramp, hind legs first, while he guided in the floppy parts by hand.

The ranger slammed the cargo gate shut. "If I'm remembering right, at our first meeting the other day, you told me about another incident involving suspicious gunshots out here."

"I did. It happened around the same time that day too. Just before sunrise. They woke us up, my partner and me. She woke first and heard enough of the blasts to know they were gunshots. She says it happened the same way this time."

"Where is she now?"

"Inside the camper. I'll get her."

***

Roz was seated at the kitchen table in the camper, focused on her laptop computer, as she had been since Harlan gave her Zach Romanelli's online password information an hour ago.

"The ranger wants to talk to you, Roz."

Her attention remained on the computer screen.

"Did you hear me, Roz? The ranger wants—"

"It's not random," she said, looking up.

"What's not random?"

"The movement of the GPS signal on the back roads that night. You said it was haphazard. But it wasn't. It was systematic."

"What do you mean?"

"The signal… the blinking dot… its movements consistently follow certain rules. I wrote them down here." She turned back to a page in her notebook and left it open on the table. "Just play the recording at higher speeds, Harlan, and see for yourself."

He took her seat as she left to speak with the ranger. Next to him was the notebook with a list entitled, "Rules Governing the GPS Signal's Movement," beginning with the following:

"1. It never exceeds 30 mph."

Harlan already knew this. He moved on to the next rule.

"2. It remains within an area bounded to the north by the Ontonagon County line, to the south by the Wisconsin state line, to the east by the Iron County line, and to the west by Island Lake Road."

To confirm this one, Harlan had to increase the play-back speed of the recording, as Roz had instructed, faster and faster, until the signal's blinking dot became a steady point of continuous light that bounced around an area of the electronic map like a ping-pong ball—an area defined by the boundaries Roz had described. *Like it's trapped in the southeast corner of Gogebic County,* Harlan realized, *unable to escape into the neighboring state or counties.*

He looked back at the final rule on Roz's list.

"3. It travels every road in that sector twice, in opposite directions."

To confirm this one, Harlan found that he had to dial down the recording's play-back speed. About midway between regular speed and ping-pong speed, he saw it. The blinking dot was not meandering aimlessly along the back roads. It was covering every one of them in the southeast sector, twice; and although the second pass did not always immediately follow the first, it was always, as Roz had described, in the direction opposite the first pass.

He stopped the recording and, thinking through Roz's list of rules, imagined a vehicle traveling up and down every single road within a specific sector of a county at speeds of less than 30 mph... immediately after a blizzard had dumped over a foot of snow on those roads.

An image of the vehicle popped into his mind.

What else could it possibly be?

Chapter 25

Harlan had more on his mind than the progress of their interview when he rejoined Ranger K and Roz outside. There was some tangible evidence of the poachers' identities that he had purposely held back during his earlier conversation with the ranger, and he was now even more intent on using it to finagle an interview of his own with the ranger's one-time partner, former Deputy Rayden Jude, given Jude's current job as head of the county road crew that plowed and de-iced roads in the Watersmeet area, including roads methodically traveled by Zach Romanelli's dead or disabled body on the night of his murder.

The exchange was winding down as the ranger, spiral notebook in hand, reviewed with Roz some highlights of her statement. "Okay, I just want to confirm a few more things, mainly about these men in the woods. You say that you heard their voices approaching the campsite a few minutes after the moose showed up, right?"

"Yes."

"And that they got close."

"Yes."

"But you never saw them."

"No, they never reached the campsite, and I didn't go out looking for them. Like I said before, I hid behind a tree."

"But you could tell from the voices that there were at least three men in the group."

"Yes."

"Coming from that direction," Ranger K said, pointing at the same spot in the woods that Roz had shown Harlan when she told him about the incident.

"That's exactly where they were coming from," Harlan said. "And there were exactly three of them."

Roz and Ranger K both reacted like they had just realized Harlan was there, though only Roz probably realized that his purpose for intervening was less about the ranger's case and more about his own.

"How would you know anything about the poachers?" the ranger asked. "You said they were gone by the time you got here."

"They were," Harlan said, "but I didn't know that at the time. So, after we called for you, I checked out the area to make sure it was secure, and the first thing I did was backtrack the trail of blood left by the moose. About fifty yards out, I started coming across their footprints."

The ranger looked surprised. "You thought to backtrack the moose? That's what I was going to do next."

"Well, of course I did. And when you do the same, you'll see what I saw—that the moose's tracks lead to the poachers' tracks."

The ranger nodded slowly. "Why didn't you tell me this before?"

"Because I didn't know the footprints were theirs until a few minutes ago, when I checked the weather online and learned that earlier it had rained enough to degrade any older footprints that might have been out there."

"You mean to say that you didn't know about it raining in the same woods where you were camping?"

"I wasn't here yesterday. Like I told you before, I was downstate, dealing with some unexpected business, and was still on my return when this poaching incident happened."

The ranger looked at him curiously. "Okay... tell me about these footprints you discovered. What was their condition?"

"Deep and clean—from the edges of their boots down to every detail of their outsole tread patterns."

The ranger glanced at his watch. "And you saw them just a little while ago?"

"That's right. If you'd like, I can take you right to them."

"I'd appreciate that." The ranger turned and began walking away. He stopped and turned back, however, when he realized that Harlan had stayed behind. "Is now not a good time?" he asked.

"No, it's fine, but don't you want to take along some casting material, you know, to make impressions of the footprints?"

The ranger seemed at a loss for words. "I... guess I don't have any. In the short time since I took this job, I've never come across a poached carcass soon enough to get evidence like this."

Harlan shrugged. "Well, ideally you want to use dental stone—the stuff dentists use to make impressions of teeth. But if you don't have that, I'm sure the hardware store in town has something you can substitute—plaster, cement, silicone rubber—really anything that'll go in soft and harden up. And you can always apply hairspray to the footprints as a firming agent."

"Hairspray?" the ranger said.

"Sure, it should work just fine to firm up any loose soil on the surface—you know, so when you pour in the casting material you don't mess up the impression."

"I... guess I wouldn't have thought of that."

"Tell you what," Harlan said, "I'll go with you into town to get what we need after we chart out the locations of the best footprints and take some photos."

For the next few hours Harlan did his best to impress his young friend with his ability to do forensics on the fly as they hiked deep into the woods collecting not only footprints but various other evidence that someday might lead to the arrest and conviction of the poachers who had killed the moose and probably a lot of other forest animals. As much as he wanted to help with the ranger's case, however, Harlan's ulterior motive was to make the ranger feel as deeply indebted to him as possible before broaching the subject of a future meeting with Rayden Jude.

Harlan waited to make his pitch until they had completed their work and were on their return to the campsite, plodding along a muddy deer trail. The biggest impediment to turning on the charm at this point was the sharp pain intensifying within Harlan's arthritic knees. No longer did the eight hundred milligrams of ibuprofen he took before they set out relieve the incessant grinding of bone spurs happening inside his feeble tibiofemoral joints.

He stopped to sit on the trunk of a fallen tree and tried massaging his knees, as if he might rub away the inflammation inside.

"You okay?" Ranger K asked.

"I'm fine."

"You don't look fine."

Harlan continued to collect himself. Maybe this was a good problem to have right now—a sympathy card that might leverage the play he was about to make.

Ranger K glanced at the sun. "We've been out here a while and come quite a way. Maybe I should hike ahead and come back with your UTV and give you a lift out of here."

"No, really, I'll be okay. I just need a little rest. Besides, there's something I've been wanting to talk about with you."

"Sure."

"Some*one*, actually."

"Okay, who would that be?"

"Rayden Jude."

"Jude? I thought we already talked about him on the phone just yesterday. I told you where his loyalties lie. He won't help with George Viola's defense."

"I know what you said, and I get it. The guy doesn't want to burn a bridge with Sheriff Mills. But Jude was your partner, and that should mean something to him. Hell, my former partner from back in the day is still on the force, but she'll do whatever she can to help me, even when I'm working for bad guys—guys a lot worse than George Viola."

Ranger K took a knee in front of Harlan, looking like a schoolboy at the foot of a teacher. "Tell me, Mr. Holmes, what was it like working for the Chicago Mob?"

Harlan fought back an urge to laugh. "If you want to have that conversation, you'll first have to ply me with a few beers. And seeing as how we didn't bring along any cold ones, how about we have the conversation I started?"

Ranger K nodded. "I get what you're saying about Rayden being my old partner and all. And I could try again, I guess, a little harder."

"No, I'm afraid you don't get it," Harlan said. "I don't want you to try harder. I want you to make it happen."

"But how?"

"Let's get back on the trail, and I'll tell you on the way."

Chapter 26

After breakfast the next morning, Roz stayed at the camper to spend more time delving into Zach Romanelli's past online activities while Harlan followed up on other leads that required another trip to Land O' Lakes. He took the UTV but opted to drive it on surface roads rather than test his limited knowledge of the area's complex system of forest trails.

Upon reaching the town, he headed west on County Road B, as he had done when he last came here to catch a flight, but this time he passed the drive on the left leading to the luxurious Gateway Lodge and instead took the next left into the parking lot of one of the Lodge's more modest competitors, the Bel-Air Motel. Efficiently designed, the compact, two-story motel housed twelve units—one row of six guest rooms stacked on top of another. According to the sign out front, each unit provided all the essentials—bed, bath, heat, and A/C—and a few extras, including Wi-Fi, color TV, and complimentary coffee.

Harlan stopped in the gravel parking lot, got out of his UTV, and stood before what he thought might be the Bel-Air's biggest attraction—a magnificent view of a PGA-style golf course carved into the woods next door on the sprawling estate of the Gateway Lodge. He wondered why Zach Romanelli—an attorney on an expense account— had settled for a mere view of the resort. Whatever the reason, it was easy to figure out which of the Bel-Air's units he had preferred to make his home away from home. It had to be Room 4, on the ground level, which still had its door sealed with police barrier tape.

A middle-aged woman wearing a colorful pantsuit approached soon after Harlan began taking photos of the scene. She smiled despite the difficulties she had crossing the parking lot in high heels that stabbed deep into the gravel with each step.

"Can I help you?" she asked as she hobbled onto a cement slab in front of Room 4.

"Sure, if you can get me inside this room. Are you the manager?"

Her smile disappeared. "No, I'm the owner, Cheri Belli."

Even better, Harlan thought. He paused before introducing himself to see how she might respond to his request. Apparently, her now stolid expression was her response.

"I'm Harlan Holmes, private investigator for the guy charged with killing a guest who once occupied this room. I need to get inside and check it out."

"George Viola? You work for him?"

"Do you know George?"

"Well... no. I just know *of* him, you know, from what people say he did to Mr. Romanelli."

"So, you've never seen George around here."

"Not personally."

"Do you know anybody who has?"

She paused over the question before replying, "Just one person, a friend of mine..."

Harlan waited through another pause, inviting her to complete her thought. After hesitating a little longer, she did. "Her name's Linda Tisdale. She works at the liquor store."

"The one down the street? LaChance's Liquorland?"

"Yes. It's the only liquor store in town. Linda is a cashier there."

"And that's where she's seen George Viola? At the store?"

Belli looked away as she nodded.

Harlan sensed that she had more to say about this. "Do you happen to know if she saw him there on the night when—"

"Yes, Mr. Holmes. She sold him a bottle of bourbon on the night Mr. Romanelli left this very room for an outdoor excursion. And never returned. The poor man."

Tears began welling in Belli's eyes with her last remark. As Harlan watched her fight them back, it occurred to him that this was the first time he had seen such a reaction from anyone other than Zach Romanelli's sister, Stevie Viola. The townsfolk from Watersmeet certainly did not miss the dark-store attorney. Nor did he seem to be missed by his adulterous wife or treacherous law partner.

"My husband and I got to know Zach quite well," Belli explained. "He'd basically lived here for his last few months and became a good friend."

Harlan looked down the row of ground-level rooms at an "Office" sign outside the end unit. "Do you and your husband live here on site?"

She nodded.

"Then, Mr. Romanelli was more than just a guest at your motel. He was a neighbor."

A tear streamed down her face as she nodded again.

"Look, Ms. Belli, I'm sorry for your loss. Really, I am. But I have a job to do here and if you could just—"

"I can't let you in there."

"I understand how you must feel," Harlan persisted, "but even if George Viola did this terrible thing, he's entitled to a defense. And all I want to do when I go inside is—"

"You don't understand, Mr. Holmes. I *can't* let you in. I couldn't even if there was no police tape on that door."

She was no longer crying; in fact, she offered a faint smile as she added, "Well, I guess I could, if I let you break it down."

Before asking anything further, Harlan looked again at the door to Room 4. Then he studied the adjacent doors to Rooms 3 and 5. All three doors had keyless locks, the kind that open with barcoded access cards. But the door to Room 4 had something in addition—a standard deadbolt lock. He stepped back and made the same comparison with the doors for the other three first-floor rooms. None of them had a deadbolt either. Only the door for Room 4. Harlan pointed his cellphone at the lock and took a photo of it.

"Who installed it?"

"The sheriff did, a few days after Zach disappeared."

Harlan thought for a moment about where he was. "Which sheriff? From what county?"

"Sheriff Caudill, from Vilas County."

"Wisconsin?"

"Of course. That's where you are right now, Mr. Holmes."

"And you say he installed it a few days after Zach went missing, not right away."

"That's right, on a return visit. That's when he taped off the room, too."

Harlan wondered about the reason for the delay as he reexamined the barrier tape crisscrossing the door. And then he wondered why the sheriff found the measures necessary at all. Zach Romanelli was reported missing on March 13, but until his body was found much later, in mid-April, the case was thought to be one of mere desertion, not murder, at least according to Mrs. Romanelli and her extramarital lover.

"Do you know why the sheriff secured the room at that point?"

"To preserve evidence at a possible crime scene, he said. My husband Bob didn't like the idea, until the sheriff said he'd look into getting us compensated for lost rent on the room."

"Was that what Sheriff Caudill called it, Ms. Belli? A possible *crime scene*?"

"Yes, those were his words."

"Did he say what crime he suspected might have happened?"

"Well, not exactly, but I could tell he thought something bad could have happened. I know Bob and I started thinking so after a few days passed and Zach didn't come back for his car or any of his belongings. It was like he up and left everything—clothes still in the closet and dresser, empty suitcases, and work-related files and office supplies everywhere."

As Belli explained the condition of the room, Harlan spotted a gap between the curtains in its window and peeked inside. A beam of sunlight streaming through a back window illuminated the files that she had mentioned, stacks of them on a table in a corner of the room. Pressing closer to the glass, he scanned as much of the room's contents as he could through the narrow opening, from left to right... the head of a double bed... a TV... part of a desk with what appeared to be a printer on it... and then the table full of files again. He repeated the process, this time from right to left, and saw the same things in reverse... plus one more item that he had missed on the first pass... a large, wood-framed mirror on the wall above the bed.

Harlan stared into the mirror and eventually discerned a reflection of the entire desk. On top of it, in addition to the printer, were more files, several of them open, a computer and its keyboard and mouse, some loose documents, a notebook, a coffee cup full of pens, a stapler, and some other items that he could not quite make out.

Harlan pointed his camera at the opening, enlarged the view of the desk provided by the mirror, and took a few photos. He then snapped some shots of what he could see directly through the gap in the curtains. As he photographed the table full of files, he noticed two shiny objects on the floor beneath it. He zoomed in with his camera and saw what they were—small stainless-steel bowls.

"What are those for?" he wondered aloud.

"Those bowls?" Belli said. "Why, they were for Eli."

Harlan turned. She was standing behind him, looking over his shoulder at his camera screen. "Eli?" he replied.

"Zach's cat. His name is Eli. Those are his food and water bowls."

"Mr. Romanelli kept a cat? In his motel room?"

"Sure. We permit pets in two of our guestrooms—this one and Room 3 next door. It's how we got Zach's business. We were the only lodging place in town he could find that let him keep his cat."

This explained why Romanelli had opted for this motel rather than the resort next door, Harlan thought. And maybe this also explained something else more relevant to his investigation. "Did you ever see the cat?"

"Eli? Why, of course. Bob and I took him in after Zach went missing. He was the only thing Sheriff Caudill would let us remove from the room. Poor little fella needed a home."

"Is he a black cat?"

"Yes, in fact he is, though not entirely. He has an interesting spot of white fur on his chest. How did you know his color, Mr. Holmes?"

"May I see him?"

"I suppose, if you must. He's just down the way in our unit. He's not a suspect, is he?"

Chapter 27

After his visit with Eli the cat, Harlan walked down the street to the Pinecone Café and ordered a Popeye Melt and Faygo Cola for lunch. Next door was LaChance's Liquorland, but his attention during the meal was focused on a gift shop across the street—the Trading Post Internationale—where he would soon meet a cashier from the liquor store, Linda Tisdale.

Harlan's thoughts digressed as he reflected on the gift shop's exact location. It was on the north side of County Road B, possibly straddling the state line running between Wisconsin and Michigan, depending on the size of its rear parking lot. Cheri Belli had arranged the meeting at the shop before he left the Bel-Air Motel. She did so over the phone but out of earshot while he was taking photos of Eli. After relaying the time and place of the meeting, Belli only vaguely explained why Linda Tisdale wanted to meet him there rather than at her workplace. It had something to do with how Tisdale's employer might feel about her assisting George Viola's PI. Specifically what the issue was, however, Belli did not say.

There she is, Harlan realized as a woman fitting Belli's description of Tisdale crossed the street and headed up the walkway toward the gift shop's entrance. He snapped a few photos of her with his cellphone and then checked the time. He was supposed to join her in five minutes.

Harlan paid his tab and then walked across the street to the gift shop. A bell chimed as he swung open the door, entered the establishment, and was met by an eclectic collection of memorabilia, knickknacks, and apparel… but no store personnel or customers.

He stopped by a glass case containing handmade Native American jewelry. On top of the case was a stack of paperback books entitled, "A Short History of Land O' Lakes," accompanied by a sign inviting customers to help themselves to copies at no charge, "Courtesy of the Chamber of Commerce." Harlan picked up a freebie and leafed through it until a woman approached him from the other side of the counter.

"That'll be a hundred bucks," she said, despite the sign right under her nose. She fit another description that Cheri Belli had provided earlier, this one of someone he would meet first—a young woman with blonde-streaked hair and skin deeply tanned from visiting the salon this past winter—who would broker his meeting with Linda Tisdale.

"You must be Charlie," Harlan said.

"And you must really want that book."

He put the money on the counter.

Charlie pointed at a door with an "Employees" sign on it. "Go through that door and down the stairs. She'll be in an office on your left."

Harlan did as instructed and knocked on the door to the basement office.

"Come in," said a woman inside.

The unmistakable aroma of freshly baked dough and melted cheese poured out as he opened the door. Although Harlan had just finished his own lunch, it smelled good. He inhaled deeply, stepped inside, and closed the door.

Tisdale remained seated behind a desk, her face hovering over a deep-dish pizza that she was eating straight from the box. She looked up and nodded at a chair across the desk. He returned a nod and sat in the chair.

"Thank you for meeting with me, Ms. Tisdale."

Her sullen expression made clear how she felt about giving this interview. She opened the pizza box and dug out a fresh slice. "Look, I only get a half hour for lunch, Mr. Holmes. How about we just cut to the chase?"

Harlan waited for her to chew and swallow a large bite. "All right then," he said, "maybe you can sum up the statement that you gave the sheriff about what you witnessed at LaChance's Liquorland on the night of March 12."

"Which sheriff?"

"Excuse me?"

"I talked to two of them—Sheriff Caudill the next day, and then about a month later that other sheriff from Michigan, up there in Gogebic County. Sheriff... uh..."

"Jake Mills," Harlan said.

"That's the one. Sheriff Mills."

"Why don't you start with what you told Sheriff Caudill, Ms. Tisdale. You say you talked to him the next day. That would have been March 13, the day Zach Romanelli was reported missing."

"That's right. Sheriff Caudill came into the store and told us about the missing person report. He had a photo of Mr. Romanelli and was showing it around to see if anyone recognized him. When he showed it to me, I remembered seeing Romanelli once at the Bel-Air while visiting with the Bellis. Eventually the sheriff got around to asking if I had worked in the store the night before, and when I told him I had, he asked if I happened to see any suspicious activity, or people, that night."

Tisdale paused for a bite of pizza.

"What did you tell him?" Harlan asked when she stopped chewing.

Tisdale seemed to strain as she swallowed before answering, "Nothing. I told the sheriff I saw nothing suspicious that night... which was a lie."

Harlan waited through another pause.

"I *did* see something—a man who scared the hell outta me."

"Who?"

"You know, Mr. Holmes. Your client, George Viola. I didn't know his name at the time, but I knew his face from having dealt with him in the past. He was a regular customer. Always came to buy the same thing, a pint of Jim Beam. Sometimes we could sell it to him, and sometimes we couldn't."

"What do you mean?"

"That sometimes he came in so drunk we couldn't sell to him. It's against the law to sell liquor to someone who's intoxicated. Harry could lose his license if we ever did that."

"Harry?"

"Harry LaChance. He owns LaChance's Liquorland. And he's very strict about us complying with that particular law."

"Was George visibly intoxicated when he came into the liquor store that night?"

"Visibly intoxicated? Are you kidding me? The man was four sheets to the wind. But like I was saying, he scared me so bad that night, I sold him the liquor anyway."

Harlan recalled from his first meeting with Viola how the man could come across. "Did he threaten you, Ms. Tisdale?"

"Not with words. But he had a gun that night. I could see it holstered inside his jacket. And he had a look in his eye—the look of a man who might use that gun if you crossed him."

"Were you working alone at the time?"

"No, Harry was there, too, but he was in the back taking inventory and didn't see what happened. Later on I decided I better tell him, even though I knew it'd make him mad. I figured, better to tell him right away than to wait for him to somehow find out later about how I broke the rule."

"Was Harry also with you the next day when Sheriff Caudill came asking questions about whether anything suspicious had happened the night before?"

Tisdale nodded. "I wanted to tell the sheriff what happened, but I could tell that Harry didn't want me to. So I lied. Of course, I didn't know then who the drunk guy was and that he had something to do with Mr. Romanelli's disappearance. I thought I was just lying about breaking the law against selling booze to intoxicated people."

"It doesn't sound to me like you even broke that law," Harlan said, "considering the circumstances. No judge or jury would expect you to kick an armed man out of your store."

Tisdale offered the closest thing to a smile he had seen from her to this point. "I appreciate you saying that, Mr. Holmes. Just like I appreciated Sheriff Caudill saying the same thing a couple days later, when I fessed up to lying about it."

"You talked to the sheriff a second time?"

"Yeah, Cheri Belli encouraged me to do it. I confided in her about what had happened when I first spoke to the sheriff, and she said I should go back to him and tell the truth. I told her I'd think about it. And then, a few days later, she called and asked if I'd set the record straight yet. When I told her I hadn't, she told me that the sheriff was coming to the Bel-Air that day to lock down Mr. Romanelli's room, and that it might be a good opportunity for me to drop by and tell him what really happened that night."

"How did he react?"

"He was very understanding. Like I said, he told me I didn't do anything wrong."

"I got that, Ms. Tisdale. What I'm wondering is whether you think the sheriff may have drawn any connection between Zach Romanelli's disappearance and the armed, drunken man you encountered down the street on the night it happened."

"Gosh, I'm not sure. I know I didn't make a connection like that. I just didn't want to lie to the sheriff."

"Did he take notes while you talked?"

She set down a piece of pizza crust and thought for a moment. "Yes, he did… as I gave him a description of the drunk guy."

"Do you know if the sheriff followed up with another visit to the liquor store? Maybe within the next few days?"

"No, not that soon anyway."

"How do you know?"

"Because if he went there asking about me selling liquor to a drunk, I would've caught hell from Harry."

"So, to your knowledge, early on in the case the sheriff never asked to see any video recording of that transaction taken by the store's security camera."

Tisdale had opened the pizza box but stopped short of digging out another slice as she took in the question. "How do you know that he *ever* asked to see that?"

Harlan pushed past her question. "When did he come back to see the video?"

She closed the lid to the box without removing a slice. "It was around the time your client was arrested, as I recall."

"Before or after you first heard about it?"

She thought for a moment and then shrugged. "I'm not sure."

"Did he bring Sheriff Mills with him?"

She nodded.

Harlan tried to imagine how the two sheriffs had come together on the case. Sheriff Caudill would have had little reason to connect Zach Romanelli's disappearance with a drunk guy who frequented a liquor store down the street and happened to do so the same night, albeit carrying a gun, until Caudill learned who the guy was and what he admitted to doing earlier that evening. *Maybe he ID'd the drunk when Viola's arrest made the news and then reached out to Sheriff Mills,* Harlan thought, *or maybe Mills reached out to him beforehand, when the body of Caudill's missing person was found in Michigan.* Harlan considered the latter scenario more likely, as it better explained why Viola was arrested on sight a week later.

"What happened when Sheriffs Caudill and Mills came to the store that day?"

"They first talked to Harry in his office. And then Harry came up front and got me and took me into his office. As we walked back, I could tell he was upset. He asked me straightaway, 'Did you tell Caudill about how you sold liquor to a drunk customer that night?' But I didn't say anything until we got back to his office."

"What happened there?"

"Sheriff Caudill introduced me to Sheriff Mills and asked me to tell Mills what I'd told him before."

"With Harry still there?"

"Yes."

"But that didn't stop you this time from telling the truth about your sale of a bottle of Jim Beam to a drunk customer on the night in question."

"Of course it didn't. I had to admit it. Sheriff Caudill already knew. There was no hiding it from Harry that I'd already fessed up to it."

"That must have put Harry in an awkward position—knowing that the sheriff knew about how he had pressured you into lying about it in the first place."

"It made Harry very forthcoming, if you know what I mean."

"With the video that had been taken by the security camera that night?"

"More than just that."

"What else did he give them?"

"His assurance that neither he nor I would say anything to anybody about our meeting him and Sheriff Mills that day, especially anybody working for Viola—like you."

Harlan pulled out his wallet. "You should have asked for more than a hundred dollars."

"Put your wallet away, Mr. Holmes. The hundred wasn't for me anyway. It was for Charlie, for letting me use this office to meet with you this way."

"You mean to say that you're doing this for nothing?"

"No, I'm doing it because it's the right thing to do. It's like Cheri Belli told me when she called; your client may be a total scumbag, Mr. Holmes, but he's entitled to a defense."

"Ms. Belli told you that?"

"Yes, and she also told me that she had a feeling about you—that you don't seem like a total scumbag yourself—especially after she saw how you got along with her cat, Eli. Cheri puts a lot of stock in how people relate to animals. She thinks I can trust you to never tell Harry about this meeting."

"You can."

"I hope so, Mr. Holmes, because the last thing I need is for you to go over to LaChance's Liquorland and follow up with Harry on what I've said."

"As much as I would like to, Ms. Tisdale, I promise you I won't. But that means I won't get to see the video of your transaction with George Viola until the prosecutor is compelled by law to produce it to the defense, which will take a while. And there's something I'd really like to know about that transaction, right now, if you can remember."

"What is it, Mr. Holmes?"

"How did George Viola pay for the bottle of Jim Beam? Cash or credit?"

Harlan still had his wallet in his hand. She stared at it as she thought about the question. He considered prompting her with another question, *Did he pay from a big wad of cash?* But he did not want to lead the witness.

"It was cash," she said. "He had a wallet like yours, black leather. And he paid with cash from it. I know because I had to give him change."

"A lot of change?"

She stared at his wallet again. "No. It was just coins. No bills."

"How much was the pint?"

"Jim Beam? Nine-something after tax."

"So, he gave you a ten-dollar bill?"

She thought some more, now staring into space. "No. He paid with a five and five ones. I remember, because I had to rearrange the singles so they'd all face the same way when I put them in the drawer, and I was trying to do that while keeping an eye on him and his gun."

"So, he was carrying his cash loosely organized in his wallet at the time."

"What do you mean?"

"I mean, he wasn't carrying it in a neat wad fastened together with something like a money clip, the way some people do."

"I suppose that's true. I don't remember seeing a wad of bills, fastened or not."

Chapter 28

Later that day Harlan returned to the Michigan side of the Ottawa National Forest and maneuvered his UTV to a point about a mile west of his campsite where the trail he was riding ended. From there, he hiked deeper into the forest to the site of a man-made mineral lick that consisted of salt blocks as big as bowling balls mounted on posts at heights providing easy access to moose instinctively craving certain elements, like sodium and calcium, required in the springtime for bone, muscle, and antler growth. Although the site had been constructed to blend into the environment, he and the ranger had found it the day before when backtracking the blood of the slain moose and the footprints of the poachers who shot him. This was the place, they determined, where the moose was baited into the sights of the poachers' rifles.

Harlan paused at a tree he had seen the day before. Its trunk remained stained with the spray of the victim's blood.

Turning from the tree, Harlan headed down a natural corridor that provided a clear line of sight through a long stretch of the woods. Up ahead he came upon a spot where, the day before, he and the ranger had discovered a metal stake poked deep into the soil. Adjacent to the stake, a square patch of landscape had been meticulously cleared of branches and brush. They surmised that the stake probably had been used to help secure a ground blind pitched there as a place for the poachers to shelter themselves as they lay in wait, watching down the corridor for a moose to enter their mineral lick. While waiting, the poachers made a mess of the place and, in doing so, left a trail of evidence—cigarette butts, food scraps, and an empty fifth of rum—that might contain their DNA or fingerprints. They also left behind several spent cartridge cases of perfect size to have housed 308-caliber bullets, like the ones the ranger later dug out of the dead moose.

All this evidence had been bagged the day before. Harlan was here today to bag certain other evidence relevant to another murder.

He crouched down by a bush and peered down the corridor. A few minutes later his mark, Rayden Jude, arrived at the mineral lick accompanied by Ranger K, both men wearing hiking boots and camo-colored clothing. Jude's appearance was consistent with the description provided by the ranger the day before: a forty-two-year-old Caucasian male who stood six foot two inches tall and weighed about one hundred eighty-five pounds. This made him a little bigger than the ranger and fifteen years older, though his stubbled face beside the ranger's boyish features—a juxtaposition enhanced by Harlan's binoculars—made the disparity in age seem even greater.

Harlan worked his way back toward the mineral lick, staying out of sight, and paused when he was within earshot. The two men had stopped at the bloodied tree. "Right here is where we think he took the first shots," Ranger K said. Jude crouched down at the base of the tree and studied the blood spray.

As Harlan crept closer, he felt his cellphone vibrate in his back pocket. He checked the device before declining the call. It was Roz.

Jude looked up from the base of the tree. "Where are the footprints you said were out here?"

"We collected the best ones."

"How'd you do that?"

"Made plaster casts of them."

"You don't say."

Harlan's phone vibrated again. This time it was an alert for an incoming text, also from Roz. "Big break on the poacher case," the message said, "and possibly our case too. Call me ASAP."

He returned the phone to his pocket and crept closer. Ranger K and Jude were now at the base of another tree, this one on the perimeter of the mineral lick. The tree contained a motion-activated camera that Harlan and the ranger had planted in it the day before.

"Here it is," Ranger K said as he pointed at the device tucked into a tangle of branches. "We got another one just like it on the other side of the lick in case those poachers ever come back."

"Who's *we*?" Jude replied.

Ranger K glanced around the woods before responding, "What do you mean?"

"You keep saying *we*," Jude said. "*We* collected footprint evidence, you said before. Now you're saying *we* got cameras in these trees. Who the hell is *we*? I thought you worked alone."

"He does," Harlan said, pushing through some brush to join them. "I just tagged along as a concerned outdoorsman."

Jude jumped back. "Who the hell are you?"

Harlan waited for Ranger K to take the lead, as they had previously planned. To this point, he had not reacted at all to Harlan's sudden arrival.

"What the hell is going on, Kole?" Jude asked. "Do you know this guy?"

Ranger K calmly nodded. "Yeah, he's the detective I was telling you about the other day, you know, the one who wants to talk to you—Harlan Holmes."

Jude glared at Harlan and then the ranger. "You set this up?"

Still calm, the ranger nodded again.

"Un-fucking-believable!" Jude shouted. "You told me you wanted my opinion on your poaching case. And now I come to find out that was bullshit? That you hauled my ass out here to see him?"

"Yeah, that's the long and short of it."

"I already told you no, Kole. Hell no! I'm not meeting with this… fucking mafia detective."

"He's just doing his job, Rayden."

"His job? Is that what this is about? How 'bout my job, Kole?"

"What job?"

"You know. The one I'm trying to get back."

"You need to get real, Rayden, and face the fact that we'll never be deputies again. We weren't furloughed, man. We were fired. Our jobs are gone."

Jude's angry expression eased a little. "Doesn't mean something won't ever open up. People change jobs. People retire."

"True," Ranger K replied, "but who will get to pick any new hires?"

"Well, Sheriff Mills."

"That's right, Sheriff Jake Mills. Same guy who canned us while keeping deputies with less seniority. And the same guy we went to for help getting real law enforcement jobs to replace the ones we lost. You remember, Rayden? You and me, we were willing to relocate—go anywhere in the state—to be cops. And what did Mills do for us? Nothing. And now look at us. You're a fucking road worker. And I'm a fucking Boy Scout."

Harlan waited through a lull in the exchange. "He's been jerking me around too."

"Who?" Jude asked.

"Your former boss," Harlan said, "Sheriff Mills. Everywhere I go I run into witnesses he's turned against the defense."

"Maybe that's because you're defending a cold-blooded killer, Holmes. Just like you've defended cold-blooded mob bosses, according to what I've heard. Is that true?"

Harlan shrugged. "What can I say? I lost my job as a cop, just like you, and when I could see there was no getting it back, I turned to the only detective work I could find. It's true; some of my clients have been criminals. But I'm beginning to think that George Viola isn't that kind of client."

"You think he's innocent?"

"Maybe."

"Well, if he didn't kill the dark-store attorney, who did?"

"I'm not sure, but I have a few suspects in mind."

"Yeah, right," Jude scoffed. "And how do you figure I can help you pin what your client did on someone else?"

"I don't know for sure, but maybe someone on your crew saw something—you know, one of your drivers out plowing all the snow you got the night Romanelli went missing."

"I thought all you wanted to know about was the de-icing program—the names of roads where we used beet-juice instead of salt."

"I'll still take that information, and anything else you might be able to tell me about the program, like who applied the beet juice to which roads that night and when they did it."

Jude laughed. "Are you shittin' me? I couldn't tell you who was out on which roads even if I wanted to."

"Why not? You're the boss, right? The one who oversees the road crew?"

"Yeah."

"Don't you keep records of their activities?"

"Well, yeah. My drivers all punch a clock when they start and end their shifts. So, I could find out who was working any given night."

"Including the night of March 12."

"Of course. But I couldn't tell you who was driving on any particular roads. We cover the entire eastern half of Gogebic County and a big part of southern Ontonagon County under a contract our county has with theirs. On a snowy night, I've got drivers all over the place."

"But certainly you assign each one a specific area to cover, right? So nothing gets missed?"

"Sure. We got the territory divided up into sectors. Six total. And if you asked me this question that night or the next day, maybe I could tell you who was driving in any given one. But I have no way of knowing that now."

"Okay. How about the names of *all* your drivers that night—can I have those, along with the times they clocked in and out?"

"So you can do what? Interrogate them one at a time?"

"Something like that."

"And when the sheriff finds out—because you know word of what you're doing will get back to him—who do you think he'll suspect gave you the names?"

"Are you still worried about that?" Harlan said. "I thought you and Kole already discussed that issue, and that he was quite persuasive on it."

They were still standing by the tree with the camera in it. Jude looked at the device. "I take it the camera was your idea, Holmes. Same with the footprints, taking casts of them—I'll bet you suggested that too. Hell, you probably showed him how to do it."

Harlan didn't respond.

"Don't you see what's going on here, Kole?" Jude said. "He's playing you, getting you to do his bidding."

"I thought about that," the ranger said. "And I figure he is, but I decided to help him anyway."

"Why?"

"Because I'd rather do his bidding than the sheriff's. Besides, it won't be long and the sheriff will have to give the defense all the evidence he's got anyway. What's the harm in us giving some of that evidence to Mr. Holmes a little sooner? Hell, it's just the names of a few of your drivers."

"The sheriff never asked me for those names," Jude said, his face looking perplexed as he stared off.

Harlan imagined the question on Jude's mind and answered it in his own—*Because the sheriff didn't replay Zach Romanelli's GPS recording from that night at high-enough speeds.*

"What do you say, Jude?" Harlan asked.

Jude remained lost in thought.

"Listen," Harlan said, "I don't want the sheriff learning of me interrogating members of your crew either."

"Why not?" Jude asked, turning back to Harlan.

"Because, for once, I'd like to know something about this case that he doesn't."

"So how would you keep a lid on what you're up to?"

"I don't know. I suppose I could pay your guys a little something to stay quiet about meeting with me."

"A *little* something?"

"Whatever it takes, within reason."

"And what about me?" Jude asked, looking more interested. "Will I get paid whatever it takes for the names you'll need to get started on your errant mission?"

"Seriously, Rayden?" Ranger K objected. "How do you think it'll go over with the sheriff if he finds out you *sold* evidence to the defense? Just give him the damn names, man. His client is entitled to a defense."

"I'll think about it."

Chapter 29

As Harlan four-wheeled back to camp, he considered calling Roz in response to her earlier text announcing a big break in the poaching case and possibly the murder case. But he would soon see her in person, and he was troubled by the uncertain outcome of his prior meeting with Rayden Jude. There was little chance of Jude delivering on the names of the plow-truck drivers, let alone providing further information that might be needed once Harlan began investigating them.

He reached for his cellphone as it bounced around the passenger seat.

"Hey Google, call Jackie Diebolt."

"Harlan Holmes?" Diebolt answered. "Don't tell me you've changed your mind and are coming to arrest me."

"No, your alibi still works for me. I'm calling to ask for a favor."

"Well, I guess you're the reason I have an alibi, so I owe you one. Go ahead. What can I do for you?"

"You mentioned being friends with the receptionist I met at Township Hall the other day—the young blonde, Julie."

"Sure, Julie LePoudre. We've been good friends since I moved to the area. She's a real sweetheart."

"Besides her pleasant demeanor," Harlan said, "she struck me as someone who might be well informed of what's happening around Township Hall, if you know what I mean."

Diebolt laughed. "Why? Because of the paper-thin wall between her desk and the supervisor's office?"

"Let's just say she has better connections inside local government right now than you do. Wouldn't you agree?"

"No shit, Sherlock. Folks downtown didn't like their nonbinary assessor even before she got fired."

"Except for Julie."

Diebolt laughed again. "What do you want her to get for you, Mr. Holmes?"

"Everything she can dig up on the comings and goings of whoever worked on the road crew on the night of March 12—especially those who drove plow trucks that night after the meeting of the Board of Review. I need to know their names, when they clocked in, when they clocked out, and anything she can find out about where each one drove that night. But I don't want her talking to anybody about this. I just want her to search whatever records there may be of the road crew's activities that night, in whatever form the records may be in—digital or paper—and make me copies. Do you think you can get her to do this for me?"

"I don't know. You're talking about county records. She works for the township. As a matter of formal government structure, she shouldn't have access."

"Can you at least ask?"

"I suppose."

"If she's willing to try, tell her I'd also like her to find out whatever she can about a pilot program the road crew was running with a new de-icing agent for the roads—beet juice. Are you at all familiar with it?"

"Familiar with it? Are you kidding? They made a mess everywhere they sprayed that crap. And it stunk to high heaven. Yes, I know exactly the program you're talking about, and I'm sure Julie does too."

"Good. Tell her I need copies of records she can find on that too. I want to know what roads they applied the beet juice to on the night of

March 12, and what times they applied it. And if there are any records of who applied it, I definitely want those."

"And I suppose you want her sneaking around for this information too—like a spy, working for you on the q.t."

"I know it's a lot to ask. If you think it might help, tell her I'll pay twenty dollars per page for the records—capped at two thousand dollars—plus another thousand up front just for trying."

***

Roz was right where he had left her earlier, still in the camper seated in front of her laptop computer at the kitchen table. He kicked off his hiking boots and plopped into a chair beside her. "Sorry I didn't get a chance to call. What's the news?"

She said nothing in response and instead placed the laptop between them, restored a page linked to a video recording, and clicked play.

In the foreground of what appeared on the screen was a thicket of bare branches from a bush or tree that interfered with, but did not block, the view of the scene ahead, which consisted of three people in a wintry wooded area. One of them was pointing a rifle at a large hollow in the base of an enormous tree while the other two were crouched down beneath the rifle peering through the opening. They seemed to be unaware of the camera operator recording them from behind the branches; but in any event, even if they were up to no good, this much of the recording would be of no concern, as they were dressed from head to toe in snow gear, including ski masks pulled over their faces.

"Who are they?" Harlan asked.

"Shh," Roz replied. "It's about to get interesting."

There came a cry from what sounded like an injured or frightened animal. The two individuals who were crouched down scooted back; as soon as they were clear, the one with the rifle fired a shot into the hollow.

Then came another cry.

And then another shot from the one with the rifle.

And then silence as the other two slowly returned to the base of the tree and peered into the hollow again. One nodded in response to an inaudible statement made by the other. They both then leaned into the hollow and seconds later dragged out a large, lifeless black bear.

They placed the bear's carcass in front of the one with the rifle, who promptly set down the weapon, kneeled beside the carcass, and raised its head in position for several cellphone selfies.

Trophy photos, Harlan imagined, wondering if vanity might result in the removal of the ski mask for at least one snapshot. *C'mon, show yourself. You know you want to.*

And then, as though responding to the dare, he did. His face was not familiar to Harlan. Roz shook her head and shrugged when he glanced at her.

After taking the selfies, the proud poacher and one of his accomplices used long knives to saw off the dead bear's paws while the third member of their party went back inside the tree hollow. That one soon returned with two lifeless bear cubs and dropped them beside the carcass of the big bear, no doubt the cubs' slain mother. The proud poacher then took some more photos of himself, this time while holding one of the dead cubs by the scruff of its neck next to his face.

When they finished cutting off the mother's paws, one of them slit open her gut, dug around inside, and pulled out an organ. "Probably its gallbladder," Roz said. "According to some online sources, they're valuable on the black market for use in certain alternative medicines."

Upon completing their work, the poachers stuffed the organ, the paws, and the dead cubs into two backpacks, picked up and pocketed their spent cartridge cases, and then hiked away from the scene, leaving behind the butchered remains of the mother bear.

Harlan had counted them picking up at least six cartridge cases before they left. "Those bastards opened fire on a family of hibernating bears," he said as the video ended.

"And Zach Romanelli managed to record everything they did after their first few shots," Roz said.

"Romanelli was the camera operator? Where did you get this video, Roz?"

"From his photo library."

Harlan recalled what Romanelli's wife, Ava, had said about her husband's practice of taking photos and videos of wildlife when he went cross-country skiing. He also recalled her saying how she had tracked certain metadata left by the sheriff when he searched the library, without success, for photos or videos that might have captured Romanelli's stalker, George Viola. According to Ava Romanelli, the sheriff's search never turned up any photos or videos that included any people.

"When was this video taken?"

"February 11, according to the posting date recorded in Romanelli's photo library—a month and a day before the murder."

Harlan's notes from his meeting with Ava Romanelli were on the kitchen table. Roz must have been consulting them as she did her research. He reached for them now, but as he did, she said, "I've already checked, Harlan. According to Ava Romanelli's statement, the metadata on the sheriff's search showed that he went back exactly one month and stopped, when he reached February 12—one day short of this video. Apparently, the sheriff has never seen it."

Roz refreshed another page on her laptop. It was the GPS recording from Romanelli's fitness app on the night of February 11, paused at 10:27 p.m. "Zach Romanelli was right here when it happened," she said, pointing at the frozen GPS signal on a map of a trail deep in the Ottawa National Forest. "The GPS recording shows him stopping there about twenty seconds before the video began posting to his photo library."

Roz then hit playback on the fitness app's GPS recording. "And, according to the fitness app, he remained in that spot throughout the entire time it took for the video to post to the photo library, plus another ten minutes. My guess is that he happened to be skiing nearby when the poachers started shooting, and not only did he stop to investigate but he had the presence of mind to record it."

Harlan thought about the video's starting time, 10:27 p.m. "How did he get such a clear recording? It should have been pitch black in those woods at that hour."

"I imagine he had a night-vision camera," Roz replied. "Remember what his sister Stevie said? He often went skiing late at night, and all of his photos and videos are as clear as day."

"And he was pretty good with that camera," Roz added, as she refreshed another page on her laptop. It displayed a zoomed-in image of the shooter after he had removed his mask for one of his selfies. "It's about as good a mug shot as you could ever hope to get from an amateur videographer."

Harlan studied the image on the computer. Together with the rest of the video, it was smoking-gun evidence that should, at the very least, bring this man down for an egregious act of poaching. It could also lead to the arrests and convictions of his accomplices for this act and potentially others, perhaps even the shooting of the moose that died in their campsite the night before.

"I definitely get your point now about this being a big break in the poaching case," Harlan said. "But your text also said it might be relevant to our murder case. Beyond the fact that this could provide other suspects in Zach's killing, is there anything else?"

"Yes, in fact there is. I dug further into Zach's digital records and found evidence showing a direct connection between this poaching incident and one of our current suspects." Roz refreshed another page on the laptop. It was from a cellphone provider's online billing statement listing incoming and outgoing phone calls in the month of February for a particular cellphone account. Roz had highlighted the account holder's name, Zach Romanelli, and all calls listed for February 11. There was only one after 5:00 p.m. that day. It was an outgoing call placed at 10:56 p.m.

Harlan thought to reach for Roz's laptop to check something, but he imagined she had already done so. "How long was that after the poachers left the scene?" he asked.

"Three minutes and twenty seconds."

"Who did he call?"

"Bernie Dufflemire."

Roz let the answer sink in before adding, "The call lasted a little less than seven minutes. You can see that on the phone record. And if you go back to the fitness app's GPS recording, the phone call plus the few minutes he waited before placing it account for the ten minutes he remained behind that bush before getting back on the trail."

"He didn't call the county sheriff's office or the Forest Service?" Harlan asked. "After what he saw those poachers do to those helpless bears?"

"Not according to his phone records," Roz said. "He called his law partner immediately after it happened, and for whatever reason, after that, he let it go."

"What are you saying, Roz? That he *never* reported this to law enforcement?"

"That's right. He just let it go."

"How can you be sure?" Harlan asked as he began scanning the computer screen for the rest of Romanelli's phone calls during the month of February.

"Because I've reviewed every call he made from February 11 through to the day he died, and in that time frame, he never once called any law enforcement agency—state, local, or federal—at least not on that phone. I think he let it go because of something that was said during his phone conversation with Dufflemire... maybe something about the guy whose face he caught on camera. I'm wondering if they knew him."

Harlan was beginning to understand the urgency of Roz's earlier phone call and text. At the time, he wondered why she tried to reach him when she knew he was working on a surprise meeting with Rayden Jude. "When you called before," he said, "you were worried about Dufflemire being alerted to your discovery of the video and phone record, weren't you?"

Roz nodded. "According to your interview notes with Ava Romanelli, she was quite adept at tracking the sheriff's metadata when he searched her husband's past online activities. I imagine she's been doing the same with us, which means she and her boyfriend Bernie Dufflemire know, or soon will know, about our discovery of this video and phone call."

"Sorry, Roz. Guess I should have returned your call sooner."

"It's okay. I don't think we could have kept the element of surprise anyway."

Chapter 30

Harlan woke the next morning to a cellphone alert. It was a text from Jackie Diebolt responding to one he had sent the night before attaching one of the proud poacher's selfies and asking if she recognized him. Diebolt's answer confirmed a hunch Roz had suggested and now repeated with her eyes still closed as she lay beside Harlan in bed.

"So, was I right? Did Diebolt just identify the shooter as the appraiser, Dave Trumane?"

"Yeah."

"Which means Romanelli also probably recognized him when he recorded the incident."

"I'm sure he did."

"Which, in turn, makes Romanelli's immediate decision to call his law partner, Bernie Dufflemire, quite interesting—don't you think?"

***

After a shower and breakfast, Harlan drove the UTV to the Ottawa National Forest Visitor Center. He went there on the ranger's invitation via a text saying that he had something for Harlan. The ranger had sent his message a moment before Harlan was about to click "send" on basically the same text message to the ranger—informing him that *he*, Harlan, had something for *him*. Harlan decided to hold back his message until the two met in person.

Inside the visitor center he spotted Ranger K stationed in his usual place, behind the information counter, fielding questions from inquiring tourists. The two men made eye contact as Harlan stood waiting across the room by one of the center's more exotic wildlife exhibits. It was a mounted black bear standing seven feet tall on its hind legs, brandishing its teeth and claws. Harlan stared into the beast's glaring eyes. *Too bad you weren't there, big guy, before Trumane opened fire.*

Harlan cued up the video of the massacre while waiting for the crowd surrounding the information booth to clear. Amidst the bustle the ranger again made eye contact with him while holding up an envelope. Harlan stepped up to the booth, took the envelope, and opened it on his return to the bear exhibit. Inside he found an unsigned note written by hand in a sloppy blend of print and cursive writing, slanting left.

From the scribble he eventually discerned two lists. One named various roads that had been sprayed with beet juice on the night of March 12, including Indian Village Road. The other named six road-crew workers on duty that night and indicated the times each had clocked in and out of work. The note concluded, "This is the best I can do. Like I said before, we don't keep records of who drove in which sectors." Harlan recalled Rayden Jude having said this the day before. The note was from him. He had decided to help after all.

Harlan paused over Jude's account of the times when members of his crew had clocked out of work that night, which ranged between midnight and 12:25 a.m. The time frame triggered a question: *What time was it when Zach Romanelli's GPS signal first arrived at the Mystery Light viewing area that night?* Harlan thought it might be later than 12:25 a.m., but he was not sure until he consulted his notebook.

According to his notes, it was 12:47 a.m. when the GPS signal got to the viewing area. *Twenty-two minutes after the last driver clocked out for the day,* Harlan thought, *if Jude's account is accurate.* That would mean none of them could have had a plow truck on the road for those twenty-two minutes while Romanelli's body was still being driven by motor vehicle to the viewing area. And that, in turn, could mean it did not matter which of them had plowed the sector that included Indian Village Road, where the transport of the body had begun.

Unless there was a handoff to an accomplice somewhere in between, Harlan thought. He reviewed his notes further, only to be reminded that the transport did not stop until it reached the viewing area. It was continuous, slowing only for turns, and otherwise maintaining speeds of at least 20 mph. *There was no pause for a handoff.*

Again the ranger caught Harlan's eye, but this time with a look that seemed to ask, *What else do you need?*

Harlan responded with a quick text message to the ranger attaching the same photo of the poacher and dead mother bear that he had sent to Diebolt the night before. "I want to show you a video of this son of a bitch killing three bears," the text said.

Seconds later the ranger retrieved a clerk from the souvenir shop to fill in for him behind the information counter, and then he gestured for Harlan to join him as he left the facility through an employee exit.

"What video?" the ranger asked as soon as they stepped outside.

Harlan brought it up on his cellphone, clicked play, and then held the device between them as they remained standing next to picnic table for employees who smoked on their work breaks. On top of the table, a tin can stuffed to the brim with cigarette butts smoldered.

As soon as the recording ended, the ranger drew in a long breath to begin what Harlan anticipated would be a great many questions. Harlan raised his hand to quiet him for a moment. "I'll tell you what I can, Kole, and I'll email you a copy of this video for your own use, but I first must have your word that none of this gets back to Sheriff Mills until I say it's okay to involve him."

"Why would you care if he knows about this?"

"Because as long as he doesn't, and I do, I may be able to stay out in front of him on the case I'm working."

"The case *you're* working? Zach Romanelli's murder? What does this video have to do with that?"

"It was taken by Romanelli a month before he disappeared. And he recognized the shooter."

"Are you saying you know who—"

Harlan raised his hand again. "First give me your word that you won't talk with anyone about this until I say it's okay."

"My word? About what exactly? A moment ago you said not to tell Mills, which I have no problem with. But now you're telling me I can't talk to *anyone* about this? Hell, first thing I have to do after I get your statement is file a report with my superiors."

Harlan stuck his cellphone in his pocket. "Go ahead and file your report then. I'm done giving you my statement. And don't expect a copy of this video anytime soon."

"Wait," Ranger K said as Harlan turned to walk away. He turned back.

"If I go along with you, you'll tell me everything you know?"

"I said I'd tell you what I can," Harlan answered. There were certain matters he simply was not going to risk revealing, like the information Roz had obtained when cross-referencing the video with Romanelli's GPS recording and phone records for the night of the incident. If Sheriff Mills ever did learn of this video, he would have to make those connections for himself.

"Well, what *can* you tell me?" Ranger K asked.

"Enough to bust all three of those bastards for poaching those bears."

"Including the two spotters who kept their masks on?"

"Absolutely. We're going to get the shooter to lead us right to them."

"How so?"

Harlan smiled. "By becoming the poachers."

Chapter 31

After his meeting with the ranger, Harlan drove west into a remote region of the Ottawa National Forest known as the Sylvania Wilderness. Deep in the region's wooded interior he came upon a staggering reminder of civilization—an enormous sporting goods outlet and canoe and kayak rental business—set back off a forest highway. According to Roz, this place, Sylvania Sports, was where many outdoor enthusiasts commenced their excursions into northern Michigan's most pristine backcountry trails and waterways.

It was also the place where George Viola had been discovered the day after the murder, in his parked truck, sleeping off a night of heavy drinking. Roz had followed up on the lead a few days ago and while here discovered a connection she had with the business's owner, Bob Lewandowski, going back to their days in middle school when they served in student government together.

Harlan parked his UTV in a clearing next to the facility and looked through its front windows at an abundance of merchandise inside as he made his way on foot along an asphalt path leading to its main entrance. Roz was right. The store was every bit as big as those corporate-owned megastores that had been avoiding property taxes via the dark-store loophole. No wonder Zach Romanelli, the leading expert on the loophole, had once tried to convince Lewandowski to get his business on board with other big retailers partaking of the tax break. It was this potential and Roz's connection with Lewandowski, Harlan hoped, that might make Sylvania Sports a perfect location to stage a scam he had cooked up for a certain real estate appraiser, Dave Trumane, who supported those tax-evading retailers behind the scenes—and who, in his spare time, poached and butchered hibernating bears.

"Hey Mister, can I get you to sign a petition to save the trees?"

Harlan spun around to see who had come up behind him and asked the question. It was a college-aged kid with short blond hair, pale skin, and a sunburned nose.

"What petition?" Harlan replied.

The kid held out a clipboard. "This one right here. It's to save the trees they're planning to cut down to build a new cell tower about a half mile out back of this place. You should sign on if you want to protect our forest from the urban sprawl."

"What urban sprawl?" Harlan said. "The only sign of civilization I've seen in all the Sylvania Wilderness is this sporting goods store, whose customers could probably use better cellphone reception. How many trees are you trying to save, anyway, by stopping the construction of a single tower?"

"All due respect, sir, it's that attitude that paves the way for the urban sprawl I'm trying to stop. Today it's a single cell tower; tomorrow it's—"

"What the hell do you think you're doing—you damn tree hugger?"

Harlan spun around again, this time to see who was coming from the store's main entrance, shouting. It was a wiry, middle-aged man with weathered skin and a gray-stubbled beard. Through the store's entrance behind him emerged Roz. She stopped on the porch as the man strode forward, glaring at the kid.

"I told you that if you want to pester my customers with your petition, you have to do it in a way that doesn't block my front door. Yet here you are, getting in this gentleman's way as he's trying to access my shop."

"I'm s-sorry... sir," the kid stammered. "It's just that this path to the front door is the way everyone comes."

"Which is why I want you the hell out of the way, so as not to create a bottleneck right where folks are trying to come inside. Now get yourself back out to the parking lot, or get off my property."

"Sorry about that," the man said to Harlan after the kid scurried off. "Is there anything I can do for you? Maybe help you find something you're looking for?"

"He didn't come here to shop, Bob," Roz said as she came down the porch steps and joined them. "He's my partner, Harlan Holmes, the one I told you about. Harlan, meet Bob Lewandowski, the owner of Sylvania Sports."

Harlan extended a hand. "Pleased to meet you. Roz has told me a lot about you. And I'm sure she's told you about the purpose of my visit. Is there somewhere we can talk privately?"

"There's no need for that," Roz said. "You're late, Harlan. Everything is all set."

Harlan glanced at Bob, who smiled back. "What do you mean, Roz?" Harlan asked.

"Just what I said. Bob and I have already talked, and we worked everything out."

"Everything? And you're okay with what we're asking of you?" Harlan asked Bob.

"Are you kidding? After seeing the video of that Trumane fella massacring those hibernating bears, hell yes, I'm all in."

Harlan glanced around the area and spotted a secluded picnic table beneath a big tree near the corner of the facility. "You two may have worked things out," he said, "but I still want to talk about this. How about we take our conversation over there by that picnic table?"

The three of them remained standing after reaching the table. Harlan glanced around again to ensure their privacy before asking, "When you say that you're *all in*, Mr. Lewandowski, you do understand *all* that we're asking, right?"

"Sure, I get how the scam is supposed to go down. I'm supposed to pretend that I'm negotiating a sale of my business property here at Sylvania Sports to a big-shot real estate developer—played by you. And

I'm supposed to pretend that I need help closing the deal because you want to be sure that after you buy the property it will qualify for the dark-store tax loophole. That's where this Trumane fella comes in."

"Right," Harlan said. "And that's where this will get tricky. We want you to reach out to Trumane—a complete stranger—and somehow get him to show up at our upcoming negotiation, here at Sylvania Sports, to help you convince your buyer—me—of the availability of the tax loophole. Do you think you can do that?"

"He already did," Roz said.

"Did what?" Harlan asked.

"Set up Trumane."

"Really?"

Roz sighed. "Tell him, Bob."

Bob shrugged. "It was easy. After Roz told me how this was going down, she gave me the number for Trumane's appraisal business, and I called. Soon as I told someone there who I was and that I needed help lining up the dark-store loophole for my business, they put Trumane on the line, and I told him about how we had a mutual acquaintance, Zach Romanelli, the dark-store attorney, and how Romanelli once came to my store and said my retail business was perfect for the loophole. Come to find out that Trumane already heard about my prior conversation with Romanelli from some partner of Romanelli's who Trumane once worked with, some guy who really wanted my business back when Romanelli was alive. Fella had an unusual name..."

"Let me guess," Harlan said, "Bernie Dufflemire."

"Yeah, that's it. Anyway, I told Trumane how, when I first met Romanelli, I wasn't interested in finagling a property tax loophole for my business on account of my standing in the community. But then I told Trumane about my plans to sell the business to a developer who was only interested in buying the property if the tax loophole was a sure thing. I explained it to him just the way Roz told me to—by saying that my prospective buyer intends to convert the property from a retail store into a gigantic water park for tourists, and he's worried about whether the loophole would apply to a water park, so he made his offer contingent on me getting a written opinion from an expert saying it would."

"And Trumane was interested in being your expert?"

"Are you kidding? The guy was saying he'd do it before I even got to the part about how I came up with his name for the job."

"It's true," Roz added. "Before the call, I'd told Bob how he might explain that, with Romanelli being dead, he wasn't sure where to find another expert who could help him out, until he read an article in the local newspaper."

Roz showed Harlan a newspaper editorial that she had downloaded from online. It was written by a disgruntled taxpayer who was complaining about big retailers not paying their fair share of the property taxes, and taking to task, by name, Dave Trumane and certain other "downstate instigators" who were behind the scandal.

"So, Bob never even had to say that this was where he got Trumane's name?"

"That's right," Roz replied. "It was just like Bob said. Trumane was tripping all over himself for the job. I heard it myself. Bob had him on speaker phone. Trumane even offered a 50 percent discount for his services if Bob would retain him to write the opinion letter."

"A discount? No kidding."

"Oh, but you haven't even heard the best part," Roz said. "Trumane's discount comes with a condition."

"And what's that?" Harlan asked.

"Bob has to make sure to introduce Trumane to his buyer—you— so he can take a crack at making you his tax client down the road, after you buy the property."

"*He* wants to meet *me*?"

Roz nodded.

"Well, that's perfect."

Chapter 32

Harlan and Roz decided to roast hotdogs over the campfire for dinner that evening. She went outside to build the fire while he remained in the camper to assemble side dishes. Before getting started he checked his cellphone, only to see that there still had been no response to either of two text messages he had sent over an hour ago: one to his former mobster client, Angelo Surocco; the other to his former partner on the police force, Detective Riley Summers.

He reread his text to Angelo. "Call me when you get the chance" was all it said. *I should have told him why*, he thought.

He sent Angelo another text, repeating his request for a return call, but this time attaching the video of the bear-poaching incident. Then he began dicing onions. In about the time it would have taken to watch the video, Angelo called. Harlan answered on speaker as he continued doing kitchen work.

"How's it going, Angelo?"

"What the hell was that, Holmes?"

"You mean, the video?"

"Of course that's what I mean. Who were the guys mutilating those bears?"

"Some guys I've never met, who I know I won't like when I do. All I have is a name and a little background information on the one who showed his face. But after he meets me, I expect he'll lead me to the other two."

"Why would he do that?"

"Oh, I don't know. Maybe to impress me after he sees how rich and influential I am."

Angelo laughed so hard he went into one of his two-pack-a-day coughing fits. It ended with him wheezing before swallowing back the phlegm. "So, you're working one of your scams on these lowlife poachers."

Harlan knew he did not have to explain. In fact, Angelo would rather know as few details as possible so he could maintain plausible deniability if he decided to get involved in whatever antics Harlan had in mind.

"What do you need?" Angelo asked.

"Tank Lochner."

This was no small request. Tank Lochner had established himself as Surocco's go-to soldier in the few years since he joined the man's crew. Previously, Tank had worked for Harlan in a similar capacity. His job was usually simple—to just be there when the boss was dealing with unsavory people. Ninety-nine percent of the time he played that role like the gentle giant he truly was. But when necessary, he could flip a psychological switch that turned him into a monster comparable in size and ferocity to a live version of the seven-foot black bear Harlan had seen on display earlier that day at the Forest Service Visitor Center.

"I take it you're planning something that could go sideways," Angelo said, as though asking for details.

Again, however, Harlan knew that he wanted no explanation. His statement was rhetorical. He already knew that Harlan's dealings with the poachers could turn violent. Why else ask for Lochner?

"When would you need him?" Angelo asked.

"Soon—sometime within the next few days, I'm guessing."

"You're guessing? You don't know what day?"

"Not yet. But when I do, I expect I'll need him on short notice."

"What the hell, Holmes? Are you asking me to stand ready to fly one of my top soldiers up to the UP on the drop of a dime?"

"Sorry, Angelo, but I'm dealing with a lot of moving parts right now."

Angelo laughed. "I see you haven't changed. Always pulling shit on your marks. Thing is, it's probably what I miss most about you."

"Does that mean you'll help me out here, Angelo?"

"It means I'll see what I can do."

"About lining up Lochner?"

"I said I'll see. No guarantees."

"Come on, Angelo. You saw what those assholes did to those bears. Let me turn Lochner loose on them."

There was a long pause. During it, Harlan could hear Surocco lighting a cigarette and taking a long drag.

"You know, Holmes, I never thanked you for not talking Lochner into going straight, along with you, back when you quit working for me."

"It was his decision, Angelo. There really wasn't much I could say when he told me about the compensation package you offered him."

"Just the same, I appreciate it. He's become one hell of an asset. And my guess is that he'd welcome the chance to work a scam with his old boss."

"Me too, with him," Harlan said. "It'd be like old times."

"Hell, if I was a few years younger, I'd probably want in on some of this action myself."

"You don't say," Harlan remarked. "No offense, Angelo, but you always struck me as a boss who got his hands dirty only on rare occasions."

"Well, this occasion kind of feels like one."

"How so?"

"You know that I spend a lot of time up there where you're at right now."

"Sure, I imagine that's how you established VIP status at the Gateway Lodge."

"That's where I go to get away from all the big-city bullshit. I love it up there. Hiking the trails, fishing the lakes and streams, *and hunting the wildlife*. But what those guys did wasn't hunting."

"I know how you feel, Angelo. What they did was a crime against everyone who feels that way, not to mention those bears."

***

Harlan waited until after dinner before texting Detective Riley Summers to ask again that she give him a call.

"I'll go inside and get started on the dishes," Roz said as Harlan began poking at his phone. "You can tell me what she says later."

After typing the message, he leaned back in his canvas chair beside the campfire and searched his photo library for an attachment. This time it would be a photo he had taken the day before at the Bel-Air Motel rather than the video of the bear-poaching incident.

Before tapping "send" Harlan reflected one last time on the irony of him asking Riley for help with his defense of George Viola. Not only was she allied with the sheriff and prosecutor; the alliance had resulted from the concerns of her boss, Captain Martin Nash, when he learned that Harlan was working for the defense. Nash had offered Riley up— one of his best detectives—to help a small-town sheriff deal with just the kind of ploy that her former partner on the force was now instigating.

He tapped "send." If his hunch was right, she had insisted on being briefed on every detail of the prosecutor's case when she was brought on board. *She'll know the significance of the photo*, he thought.

Riley's call was instantaneous. "Where did you get this?"

"Hello to you too, Riley. Aren't you going to ask why I sent it in the first place?"

She did not respond.

"Well, I'll tell you anyway. You're looking at George Viola's alibi."

"His alibi? Is a fucking cat?"

"I take it that nobody on your side of the case has ever met Eli."

"So, that's the name of the furry critter Viola claims to have been with on the night of the murder—at his make-believe support-group meeting."

"Listen, Riley, that cat is central to George Viola's defense. And I'm willing to tell you all about it if—"

Riley burst out laughing. "Please Harlan," she begged when she caught her breath. "Just stop it, would you? I mean, you've been working this case for what, almost a week now? And this is all you got? Eli the cat?"

"There's more, Riley. I assure you. A lot more. And like I was about to say, I'm willing to tell you all about it if you'll do something for me."

"Sure you will, Harlan. I'm all ears. What can I do for you?"

"I want you to be my partner again."

"Would you stop joking around, Harlan, and just tell me what you want?"

"I'm serious. I want you to be my partner, for just one more day out of your life."

"Okay, look, assuming you're serious—which I never can tell with you—you know that's not possible."

"Why? Because of your association with Sheriff Mills?"

"Obviously," she replied.

"What if I said that you can tell him everything—after the one day is over?"

He took the silence that followed to mean he had her attention. "Mills doesn't know the whole story, Riley. And I can assure you, if he doesn't hear it soon—from you—George Viola's defense attorney will spring it on the prosecutor at the most inopportune moment he can find."

"What would you have us do during our last day as partners?"

"It's not all worked out yet. I'll have to bring you up to speed when the day comes."

"What day?"

"I'm not exactly sure of that either. But it'll be soon. And there won't be much notice."

"What are you saying, Harlan? That sometime soon you're going to call and tell me I need to drop everything and get my ass up to bumfuck Yooperland on the spot, for some assignment you're going to make up as we go along?"

"Well… yeah… I guess."

"And what do you guess the captain would say if I took this to him?"

"I don't know."

"I do," Riley said, "because the budget he's on couldn't handle the expense of flying me up there on a moment's notice for a day in the life of Harlan Holmes."

"But I already have the flight worked out. At no charge."

"Who the hell would provide that service for free?"

"Surocco Imports."

There was an audible gasp followed by a long silence.

"I thought you were done working for those hoods," she said.

"I am. I'm just borrowing one of Surocco's guys for something I've got going, and I figure his flight can stop off in Traverse City and pick you up on the way."

"You have *got* to be kidding."

He waited for her to answer herself.

"Of course you're not."

Chapter 33

Harlan and Roz were already five minutes late for a 6:30 meeting the next morning when they pulled into a parking lot located still a half mile's hike from their destination. They had been assured, however, that the hike would be quick and easy.

Harlan paused outside the Jeep for a look at the two other vehicles parked in the lot. One was a monster SUV that he recognized as belonging to one of the participants in their upcoming meeting, Jackie Diebolt. The other was a light-duty pickup truck that he imagined belonged to the other participant, Julie LePoudre, who had asked her friend Jackie to coordinate the meeting at this time and place.

Jackie was right about the short hike. Most of it was a stroll in the woods on an elevated boardwalk designed for individuals who might require special accommodations to access the tourist attraction ahead—a waterfall known as Bond Falls. Along the way, crashing water that began as rumble of distant thunder grew louder and louder, until the circuitous boardwalk led them into the mist of the waterfall's plunge basin, where the thunder rose to a nonstop, deafening explosion.

When she had called to arrange the meeting, Jackie described Bond Falls as the most impressive waterfall in the entire state of Michigan. At the time, Harlan disagreed. "Ask anyone and they'll tell you that the Tahquamenon Falls are the best," he argued, referring to the well-known site in the eastern UP. Her rejoinder—"You must not know anyone who's seen this one"—now rang true.

Bond Falls' massive wall of crashing water began forty feet above their heads. Further up, feeding the beast, torrential cascades and rapids added another twenty feet to the raging river's precipitous elevation change.

Those two distances, combined, stood between them and their meeting place, which meant they now had to leave the boardwalk and hike up the steep, sixty-foot slope adjacent to the falling wall of water, over moss-and-water slickened boulders lying in wait in the mist ahead.

"What the hell is this?" Harlan shouted over the exploding plunge basin. "She said it was a hill!"

"Well, that's what it is!" Roz yelled back. "A *really treacherous* hill!"

Harlan waited for Roz to go first so that he could be there for her if she slipped or stumbled. She, in turn, seemed to be doing the same, waiting for him to take the lead. He understood why. She knew that his arthritic knees had already been challenged by the leisurely stroll along the boardwalk. On the dicey stretch ahead, he would be more likely to fall.

He waited her out nonetheless, until finally she ducked under the rail at the end of the boardwalk and led their ascent.

Harlan reached the summit a full minute behind Roz. "You're late!" Jackie Diebolt shouted over the roar of the rapids the moment he arrived.

He coughed hard several times trying to catch his breath, before shouting back, "Better late than dead! Why not just meet in the parking lot? I can hardly hear you up here!"

"I'm sorry, Mr. Holmes!" yelled Jackie's friend, Julie LePoudre. "It's just that—"

"Or you could've just left the damn documents with Jackie to deliver if you're afraid of getting caught!"

"Harlan!" Roz bellowed. "Let's just get on with it!"

He chalked it up to youthful indiscretion. The young woman probably was excited to play a role in a murder investigation, but at the same time had to guard against her boss finding out about it after the way he and Harlan had butted heads on the first day Harlan took the case.

Harlan directed Julie to the shelter of a large bush and stepped close to her so they could stop yelling. Roz and Jackie joined them and the four formed a tight huddle behind the bush.

"I imagine your boss, Mr. *Tee*, might be a little upset if he learned about this clandestine meeting," Harlan said.

As Julie nodded, Jackie replied, "A little? You think? Shit, he'd fire her ass in a heartbeat, the way he did me."

"No offense, Mr. Holmes," Julie added, "but my boss really dislikes you."

Harlan smiled. "Well, I guess hearing that has already made the death-defying hike up here worthwhile. My apologies for getting chippy about it. What other good news might you have for me, Ms. LePoudre?"

She unzipped her backpack, removed two Redweld folders, and handed them to Harlan. He opened the thinner of the two first. It contained only a few pages of documents.

"That's all I could find on the plow-truck drivers who worked that night," Julie said as Harlan skimmed the first page. It was a county road-crew schedule listing the names of six drivers scheduled for the night shift on March 12. According to the document, two had been scheduled in advance; the other four were called in that day, on short notice, due to an "unforeseen snowstorm." The crew supervisor listed for that evening was Rayden Jude.

Harlan reflected on the note that Jude had previously provided about the same night. This document seemed to confirm the list of names he had given Harlan.

The other few pages in the file were time records that also confirmed what Jude's note had said about the crew having worked a late shift, with the last of the drivers clocking out at 12:25 a.m., March 13.

"It doesn't match up," Roz said as she shared a look at the time sheets.

"What do you mean?" Julie asked. "I downloaded those records straight from the County Road Commission's database."

"I'm sure you did," Harlan said, recalling the exact time that night—12:47 a.m.—when Zach Romanelli's GPS signal had reached the Mystery Light viewing area on Robbins Pond Road. It was the same thing he had learned from Jude's note about that night. The facts simply did not support the theory of an assassin on the road crew. How could any of them have used a plow truck to deposit Romanelli's body at the viewing area at 12:47 if the last one on duty clocked out twenty-two minutes *beforehand*, at 12:25?

Although it seemed not to matter, Harlan still wanted to know which of the drivers plowed and de-iced the area that included the scene at Indian Village Road where the transport of Romanelli's body had begun that evening. Jude had said they kept no such records, but Harlan wanted to make sure nothing was overlooked.

"What about routes?" he asked. "There's nothing in here about who drove where that night."

"I'm sorry, Mr. Holmes," Julie replied. "I searched the Commission's database every which way I could and came up with nothing except for a map showing the six sectors they plowed and de-iced. I never saw anything saying who plowed which sectors."

"Did you get a copy of the map?"

"Sure, it's in the other folder, right on top."

Harlan opened the other folder. It contained a stack of documents much thicker than the first, at least three hundred pages he estimated. On top was a map showing a large region of the western Upper Peninsula that included eastern Gogebic County and the southern half of Ontonagon County. The region was divided into six sectors outlined and numbered in red. Sector Two included Indian Village Road, which was among many roads in the sector highlighted in yellow.

A legend beneath the map defined the highlighted roads with a term Harlan did not understand. "Program Roads?" he asked, reading it aloud.

"Roads that were part of the beet-juice pilot program," Julie replied. "You said you wanted information about them. Turns out, there were lots of documents."

"I see," Harlan said as he flipped through the rest of the thick folder, stopping on the last page. It offered a summary outline of the cost savings yielded by using beet juice rather than conventional road salt to de-ice the program roads. A look from Roz showed that she shared his impression of this document and probably the rest in the thick folder—they seemed useless to their murder investigation.

"You asked for it," Roz said. "And how much did you say you would pay Ms. LePoudre for this *evidence* that we just risked our lives to get?"

Harlan shrugged. "Twenty bucks a page, up to two grand, and another thousand up front."

"Well?" Roz said.

Harlan dug into his pocket for an envelope containing the $3,000, as promised.

Roz rolled her eyes. "And now we get to scramble down from this cliff and hike back to the parking lot."

Chapter 34

Compared to the rental UTV that Harlan had been driving lately, the Jeep purred quietly during their return trip to the campground, making a break in their conversation markedly silent. Roz, though driving, looked over at him for longer than a glance.

"What are you thinking about?" she asked.

"The dead end we've run into, twice in the last two days."

Roz returned her stare to the road ahead. She no doubt knew he was talking about their theory of a homicidal road worker being undermined by evidence from two sources suggesting that none of the crew was still on the road when Romanelli's body arrived at the Mystery Light viewing area. "Well, all is not lost," Roz said. "We still haven't ruled out the cheating wife and her tax-evading boyfriend."

Harlan's thoughts turned to those two suspects: Ava Romanelli and Bernie Dufflemire.

"That theory has its problems too," he said.

"It doesn't have to be perfect, Harlan. We just need enough evidence to raise reasonable doubt as to George Viola's guilt."

"I doubt we have even that."

"What do you mean? They had one of the oldest motives in the book—to rid her of an unwanted husband while keeping his entire estate. And that unwanted husband may have been more than an inconvenience if he was catching on to Dufflemire's tax evasion, which was a distinct possibility. After all, Zach Romanelli was the brilliant dark-store attorney; it might not have taken until the meeting of the

Board of Review for him to suspect Dufflemire of rigging the comps on all those big-box stores."

"I get all that, Roz, but I'm still not convinced."

"Why?"

"Because when I met the lovebirds in Traverse City, it sounded to me like Ava Romanelli had come clean with her husband about her affair and worked out an amicable separation from him. And Dufflemire admitted to having run his scam on the comps since the beginning, right under Zach Romanelli's nose, with no worry of Romanelli catching on. Hell, even if Romanelli did figure it out, he was the front guy—the attorney making all the cases for their retail clients based on those rigged comps. He couldn't roll over on Dufflemire without implicating himself."

"Just what are you saying, Harlan? That you don't like a murder theory against a cheating wife and her tax-evading boyfriend because they told you they didn't do it? Since when do you take liars and cheats at their word?"

"I didn't say I believe them. I'm just saying that we don't have enough on them—not yet anyway. Based on what we know so far, their lying and cheating lives had been going along smoothly for quite some time. For the narrative to work, it would help if we could find some event that pushed them over the edge and induced them to whack the guy."

"A precipitating event," Roz said.

"That's right, and I have one in mind, but there's a lot we don't know about it."

"You're talking about Zach Romanelli's telephone call on the night he witnessed the expert appraiser, Dave Trumane, slaughter those three bears."

Harlan nodded. "After witnessing that carnage, Romanelli should have called the cops. But instead he called his sleazy law partner, Bernie Dufflemire. Why *him*? And what might Dufflemire have said—or done—to stop Romanelli from ratting out their crooked appraiser for what he did to those bears?"

"I've wondered about those things too," Roz said. "But we'll never know because Dufflemire is the only living witness to that phone call and we won't have the element of surprise when we catch up with him to interrogate him about it."

Roz's latter point, Harlan knew, was based on what Ava Romanelli had told him she did after she shared her husband's online password information with Sheriff Mills. Tracking the metadata left when the sheriff visited her husband's online accounts, Ava Romanelli was able to discover every bit of information revealed by the sheriff's online investigation. She undoubtedly was doing the same during Harlan and Roz's subsequent investigation of those same online accounts, which meant that she and Dufflemire already knew of Harlan and Roz's discovery of the bear-poaching video and Zach Romanelli's subsequent phone call to Dufflemire about it.

"It's going to take some creativity to come up with a 'gotcha' interrogation for Dufflemire," Harlan said as Roz steered the Jeep into the campsite.

"Well, you better get creative fast," Roz said, "because based on your description of the lovebirds, it looks to me like that's them up ahead, paying us a visit right now."

Harlan looked up. Sure enough, it was them, the extramarital soul mates, Ava Romanelli and Bernie Dufflemire, getting out of a Cadillac Escalade parked in Harlan and Roz's campsite.

***

After introducing Roz to their unexpected guests, Harlan invited everyone to seat themselves in canvas camp chairs around the charred remains of last night's campfire.

"My, isn't this a romantic setting," Ava Romanelli commented as her smile at Bernie segued into a giggle that ended with an abrupt snort. Bernie smiled back, giggled the same way, but then, in an apparent effort to suppress snorting himself, nervously squirmed in his chair.

Harlan watched Roz, her mouth slightly ajar, as she examined the couple, their chubby, chalk-white faces and tiny eyes hidden beneath thick, horned-rimmed glasses—both of them. Today, they even dressed alike in plaid flannel shirts and blue jeans rolled up at the bottom revealing their matching argyle socks and high-top PF Flyers.

What did I tell you? Harlan thought as he continued to watch Roz size up their guests. *They're twins… a couple of geeks. If it's true what they say about likes attracting, poor Zach Romanelli never had a chance.*

Harlan turned to their visitors. "So… what brings you to our humble campsite at this early-morning hour? You two must have driven through the night to get here. It must be something important."

Of course, he knew the reason for their long, late-night journey and why neither of them was quick to explain it. They, too, had never reported Zach Romanelli's video recording of the heinous crime against nature committed by a man who had conspired with Bernie to defraud local tax collectors throughout northern Michigan. *This should be interesting*, Harlan thought.

"Well… uh…" Ava stammered. "Uh… tell him, Bernie."

Bernie squirmed again in his chair, his gaze darting every which way, except at Harlan or Roz.

"What's on your mind, Bernie?" Harlan pressed.

Bernie finally looked at him. "You know… the video of… what happened that night."

"You mean the video Zach Romanelli recorded a month and a day before his murder? What about it?"

"You're probably wondering about the phone call Zach made after… why he called me."

"You think?"

"You haven't told anybody, have you?"

Harlan felt no compunction about lying to this man. "Of course not, Bernie. Who would I tell? The forest ranger whose office is just a few miles from where those bears were butchered?"

"You're not going to tell him, are you? I mean, it really has nothing to do with your case."

"Really," Harlan said, his tone sarcastic. "Zach Romanelli witnesses your coconspirator in tax fraud commit a brutal felony, confronts you about it, and a month later gets whacked. And you're telling me there's no connection?"

"You're mischaracterizing the phone call. There was no confrontation."

"Then enlighten me, Bernie. Why the hell did he call you—if *not* to rip you a new one for entangling him in your felonious scheme with that scumbag appraiser, Dave Trumane?"

"I'm telling you, that's not why he called."

Bernie glanced at Ava. "Go ahead," she said. "Just tell him the truth."

"Why should I?" Bernie replied. His frustration was palpable. "What's the point? He won't believe me."

Ava turned to Harlan. "Look, Mr. Holmes, Bernie wants to be straight with you right now, just like he was when you met us in Traverse City. My husband, Zach, had no idea Bernie was bribing Trumane to manipulate the data on those big-box store appraisals—not until later, on the night of the meeting with the Board of Review, when the data came in the way it did, all skewed in favor of their clients. *That's* when he ripped into Bernie, a month later when both he and the local assessor figured it out. I heard it myself, and so did you when we let you listen to the voicemail Zach left that night for Bernie."

Harlan recalled the hostile message Zach had left that night shortly after his shocking discovery of Bernie's fraud. "Okay," Harlan said, "so let's say that a month earlier, when Zach witnessed the bear-poaching incident, he didn't know Bernie had been bribing Trumane. That still doesn't explain his immediate phone call to Bernie. Why would he call his law partner after seeing what Trumane did to those bears, and not the sheriff or the ranger?"

"He wanted my legal counsel," Bernie replied.

"Your counsel? About what?"

"Whether he *should* report Trumane to the cops."

"Why would he even hesitate? As upset as he must have been at the sight of Trumane shooting that mother bear and her cubs—in their sleep—his impulse should have been to alert the authorities."

"I'm telling you, Holmes, when Zach called that night, he wasn't the least bit upset about anything—not with me, Trumane, or anyone else. He was as calm as could be, trying to make a decision, and was just reaching out to me, his law partner, as someone he could talk to about what was making him think twice about calling the cops."

"What possibly could have made him hesitate about reporting those poachers?"

"Whether he should give a damn about Nimrod Nation."

"Nimrod Nation? You mean, the town of Watersmeet?"

"That's right. The people of Watersmeet, the Nimrods. Them and pretty much every Yooper north of the Mackinac Bridge—but especially them. If you know how they were treating him, and I'm sure you do, then you know why he was questioning whether he should give a damn about what he'd just witnessed Trumane do in their forest."

"I've heard some things," Harlan acknowledged.

"Including the vicious lies and rumors about him sleeping with Stevie Viola? His sister, for crying out loud."

"I guess I can understand him being upset."

"Dammit, Holmes," Bernie complained, "you're not listening. He wasn't upset; I'm telling you, he was calm—emotionless—like he was feeling no sense of duty to the people up here, despite what he saw Trumane do to those bears."

"What'd you tell him?"

"I told him he had no duty. Under the law, a bystander to a crime has no duty to report it to the police. I'm sure you know that. Like those people in New York who once shut their windows to the screams of a woman being raped on the street below, Zach Romanelli owed no duty to the people around here—or, for that matter, to those bears. That's what I told him."

"And that advice worked out nicely for you, too, didn't it, because my guess is, you had something to do with what Trumane did to those bears."

Harlan was fishing with this accusation. If it was off base, however, Bernie should have looked surprised, and he did not. Nor did Ava, who nodded at him.

"You're right, Holmes. I had a hand in it."

Harlan waited for the admission. It took another nod from Ava.

"You remember us discussing how Trumane got picked for the job he did on the property tax rolls, don't you?"

"Sure," Harlan said. "The local officials up here in the UP wanted all the assessments on your clients' big-box stores reviewed by an independent appraiser, and the agreement reached was that they would get to create a list of five candidates for the job, and from that list, your firm would pick one. And your firm picked Trumane."

"No, *I* picked Trumane," Bernie amended, "on behalf of the firm. And before doing that, I did some homework and learned not only that the man was having some financial issues, which made him potentially receptive to a bribe, but that for the past twenty years he'd entered the state's annual lottery for one of the few bear-hunting licenses they issue—and had never once been drawn for it."

"So, part of your bribe was a promise to get him a bear hunt."

Bernie nodded. "I know what you're thinking, Holmes. There's nothing stopping you from turning me in for solicitation of the poachers who took Trumane out for the hunt. But it won't matter if you do. I'll never go down for it."

"Why not?"

"You think I'm just some socially inept legal nerd who doesn't have connections like yours—don't you, Mr. Mafia PI?"

"I never said that."

"You didn't have to. It's written all over your face. Hers too," Bernie added, glancing at Roz. "The two of you think that Ava and I are a couple of bumbling geeks. Well, think again. We're not going down for shit, no matter what you decide to do with anything your investigation uncovers. Do you really think we would've given you access to Zach's online activities if there was even a chance of that? Like I said—think again."

Harlan glanced at Roz and again caught her with her mouth slightly ajar, examining their guests. "If you two have things so under control right now," he said, "then why did you drive 370 miles through the night to speak with us about it? And why, when you first got here, did you ask whether we had told anyone about the poaching incident and Zach's call to you afterward?"

"I'll take your second question first," Bernie replied. "Make no mistake, I don't want you to report the incident, and I came here, in part, to see if I could head that off, assuming you haven't reported it yet. But I *can* handle it if you report it anyway. I just don't need a nuisance like that in my life. As for your other question, I'll let Ava respond."

"We also came here," Ava said without missing a beat, "for the same reason we gave you access to all of Zach's online activities—because, believe it or not, we want to make sure that they prosecute the right person for the murder of my late husband and Bernie's late law partner. We came here intending to help you get to the truth, Mr. Holmes."

This time Harlan caught himself with his own mouth ajar as he examined the couple. He did not know how to respond. *What the hell are they up to?*

"And, although I'm pretty sure George Viola did it," Ava continued, "I have to admit some doubt after the last time I saw his wife, Stevie. She believes in her husband's innocence, and I've come to love and trust her—Zach's flesh and blood—like she's my sister too. We want to see that you get to the truth of the matter as much for her as we do for ourselves."

"You say that with such conviction," Harlan scoffed.

"Fuck you, Holmes!" Bernie shouted. "Let's just get out of here, Ava. They don't want our help."

"Wait a second," Roz said. "Maybe my partner doesn't want your help. But I do."

Ah, good timing, Roz, Harlan thought as he watched the disdain in Bernie's expression ease a little. *Perfect time for the arrival of the nice PI.*

"It sounds like you two may have come here to talk about something else," Roz said, "besides this bear-poaching incident. It'd be a shame for your long trip to have been a waste. Please tell me what you came here to say. And please accept my apologies for my partner's behavior. Sometimes he can take his hard-boiled detective routine too far."

Okay, Roz, you don't have to be that nice.

"Why don't you tell them, Bernie," Ava said. "You're the one who figured it out."

Bernie shifted in his chair, turning a cold shoulder to Harlan, and faced Roz. She stared back at him without expression. "I know what you're thinking," Bernie said. "Why would this guy who's having an affair with Zach's wife, and who bribed that appraiser behind his back, care about getting to the truth of his murder."

"I guess the question crossed my mind," Roz said. "But then I see the way you two are together—you and Ava—the way you look at each other and interact, and I get it. What you have is real. And I imagine Zach saw that as well when you two told him about it. From what I understand, his separation from Ava was amicable. Sometimes life just doesn't introduce us to our true soul mate until late in the game." Roz glanced at Harlan and added, "I know that from my own experience."

"I appreciate you saying that," Bernie said, his expression easing further. "You're spot-on."

"And I think I also get why you kept Zach in the dark about your dealings with the appraiser," Roz said. "You were protecting him, the way you always did when you massaged the comps as needed to make his dark-store tax loophole work. You knew that if those bogus appraisals ever went to court, Zach would be the one submitting all the pleadings and affidavits. He would be the one on the hook for tax fraud and perjury if he knew what was going on. You had to keep it from him, for his own good."

"Damn straight, I did," Bernie said, scowling at Harlan before shooting a pleased look at Roz. She leaned forward in her chair, toward him. "Tell me, Mr. Dufflemire, what have you come here to do this time for your friend Zach, or his memory?"

"It's not something I'm doing today. It's something I did in the past for him that I want to tell you about."

Bernie nodded at Ava, and she removed a piece of paper from her purse and handed it to Roz. After looking at it, Roz gave it to Harlan. It was an article printed from an online newspaper about Zach Romanelli's murder and the charges brought against George Viola for it. A sentence was highlighted in yellow: "Witnesses at the Roadhouse Tavern say that the suspect, George Viola, seemed to show up out of nowhere on the night of his capture, oblivious to the warrant out for his arrest, claiming to have been wandering in the woods during the six weeks since the victim's disappearance."

"Zach Romanelli once did something like that too," Bernie said.

"Did what?" Roz asked.

"A recovery hike."

It took everything in his power for Harlan to avoid jumping in as a flurry of questions flew through his mind, starting with, *Where did he get that label, "recovery hike"? That's what George called his method of attaining sobriety, and it's never been released to the public.*

"I'd be interested in hearing about that," Roz said.

"I'm sure you would," Bernie replied. "It happened five years ago, before Zach was made a partner at the firm. He and I were working long hours in those days, booting up our brand, spanking new dark-store tax loophole for our mega-retail clients. We were also hitting the booze a lot back then—drinking as hard as we were working. For Zach, it was becoming a problem. Nobody but me knew about it, not even Ava, but I could see that his drinking wasn't going to stay a secret for much longer, and that it could cost him his chance to make partner at the firm."

"So, you did something to help him," Roz said, "to protect him, the way you always did."

"That's right. I talked with Ava about it, and we did one of those interventions with him, just the two of us, to encourage him to admit his addiction and get some help. Thing is, it didn't work so well. He refused to do the necessary rehab and counseling. It wasn't until sometime later that he came up with his own way to get clean and sober—a recovery hike he called it."

"That's the second time you've described it that way, Mr. Dufflemire," Roz said, "as a *recovery hike*. Are you sure that's what Zach called it?"

"That's exactly what he called it," Ava interjected. "He took a leave of absence from work and went to the Rocky Mountains, alone, and after seven or eight weeks of hiking around in the wilderness—far removed from liquor stores and bars—he came home clean and sober. And from that day until he died, he remained that way—recovered."

Roz leaned over toward Harlan for another look at the highlighted sentence in the news article describing how George Viola, a reputed alcoholic, had disappeared for a similar length of time in the wilderness.

"It struck us as a strange coincidence," Ava said, "especially because Zach made Bernie and me promise absolute secrecy about his addiction. Nobody but us knew about it, or his hike in the Rockies, not even his sister Stevie."

"How do you know she didn't?" Roz asked.

"Because of something she said after the funeral, while she and I had a glass of wine together. She commented about Zach never drinking alcohol because, he had told her, he didn't like the buzz. And all I could think at the time was how *untrue* that was. His recovery hike never stopped his craving for the buzz. I'm sure her husband George would tell her the same thing if he happened to have the same purpose as Zach had for taking his hike."

"He didn't just *happen* to have the same purpose," Harlan muttered to himself, but more loudly than he realized. Bernie responded, "That's the first thing you've said that makes sense, Holmes."

Harlan ignored Bernie and, turning to Roz, asked, "What do *you* think about Romanelli taking a recovery hike?"

As so often happened between them, Roz knew where Harlan's train of thought was going. As he started working his cellphone, she answered, "I think he must have taken a lot of supplies to survive that long in the Rockies."

"Yeah, supplies like these," Harlan said as he pulled up the surveillance-camera image of the handwritten shopping list used by George Viola at Sylvania Sports when he went there to gear up for *his* hike.

Harlan reached across the charred remains of last night's campfire and held his phone in front of Ava Romanelli. "Where did you get that?" she asked, her eyes opening to a near normal size beneath her thick glasses.

"Have you seen it before?"

"No, but the writing is his."

Chapter 35

Dark clouds rolled in later that day in advance of a storm forecast to begin during the early evening hours. For Harlan and Roz, there would be no outdoor dining by the campfire tonight. Eating indoors, however, still might not spare Harlan from getting wet. It was 5:00 p.m. when the first few drops began tapping at his Jeep's soft top on his return from town with Chinese takeout.

Minutes later, as he pulled into the campsite, the storm broke. He parked as close to the camper as he could and waited, hoping for the torrent to dial back, if just for the few seconds it would take him to dash to the camper. Meanwhile, the tantalizing aroma of his Hunan beef filled the Jeep. He considered digging into it right there, until a bolt of lightning and simultaneous explosion of thunder lit up the campsite and rocked the vehicle.

He grabbed the food and made a run for the camper.

Harlan returned to the kitchen table after changing into dry clothes and plopped himself into the chair in front of his Hunan beef. Roz sat beside him eating her cashew chicken with the wooden chopsticks that came with the meal. With her free hand she was shuffling through stacks of papers also on the table. They were the documents that Julie LePoudre had delivered earlier concerning the experimental beet-juice de-icing program conducted in parts of Gogebic County this past winter. The couple had spent most of the day organizing the documents, and Roz was now close to completing the task.

After several failed attempts with his chopsticks, Harlan snatched up a fork. "Find anything useful yet?" he asked.

Roz slid him a stack of documents. "Those continue to be the most interesting ones, so far."

They were copies of a form filled out by plow-truck drivers on program roads whenever they sprayed those roads with beet juice. The stack included those they had found for Sector Two—the sector that included Indian Village Road.

Harlan slid the top sheet from the pile. It was a one-page, one-sided document dated November 10 from the prior year. He thumbed through the rest of the stack. Roz had organized them chronologically while he was out; the most recent one was dated February 27, just two weeks prior to the night of Romanelli's murder. "I take it you haven't found any for March yet."

"I have, actually, but none yet for Sector Two," Roz answered.

Harlan reviewed portions of the form for November 10 that he had highlighted earlier when he first found it. Above the date, at the top of the form, was the caption: "Pilot Program: Driver's Feedback." On the line beneath the date was the typewritten word "Sector" followed by a handwritten "2." Beneath that there followed a series of typewritten phrases—"Weather conditions," "Volume of beet juice sprayed," "Start and finish times," and "General observations"—followed by handwritten responses, which for that day in November were "5 inches of snow with heavy drifting," "2/3 of the tank," "2-8 p.m.," and "Stuff made a mess but got the job done." At the bottom of the page there was a space for something potentially important to their case—the name of the driver who had completed the form—if they could just find a form completed for Sector Two on the night of March 12. For Sector Two on that day in November, the driver was "Joe Abraham."

As Harlan reviewed another form, Roz called out, "Here it is, finally, the one for March 12—Sector Two." After looking at it, she gave it to Harlan and then grabbed the other file folder LePoudre had provided, which contained employee time records for that night.

Harlan skimmed the form. The driver that night reported "15 inches of wet snow and ice" and claimed to have "drained the tank" of beet juice. At the bottom was his name, "Mark Smith."

Roz called out again, "Got it."

"Got what?"

"Smith's time records."

Harlan scanned up the form for the "finish" time. "Says here that he returned the truck to the garage at 12:15 a.m., March 13."

"That's consistent with his time records," Roz replied. "He clocked out at 12:25, along with his supervisor, Rayden Jude." Roz shuffled through a few more documents. "They were the last of the road crew to clock out that night."

Twenty-two minutes before the transit of Romanelli's body had been completed, Harlan recalled. He looked again at the form, this time to study the handwriting. It looked familiar. *Where have I seen writing like this: sloppy, slanted left, half cursive/half print?*

"I got it," Harlan said as he headed for a stack of papers on the kitchen counter.

"Got what?" Roz asked.

He dug through the stack until he found it. "This. It's the note Rayden Jude wrote me saying who worked on his crew that night and the times they checked in and out." Harlan compared the note and the feedback form and then handed both to Roz. "The form may say it was filled out by this guy Mark Smith, but I don't think so."

Roz made the same comparison. "I'd say that's a match—a perfect match—which makes you wonder, why did Jude fill out the form and enter Smith's name?"

Harlan mulled over the question. "Maybe he was just doing the guy a favor, you know, completing the form while Smith was busy with something else. Or maybe Jude drove the Sector Two plow truck himself that night... but wanted it to look like someone else did."

"Why would he do that?"

"For the same reason he lied to me about having no record of who drove which roads that night," Harlan replied as he began rifling through other documents on the table. "The map outlining all the sectors. Where is it?"

Roz dug the map out from a pile of documents and gave it to Harlan. He reviewed the roads traveled by Zach Romanelli's GPS signal that night in Sector Two, confirming his recollection of them. His thoughts returned to what had become a nagging issue. "It just can't be a coincidence that the movement of Romanelli's body was confined to this sector," he muttered. "There must be some reason for it."

Roz scooted close to look at the map with him. "Maybe there is."

"What are you suggesting, Roz?"

"Nothing specific. I don't get it either. Until it entered Ontonagon County en route to Robbins Pond Road, Romanelli's body never left Sector Two. Like you said, that can't be a coincidence."

Still studying the map, Harlan traced his finger over the last segment of the ride Romanelli's body took that night, north along Highway 45, but stopped his fingertip short at the county line. There was something in fine print written on each side of the line. He squinted and adjusted the distance between his aging eyes and the map but could not bring it into focus. "Can you make this out, Roz?"

She took the map from him. "Where?"

"Right where Highway 45 crosses the county line between Gogebic County to the south, and Ontonagon County to the north."

Roz struggled the same way Harland did, and then retrieved a set of keys from her pocket. On it she had a tiny magnifying glass. Harlan leaned in as Roz held the lens over the fine print, increasing its size several times. On the Gogebic side of the line, the notation said, "Central Time Zone." On the Ontonagon side, it said, "Eastern Time Zone."

Harlan snatched his cell phone off the kitchen counter and called George Viola's attorney, Kerry Jammer.

"Jammer, this is Harlan Holmes. I need you to arrange a meeting with our client."

"Sure, I'll call the county jail tomorrow, first thing. What's going on?"

"No, I want to see him now—tonight."

"Tonight? It's raining cats and dogs here in Bessemer."

"So what? We'll meet inside this time. And I want his shrink to be there, you know, the therapist you told us about who's trying to help George recover his memories about the night they say he killed Zach Romanelli."

"Dr. Goodwin? She's over a hundred miles away, in Marquette."

Harlan looked at his watch. It was 6:17 p.m. "Okay, then schedule the meeting for a couple hours from now and tell her she *has* to be there."

"Why?"

"Because we need an expert on hand when I try to unlock George's repressed memories of what happened that night."

"When you... what?"

"When I help George recall why he's innocent."

"How are you going to do that?"

"You just tell the good doctor that she'll see when she gets there, and so will you, if you're able to join us."

"Even if she can make it, I have no idea whether the sheriff is going to—"

"Just make this meeting happen, Jammer."

Harlan ended the call and rejoined Roz at the kitchen table. She had the recording of Zach Romanelli's GPS signal from the night of March 12 running on her laptop. "Watch this," she said, as she reset the recording to the point where the GPS signal was a short distance south of the county line. She then opened the app's timer, which displayed on the side of the screen, and hit play. Seconds later, as the signal crossed the border, the timer switched from 11:40 p.m., March 12, to 12:40 a.m., March 13.

Chapter 36

Kerry Jammer was able to arrange the meeting, though a little later that evening than Harlan had requested. It was almost 10:00 p.m. when a deputy led him and Dr. Doreen Goodwin into a small, windowless interrogation room in the county jail. Harlan took a seat at a gray metal table in the middle of the room while Goodwin remained standing to his left, pointing her cellphone at him.

"Smile for the camera, Mr. Holmes."

Harlan rolled his eyes as he turned to face her. Too bad the deputy wouldn't relax the two-visitors-only rule, he thought, so that Roz or Jammer could have been here to help him deal with this woman. She returned a big smile that lit up her perfectly round face and eyes.

"I'm just so excited about this, Mr. Holmes."

Her optimism bordered on annoying, like that of a bubbly cheerleader he once knew in high school who could remain oblivious to her team's circumstances no matter how dire. Never mind that she had been hailed to this jailhouse in the middle of the night during a downpour that had flattened her big hair and streaked her mascara, potentially for naught. She really *was* excited to be here.

"I think you have a great plan, Mr. Holmes. But always remember what I said. You must not…"

"I know," Harlan replied. "I got it the first time—don't lead the witness."

She continued smiling despite his reprimanding tone. "I'm sure I must sound like a broken record, but I can't emphasize it enough.

Whatever memories George might recover tonight, they must be *his* memories, resulting from *his* independent recollection. You can facilitate his recollection of those memories, but you must guard against creating them. Never forget how vulnerable he is to suggestion, especially any suggestion coming from you—his PI."

Her point about George Viola's vulnerability was another one she had made already during a half-hour meeting in Jammer's law office before going to the jail together. She had said that there is an expected degree of suggestibility among amnesiacs who, like George, desperately want to remember the events of some forgotten time frame. And in George's case, she said, his suggestibility to Harlan had been enhanced even more by something Harlan said when he and George first met. Believing at the time that George probably was guilty of murder, Harlan had pointedly asked him, "Do you really want a couple PIs looking into this? Because we *will* figure out who did it." According to Dr. Goodwin, George had taken those words to heart.

The heavy metal door to the interrogation room jerked open, and two deputies led George Viola into the room, cuffed and shackled, and directed him into a seat at the table opposite Harlan's. The deputies then left George and his two visitors alone in the room.

Harlan was about to begin making some introductory remarks, but George's appearance cut him short. "What's wrong, George? You look pale, like you're scared."

"That's because I... I am," George replied, unable to make eye contact. "I'm afraid of hearing what you might say I did that night."

Harlan glanced over at Dr. Goodwin, who gently shook her head. Her meaning was obvious: *Don't* tell him he's innocent. *He* must recall that.

Harlan skipped his introductory remarks, powered up his cellphone, and opened it to a collection of photos that he and Dr. Goodwin had put together before the meeting. "During the course of the investigation, I've collected some photos of a few places and people that I want you to see, George, and comment on if you can."

George looked at Dr. Goodwin and then back at Harlan. "You came here at this hour, in the middle of a storm, just to show me some pictures?"

Harlan shrugged. "That's exactly what I came here to do. And Dr. Goodwin insisted on coming along to make sure I didn't say anything that might mess up your therapy. I guess during my first visit a few days ago, I got a little too heavy-handed with you."

George again looked at the doctor, who offered a wink and cheerleader-like smile.

"Okay…" George said.

Harlan brought the first photo up on his screen. It was one of the calico cat that Roz had taken in the basement of Pastor Ed's church the day after they met George.

"That's Marty," George said, "one of Pastor Ed's cats. I've seen him before at some of the pastor's support-group meetings."

"Including the meeting you may have attended on the night of March 12?"

George seemed surprised by the question. He opened his mouth but said nothing.

"Reason I ask, George, is that in your prior statements you've said that you may have gone to a meeting that night at Pastor Ed's church and saw a cat there."

"Well, yeah, but I also told you and your partner that the cat was black. It wasn't Marty."

Harlan retrieved a small notebook from his pocket, opened it, and thumbed through it as though he was consulting his notes. He stopped on a blank page. "You're right, George. You specifically said that the cat you saw that night was black… with a white patch on its chest."

"Yeah, a black cat with a white patch, shaped like Superman's patch. It's one of the few things I remember from that night."

Harlan continued holding the photo of Marty in front of George. "So, different cat, but the same location as where you met the guy who told you about the recovery hike, right?"

"I think that was the place."

"What makes you think so?"

George nodded at the photo of Marty. "See the office equipment behind him, in the background? The computer, the printer, and other stuff? That's Pastor Ed's office in the basement of the church, where he held the meetings. My memory of it that night is foggy, but I think I remember seeing that stuff when I met the guy who told me about the recovery hike."

"And you're sure that the cat with you was mostly black?" Harlan asked.

Dr. Goodwin cleared her throat, apparently cautioning him against leading the witness by highlighting a point he had already made.

George continued staring at the screen. He hesitated before nodding. "Yeah... I'm sure."

Harlan tapped the screen to advance to the next photo. As it came up, he could feel Dr. Goodwin's stare. She had specifically told him *not* to explain what he was doing from this point forward—that is, walking George through a series of photos that, Harlan believed, chronologically depicted some of George's actual activities on the night of March 12. A visit to Pastor Ed's church was *not* among those activities, Harlan thought.

The series began with a photo of the pavilion across the street from Watersmeet Township Hall. To no surprise, George's expression showed recognition. Harlan asked anyway, "What do you see, George?"

"Same as I said the first time we met. That's where I was that night, getting drunk, waiting to gun down Romanelli. But it's like I told you before. I never shot the gun. I know I didn't. It still had all the bullets the next morning."

"And as for your whereabouts in between," Harlan said, "from the time you were at the pavilion until that next morning when you checked the gun, have you been able to recall anything you haven't already told us?"

"No, I still got nothing... except what I told you about the support-group meeting."

"Which is still kind of foggy."

George stared blankly at the photo, nodding.

Harlan tapped the screen, advancing it to a photo of a person whom he believed George saw later that evening after following Romanelli to his motel and then taking a short detour to a liquor store down the street—LaChance's Liquorland—for a fresh bottle of bourbon. It was a photo of the cashier at the store that night, Linda Tisdale, which Harlan had obtained when he met her at the Trading Post Internationale.

George's eyes showed recognition as he studied the photo. "I know her... from LaChance's. She works there."

"What's her name?"

"Hell if I know. I've just seen her before, you know, when I went there to buy booze."

"How many times?"

"I dunno. A few, I guess."

Harlan paused to consider how to proceed with this line of questions. If he asked whether George visited the liquor store on the night in question, he would no doubt hear Goodwin clear her throat again. But he might not have to lead the witness, he thought, as he watched George's brow furrow as though he might be trying to make a connection himself.

"They say I went there that night," George said, "to get another bottle of bourbon."

"Who says you went there?"

"A couple deputies here at the jail. They told me I stopped at the store while I was stalking Romanelli. But I don't remember it. Do you think I did that, Mr. Holmes? Did I follow Romanelli that night?"

"George!" Dr. Goodwin intervened. "You know what I've told you about what others say you did that night. You need to ignore their accusations. Those are *not* your memories, which is all that matters right now. This is a therapeutic intervention, George, not an interrogation."

"Bullshit!" George objected. "If this is therapy, then how come he's asking the questions and not you? And why the hell now, at night, in the middle of a fucking storm?"

"Easy, George," Harlan said, raising a hand to him. "You're right, I'm not here for your therapy. But the doc's right too. What other people might think you did that night—myself included—doesn't mean shit right now. It's like she says, all that matters is what *you* can remember. And I've reached a point in my investigation where I think I can help you with that, but I don't want to mess it up and put any of my own thoughts in your head. That's why the doc is here. To make sure I don't fuck up. And she's doing this for us tonight, in the middle of a storm, because I asked her to. We're running out of time, George. The preliminary hearing is in just a few days, and the prosecutor may well use the occasion to lay out all her cards and tell a very persuasive story of what she thinks you did that night, for you and the whole world to hear. If you hear that story before you remember your own, the doctor fears it could forever obstruct your independent recall of that night. That's why this can't wait any longer."

George seemed satisfied with the explanation. He looked back at the photo of Linda Tisdale. "All right then, if you're asking whether I remember her from that night, the answer is no. I don't remember going to LaChance's Liquorland that night."

"How about here?" Harlan asked as he tapped the screen and advanced it to a photo of the next place he believed George had gone that night. It was a photo of the exterior of the Bel-Air Motel.

George had been shaking his head during his prior response and continued shaking it as he again answered, "No, I don't remember going there either. Not *that* night, anyway."

"Some other night?"

"A few times," George said. "Like I've told you before, I'd been watching him for a while. I've seen his motel."

"As close as this?" Harlan asked as he tapped the screen and brought up a close-up photo of the door for Room 4.

George shook his head. "No, I never..."

"Or maybe inside?" Harlan asked as he tapped the screen and brought up one of the interior shots of the room that he was able to get through the gap in the curtains during his recent visit to the motel.

George stopped shaking his head as his stare locked onto the photo. Harlan then tapped the screen several times in a row, pausing briefly between taps to allow George to see all his interior photos consecutively. Among them were close-ups of the desk, computer, printer, and copy machine that Romanelli had been using to work remotely for his law firm back in Traverse City. Harlan stopped tapping on the last of the interior photos, which showed the table Romanelli used to organize his working files.

George remained silent through the series of photos. His stare then shifted to the left. That was the direction Harlan recalled him looking during their first meeting when he was trying to access his memory.

"What is it, George?"

"Can I see them again?"

Harlan backed up to the first of the interior photos.

"The door too," George said. "I want to see it again, along with the rest."

Harlan tapped through them all, starting at the door, and stopped again at the table full of files.

For the first time during the meeting, George tried to bring his hands up above the tabletop, but his shackles prevented him from doing so. Harlan took this to be an attempt to reach for his cellphone. He moved the device closer to George and tapped through the series again. George's stare intensified with each changing photo.

This time, however, Harlan did not stop at the table full of files.

"How about this one, George?" he said, as he tapped one more time.

George's eyes bulged. "Holy shit—that's him! The black cat! Eli! Where did you get that?"

"I'd rather hear from you where you met him, George, and who told you his name. You think you can tell me?"

George nodded slowly. "I remember."

"What do you remember?"

"Everything."

"Good. Then let's back up to the pavilion and start over."

Chapter 37

"I remember waiting by the pavilion for a couple hours, until a bunch of people started coming out of Township Hall across the street. The big meeting they were having must've been over, I thought. Romanelli was one of the last ones out. I watched him get in his car, parked there on the street. And then—"

George's voice cracked and his body stiffened. He then went silent.

Dr. Goodwin lowered her camera. "Are you okay, George?"

He hiccupped while trying to catch his breath. "That's w-when I followed him to Stevie's house, where I was gonna... you know..."

A tear streamed down George's face as he again went silent, this time for much longer, as though he might be shutting down.

Harlan caught himself sighing, but too late.

George turned to him. "I'm sorry, Mr. Holmes, but I was in a bad frame of mind, and rehashing it is..."

"It's okay, George," Dr. Goodwin said. "Difficult feelings are perfectly normal in these circumstances. Would you like to talk about them?"

"Look, I don't mean to be insensitive," Harlan said, "but you two can talk about feelings later, okay? Please, George, can we just get to what happened?"

George lifted his hands as high as his shackles permitted, lowered his head, and used the back of his forearm to wipe away the tear. "I guess I can, but I just want to put it in context, so you and the doctor understand why I was behaving the way I was. I mean, I thought Romanelli was fucking my wife."

Harlan shrugged. "I get the picture, George. You misunderstood the guy's intentions, and it pissed you off to see him go to your wife's house. Like the doc says, it's all perfectly understandable. Now please just tell us what happened when you got there."

***

You bastard, I'm gonna seriously fuck you up, George thought as he watched Zach Romanelli's car turn onto Allen Lake Road and head toward Stevie's house. Before making the same turn, George clicked off his headlights and slowed down to put more distance between their vehicles. Soon after, as he watched Romanelli pull into Stevie's driveway, George sped up for a few seconds and then dropped his truck into neutral, killed the engine, and glided to a stop on the shoulder of the bend in the road beyond the house.

He had done this before. From this spot he would have a clear view of the entire house between the branches of the surrounding trees. Never before, however, had he left his vehicle for a closer look at what they were doing inside. Tonight he would, he thought... after he finished his bourbon... and smoked a cigarette... and then another.

Twenty minutes later, George slipped out of his truck and scampered through the woods toward the house until he reached its southeast corner. He paused there and caught his breath before sneaking a peek through a window... at what turned out to be an empty bathroom.

George continued slinking around the perimeter of the house, peeking through windows, until he found them in the kitchen. Thank God they were still dressed and were just talking... about something in Romanelli's hand, it seemed. It wasn't clear what the object was until Romanelli peeled off several bills from it and set them on the kitchen counter.

It's a wad of cash, George realized. *What the hell? She's making him pay for it?*

Romanelli then returned the rest of the cash to his pocket and took Stevie into his arms for a long embrace. George's heart pounded as he slid his hand inside his jacket. When he reached the butt of his gun, however, he paused. There was no kiss accompanying the embrace. Indeed, the show of affection ended with Romanelli rubbing his hand on top of Stevie's head, playfully mussing up her hair, and Stevie laughing in response while slugging his shoulder.

***

George struggled against his shackles to wipe more tears from his eyes. "I didn't know what to make of it. I had no idea he was just her brother."

"What happened next?" Harlan asked.

"I froze with my hand on the gun, and next thing I knew, he was leaving through the kitchen door that goes into the garage. When I came around to the front of the house, he was already getting in his car."

"And then what did you do?"

George lifted his shackled hands to the edge of the tabletop in front of him. "Can I scroll through those pictures?" he asked, nodding at Harlan's cellphone on the other side of the table.

Harlan brought up the last photo they had viewed, of Eli the cat, and set the phone within George's reach. "I followed Romanelli from Stevie's house to Land O' Lakes," George said as he tapped the left side of the screen, backing through the photos. "Romanelli went to his motel, and I continued down the street to the liquor store to get another bottle of bourbon."

George had stopped on the photo of Linda Tisdale. "I could tell she was scared of me," he said.

"Who?" Harlan asked.

"Her, the cashier at the store. I think she saw my gun, but she didn't make a fuss."

George tapped the right side of the screen and took a long look at the next photo—the façade of the Bel-Air Motel—before continuing his account.

***

George killed his headlights before turning into the motel's gravel parking lot. A short distance ahead he stopped and backed up his truck, just off the premises, and parked it in an adjacent patch of tall weeds growing beneath a willow tree. This was another location he had used in the past when stalking Romanelli—a place deep in the rough alongside one of the fairways on the Gateway Lodge's golf course next door. In a narrow gap between the top of the weeds and the bottom of the willow branches, he could look directly at Romanelli's motel room and, if the curtains were open, as they were tonight, see inside.

Romanelli was suiting up for one of his cross-country ski outings.

George gulped down several ounces of bourbon, trying to work up the nerve to finish what he had set out to do this evening. After a final swig he crept from the truck, staying low beneath the weeds until he reached the parking lot, where he paused for another look.

Romanelli was about to pull a sweatshirt over his head and for the next few seconds would be blind. Now was the time, George thought.

He bolted across the parking lot, lowered his shoulder, slammed into the door—and bounced off. From his backside there on a slab of cement in front of the room he looked up at the number on the door. Room 4. Then he heard a window slide open, up and to his left. Through it he saw Zach Romanelli's face staring down at him.

Romanelli pressed close to the screen. "George Viola? Is that you? Are you okay?"

Still on his butt, George drew his gun. "Step back from the window, asshole!"

Romanelli showed his empty hands. "Wait a minute, George. Let's talk about—"

"Goddammit! I said get back!"

Romanelli complied as George staggered to his feet, elbowed his way through the screen, and climbed into the room. The two men stood on opposite sides of the bed. George again raised his gun. "On your knees," he seethed.

"Please, George. I need to tell you something about..."

George cocked the hammer on his revolver. "On your knees, dammit! Now!"

Romanelli fell to his knees as George came around the bed, shouting: "How the hell do you know who I am?" He pressed the gun's muzzle into Romanelli's temple. "Answer me!"

"F-family photos, George... in Stevie's house. Of you... along with some of her, little Bobby, and... me."

It took a moment for Romanelli's description of George's *family* to register. When it did, George pressed the gun harder into Romanelli's head. "You gotta lot of fucking nerve."

Romanelli's hands were at his sides, trembling. He slowly raised one and pointed at his face. "Look at me, George... my face... and think of Stevie's face. Hasn't she ever told you?"

George acquiesced to what he assumed would be Romanelli's dying request and proceeded to study the man... his thin, asymmetrical face and crooked nose, which he had never seen up close this way during any of his prior stakeouts. Its familiarity stimulated a thought that began nudging its way into his drunken consciousness... a connection to something Stevie had said in the past, maybe more than once.

"She's told you," Romanelli said. "I can see that she has."

George continued struggling to remember. "Told me what?"

"I think you know."

George's mouth dropped open. "Are you..."

"Yeah, George—*I'm her twin brother.*"

George's knees buckled and both he and his gun fell to the floor—him to one side of Romanelli, the gun to the other. Romanelli reached not for the gun, but for George. "Which makes me your brother, too, George. Let me help you up."

Chapter 38

"Is everything okay in there?" shouted a deputy from outside the door. Inside the interrogation room, Dr. Goodwin had taken George into her arms as he cried hard.

"Everything is fine," Harlan shouted back. "Just need a few more minutes."

"Hold on, Mr. Holmes," the doctor said. "I think George needs a break."

"Is that right, George?" Harlan asked. "Am I pushing you too hard?"

George broke free from the doctor's hug and returned his attention to Harlan's cellphone, which remained on the table in front of him. He scrolled once more through the photos of various office equipment and supplies inside Romanelli's motel room and stopped on the close-up of Romanelli's work files piled on top of the table next to his desk.

"That's where I hit the floor, in front of the table," George said, "next to Zach. It's also where I hit rock bottom after all the years of drinking."

Harlan leaned over to see George's face better. His nose was so close to the cellphone, he was fogging up the screen. The image seemed to have him mesmerized. "What else happened there, George?"

George remained glued to the photo. "Zach understood what I was going through, cuz he'd been there before, just like me, years ago… in a hole so deep, you think you died and went straight to hell."

"Romanelli told you about his battle with alcohol addiction?"

George nodded. "We sat there on the floor together, sharing our stories and crying about them, feeling each other's pain. It was like something I've seen other addicts do at support-group meetings where someone, for the first time, comes face-to-face with their demons."

"And that night it was you," Harlan said, "facing your demons in a setting a lot like the space in Pastor Ed's basement—an office environment—where you'd seen others do the same."

George looked up from the phone. A tear streamed down his face. "I was about to kill my wife's brother... my brother... on account of those demons. And what'd he do? He took me in his arms, forgave me, and helped me fight them off."

"How did he help you?"

"By giving me a way to do it... a concrete way to recover from my addiction."

"And what *was* that, specifically?"

"I've already told you, days ago, when we first met."

"I know," Harlan replied, "back when you thought you had met someone from Pastor Ed's support group. You're saying, now, that the guy was Zach Romanelli."

"Yeah, it was him. Zach was the one who told me about the recovery hike he did years ago to get clean and sober."

"Where did he do his hike?"

"The Rocky Mountains. He said he spent nearly two months out there, deep in the wilderness, away from the bars and liquor stores and all the things that triggered his urge to drink. And he came out on the other side recovered."

Right answer, Harlan thought. *And who else would have told him if Zach Romanelli had kept his addiction and method of recovery secret from everyone in the world except his wife Ava and law partner Bernie Dufflemire?*

"Who came up with the idea for you to do the same thing in Michigan's UP?"

George paused over the question. "I'm not sure. It's like the idea just grew out of our conversation. At some point, Zach drew up a map for me to follow. He knew every square inch of the western UP from all the cross-country skiing he did. And he knew what I'd need for the hike, so he wrote that down for me too."

"A list of supplies," Harlan said as another corroborating fact came to mind... *a list created in handwriting identified by his wife Ava as his.*

"And if that wasn't enough," George added, "he gave me money to buy those supplies, a big wad of cash. The same cash he had on hand earlier at Stevie's house, I think." Another tear streamed down George's face. "I set out to kill him that night—and he saved my life."

Harlan reached across the table and advanced the photo collection to the final one, of Eli the cat. "When did he join you two?"

George shrugged. "Not exactly sure. Somewhere in the middle of it all, I guess. We were still sitting on the floor, and Eli came out from under the table and climbed into my lap."

George smiled for the first time since the interview had begun.

"What is it?" Harlan asked.

"Something I just remembered about that dang cat. Little son of a bitch bit my hand while I was trying to pet him. It was his idea of play, Zach told me." George began rubbing the back of his right hand, apparently where he had been bitten. His smile disappeared. "I remember thinking that I had it coming—and a hell of a lot more—for what I almost did."

Dr. Goodwin returned to George's side and placed her hand on his shoulder. "But you didn't, George. And if you ask me, I'd say you've had more than your share of comeuppance. It's time for it to end. Wouldn't you agree, Mr. Holmes?"

When Harlan didn't respond, the doctor pressed, "What is it, Mr. Holmes? You *do* believe him, don't you?"

"Of course I do—even if Eli the cat is the only living being, besides George, to have witnessed what happened in the motel room that night."

"You say that like maybe you're not sure," Dr. Goodwin replied, frowning.

"Don't worry, Doctor, we're on the same page. And I know we have more than just George's word about what happened."

George came out of a blank stare. "What do you have, Mr. Holmes?"

"Evidence that corroborates some of the things you've said. Take Zach Romanelli's experience with alcohol addiction. It seems only two people in the world, besides Zach himself, knew about that, and they tell it the same way you do. And your account of Zach writing down the list of supplies needed for your recovery hike can also be supported, because the list was caught on video at Sylvania Sports, and his wife has identified the handwriting as his."

"That's more like it, Detective," Dr. Goodwin said.

Harlan paused to reflect on some other key evidence concerning that night—evidence provided by Romanelli's fitness app—and the possible synchrony between its GPS recording of Romanelli's movements and the route driven by the plow-truck driver in Sector Two. *Nobody can deny that it's possible...*

"But we don't have enough... not yet... not for a prosecutor who's already gone on record saying she's got George dead to rights. She'll want more before she backs off."

"Like what?" the doctor asked.

"A better case against the guy who actually did it."

Chapter 39

I look ridiculous, Harlan thought as he stared at his reflection in a window above the camper's kitchen sink. He looked down at the counter to reexamine the source of his frustration—a tube of hair-coloring gel. It was advertised as "just for men" and came with an insert promising "salon-quality silver hair" by simply applying the product like ordinary styling gel, which was what he thought he did. But his hair came out chalk white. Nothing like the silver-streaked locks of the babe magnet whose picture was on the package. *I must have overdone it.*

"How are you coming along, Harlan?" called out Roz from across the camper.

"Not so good. How about you?"

"I'm pretty much done. Why don't you join me, and I'll see if I can help?"

Harlan snatched up the coloring gel and headed for the bathroom. He found the door open when he arrived and Roz standing inside in front of the mirror touching up her mascara.

Holy shit, he thought. Beneath her skimpy white top she wore an even skimpier, tight-fitting skirt and a pair of strappy dress sandals with four-inch stiletto heels. The outfit drew his gaze downward, from her compact backside down the length her bare legs, and then slowly back up. A close shave and sunless tanning lotion had rendered them silky smooth, bronze, and flawless.

After squeezing into the tiny bathroom with her, he stared at her face in the mirror. It, too, looked amazing, even more so than the rest of her. Between the cappuccino-brown hair coloring and just the right blend of makeup, she looked fifteen years younger, at least.

"I'm glad you approve," Roz said. She snapped shut her makeup kit. "Unfortunately, you were right. I can't return the compliment. Let's rinse that mess out of your hair and start over."

When Roz was done with his hair, he still did not look like the stud on the gel's package. But that was not the goal. All he was aiming for was a little more gray than he already had, and for Roz, who long ago had been a professional hairstylist, that was an easy do.

Next came the tricky part, adding years to his face. Roz started the process by applying highlighting makeup to his more prominent facial features—his forehead, cheekbones, chin, and jaw—to give his face a bonier appearance.

"Now I need you to squinch your face in different ways," she said.

"Squinch my face?"

"Yeah, like this," Roz said as she grimaced at him in the mirror.

"What for?"

"So I can see all your natural creases and wrinkles, including those you don't have yet, but someday will. We're going to deepen the ones already there and give you some new ones ahead of schedule."

As Harlan made twisted faces, Roz used thin brushes dabbed in various shades of brown eyeshadow to trace over existing lines and add a few new ones. Then she patted the lines with a sponge to soften the edges. She did the same thing with the natural circles under his eyes—outlined them with brown eyeshadow—and then blended in a tiny amount of highlight above the shadow, onto the fleshy part beneath each eye, to enhance the appearance of puffiness.

"I think that should do it," Roz said, "after you put these on." She handed him a pair of costume bifocal glasses. He popped them on and studied the couple looking back at them in the mirror.

"Well, what do you think?" Roz asked. "Are we going to pass for a lecherous old real estate mogul and his sugar baby?"

A half hour later, the disguised couple arrived at the Roadhouse Grill, driving their rental UTV. Roz's friend Patty was there waiting behind the wheel of her car in the parking lot. She had been informed of the couple's plan but still looked surprised as they pulled in and parked alongside her. She, too, surprised them, though not by her personal appearance.

"Very cool," Harlan murmured as he and Roz got out and began circling around to the driver's side of Patty's car—a classic, late-1950s model Ford Thunderbird Roadster. During a prior phone conversation with Roz, Patty had promised to provide Harlan with a "fancy" vehicle for a grand entrance he would soon be making at an upcoming meeting, but this... this thing of beauty... far exceeded his expectations. There was not a single scratch, dent, ding, or flaw of any kind visible anywhere on its shiny bronze exterior or colonial white hardtop.

"You look more pleased by the sight of this car than you did by the sight of your sugar baby," Roz remarked.

"I might be," Harlan confessed. "It's a pretty close call." He stopped at the rear of the vehicle and examined its signature trunk ornament—the iconic T-Bird, its wings outspread. "Where did she get it?"

"It was my father's," Patty said as she joined them. "He died not long ago and left it to me. I hope it's what you had in mind."

"It's perfect," Harlan replied, his hand extended. "Glad we finally get to meet. Roz speaks fondly of you."

"She does of you, too," Patty said, staring into his age-enhanced face as she shook his hand. "You must clean up well."

Harlan turned back to the T-Bird—its original chrome-spoked wheels, front-hood scoop and ornament, and white-leather interior—as Patty turned to Roz. "My goodness, girl, I don't think I would have recognized you if I didn't know you were coming. You look drop-dead gorgeous."

"I guess I'll take that as a compliment," Roz said.

"You know what I mean. You could pass for my daughter right now, while your partner over there... geez... he looks worse than my old man did on his death bed."

Harlan came full circle around the T-Bird, back to the other two. Patty handed him a set of keys. "If you want to know what's under the hood, there's a spec sheet in the glove box. But my guess is you're more interested in what's in the trunk."

Harlan returned to the rear of the vehicle and noticed for the first time its out-of-state license plate from Wisconsin, as he had requested. "Where did you get the plate?"

"From right here," Patty said, pointing at the Roadhouse Grill. "It's usually hanging on a wall inside as a decoration, along with all the other road-related stuff they have in there. The manager is an old friend and let me borrow it, no questions asked."

Excellent, Harlan thought as he proceeded to open the trunk. Inside he found one more thing that Patty had promised. He lifted it out and stood it on the rear of the car after closing the trunk. Through its glass eyes, it stared back at him—a long-dead black bear cub, now stuffed, about the size of a bulldog. Harlan reached up and rubbed his hand over a deep dent in the left side of the critter's head. It was the only imperfection, but a quite noticeable one.

"Got that from my daddy too," Patty said. "Poor little fella ran onto the road in front of this very car one day and got himself killed. That's where the dent in the head came from. Don't know why the taxidermist didn't fix it. Hope that doesn't mess up what you have in mind for it."

"Not in the least," Harlan said. "It's perfect too. Everything is. I can't tell you how much I appreciate all of this." He placed the stuffed bear cub into the UTV and thanked Patty again. "Talk to you in about twenty minutes," he said to Roz before driving off in the T-Bird.

Chapter 40

Harlan pulled the T-Bird into a wheelchair accessible parking space near the storefront of Sylvania Sports and feigned difficulty getting himself out of the vehicle, fumbling with a cane he had brought along to enhance his old-man persona.

"Can I help you, sir?" asked a young man who approached with a clipboard in hand.

Harlan recognized him. He was the college-aged kid with the save-the-trees petition who got in trouble the first time they met here.

"What do you have there, son?" Harlan asked, glancing at the clipboard.

The kid's expression showed no recollection of their past encounter. "It's a petition to stop them from destroying trees and building a cellphone tower in our woods."

"You don't say. Well, I like trees. Let me have a look."

As Harlan reached for the clipboard, however, the kid jerked it back and his eyes widened. "Uh-oh," he said, looking toward the store's front door.

Harlan turned that way and saw Bob Lewandowski and another man coming. "What the hell do you think you're doing?" Lewandowski called out.

"I'm sorry, sir," the kid replied. "I know I'm supposed to stay in the parking lot with my petition. But this gentleman looked like he was having trouble getting to the door, and I was just offering to help him."

"Looks to me like you're trying to get his signature."

"That's my fault," Harlan said. "I asked to see his petition. And I still want to. Sounds like a good cause."

Harlan took the kid's clipboard and printed and signed the name "John Barron" as Lewandowski looked on.

"Mr. Barron?" Lewandowski said. "I wondered if that was you, but…" He paused and looked back at Harlan's car, the mint-condition 1957 Ford Thunderbird. "I should have known," he said, extending his hand. "I'm Bob Lewandowski."

Harlan fumbled with the clipboard and his cane to free up his right hand for the greeting. "How could you have known, Bob? You've only met my people."

"Because who else would drive a car like that on our forest roads, other than…"

"Other than the one and only John Barron," the other man piped in as he stepped in front of Lewandowski and extended his hand.

Harlan let the man's hand hang for a few seconds before shaking it. "You also know me?"

"Of course I do. Bob told me all about you. You're the *man* with the *plan* from the Wisconsin Dells. And I'm here to make it happen. Name's David Trumane."

"Never heard of you," Harlan replied. He turned his back to Trumane and returned the clipboard to the kid. "You keep up the good work, son."

"Thank you, sir. And by the way, I like your car too. It's a sweet-lookin' ride."

Harlan smiled at the kid. "You sure about that? Did you know it burns regular gasoline?"

"I guess… I didn't."

"Do you even know what I mean by *regular* gasoline?"

The kid shrugged.

"I best not tell you, the environmentalist that you are. Now get yourself back in that parking lot and save us a lot of trees."

"Okay then, where were we?" Harlan asked as he turned back around. Trumane was again in his face, in fact so close now that Harlan could see the pores in his bulbous forehead and a breakfast remnant hung up in his thick mustache. "Oh yeah," Harlan said, "you wanted to tell me something."

"I sure do," Trumane replied. Despite the cool morning breeze, a bead of sweat had formed at the peak of his receding hairline and began its long, slow decent. "I'm the appraisal expert your people asked for, the one they wanted Bob to retain for an analysis of the tax consequences of the transaction you're here to consummate today."

"Consummate?" Harlan grumbled as he poked his cane into the ground and stepped around Trumane. "Talk to me, Bob. Who is this guy? And what does he think you and I are gonna do out here in these woods today?"

"It's like he said," Bob replied. "Your people said your purchase offer was contingent on a favorable expert opinion on a property tax issue that may arise if you buy this place and turn it into a water park. Mr. Trumane is the expert I retained for that opinion. In fact, he came all the way from Vestaburg, Michigan, to explain his findings in person."

"What I asked for was a letter," Harlan said, "something with his John Hancock on it saying all the right things. That's all I need—his ass on the line, in writing, saying we're good to go on that tax loophole you promised my people we'd have."

Bob turned toward the storefront and began waving, it seemed, for someone inside to join them. "Don't worry, Mr. Barron, we got the letter."

"Who's got the letter?"

"My attorney. We left him inside when we saw what we thought might be your car pulling in. In fact, he was printing off an extra set of the closing documents for you when we stepped out."

"Closing documents?" Harlan complained. "Is that what you think we're gonna do here today? Close this deal?" Harlan returned his stare to Trumane and added, "Or should I say, *consummate* it?"

"All due respect, Mr. Barron," Trumane replied, "I was led to believe that the tax issue was all that had to be resolved for this to be a done deal. If that's not true…"

"It *is* true," Harlan said. "But it's a *big fucking issue*. I have to know, for sure, that I'll get that loophole—that dark-store loophole Bob told my people about—or there will be no deal. So, all I need to see right now is your letter. Then maybe we can talk about it."

"Here he comes now," Bob said.

Harlan not only recognized the man coming from the store but he was also fully expecting him. "Who's he?" he asked anyway.

"Like I said," Bob answered, "my attorney—Kerry Jammer."

"Jammer..." Harlan muttered. "Where have I heard that name before?"

"Probably from your real estate dealings in Wisconsin," Bob responded. "Mr. Jammer represented a couple of the sellers you dealt with a few years back."

Harlan nodded and began smiling. "Is that really you, Jammer? As I live and breathe. How long has it been, old man?"

"Who you calling old, Barron? You mangy, gray-haired dawg."

The two men exchanged a vigorous handshake and hard shoulder slaps. "Since when did you practice law in Michigan?" Harlan asked.

"Hell, since well before I ever practiced in Wisconsin. I'm a Michigander, born and raised. Genuine Yooper, if you know what I mean, eh?"

"No kidding. Well, I'll tell you what, it gives me some comfort to see you on the other side of this deal. These two were starting to make me nervous."

"About what?"

"They're talking like we got us a done deal, and I've never even seen the place."

"Well, what are we waiting for?" Jammer said. "Let's start the tour right now."

"In a minute," Harlan said. "Bob says you got that tax letter with you. I'd like to see it first."

Jammer held out a folder stuffed with papers. "I've got more than that. Here, these are all the closing documents for the deal, a complete set, for you."

"See, now you're doing it too."

"Doing what?" Jammer replied.

"Making me nervous. I'm just passing through here on a little road trip into the UP to check out this place and a couple others I'm eyeing, and next thing I know, your client is coming at me with his hard-selling appraiser talking of us *consummating* something here today. And now you're doing it too. I mean, get real, Jammer. You know I won't be signing anything here and now, all by my lonesome."

Jammer pulled back the documents. "Maybe I should just email these to your attorney."

"That's more like it," Harlan replied. "Except as long as I'm here, I may as well have a look at this fella Trumane's tax letter."

"Sure," Jammer said. "Why don't we go inside and sit down somewhere quiet to review it?"

Harlan shook his head. Roz would be joining them soon, and he wanted Trumane to see her coming—strutting across the parking lot— before her introduction. "Tell you what," Harlan said, "it being a nice morning, why don't we have a seat at the picnic table over there by the corner of the building? And maybe someone can fetch us something to drink. Something cold sounds good right about now, even if it's just water."

"You got it, Mr. Barron," Bob replied as he hustled back to the store.

Placing heavy reliance on his cane, Harlan shuffled his way across the store's front lawn toward the picnic table. Trumane came up on the side of his free hand. "Would you like to take my arm, sir?" he asked.

"I appreciate it," Harlan replied, slipping his hand inside Trumane's arm and grasping his forearm. As they advanced, he tightened his grip and made his hand tremble.

"I got you, Mr. Barron," Trumane assured.

Harlan glanced to his other side and caught Jammer rolling his eyes.

Trumane assisted Harlan all the way to the picnic table and into one of its built-in bench seats, and then he remained standing at Harlan's side, watching as Harlan read his letter. Meanwhile, Jammer pretended to peruse some other documents in the folder while sitting on the other side of the table.

The letter was only a page long, but it was packed with property-tax terminology that made for difficult reading. Harlan would have understood little of it had he not been tutored on the dark-store loophole by Jackie Diebolt the other day. During the reading, Bob returned with four bottles of spring water. Nobody said a word to him as he placed them in the middle of the table and took a seat next to Jammer.

By that time, Harlan had reached the letter's concluding sentence. He traced under it with his finger as he read it out loud: "In light of the foregoing, a substantially reduced state equalized valuation of the subject property is probable."

Harlan stopped his finger on the last word and looked over his shoulder at Trumane.

"I don't do *probable.*"

"Excuse me?" Trumane replied.

"You heard me. How many times do I have to say it? This so-called dark-store tax loophole has to be certain, or there's no deal."

Trumane took a deep breath as he sat down next to Harlan. "Listen, Mr. Barron, no appraiser worth a lick would make a guarantee like that. Valuation of big commercial properties involves a complex process of assessment and equalization. And when the locals see you trying to lowball yours, they will fight you every step of the way."

"Sounds to me like you're backpedaling even more right now."

"No, that's not my intent. I just want to make sure you're going into this with your eyes open. You should know that the dark-store loophole is a relatively new tax strategy; to date, it's been used only on big retail properties. But I'll tell you what, bottom line: I think it can be adapted to any special-use business property."

"Special use? What's that mean?"

"It's all in the letter you just read."

"What I read was a bunch of mumbo jumbo. Give it to me straight, Trumane."

Trumane opened one of the water bottles, placed it in front of Harlan, and then helped himself to another. "Okay, look, special-use property is just what the term says—property used in some special way, differently than any other property in the locale, like the first and only ginormous big-box store in town. Thing is, if someday the business dies—maybe because too many folks in town discover Amazon—who would buy that dark and vacant monster? And what would they pay? Certainly nowhere near what it cost to build it. In the appraisal business, we have a label for that prospective problem with resale. It's called *functional obsolescence*; it's what drives down the ginormous store's market value today, even while it's a thriving business, which in turn drives down its value for property tax purposes."

Harlan took a long swig of water as he recalled something Jackie Diebolt had said during her tutorial on the same subject. "It'd be like me building a mansion in some odd place," Harlan said, "like a farming community or working-class neighborhood. If I go to sell it, I won't find a buyer who'll pay anywhere near what it cost me to build."

Trumane smiled. "There you go. You got the idea. The mere prospect of a buyer someday down the road who will incur costs to renovate that misplaced mansion, maybe to turn it into an apartment building, drives down its value today. The same thing is true of a Walmart or Target that someday a buyer may have to convert into something else, like a skating rink or rec center. And the same thing, I think, should be true of a ginormous water park plopped down out here in the middle of the wilderness in the western UP. For valuation purposes, it's a mansion built in the wrong neighborhood—a white elephant."

"Even while it's a thriving business, you say?"

"Right on, once again, Mr. Barron. That's why the loophole annoys the hell out of tax collectors. They see that white elephant up and running and can't understand how it's market value can be so low. But under the dark-store theory, the business is separate from the facility and adds nothing to its value. And that, in a nutshell, is how the loophole works for mega retailers, and how I think it'll work for your mega water park."

Harlan nodded and, for the first time since meeting Trumane, smiled at him. "Tell me more about your bottom line, Mr. Trumane. What's your conservative estimate of how big this loophole could be for me?"

"At the very least, a 50 percent tax write-off. But I've seen bigger. Much bigger."

Harlan looked away, as if reflecting on it. "Fifty percent..." he eventually muttered and then smiled again.

"And so far," Trumane added, "all we've been discussing is this one water park, the one you're planning to build here."

"What are you saying?" Harlan asked.

"Mr. Jammer told me about your other water parks. He says you're the silent partner—principal investor—in practically every water park in the Wisconsin Dells. What I say in that letter, and everything I've been saying here, should apply to all those water parks too."

"All of my business holdings? In Wisconsin too?"

"Why not? The dark-store loophole is a manipulation of standard appraisal principles used throughout the nation. Michigan's big-box stores just happen to be where it got its start—the mere tip of the iceberg, if you ask me."

"A manipulation of standard appraisal principles, you say," Harlan remarked. "I suppose I'd have to hire someone to do all that manipulating for my many water parks."

Trumane slid closer to him on their shared bench seat, eliminating any semblance of appropriate social distance between them. At this range, Harlan could make out the breakfast remnant stuck in his mustache. It amused him. There was literally egg on the face of the chump who was about to make his big move on John Barron, the phony real-estate mogul.

"That's right, Mr. Barron. And I'm the man you want for the job."

Harlan used the last few inches available to him on the bench seat to put a tiny amount of space between him and his mark. "At what cost?" he asked.

"My standard rate. Ten percent of the tax savings."

"That's a pretty steep appraiser's fee. Are you an attorney too?"

"No, but you don't need one for the job."

"Is that right, Bob? Didn't your people say that the guy who tried to sell you on this loophole in the first place was some bigshot attorney from Traverse City?"

Bob nodded. "That he was. Fella named Zach Romanelli, from the law firm of Lesko & Craine. I checked 'em out myself back when Romanelli made this same pitch to me."

"Maybe so," Trumane chimed back in, "but guess who Lesko & Craine relied on for the expert appraisals needed to make the dark-store loophole work?"

The question hung in the air as Trumane once again closed the distance between them, causing Harlan to slide one of his butt cheeks off the edge of the bench. "Me," Trumane said, "I'm the expert appraiser who made that loophole work for every big-box store in the UP. And I can make it work for you—for every single one of your water parks, here in Michigan *and* in Wisconsin. If you hire a law firm, all they'll do is subcontract the work out to a guy like me, and then charge you three times what I would. Do you want to pay them 30 percent for work I'll do for 10?"

At that moment, Harlan's phone rang. He glanced at the caller ID. It was Roz, calling as planned. "I should take this," he said.

Thankfully, Trumane slid over and gave him some space as he took the call and proceeded to carry on a one-sided conversation that Roz, like his live audience, only listened to.

"Hey, what's happening, baby... Uh huh... Good... Yeah, I'm still here... Nope, still haven't taken the tour. We're just talking... Well, okay, let me see."

Harlan covered the phone with his hand. "You guys won't mind if my lady friend joins us for the tour, will you? She's finishing up with an errand not far from here."

"No problem at all," Bob said. "The more the merrier," Jammer added. Trumane, however, said nothing. He was preoccupied, Harlan imagined, with trying to figure out a way to close his part of the deal and land John Barron as a new property-tax client.

"You're on, baby," Harlan said after returning to the phone. "Uh huh... Sure, love you too. See you in a few."

Chapter 41

Roz pulled into Sylvania Sports and parked the UTV smack in the middle of the store's front lawn, in plain view of the four men at the picnic table. Her short skirt hiked up even higher as she swung her tanned legs out of the vehicle and stabbed her high heels into the grassy surface. And then, everything seemed to stop—the coming and going of several store customers, the activities of the petitioner in the parking lot, and of course the conversation at the picnic table—as she strutted across the lawn like a model on a runway.

Harlan's three associates scrambled to their feet on Roz's arrival. "You boys havin' any luck?" she asked, looking straight into Trumane's bulging eyes before leaning over and giving Harlan a long kiss on the lips.

"With wh-what... ma'am?" Trumane answered, his mouth remaining open.

"Why, catchin' flies, of course. What else would you *gentlemen* be doing with your pie holes wide open that way."

Trumane snapped his mouth shut, as did Jammer and Lewandowski.

During this exchange, Harlan had been feigning difficulty getting up from the picnic table.

"Let me help you, darlin'," Roz said.

His cane fell to the ground and both of his hands groped her body as he struggled to his feet. One hand found its way to her ass and remained firmly planted there well after he caught his balance. "Thank you, Sweet Pea," he said, squeezing with that hand while giving her a peck on the cheek.

Roz turned back to the other three. "There you boys go again, catchin' more flies. Is that all you do around here? I thought this was supposed to be *the* place in the western UP for outdoor adventures. At least that's what the brochure said about it."

"Brochure?" Bob asked.

"Sure, the one there in the taxidermy shop alongside a huge poster about this supposedly action-packed place, Sylvania Sports."

Bob nodded. "Oh, okay, you must've visited the taxidermy store just down the road apiece. Stan Lewandowski's store. I'm his brother, Bob, the owner of this place. We advertise for each other."

"Well, if I was you, I'd get my brochures and poster the hell outta his taxidermy store."

"Why?"

"Cuz I wouldn't want people to make the association. No offense, but your brother's work sucks."

"What?" Bob objected. "Why would you say such a thing, Ms...."

"What happened there, Sweet Pea?" Harlan asked.

"I'll tell you what happened," Roz said. "Critter he stuffed for us looks like shit—even worse than when you bagged him."

"Now just a minute," Bob said. "I don't know what work my brother may have done for you, but I can tell you, he's the best darn taxidermist you'll find in these parts. This must be some kind of mistake."

"Oh, there's been a mistake all right; that's for damn sure," Roz replied. "I'll show it to you." She turned and strutted back to the UTV.

"Dude," Trumane said as he elbowed Harlan's side while watching Roz wiggle away. "You *are* the man. Do tell, where the hell did you bag your little Sweet Pea?"

Harlan was not entirely surprised by the choice of words, coming as they were from a ruthless poacher. Perhaps that illicit avocation, or a personality trait of some drawn to it, also explained why Trumane did not ask whether the woman had a name other than Sweet Pea, which for this occasion was going to be the pseudonym Rainy Daniels.

Apparently, knowing what he thought she was to John Barron—a trophy—would suffice.

Roz returned with the stuffed bear cub that she and Harlan had borrowed earlier from her friend and stood it on the picnic table. "Just look at this mess," she complained as she stroked her hand over the dent in the cub's head.

Bob stepped close and studied the deformity. "Why is his head all bashed in that way?"

"It's where I hit him with my car," Harlan replied, "the other day, after we crossed the state line. Little fella came busting out of the woods right in front of us. Can't imagine why your brother didn't fix it."

"I can't either," Bob said. "But if you take it back, I'm sure he will. In fact, if you'd like, I'll call him myself and tell him he needs to make this right."

Harlan paused to consider the offer as he looked again at the defective condition of the cub's head. "What do you think, Sweet Pea?"

"You know what I think, because I know how important this little bear is to you."

"This little guy?" Bob remarked. "What makes him special?"

"It's a long story," Harlan said. "Been going on for sixty years."

"What's that?" Bob asked.

"State lotteries for limited bear-hunting licenses—here in Michigan and in Wisconsin—that's when they started, about sixty years ago. And every year since, I've entered my name for the drawings, but not once have I ever been picked. Talk about shit luck."

Bob's mouth fell open even wider than it did for Roz's provocative entrance. "Are you telling me that you've been a hunter for sixty years, and you've never taken down a black bear—except for this little guy that you hit with your car by accident?"

"Total embarrassment is what it is," Harlan said. "But what can I do without a license to shoot one dead?"

"Well, what about another state? Hell, you can buy a license to hunt grizzlies out west."

"Of course you can. And I have. But my trophy collection is still missing a black bear from these northern woods, which I consider home." Harlan stroked his hand over the dent in the cub's head. "Can't even imagine putting this deformed thing in my game room with all my real trophies."

During this exchange Harlan had been sneaking peeks at Trumane, trying to get a read on whether he might take the bait. At the moment he was staring into space, perhaps considering it. *It's time to see how much he wants John Barron's business*, Harlan thought.

"What would you do, Bob?" Harlan asked. "Fix this damn thing and display it like it's something special? Because I'll tell you what, at my age, I'm running out of lotteries and don't see myself ever bagging a real black bear the way God intended when he created man and gave him dominion over all the beasts."

Trumane then made eye contact with Harlan and the two held each other's stare. "You got some thought on the subject?" Harlan asked.

"Maybe. Guess it depends."

"On what?"

"How risk averse you are."

"About what, Trumane?"

Trumane raised his eyebrows and shrugged. "I was just thinking that maybe you don't have to hit the lottery to go bear hunting in these woods."

"What?" Harlan replied. "Either you're not listening, or you're not a hunter—or maybe both, Trumane—to not understand the limited availability of bear-hunting licenses."

"All due respect, Mr. Barron, but you're wrong. I *have* been listening, and I *am* a hunter. And I'm telling you that you don't need no stinkin' license to take down a black bear in these woods."

Kerry Jammer reached over and tapped his client on the shoulder. "I think that's our cue, Bob."

"For what?" Bob replied.

Jammer looked at the others. "If you'll excuse us, gentlemen, and... uh... Ms. Sweet Pea. I do have a stinkin' license—my law license—

which I'd like to keep. So, if it's just the same to you folks, you'll have to continue this discussion without us."

Harlan waited for Jammer and Lewandowski to get out of earshot. "What are you suggesting, Trumane?"

"You know damn well what I'm talking about."

"If it's poaching, I'm not into it."

"I don't think of it that way. I agree with what you said before about it being our God-given right to exercise dominion over wild animals. It's the natural order of things. No law on the books can change that."

"Maybe so, but those laws still say it's a felony, and I'm too damn old to do time for committing one."

Trumane smiled. "That only happens if you get caught."

A glance from Roz told Harlan that she shared his thought. *Wait for it...*

Trumane pointed at the surrounding woods. "There's a million acres of forest out there, and only a handful of rangers patrolling it. And there are people who know how to avoid them."

"What people?" Harlan asked.

"People I know who take folks hunting in those woods for all kinds of big game, including bears, and *never* get caught."

Harlan paused as if reflecting on what Trumane was suggesting. "How would you know these people?" Roz remarked. "I'll bet you're not even from these parts. You sound more like a flatlander to me."

"True, I'm from downstate. But I'm telling you, I know these guys. Hell, they took me out not long ago, and I picked off three black bears in these very woods."

"Three?" Harlan said.

"John Barron!" Roz objected. "Don't tell me that you're—"

"*Sit down*, Sweet Pea!" Harlan snapped as he thumped his cane on the seat of the picnic table behind them, like he was commanding a disobedient dog to behave. "I want to hear what Mr. Trumane has to say about his hunting buddies."

Trumane smiled. "They're not typical hunting buddies, Mr. Barron—weekend warriors like you and me. No, these guys are pros.

Guiding clients to big game is what they do, year-round. And like I said, they don't get caught."

"It's interesting how you keep saying that," Harlan said, "about them always getting away with it, like it's a sure thing."

"It is."

"Yet just a few minutes ago, you sounded like the kind of guy who doesn't guarantee anything. Remember what you said about my tax break? How nobody could guarantee something like that?"

Trumane moved in close, the way he did earlier when trying to close the tax deal with him. "Well, maybe I was being a little coy with you about the dark-store loophole. I mean, after all, you and I had just met."

"And now what? All of a sudden we know each other so much better?" Harlan said as he resisted the urge to put some space between them.

"I think we understand each other," Trumane replied.

And I think you couldn't be more clueless, Harlan thought as he nodded in agreement. "Maybe we do. So tell me, how much would these hunting guides charge me for their service?"

"For you, Mr. Barron, nothing. I'll pay for it myself from my 10-percent fee for the tax work you're going to hire me to do... if that works for you."

Harlan turned and raised his hand to Roz as she drew a breath and opened her mouth to say something. "I told you to be quiet, woman. This has nothing to do with you." He then took his cellphone from his pocket, pulled up his calendar, and turned back to Trumane. "Longest I can stick around this area is two days. Would that be enough time to put something together with these guys?"

"I'll see what I can do."

Chapter 42

It was 7:30 a.m. the next morning when Harlan completed a short drive south to a familiar destination, the Gateway Lodge, located on the Wisconsin side of the state line. This being his third visit here, his connection to a lodge VIP was well established, and as a result he was waved on by a woman he recognized as the manager, who let him drive his Jeep onto the golf course. "Just watch out for players!" she shouted as he maneuvered around the first tee and onto the cart path.

He made his way across the course to the lodge's private airstrip adjacent to the fairway for the fifteenth hole. A teenaged kid in a polo shirt and khakis stepped out of a caddy shack, which doubled as a hangar, and directed him to a spot between the fairway and the airstrip in the first cut of rough, next to a bunker.

Harlan stood waiting outside the Jeep for his guests to arrive. They would be an odd couple, for sure—a good cop and a badass.

In the time it took a threesome to play through behind him, the plane had landed and slowed to a stop directly in front of him. Its twin engines quieted as a short set of stairs unfolded from its fuselage and descended slowly to the ground.

His former partner on the force, Detective Riley Summers, appeared first on the stairs, carrying a small suitcase. Given the premium she had always placed on efficiency, everything she brought for the trip probably was in that one bag.

Riley's demeanor was as he remembered it—serious—though this may have been the first time he had ever seen her during business hours not wearing business attire. This morning, she wore jeans and a hoodie from her alma mater, Grand Valley State University. As he recalled, she could have still passed for a student there the last time he saw her, but today, as she drew near, he had his doubts. *Perhaps a grad student,* he thought, *maybe one who took a break from studies to have a couple kids and raise them through elementary school... no, make that middle school.*

"Thanks for coming, Riley," Harlan said. "Can I take your bag?"

She tossed it into the rear of the Jeep without a reply.

"How was your flight?"

"Fine, considering the company."

They both looked back at the plane. A man of impressive stature was now on the steps disembarking, also with one suitcase in hand. Harlan recognized him, though he was not the former associate Harlan was expecting, Tank Lochner. He was another of Angelo Surocco's soldiers, Phoenix Wade, whom Surocco often trusted for challenging assignments. Harlan had worked with Wade a few times in the past and had come to regard him as a capable badass, comparable to Tank Lochner. But nobody was Tank's equal in that department. Tank was a near seven-foot tall, three-hundred-pound monster whose mere scowl brought adversaries into submission 99 percent of the time. At half a head shorter and eighty pounds lighter, Wade relied more on intellect, camouflaged beneath a cliché street-kid persona, to deal with adversaries.

The persona included a pair of mirrored sunglasses that Wade wore no matter the weather or time of day, as he did this overcast morning in the lingering remnants of an earlier fog. "Yo, Holmes!" he shouted as he neared. "What it is, Brotha?"

Harlan shook Wade's hand but looked past him, back at the plane.

"Whatchu lookin' for, man?"

"Lochner. Isn't he on board?"

"Shit, you serious? Would've needed a jumbo jet to get that freak's big ass here. Is that a problem?"

"Yes, in fact it is, because I specifically told Angelo that I needed him for this job."

"So I heard," Wade said, making eye contact over the top of his shades. "And he was gonna be your muscle, 'til I pulled rank on him."

"Rank? You? Over Lochner?"

"Seniority, man. I got three years on him. And when I saw that video you sent of those fuckin' poachers, I wanted the job."

"Really," Harlan replied. "Since when do you give a shit about unethical hunters?"

Wade reached up and turned around a baseball cap he had been wearing backward. Embroidered on the front was an orange "C."

"Since the day I became a fan of the Chicago *Bears*," he replied.

"Very funny, Phoenix."

"What are you two talking about?" Detective Summers asked.

Harlan turned to her, wondering whether her curiosity was real. "Well, you know, Riley—the poachers we're taking down tomorrow."

"What poachers?"

"Oh, c'mon, Detective, you can't tell me you don't know—not if you've been working closely with the Gogebic County Sheriff on this case."

"I *have* been, and I'm telling you, there are no poachers involved that we know of. Talk to me, Harlan. What are you getting me into up here?"

Her continuing denial seemed to confirm his suspicion that the sheriff never took his search of Zach Romanelli's photo library back far enough to see it. Harlan got out his cellphone and pulled up the video of the poaching incident. "Why don't you have a look at this," he said, "while Phoenix and I sort out our issue."

"All right, where were we?" Harlan asked, turning back to his other guest.

Phoenix scowled. "At the point where you were about to thank me profusely for coming all this way from Chi-Town, *pro bono*, to open a can of whoop-ass on some lowlifes who deserve a helluva lot worse."

Detective Summers glanced up from Harlan's cellphone, rolled her eyes, and then returned her stare to the device.

"Okay, Phoenix," Harlan said, "I do appreciate your willingness to help, but I don't think you understand the play I want to make on these guys."

Phoenix removed his sunglasses, which meant no more of the cliché street kid for the moment. "Then enlighten me."

Harlan thought for a moment about how to explain his preference for Tank Lochner before responding, "Look, I didn't ask for Lochner just because he can be an intimidating beast, which I know you can pull off too. I also wanted him because of the role he was supposed to play before he would have had to become the beast."

"What role?"

Harlan sighed. This was going to get awkward. "In this scam, I'm supposed to be an old man, a real-estate mogul well into his seventies, who brings along a companion—a hunting buddy—to go with him and these poachers on a bear hunt. And this companion is supposed to be…"

This was where it would get difficult.

"Supposed to be who?" Phoenix asked.

"My son. In fact, I've already told them that. These poacher guides are expecting me, John Barron, and my son, John Barron Jr."

Phoenix nodded slowly. "I see, and you think I make that a harder sell."

Harlan drew a breath to say something…

"Because I'm *black*," Phoenix interjected.

"Okay, Phoenix, let's not—"

"Since when can't a white guy have a black son?"

"He's right," Detective Summers said, looking up from Harlan's phone. "Maybe in his past love relationships, your John Barron wasn't a *racist*—like perhaps some people I know."

"What the hell, Riley? Who asked you? And who are you calling a racist?"

"I'm just saying…"

"Oh, for God's sake. You know me better than that. We were partners for years. What you don't know is the character I've created with John Barron. He's not exactly the open-minded kind of guy you'd meet at a Black Lives Matter rally. He's a filthy-rich, narcissistic white guy with no moral compass. Just ask my partner Roz, when you see her, how John Barron treats the character she plays in this scam, his current girlfriend. She'll tell you. He's a bigot."

Phoenix laughed as he slipped his shades back on. "Sounds like you may have tapped into a deeply disturbed alter ego, Brotha. Or should I call you Pops?"

Harlan took Phoenix's bag and tossed it into the Jeep as his guests went around to the passenger side of the vehicle. "Go ahead and take shotgun, Mr. Wade," Riley said. "You two obviously have a lot to discuss."

"And you two don't?" Phoenix replied.

"Oh, we definitely do, but I can wait my turn. Besides, I'd like to watch some more of this video."

Phoenix waited until they were most of the way across the golf course. "All right, tell me what you know about these poachers."

Harlan shrugged. "Not much more than what you've already seen in the video and probably heard from Tank Lochner when you took the job from him."

"I spoke with him. And he says that you think these guys may not have limited their poaching to the wildlife."

"It was just a theory I was considering earlier in the case," Harlan replied, catching eye contact in his rearview mirror from Riley in the back seat. "But I've come to realize that the theory doesn't hold up."

"Well, the guy who set up the slaughter of the three bears—the downstate lawyer—he knew about the video and the dude who made it, right?"

"He did."

"And that would mean the poachers he retained may have learned of the video and the dude who made it, right?"

"It's possible, but I doubt it."

"What dude?" Riley asked. "Who made this video, Harlan?"

He held her stare in the rearview mirror. She really did not seem to know. "Zach Romanelli," he said.

Harlan maneuvered the Jeep around the first tee and waved at the golf-course starter as he drove back onto the resort's driveway. Sensing Riley's stare, he glanced again into the rearview mirror.

"What downstate lawyer set up the hunt?" she asked.

"Romanelli's law partner, Bernie Dufflemire. But like I just told Phoenix, he and his poachers are no longer suspects."

"How can that be?" Phoenix argued. "According to Lochner, you said Dufflemire was pulling all kinds of shit on Romanelli—fucking his wife and setting him up for a tax-evasion rap. And then Dufflemire finds out that Romanelli videotaped his poacher buddies, and what does he do about it? Nothing? Seriously?"

"Tax evasion?" Riley said.

"Hold your questions, Detective," Phoenix said. "I get to go first, remember? And I want to know why Dufflemire and his band of bear killers are no longer suspects."

"Because I've learned a few things since talking to Tank," Harlan replied, "and it turns out there are a lot of problems with pointing the blame at them."

"What problems?"

"Well, for starters, they didn't do it." Harlan looked in the rearview mirror. "And neither did George Viola."

"Then who did it?" Riley asked.

"Hey, stand down, Detective," Phoenix said. "I'm not done yet." He then leaned over, into Harlan's space. "Stop the fuckin' Jeep, Holmes, and look at me."

They were on County Road B at this point, approaching Highway 45. Harlan pulled into a gas station at the intersection and turned to his front-seat passenger.

"If these poachers are no longer suspects," Phoenix said, "then why the hell do you still want to take them down?"

Harlan looked up at the embroidered "C" on Phoenix's hat and then down at his reflection in the man's mirrored sunglasses. "For the same reason you do. Because I'm a Bears fan too, Brotha. Or should I call you Son?"

Chapter 43

Harlan brought his guests back to the campsite, where Roz had breakfast ready and waiting on the kitchen table—four bowls of steaming hot oatmeal topped with granola and raisins. Phoenix surveyed the meal and Harlan's placement of his bag next to a reclining chair. "You can't be serious, Holmes. That's her idea of my morning breakfast, and your idea of my bed tonight?"

"Guilty on both counts," Harlan said. "But I assure you, the oatmeal is better than it looks. And as for your bed, it won't matter. We have a lot to do between now and tomorrow's predawn hunt. You'll be lucky if you get a short nap tonight."

After breakfast, Roz remained at the kitchen table with Phoenix and, using various online maps, began tutoring him on the geography of the location of his and Harlan's upcoming bear hunt. Meanwhile, Harlan took their other guest out for a live tour of the more immediate vicinity.

"I appreciate the hospitality," Riley said as Harlan backed the Jeep away from the Winnebago. "But why did you want me to come here? You know I won't aid and abet the vigilante justice you have in mind for those poachers."

"I don't expect you to."

"Why are you even messing with those guys anyway? Didn't I hear you tell Wade that their poaching is irrelevant to your client's case?"

"I never said it was irrelevant. All I said was that they didn't murder Zach Romanelli."

"Then who did?"

"That's what I intend to show you. But first, you need to have a little context."

Harlan steered the Jeep through a bend in the forest drive as he handed Riley his cellphone. It was cued up to a series of items in his photo library; the first, a photo of Eli the cat, was already on the screen. It was the same photo that he had sent her by text message when arranging for her visit.

Riley reacted to the image almost immediately. "Oh, please, don't tell me you're serious about this cat being your client's alibi."

"Sure I am. You have to admit, Riley, little Eli has unusual coloring that precisely matches George Viola's description of the cat he met that night."

At that moment, the Jeep slammed through a deep hole flooded with muddy water, jerking the two of them against their seatbelts as brown stuff rained down on the windshield.

"Holy shit!" she exclaimed.

"Sorry, Riley."

"For what, Harlan? Dragging my ass to the middle of nowhere to talk about some fucking cat your client claims he met that night—at a support-group meeting that never happened?"

"Oh, it happened, Riley, I can assure you of that. Just not at Pastor Ed's church."

She took a deep breath. "All right, Harlan, I'll go along with this a little longer. Where do you think this alleged meeting took place?"

"Tap the screen on my phone, and you'll see."

She did so and brought up one of the photos Harlan had taken of Zach Romanelli's room at the Bel-Air Motel, the one of his table full of work files. Her expression showed recognition.

"You've seen that table before," Harlan said.

"Sure, in a photo much like this one."

"Taken by whom?"

Riley thought for a moment. "A sheriff from Vilas County, Wisconsin... Sheriff..."

"Caudill," Harlan said, "the one who followed up on the missing-person report that was filed before Romanelli's body was found."

Riley nodded.

"What about Sheriff Jake Mills from Gogebic County? After the body was found here in Michigan and it became his murder case, did he ever bother going back to Romanelli's Wisconsin motel room for more photos?"

"I don't know. Are you saying he should have?"

"What I'm saying is that he shouldn't have been so damn quick to assume George Viola's guilt. If he had kept an open mind and conducted an independent investigation of the motel himself, maybe he would have discovered material evidence under the table you're looking at."

Harlan watched her squint at the screen. "You don't see it?"

"See what?"

"Zoom in on the floor beneath the table—on the two items down there."

He watched her enlarge the image of two shiny metal bowls and then flip back and forth a between them and the image of the cat. She stopped on the cat and looked up. "Are you saying that this cat belonged to..."

"Yes, I am. Like I said before, his name is Eli."

"You've met him?"

"Of course I have. I took the photo myself. He still lives at the motel, nowadays with the couple who own the place."

Riley pulled a notebook from her pocket and paged about a quarter of the way into it. After reading notes on the page, she looked back at the photo of Eli. Harlan imagined the notes had been taken when she watched the videotaped statement George Viola gave on the night he was taken into custody by the LVD Chippewa Police, the part where he described the cat he claimed to have met at the support-group meeting on the night Romanelli disappeared.

She looked up from the phone and her notes. "If what you're saying is true, all this does is further incriminate your client—by placing him inside the victim's motel room at some point, perhaps on the night of the murder."

"Now *you're* doing it," Harlan said.

"Doing what?"

"Assuming my client's guilt, without looking at the whole picture."

"What picture?"

Harlan took the phone back from her and opened it to the video of George's more recent interview with him and Dr. Goodwin. "This picture," he said, holding the phone in front of Riley. He pulled it back, however, when she reached for it. "Before you get to see it, I have to know that you're going to keep our bargain."

"You mean the deal that has me working as your partner again for a day? I already agreed to that."

"I just want to be sure you understand the full implications of the deal, Riley. It means twenty-four hours of silence as to everything you're going to learn about my case. And along the way, I expect you to have an open mind to what I'm saying, the way you did when we were partners on the force."

"Why would that matter to you? I'm not the one you have to prove your case to."

"No, but I intend to ask you for a favor or two along the way, and I want you to have an open mind about things when I do."

Riley tilted her head. "And if I still say no?"

"That's your prerogative, but I don't think you will, as long as you keep an open mind."

"All right... partner."

He started the video, turned up the volume, and handed her the phone.

Riley had reached the last minute of the video recording by the time Harlan parked the Jeep at their first stop—the intersection of the Agonikak Trail and Indian Village Road—and looked over at her. She was still riveted to George Viola's tearful account of bonding like a brother with Zach Romanelli.

"What do you think?" Harlan asked when the recording ended. "Does he come across as someone who killed Romanelli that night?"

Riley paused over the question, staring down at Harlan's phone. At its conclusion, the video had returned to a still shot of the first frame. It was an image of George Viola, in shackles, being escorted into the visiting room, free of tears and looking like his usual self—an imposing linebacker in an orange jumpsuit.

"I don't know, Harlan. Maybe he's just had some time since his arrest to come up with a story."

"Really," Harlan countered, "he somehow learned about Romanelli's experience with addiction—and about his cat, Eli—and concocted that story? Is that what you're saying?"

"I'm not sure what to say. You've sprung this on me. I need to think about it some more."

"Fair enough. While you're giving it more thought, think about this." Harlan reached over and tapped the screen on his phone. An image of a shopping list popped up.

"What's this?" Riley asked.

Harlan studied her. She really did't know. "Apparently, it's more evidence that the sheriff overlooked in his zeal to prosecute Viola. Whether you realize it or not, I'm sure you've seen it before."

"I don't know what you're talking about."

"The day after the murder, when George Viola visited Sylvania Sports, he showed up there with a shopping list—this list—and it was captured on a security camera there on-site. The sheriff has a copy of that video footage, right?"

Riley nodded.

"He's just never stopped it on this particular frame," Harlan said. "And why would he? What relevance could a shopping list possibly have to his misguided theory of George's guilt?"

"Well, what relevance does it have to his innocence?"

"I'll tell you what, Riley, when your twenty-four hours are up, why don't you advise the sheriff to show this list to Zach Romanelli's wife, Ava, and ask her that question."

Riley looked back at the shopping list on Harlan's phone. Her intensifying stare soon showed concern. Harlan knew what she was realizing—that he had corroborated what she had just heard George Viola say in his interview about Zach Romanelli creating the list for him.

"I know that look on your face," Harlan said. "I've seen it before, back in the day when we worked together. You're experiencing some doubt about George Viola's guilt."

Riley remained silent, still staring at the phone.

"And to think," Harlan added, "we're just getting started."

Chapter 44

Riley looked up from Harlan's cellphone and gazed down the tree-lined trail that crossed the road in front of the spot where he had parked the Jeep.

"I'm sure you know where we are," he said.

"I've seen photos. It's the intersection of the Agonikak Trail and Indian Village Road, where Zach Romanelli was run down by a motor vehicle while cross-country skiing on the night he went missing."

"Do you know what time that happened?"

"Around 11:00 p.m."

"How do you know?"

Riley paused to study him, no doubt realizing that he had obtained evidence critical to the prosecution's case. "The same way you do, I'm sure. Because Romanelli was using a fitness app that night, and it tracked his movements with GPS technology. His whole journey was recorded, and it was here where he stopped skiing for a few minutes, and then, around eleven, began a vehicular-speed trip around the back roads."

Harlan reached over and tapped the screen on his phone, bringing up Romanelli's GPS recording from the night he died. "Actually, as you can see here, Riley, it wasn't quite eleven o' clock when the vehicle transport of his dead or disabled body began."

Riley rolled her eyes. "Is this supposed to be another *gotcha* moment, Harlan?"

"No, it's just important to be precise about the chronology of events that night, for what we're going to do next."

"Okay," she said, raising the phone. She tapped the play button and waited a few seconds for the recording of the vehicle transport to begin. "It was exactly 10:47 p.m."

"And what time is it right now?"

She looked at her wristwatch. "10:50 a.m."

Harlan put the Jeep in gear and made quick U-turn.

"Where are we going? And what's your hurry?"

"We're going to track the movements of Romanelli's GPS signal from that night, and we need to make up the three minutes we're behind."

"Why would we do that when we can just scroll through the recording of the entire journey right here on your phone?"

"You'll see. Right now, though, I want you to get out your notebook and start jotting down the names of the roads we're traveling and the direction we're heading on each."

"Are you kidding? Why write down information we already have right in front of us on your phone?"

"Please, Riley, just do it, would you?"

She eventually made the first notation: *West on Indian Village Road.*

Harlan soon caught up with the GPS signal and then continued driving the Jeep along the same roads and at the same speeds as the GPS signal had moved on the night of March 12. This resulted in his Jeep reaching various points along the way at the exact same times— minus twelve hours—as Zach Romanelli's body did during its transport that night. Along the way, Riley continued to note each road they traveled, until...

"You missed that one," Harlan said after making a turn. "We're now on Duck Lake Road, heading east."

"Oh, for crying out loud," Riley complained. "What difference does it make? This part of the transport was random. Whoever was driving was searching aimlessly for a place to ditch the body. The names of the roads are meaningless."

"No, they're not," Harlan replied. He reached for a folder in the back seat and handed it to her. "The first document inside is a map of the area. It's divided into six numbered sectors. Based on the street names you've written down so far, you should be able to tell which sector we've been driving in this entire time."

Riley compared her notes and the map. "Sector Two, apparently. Whatever that means."

"It means the journey that night wasn't random. It was confined to that specific sector."

Riley continued making the comparison of the street names she had been recording with those on the map. "Where did this map come from?"

"It was created by the Gogebic County Road Commission. It includes large portions of Gogebic and Ontonagon Counties, where the roads are cleared of snow and ice by a crew that works out of Watersmeet. The area is divided into six sectors, one for each driver on the crew to clear whenever there's a heavy snow, as there was on March 12."

"And you're saying that the movement of Romanelli's body that night stayed within this particular sector—Sector Two—the whole time?"

"That's right. The GPS signal was confined to that sector until the driver finished plowing it, and then the signal left the sector in a hurry, heading north on Highway 45 to the place where the body was ditched."

Riley traced her finger over the map, along the last few roads they had traveled, before noting their current course, *East on Duck Lake Road.* "Only the roads in this sector," she repeated. "Are you sure?"

"Actually, every road twice," Harlan replied, "once in each direction—you know, the way someone would if they were plowing and de-icing both sides of the road."

He gave her some time to continue comparing her notes with the map. "See what I mean? Maybe not right away, but at some point, we always manage to travel each road a second time, and always in the opposite direction. In fact, I can assure you, eventually we'll travel this road again, Duck Lake Road, only when we do, we'll be going west."

He could see in her face frustration with herself for having missed this pattern when she had previously reviewed the GPS recording. "If it's any consolation, Riley, I didn't see it either."

"Then how did you figure it out?"

"I didn't. Roz did. She played the recording at various speeds and discovered certain parameters to the GPS signal's movements, like the boundaries it wouldn't cross."

"And the speed it wouldn't exceed," Riley muttered as she glanced at the Jeep's speedometer and then back at the GPS recording. "Never more than 30 miles per hour."

Riley helped herself to the next document that Harlan had placed in the folder. It was the handwritten note from Rayden Jude naming those who had worked on his road crew on the night in question and the times each had clocked in and out of work that night.

"Which one drove in this sector?" she was quick to ask.

"You'll see. Just work through the rest of the documents in the folder."

The other documents were those that had been downloaded for Harlan by Julie LePoudre from the county's digital files, beginning with copies of official time records corroborating Jude's report of the shifts worked by his crew that night. Next came documentation of the county's pilot program involving the experimental use of a beet-juice de-icing agent on the roads that winter.

As Riley studied the documents, she no longer kept track of the roads they were traveling. Harlan let it go. He was sure she had seen enough to accept his assurance that the journey would be confined to Sector Two until they reached Highway 45.

Riley was still studying the documents when Harlan stopped the Jeep at the turn onto the highway. He let the vehicle remain standing at the intersection until she looked up.

"Here's where the plowing stopped," Harlan said as he made the turn north and began accelerating to the GPS signal's increased speeds of 70-plus miles per hour. "How are you coming along with those records?"

"Well, I guess I'm learning more than I ever wanted to know about the economics of using beet juice as a salt substitute for de-icing roads. Can you help me speed this up?"

"Sure, just go to the last document. It should be a form entitled, Pilot Program: Driver's Feedback, dated March 12. It was filled out by the guy who plowed and de-iced Sector Two that night."

Riley slid out the last document and skimmed to the space at the end for the name and signature of the driver who completed the form. "Mark Smith? He's your suspect?"

"No. The guy who forged his name is."

"What guy?"

"Look again at the handwriting, Riley. You've seen it before, just a little while ago."

She shuffled back through the documents to the first note she had read, removed it from the folder, and held it next to the driver feedback form. "Who wrote this note?" she asked.

"The crew supervisor, Rayden Jude."

"You're saying that this guy Jude gave you a note linking himself to the crew on duty that evening?"

"At the time, he didn't think he was giving me anything incriminating, and in fact he wasn't, other than a sample of his handwriting."

"So, he's your suspect."

"One of them," Harlan said.

"You think he had an accomplice?"

"Yeah, I'm pretty sure."

"Who?"

"That's why I invited you to join me on this case, so *you* can tell me."

"How am I going to do that?"

"I'll explain in a minute. But first, I was hoping you might have some insight on another loose end that's been troubling me." Harlan reached into the back seat again and retrieved a notebook. It was the one Roz had been using while working the case. He opened it to a tabbed page and handed it to Riley. She read the first line out loud—"Meeting with Stuart Lamar"—and burst out laughing. "You must be kidding, Harlan. You think I can help you understand this crackpot?"

"So, you and Sheriff Mills don't think Lamar actually talked to a ghost on the night he and the professor discovered Romanelli's body?"

She stared at him. "Is that a serious question?"

"Well, if the Paulding Ghost didn't lead him to the body, how do you think he found it?"

"You *are* serious."

"You have to admit, Riley, if you don't believe in ghosts, this is a loose end. I mean, what else led those two academics into the woods on that frigid winter night—Lamar wearing nothing but khakis and a hoodie?"

"I'm sorry, Harlan, but I don't have an answer to that question."

"Roz does."

"Your Roz?"

He nodded.

"Don't tell me..."

He kept nodding.

"But she's always seemed so... normal."

"Those are her notes, the ones she took when she met Lamar in person. And even though she had her doubts at the time, she's come to think that we should keep an open mind to his story. Apparently, he's not the first person she's ever met who's had that kind of experience with the Mystery Light. She grew up near here, and she's met some folks who tell similar stories."

"But... but... surely, you don't believe those stories, do you?"

Chapter 45

They turned left from Highway 45 onto Robbins Pond Road and proceeded directly to the Mystery Light viewing area a half mile ahead, in sync with the blinking GPS signal recorded by Zach Romanelli's fitness app on the night he disappeared.

"What time you got?" Harlan asked when they stopped.

Riley looked at her wristwatch and then his cellphone. "We're right on time. It's 12:47, exactly when the GPS signal reached this point."

"It dies here in a few minutes," Harlan said.

She placed the phone on the console between them, and they watched together until the screen went dark. "Let's get out and have a look around," she said. "I've only seen photos of all this. I'd like to see it live."

"Sorry, Riley, not right now. We have to keep following the route driven by Rayden Jude that night, and I estimate that he left around the time the GPS signal stopped transmitting."

"How could that be? Didn't he first have to drag the body into the woods and bury it?"

Harlan paused to let her to figure it out.

"Oh yeah, you think he had an accomplice—the one I'm supposed to help you bust. How do you know they didn't both drag the body out there?"

"Because based on the road-crew records, Jude couldn't have done that and still returned his plow truck to the municipal garage when he did."

Riley turned back to the folder containing the records. She frowned as she reread the paperwork Jude had filled out for the beet-juice pilot program that night. "According to this form, it's already too late. It says here that he returned the truck to the garage at 12:15. That would have been thirty-two minutes *before* the body even got here."

Harlan shook his head. "No, Riley. That would have been twenty-eight minutes *after* he and the body got here, which means he hung around for a few minutes at most before returning to the garage."

She looked at her watch again. "How do you figure?"

"You'll see."

The next leg of their journey was a return trip south on Highway 45. "We're going to the municipal garage in Watersmeet," Harlan said as they got underway. "It's about seven miles from here."

Two miles later, as they were about to leave Ontonagon County and cross back into Gogebic County, Harlan pulled the Jeep onto the shoulder and slowed it to idling speed. "Why are you stopping?" Riley asked.

"It looks to me like your wristwatch has built-in GPS," he said as they approached the county line, "same as Zach Romanelli's fitness app did."

"Sure, it's a Fitbit. It keeps track of everywhere I go and the number of steps I take during the day. Why do you ask?"

"What time does it say it is right now?"

"1:00 p.m., on the dot."

"Keep watching the time," Harlan said as the Jeep crept forward.

Seconds after they crossed the county line, her eyebrows curled. "What the...?"

"What's wrong, Riley?"

"It just fell back to straight-up 12 noon."

Harlan stopped the Jeep. "Just like the time fell back to around 12 midnight when Rayden Jude returned to Gogebic County that night. Come on, I'll show you why."

He walked her to a sign on the side of the road that had been nearly flattened to the ground, apparently by a wayward driver. The side facing up said, "Entering Gogebic County, Central Time Zone." Riley crouched down to see the opposite side underneath, which said, "Entering Ontonagon County, Eastern Time Zone."

"The time also changed on Romanelli's fitness app while the body was being transported north," Harlan said. "If you look back at the recording with its timer open, you'll see it spring forward an hour when the signal crosses the county line; it goes from 11:40 p.m., March 12, to 12:40 a.m., March 13. I can't tell you how many times I scrolled the GPS data from that night without ever just playing it straight through, from beginning to end, to see that the entire journey was one hour, not two."

"I guess that makes me feel better," Riley said. "So, how did you figure it out?"

"From the map we were using back when we toured the Sector Two plowing route. It notes the change of time zones at the county line."

Riley looked up from the county-line sign. "Okay, Harlan, you have my interest. What's your theory?"

"I'm not sure. It could have been an accident. Or it could have been planned. But either way, I believe that Rayden Jude was the one who ran down Zach Romanelli that night."

"Why might he have planned it?"

"Because Romanelli's dark-store tax loophole cost him his career in law enforcement."

"Jude was a cop? And then became a road worker?"

"That's where he landed after the loss of local tax revenue forced the county to downsize its sheriff's department and lay off most of its branch-office deputies."

"And you think he may have killed Romanelli for that?"

"Maybe. Or like I said, it could have been an accident, though that theory would require some innocent reason why Jude, the road-crew supervisor, just happened to assign himself to Sector Two on that particular night."

"So, you're leaning toward a murder theory."

"Yeah, just like the sheriff—a murder, except in my view, *not* one committed by the man he has locked up for it. I mean, think it through;

everything about the movement of Romanelli's body that night points at the plow-truck driver in Sector Two, and everything in those county records points at Jude as being that driver."

Nothing was said for a while after they returned to the Jeep and resumed their course south into Watersmeet. During the drive, Riley studied the map, beginning with a close look, Harlan imagined, at the fine-print notation of the time change at the county line.

Harlan stopped the Jeep in front of the municipal garage and glanced at the time on his cellphone. Riley did the same using her wristwatch. It was 12:12.

"Well?" Harlan asked.

"Well what?"

"What do you think? Is George Viola still your guy?"

Riley stared ahead. "I don't know. I'm still processing all of this."

Harlan put the Jeep in park, folded his arms, and leaned back in his seat. "Okay, Riley, tell me when you're done processing."

"Give me a break, would you? You can't expect me to digest all of this information and answer that question right here and now."

"Why not? What else do you need to know?"

"Lots, like whatever you can tell me about the accomplice you mentioned earlier and how I'm supposed to help you bust him or her."

"Well, for starters, I'd say that the accomplice was more *him* than *her*."

"What the hell is that supposed to mean?"

"Just something I've learned since taking this case. About gender. I've come to think that for most of us it's more a matter of degree than being one thing or the other."

"If that's supposed to be a hint as to someone's identity, I have no idea what you're talking about."

"I'm just saying…"

"How about just saying his damn name?"

"I think it would be better if you found that out for yourself."

"And how might I do that?"

"Think about a critical point in the chronology, Riley—the moment Jude stopped his truck at the Mystery Light viewing area. The fitness app said it was 12:47 a.m. Eastern Time, making it 11:47 p.m. Central Time here in Watersmeet."

Riley looked again at her watch. It was now 12:15 Central Time. "Okay, if he did it, he would have needed an accomplice to dispose of the body in order to get himself back here in twenty-eight minutes— assuming he didn't drop the body in some temporary hiding spot near the Mystery Light viewing area and return later to ditch it himself."

"I don't think he worked alone," Harlan said.

"Why not?"

"Because Jude's transport of the body proceeded directly down Robbins Pond Road, all the way to the Mystery Light viewing area, without stopping along the way for an obstruction that should have been there."

"What obstruction?"

"I'll tell you later. For now, suffice it to say that I have more than a hunch about there being an accomplice and what he did that night."

"And what did he do?"

"He was there at Robbins Pond Road waiting for Jude so that Jude could drop the body and turn right back."

"You're suggesting a meeting that had to be coordinated," Riley said.

"Yes, a precisely timed handoff that couldn't have been arranged until after Jude ran down Romanelli. I mean, if it was an accident, Jude wouldn't have even known of the need to dispose of the body until after it happened. And if it was a planned execution, he still couldn't be sure about the timing. Hell, that night might not have even been the first time he ever lied in wait for the guy. He couldn't know for sure if he'd show up at all, let alone when he might."

"So, you think he arranged the drop somewhere between the time when he ran down his victim on Indian Village Road, and the time when he finished his snow-plowing route and deviated north to the Mystery Light up in Ontonagon County."

"Now you're getting the picture," Harlan said. "And now I'll bet you see how you can get that name."

Riley nodded. "You want me to get a warrant for Jude's cellphone records that night so we can learn who he may have called while driving around with Romanelli's body."

"No, Riley, I want you to get those records so *you and the sheriff* will have something more to go on than my hunch about the identity of the person who hauled the body into the woods that night and buried it."

Chapter 46

Harlan and Roz were in the camper's bathroom with the door open, him in his black knit boxers and a white tank tee and her in a fuzzy set of flannel pajamas. He watched in the mirror as she completed the finishing touches of his John Barron makeover, adding years to the number he had accumulated to this day, a birthday he would just as soon miss were it not for the alternative.

He fussed nervously with his phone, pausing at its clock. It was 4:05 a.m. According to old family records, he was born exactly ninety minutes from now on this date, six decades ago.

"You seem anxious," Roz said. "Would that be because you'll soon reach another birth-moment milestone? Or because you'll be meeting up with those poachers around the time you do?"

Following the comment, one of their house guests, Riley Summers, appeared in the doorway. She froze, mouth ajar, as her eyes met his in the mirror.

"Sorry, do you need the bathroom?" Harlan asked.

Riley shook her head slowly, still mesmerized. "No, I just wanted a drink of water, which I can get in the kitchen. Did I hear something about it being your birthday?"

"I'm afraid so."

Riley smiled. "And to think, you don't look a day over eighty."

Harlan smiled back at her in the mirror. "It's because of the good night's sleep I got. How was yours on our old air mattress?"

"Not bad, until your friend Phoenix woke me."

"Phoenix?"

"You didn't hear him? He left with your UTV about two hours ago."

"Where to?"

"I don't know."

Roz snapped shut her makeup kit. "He went out to recon the vicinity of your rendezvous with the poachers."

"He told you he was going to do that?" Harlan asked.

"He didn't have to. I could tell when we went over the maps online that he didn't like the lack of detail."

It sounded like the Phoenix Wade whom Harlan had worked with a few times in the past. He would do everything he could, Harlan knew, to avoid being hometowned in these remote woods by local outdoorsmen who would know every bit of the terrain.

Riley left them for a minute before returning from the kitchen with a bottle of water for herself and one that Roz had requested. "He needs it, not me," Roz said when Riley tried to hand her a bottle. She gave it to Harlan, and he used it to swallow an 800-milligram tablet of ibuprofen and three 500-milligram tabs of acetaminophen. He then gulped down the rest for extra hydration to reduce the risk of kidney damage that could result from the high level of pain medication.

After taking the oral meds, Harlan sat down on the toilet seat and slathered a thick coat of topical anti-inflammatory gel onto his arthritic knees. He then covered them with tight compression sleeves as Roz retrieved a set of bandage wraps. Riley watched, her expression showing concern, as Harlan wrapped a bandage around one knee and Roz the other for a second layer of support that was even tighter than the first. By the time they finished securing the old joints as best they could, the UTV could be heard returning to the campsite.

Chapter 47

Phoenix drove them in the UTV northwest along one of the wooded banks of Sucker Creek until they reached Sleepy Hollow Road, which they took due west for five miles to the southern tip of Lake Gogebic. Near the water's edge they veered off the paved road and headed back into the dark forest.

"Their camp is at the end of this trail," Phoenix shouted over the roar of the engine.

"What trail?" Harlan shouted back. He squinted into the area ahead revealed by the UTV's overhead row of LED lights. As far as he could tell, they were four-wheeling freestyle through the woods.

The UTV's lights remained on for a while after they stopped, illuminating the poachers' base camp. It looked just as it did in some photos Phoenix had taken earlier during his surreptitious surveillance of the site—a small camper trailer parked between a shed and a large dog kennel enclosed in a six-foot chain-link fence.

Inside the kennel was a pack of dogs that Harlan had also seen in the photos. According to his prior Google search, they were a rugged, relentless breed, known as Plott Hounds, whose speed, stamina, and tracking ability made them ideal for hunting large game like bear and wild boar. When not at work, however, the breed was supposed to be mellow and accepting of people, including strangers, as this pack seemed to be.

A door to the trailer opened and two men wearing camo clothing stepped out. They fit the descriptions of the poacher guides that David

Trumane had provided when he arranged the hunt. Trumane had said they were brothers, which explained why they looked so much alike, both light-complected white guys with average builds and shaggy brown hair. Both also looked to be in their thirties, though one a little further along than the other.

In one of his photos, Phoenix had caught another, much larger and more athletic-looking man who now was nowhere in sight. As Harlan considered the possibility of the third guy being somewhere close enough to be watching them, Phoenix completed the thought. "I'll bet we don't see the big dude," he said under his breath, "until something happens that these two can't handle."

"You must be John Barron," the older of the approaching brothers said to Harlan. He stopped too short for a handshake, however, his gaze turning to Phoenix.

"And you must be…"

He paused, glanced at his brother, and then turned back to Phoenix. "John Barron… *Junior?*"

Phoenix flashed a broad smile that glowed bright white beneath the full moon, in sharp contrast with the rest of his black face. "In the flesh, Brotha. But feel free to call me Chip, like my daddy does."

Harlan fought back the urge to sigh as Phoenix stepped forward and stuck out a fist, which the brothers each bumped with theirs. "Chip?" the younger one asked. "As in, chip off the old block?"

"You got it, Brotha. Just keep studying us, and I'm sure you'll see the likeness."

"You're shittin' me, right? I mean, you and this old cracker can't possibly be…"

"Jasper!" the older brother shouted. "It don't matter none. We won't be gettin' to know these guys anyway."

"Maybe so, Monte, but you gotta be at least a little curious about how a guy as white as you and me could possibly have a son who's blacker than—"

"Hold on," Harlan said. "What do you mean about not getting to know us?"

"The same as what I told you in my message," Monte replied.

Harlan stepped closer to him. "What message?"

"The voicemail I left a little while ago."

"I didn't get any voicemail."

"Well I left one, at the number you used to set up the hunt."

"I didn't set it up. A friend did. Someone you once took out for a bear hunt, Dave Trumane."

"Oh yeah, he did," Monte said. "And Trumane didn't pass along the message?"

"It's 5:30 a.m., man. I'm sure he knows nothing about it. What's going on?"

"Well, I'm sorry to say that the hunt is off for today. We had us a few bears at the bait site earlier, but now we're down to just one."

"So what? I only need one."

Monte turned to his younger brother. "You tell him, Jasper. You're the one who fucked this up."

Jasper shrugged. "Guess I did, but there ain't no point in getting into it. Fact is, the hunt's off."

Phoenix glared at them. "My daddy asked what's going on. And now I'm asking. How did you fuck things up, Jasper?"

"Look, I'm sorry, but I somehow got us double-booked today with you guys and another hunting party. They should be here any minute. If there was more than just the one bear, we could take you all. But it's like my brother said, we got just the one at the bait site right now. A big fella who chased some others away. Here, look for yourself."

Jasper held out his cellphone. Running on it was a live camera feed from a clearing somewhere in the woods showing a bear snarfing down food on the ground near a barrel. "That black monster's hungry," Jasper said, "and he's diggin' my special concoction of doughnuts, dog food, and peanut butter. Won't be long and he'll be into the barrel finishing up the rest of the bait."

"Then we ought to get out there now," Phoenix said, "and shoot him dead."

"I'm telling you, Chip, no can do. Our other hunters got priority."

"Why? We're here first."

"It don't work that way, dude. We have to give them the hunt."

"You do?" Phoenix pressed. "What makes them more important than my daddy, John Barron Senior?"

"Well… uh… it's kinda complicated."

Phoenix laughed. "I'll tell you what, Jasper. We'll all hang right here until these other folks show, and then we'll see how complicated it is."

Jasper looked to Monte, whose only response was to look down at the ground.

"Let me see this monster," Harlan said. Jasper held out his phone. The bear was now at the barrel, feeding from a hole cut in its side. As Harlan watched the animal take the bait, he contemplated whether there remained a need to continue the sting operation. The camera feed alone was evidence of Jasper and Monte's conspiracy to poach the animal, as was the admission Monte had made about setting up the hunt with David Trumane. And that admission had been transmitted live to Ranger K, standing nearby, via a wire Harlan was wearing beneath his clothing.

What Harlan did not have on Jasper and Monte, however, was evidence of an attempted felony—specifically, evidence of an overt act on their part toward the actual commission of an illegal hunt. All they had done so far was plan and prepare for it. Continuing his observation of the bear feeding at the barrel, Harlan decided he would try to get evidence of the crime's attempted perpetration.

"Is he feeding from a standard-size fifty-five-gallon drum?" Harlan asked.

Monte, still looking down at the ground, nodded.

"Which puts him at the far end of the size spectrum for a male black bear, upward of seven hundred pounds," Harlan added. "Wouldn't you say?"

Monte continued nodding and avoiding eye contact.

Harlan turned to Phoenix. "You know why the other hunting party has priority, don't you, Chip?"

Phoenix smiled. "Sure. Because the other hunting party is them, these two clowns, Jasper and Monte. They want that prize for themselves."

Jasper stepped back, slipped his hand onto a side arm holstered on his hip, and glared at Phoenix. "Enough playing nice with you assholes. You got five seconds to turn and leave—*Brotha*—or I'll be bagging me two big black ones today."

Phoenix glared back as Harlan stepped between them. "Relax, both of you. I'm sure we can figure out an arrangement that'll work for both hunting parties."

"Like what?" Jasper said, his hand still resting on the butt of his pistol.

As Harlan began formulating a proposal, Monte finally looked up at him. "With only the one bear, that doesn't seem possible, Barron. What do you have in mind?"

Harlan turned his stare to the dog kennel. "I'll tell you what I *don't* have in mind—and that's shooting an unsuspecting bear while his head is stuck in a barrel of doughnuts and dog food. I came out here for a real hunt, one I can tell folks pitted me against a beast in the wild that had a fighting chance to survive."

"You're right," Phoenix said, his expression showing realization of Harlan's train of thought. "That bear deserves our respect. If he's to be killed today, it ought to be at the hands of a real hunter—the best among us."

"What are you two talking about?" Monte asked.

"We want you to turn those dogs of yours loose on that bear," Harlan replied, "and let them chase him off deep into the woods, where the first of us to catch up with him gets to take the shot. Now that would be real sport, letting the bear run and the best hunter win. What do you say, boys? You up for a little contest?"

"Hah!" Jasper blurted. He then smiled broadly and added, "Can you even believe this guy, Monte? Challenging us to a race in our own woods. Shit, just look at the old fart, using a cane to get around our campsite. Doesn't even look like he could carry a rifle."

"That's why I'm here," Phoenix said. "This is going to be father and son versus brother and brother."

Jasper stopped smiling.

"No deal," Monte said. "This is your daddy's challenge, Junior. And he's obviously not up to it."

"Why don't we see about that?" Harlan said. "That is, if you think you can take an old fart like me."

A smile returned to Jasper's face. "I think he's serious, Monte. Old man Barron actually thinks he'd have a chance against us."

Monte glanced at the dogs. "It'd have to be your hunt, Barron, not your boy's. You'd have to beat both my brother and me to the bear."

"That's fine with me. But my son gets to carry my rifle. And you have to give me access to the GPS tracking signal I'm sure those dogs' collars will be sending you after you turn them loose."

Chapter 48

Ten minutes after the arrival of morning twilight—and seven minutes plus sixty years since the moment Harlan was born—the poachers turned loose the hounds and the chase began, along barely visible trails snaking through the undergrowth. Bumpy roots and fallen trees were among the many hazards unseen in a forest that would not yield to the dawn.

"Let's go, Harlan, move it!" Phoenix shouted. "You can stop pretending to be an eighty-year-old man. They're getting way ahead of us."

To respond would require using breath he could not spare for words that could not describe the hellfire erupting in his arthritic knees with the impact of every step, despite the excess of pain medication coursing through him.

A brief respite from the torture did not arrive until two miles into the chase when they came upon an obstacle—the Cisco Branch of the Ontonagon River. They stopped and listened for the barks and growls of the dogs over the roar of rushing water. "They're no longer on the move," Harlan said between heavy breaths. He refreshed the screen on his cellphone, which was running the app for the dogs' tracking collars. According to the GPS signal, the dogs were stopped a mere two hundred yards away on the other side of the river, where they must have cornered or treed the bear.

Using night-vision binoculars, Harlan looked up and down the river for somewhere to cross, but the spring melt had swollen the waterway and made its current too fast to do so safely. He paused and listened again over the noise of the torrent, wondering whether at any moment he might hear Jasper and Monte shoot the bear... or whether the backup provided by Ranger K might have already intercepted them. He switched over to another app on his phone; this one was programed to transmit, via GPS, his location to the ranger. The signal was still sending.

"What do you think?" Phoenix asked as he and Harlan studied the raging river. "Would our hunting buddies and the ranger's crew have swum across?"

"Not a chance," came a response from the dark forest behind them. Harlan and Phoenix wheeled around and saw Ranger K himself pushing through the underbrush to join them. "Nobody but the bear and dogs would dare pull a stunt like that," he added.

"Then where did everyone go?" Harlan asked, noticing the absence of the two LVD tribal police officers who had accompanied Ranger K for the operation.

The ranger pointed upstream. "To a bridge about a mile and a quarter that way."

"When?"

"My guys, less than a minute ago. The poachers, maybe a minute or two ahead of them. It's hard to say for sure."

"So, you don't know if they'll catch them before they get to the bear," Harlan said.

"No, I don't."

Without saying a word, Phoenix dropped Harlan's rifle and, in an instant, vanished into the woods, heading upstream.

Harlan turned the other way and hiked downstream to a bend where the river narrowed to about twenty yards in width. Due to the narrowing, however, it was also a point where the water gushed hardest, its rapids spraying a mist so cold that it stung his face. He stopped there and imagined the time it would take for the poachers to travel on foot a mile and a quarter upstream and then the same distance back to reach the bear, who was just a short distance dead ahead, though on the other side of the rush of frigid water at his feet.

Ranger K came up alongside him. "You mind me asking, why?"

"Why what?"

"Why the hell did you challenge those poachers to this chase? Your wire already gave us enough to charge them with conspiracy to hunt this bear and with aiding and abetting the past bear hunt they did with Trumane. What were you trying to accomplish with this challenge?"

Harlan paused over the question. When he issued the challenge, he had told himself it was to lure the poachers into an overt act toward the commission of the illegal hunt, which in turn would add an attempt crime to the list of charges that could be made against them. But as he thought about it now, facing the prospect of the crime being completed and an innocent bear slaughtered, an ulterior motive began dawning on him much like the rays of the rising sun that were beginning to penetrate the dark forest.

"How could you even think you had a chance to outrun these guys?" Ranger K continued. "You're what—pushing sixty? And you move like you're even older. These guys are half your age, Harlan, and they live in these woods. You never had a chance. And now that bear's only chance is if our guys can catch up with them."

The confrontation chipped away at Harlan's surface reason for issuing the challenge and lay bare an insidious enemy from within... his persistent denial of his age and physical deterioration, and the effects of these inescapable realities on his ability to serve as a PI in the field. Acceptance of those realities, however, would have to wait for another day.

He stripped off his boots and jacket. Steam rose from his sweat-drenched torso into the cold morning air. The perilous river before him was now his due.

"Harlan! What the hell are you—"

Chapter 49

Stabs of freezing pain jolted Harlan into hyperawareness of his body's every twist, turn, and tumble until the frigid deluge slammed his head into something hard.

His next awareness began with a blast of smelly air and the blurry vision of a dog closing in, tongue waggling. As the dog licked Harlan's face, the blurriness subsided, and he found himself lying on dry land. His head throbbed and his body, chilled to the bone, shook violently beneath a heavy, wet coat that was not his own. The protective covering belonged to the person who lay beside him, whose face slowly came into focus, blood streaming down it from a gash to his forehead.

Harlan reached over and shook him. "Ranger K! Wake up!"

He did not respond.

Harlan shook him again, harder.

Still no response. Not even the slightest. His perfect stillness suggested an advanced stage of hypothermia, beyond shivering, as did the bluish hue to his lips and his pale, cold skin.

Is he even alive? Harlan wondered. He slid over and lowered his cheek toward the ranger's mouth and pressed two fingers to the side of his neck while watching his chest. There was a pulse and breathing, but both were weak.

It was only then that Harlan first noticed the rest of the pack of dogs across a clearing at the base of an enormous oak tree. They were growling at something overhead. He looked up into the oak's canopy, still barren of its springtime leaves, until his gaze met that of the monster black bear. The beast just sat there, straddling two fat branches, and stared back, panting.

Turning back to Ranger K's nearly lifeless body, Harlan imagined how the man must have followed him into the river, helped him across, and then dragged him here before passing out from the effects of the cold and his loss of blood.

The bleeding, Harlan thought, *it has to be stopped.* Suppressing as best he could his convulsive shivering, Harlan stripped off his own outer shirt, wrapped it around the top of the ranger's head, and tied it off. He then tried to focus on the ranger's next most urgent need—warmth. But there was nothing on hand to cover him with—no blanket, tarp, or extra clothing—other than the ranger's own coat, which was still soaking wet.

Harlan went ahead and covered his fallen partner with the wet coat and then fought through spells of dizziness from his own head injury as he scrambled on his hands and knees looking for anything dry that the forest floor might provide. Dead leaves, brush, twigs, branches—even the dirt underneath—became the blanket that Harlan, in his compromised state of mind, hoped might provide the ranger some degree of dry insulation.

During the burial, the dog that had woken Harlan alerted to something in the woods. Whatever it was, Harlan could not hear it; but the dog, ears and hackles raised, obviously could.

Someone's coming.

He sped up the burial, and just as he completed it with an armload of dead debris over the ranger's face...

"What the hell are you doing, Barron? Playing in the dirt?"

Still on all fours, Harlan turned and looked up at them—Monte and Jasper—now accompanied by their associate, the big guy whom Harlan recognized from Phoenix's surveillance photos. Pain shot through his legs as he tried to stand up, though what stopped him from rising was not his arthritic knees; it was yet another bout of dizziness.

The poachers laughed as Harlan crumbled back to the ground. One of them, Jasper he thought, also said something that he could not make out, except for the phrase "dumbass old man."

Harlan tried again and this time made it to his feet, realizing then for the first time that he was no longer wearing boots. He recalled taking them off, along with his jacket, before diving into the river. The thought of losing his jacket also made him realize that now, minus the outer shirt he had used to bandage the ranger, he was wearing nothing but a T-shirt over the undercover wire and mic taped to his torso. He folded his arms over his chest to try to conceal the bump of the wire beneath, which they might have already seen, and wondered whether they had also already seen his sidearm, which he felt still holstered against the small of his back, no longer concealed beneath his jacket and outer shirt.

As it turned out, their attention was drawn not to his wire or gun but to his face. "What the hell happened to all your wrinkles and gray hair, Barron?" Jasper asked.

The answer, Harlan thought, must be obvious given his current condition, soaking wet, and the only explanation for it. The river had washed away his disguise.

"I bet that's not even your name," Monte added as he glanced at the bear overhead and began surveilling the immediate area. "And I sure as hell know that the black dude ain't your boy. Where is he, *Barron*?"

Harlan remained silent, arms folded, struggling to stay upright through continuing bouts of dizziness.

Jasper laughed again. "Who knows, Monte? Maybe his boy Chip ain't no smoke after all and is still in the river scrubbin' off his dark face."

Monte stopped his search and glared at Harlan. "Answer me, Barron. Where the fuck is he?"

Harlan staggered once to keep his balance as he glanced into the woods. "I don't know. Guess he was too scared to cross through the river."

"You sayin' you pulled that crazy fucking stunt alone? Without your *chip* off the old block?"

"Like you don't know already that he's not family," Harlan replied.

"Then who is he? And who the hell are you?"

"He's just a guy who works for me, but not anymore. Damn coward. And I'm just a guy who wants to shoot a bear, which is what I intend to do."

Harlan reached back and drew his gun, intending to use it to take them into custody, but his dizziness surged and he dropped the gun and fell back to the ground.

Monte stepped close and kicked the gun aside. "You're not shooting any bear, asshole."

"Why not?" Harlan replied, crawling toward the gun. "I got here first, so I get the shot. That was the deal."

"Where do you think you're going, old man?" Monte shouted as he drew back one of his steel-toed hiking boots to deliver another kick, this one to the side of Harlan's face and still-throbbing head.

The surrounding forest became a merry-go-round of whirling images, among them one of Jasper... first raising his rifle... then pointing it toward the big oak tree... and then...

Chapter 50

Harlan remembered none of the counterattack that ensued even though he himself was credited with having led it and the allies who burst onto the scene in time to see him rebound from the forest floor and thwart Jasper's attempt to shoot the bear. At least that was the account given by one of the allies, his partner Phoenix Wade, when Harlan woke up later that day in a hospital bed. The rest of the cavalry, Phoenix said, consisted of two LVD police officers, one of them Officer Frank Wolcott, the young cop who several weeks ago arrested and interrogated Harlan's client in connection with the death of Zach Romanelli.

It was now two hours after Harlan's release from the hospital, that same day, and time for him to refocus on his client's case.

"Are you sure you're up for this?" Roz asked after pulling the Jeep into the Watersmeet Plaza and parking it near the same neon sign they had seen when they first arrived in this town a week ago. The sign's registered logo—"Home of the Nimrods™"—glowed in the evening twilight, casting a bluish hue on Roz's face.

Harlan leaned over and examined his own face in the rearview mirror. "I'll be fine. The swelling is already going down."

"It's not your face I'm worried about, Harlan. It's your head and the continuing effects of the concussion it suffered this morning."

He chose not to debate the point any further and waited for her to hand him the keys to the Jeep. She then joined Detective Riley

Summers, who had followed them in the rental UTV, and he headed across the parking lot alone on foot to the Roadhouse Tavern.

He paused at the tavern's door and watched the UTV's taillights disappear as it headed north on Highway 45, toward the Robbins Pond turnoff.

The buzz of a big crowd inside poured out as he swung the door open. And then, as he entered the establishment and their heads turned and eyes met his, they came to their feet and erupted into a thunderous ovation.

What the...? Harlan wondered. He turned and looked back to see who might have followed him in. Apparently, the applause was for him.

He spotted Ranger K across the room seated at the bar and began working his way through the crowd toward him. Along the way he suffered a hard slap on the back followed by a shout from a familiar voice. "Way to go, Inspector Holmes!"

Harlan turned and found himself facing Doc Charlevoix propped up behind his walker the same way he was when the two first met a week ago at the Roadhouse Grill next door. "You're the man!" Doc shouted again.

"The man?" Harlan replied. "What makes you say that?"

"Oh, don't be so modest, Inspector. You're the man of the hour, and a lot of folks here would be honored to buy you a drink, myself included. What do you say? Can I get you one of our local brews?"

Harlan shook his head. "Thanks, Doc, but I can't partake, as I'm sure you can understand, because of my head injuries."

"Well, you have to drink something, Inspector. And your money's no good here."

"Got that right, Doc," chimed in another familiar voice from a few tables over. It was Lanny Lynchowski, the other guy whom Harlan had met that first night at the Grill. "Everyone hear that?" Lanny shouted over the noise of the crowd. "Whatever Inspector Holmes is drinking tonight is on Doc and me."

"And me," came another familiar voice from another direction. It was Bob Lewandowski standing by the dartboard drinking a beer alongside the same young man whom Bob had scolded a few days ago for pestering his store customers with a save-the-trees petition. "Check it out, Holmes," Bob shouted as he wrapped his arm around the kid's shoulders. "For the first time in my life, I'm hugging a tree hugger, cuz he and I can agree on at least one thing for sure—that those damn poachers you busted today got what they had coming."

Another earsplitting ovation broke out and continued as Harlan finished his trek across the establishment and took a standing-room-only position next to Ranger K seated at the bar.

"What the hell is going on here, Kole?"

"Well, what does it look like?"

"I asked you to meet me here. Just you. Not the whole damn town. Did you invite all these people?"

"Not exactly, though I may have mentioned to a few folks that you'd be here tonight."

"A few?"

"What can I say? It's a tight-knit community. People talk. And they all want to celebrate the guy who took down the lowlifes who've been poaching so much of the big game in their woods, including the moose that died in your camp this week. You know those footprints we cast? Turns out, they were perfect matches for the boots of Monte, Jasper, and their other associate. You nailed them good, Detective."

"Why do people keep saying that?" Harlan complained. "I didn't nail shit. Hell, I was as unconscious as you when the guys who did nail them got there."

"That's not what they say."

"Who have *you* been talking to?"

"Frank Walcott himself, one of my guys who burst onto the scene along with your guy Phoenix Wade. Frank saw firsthand how you wrestled the rifle away from that Jasper fella and caused his shot to miss the bear. You're a hero, Harlan."

"I'm telling you, it didn't go down that way. I was out like a light through the whole thing. These guys Frank and Phoenix are just messing with us, I'm sure."

"Look, Harlan, all I know is that you couldn't have been unconscious the whole time."

"How would you know? You were out cold too."

"That's how I know."

"How you know what?"

"That you must have been lucid enough to show those guys where you buried me. Hell, Frank said that they weren't even looking for me; they had no idea that I followed you into the river. Are you saying you don't remember leading him and Phoenix to where you hid me?"

Harlan shook his head. "I don't remember doing anything after getting kicked in the face."

"Well, you did something. You saved my life."

Harlan smiled at his friend. "After you saved mine."

"Okay then, we're even. And we're going to get even with those poachers, too, and not just for what they did to that moose and the bear they chased today and the three they butchered last winter."

"We got them for more?"

"Damn right we did, for numerous counts of poaching our wildlife."

"How so?"

"Frank Wolcott kept Jasper under the light all afternoon, leaned on him hard, and broke the little son of a bitch."

Harlan drank some water from a glass the bartender had brought him. As he set it down, he turned to stare at his friend. "So, you really think we're even, Kole?"

The ranger looked surprised. "Sure. I mean, why wouldn't we be?"

Harlan took another drink rather than respond.

"Why did you ask me to meet you here tonight?" the ranger pressed.

Harlan resumed his stare. "Because you *do* still owe me."

"I do? For what?"

"I helped you with your case, getting the poachers, but you haven't finished helping me with mine."

The ranger straightened up in his chair. "Your murder case? How can I still help you with that?"

Harlan leaned in close to the ranger so he could continue the conversation without being overheard. "You see, Kole, I have the whole thing figured out, except for one loose end that's driving me crazy. It has to do with the witness you interviewed when the case first broke—the grad student from MTU, Stuart Lamar, who found the body. I just can't figure out why he went out looking for something in the woods that night not even half dressed for the wintry conditions out there."

The ranger shrugged. "I don't think I can help you with that. He's never answered the question."

"But that's not true. As you well know, he told his colleague, Professor Rybicki, his reason for going out there that night. He just won't say it again for the record."

"Because what she says he said is ridiculous," the ranger said.

"Ah, but you see, my partner Roz was able to get him to talk about it, off the record, and she's come to think there's something to his story that's *not* ridiculous."

"Are you serious? What could not be ridiculous about a guy who says he met a ghost that told him, telepathically, to go off into the woods, half dressed, looking for something that had to be found before the spring melt?"

"Well, for starters, his ghost was right about the need to preserve evidence. I mean…"

"*His* ghost? What are you driving at, Harlan?"

"It's not so much my theory as it is Roz's. She grew up in this town, and she knows people who claim to have had experiences like Lamar's."

"Your partner believes him?"

"Kind of, though her theory is a little more nuanced than just taking the guy at his word."

"Well, what's the theory?"

Harlan paused and leaned in even closer to him. "You know, Kole, I came here tonight intending to explain it to you myself, here and now, but I'm beginning to think it'd be better if you heard it from her…

yeah, straight from her... out there by the Light itself, where she explains it best."

"What? Are you kidding? You want me to meet your partner in the middle of the woods, so she can tell me a ghost story?"

"I know it sounds off the wall, but I've worked with Roz for a long time, and I trust her instincts. And those instincts are telling her that there's something to Stuart Lamar's story and the idea that maybe, once in a while, the Light folks see out there really is a mystery."

Ranger K laughed. "Listen, Harlan, you already know what I think. Like I told you before, folks are seeing nothing but headlights out there—from cars traveling a stretch of highway five miles north of Robbins Pond Road. It's that simple. There's no mystery to it. And certainly no ghost."

"I hear what you're saying and tend to agree. But what would be the harm in you coming out there with Roz and me, where we can watch the Light for ourselves and talk about it? What do you say? The damn thing traipses around in your national forest, just like those poachers used to. I helped you deal with them. How about helping me deal with this?"

"I... suppose I could. When?"

"How about right now?"

The ranger glanced around the room. "Now? During this party for you, the man of the hour?"

"Well, okay, how about an hour from now?"

Chapter 51

It took them two hours to free themselves from admirers at the tavern, making their time of arrival to the Robbins Pond turnoff about 11:00 p.m. Harlan was first to turn onto the road's loose-dirt surface, driving his Jeep, with Ranger K following directly in his pickup truck. Before reaching the Mystery Light viewing area, however, they had to stop for an outstretched chain blocking the way.

Harlan had pulled over and was still in his vehicle reading a text message when Ranger K approached on foot. "What's the story?" he asked as Harlan lowered his window.

"Roz blocked off the road so we could have the viewing area to ourselves tonight. She texted earlier to tell me where she stashed the key for the lock. I'll get us through in a minute."

Ranger K watched as Harlan unlocked the chain and removed it from the posts it was fastened to on each side of the road. "You know, Detective, these posts belong to the United States Forest Service, which technically speaking means that your partner Roz was making unauthorized use of federal property."

"Well, I guess you'll have to arrest us both because I intend to rehang the chain after we pass."

The ranger laughed. "I have a better idea; we'll use my chain for the rest of our stay and pretend I'm doing something more official than chasing a ghost."

They parked their vehicles beyond the posts and Harlan watched as the ranger hung a much heavier chain across the road. "That must be the chain you told me about the first time we met out here."

Ranger K paused and looked up. "I told you about this rusty old chain?"

"Sure. You don't remember? I saw these posts that day and asked you about them, and you told me about the chain in the back of your truck that you use to block off the road when there's been a lot of rain or snow, so people don't try driving out here to see the Mystery Light and get themselves stuck in the middle of nowhere."

The ranger nodded. "I remember the conversation now, and then how we got talking about whether the road might have been blocked the night Stuart Lamar found Romanelli's body out here, after a winter storm."

"That's right," Harlan said as he retrieved a small notebook and penlight from his pocket. "My notes about our conversation are right here. Let's see... Oh yeah, you said you thought about blocking the road that night but decided not to because the snow accumulation didn't quite reach your minimum threshold of... what was it...?"

"Eight inches," Ranger K said.

"Yeah, that's what I wrote down here, eight inches, and that day there had been only six."

Ranger K finished locking the chain to the posts, and on the return to their vehicles Harlan said, "You know, I've been meaning to ask the same question about the night of March 12—the night Zach Romanelli was killed by someone who must have tried using this road to ditch his body out here. There was a lot more snow that day, over a foot according to weather reports. Do you remember whether you chained off the road that day?"

It took a moment for the ranger to answer, "I... guess I don't have a specific recollection one way or the other. We had so many big snow events toward the end of February and into March, I can't say for sure."

"But certainly the snowfall on March 12, which far surpassed eight inches, would have led you to do that, right?"

"Probably."

Roz and another person, Detective Riley Summers, were there when they arrived, waiting by the guardrail barrier at the road's dead end. Extending north beyond them, beneath the lights of a clear night sky, was a narrow path carved deep into the dense forest ahead by a power line right-of-way. Where the path disappeared, trees to each side formed a distant notch on the moonlit horizon.

It was in that notch, Roz had told Harlan, that she herself had seen the mysterious orb appear many times back in her childhood. It might even make multiple appearances any given night, she said, floating in the distance along the power line's path for up to several minutes each time.

Harlan studied the notch, hoping for his first encounter with the orb as Ranger K greeted Roz and introduced himself to Riley.

"I think we've already met," Riley said.

"We have?"

"I'm Detective Riley Summers of the Michigan State Police. You called me on the phone last week about my former partner over there, Harlan Holmes, to see if he was being straight with you about his good standing with MSP."

"My gosh, it is you, Detective Summers. I recognize your voice. You know, it's funny how someone can look so different than how you imagined them when you've only talked on the phone."

"No kidding," Riley replied. "Knowing how you work and live way out here in the sticks, I figured you to be a grizzly old woodsman."

Harlan turned back to join the conversation between his partners and the ranger, whose appearance this evening, in his drab-green tactical shirt and cargo shorts, was far from grizzly and old. His fair complexion reflected the light of the moon as he spoke. "So tell me, Detective Summers, what brings you way out here to these sticks? Is MSP now working with George Viola's defense team?"

"Not quite yet. Truth is, I'm a tad bit off the reservation right now, giving Viola's PIs a chance to explain why they think he's innocent."

"And what does the Mystery Light have to do with that?"

"You'd have to ask them; I got here just before you," Riley said, lying.

"The Light has everything to do with the defense theory we've put together," Roz replied.

The ranger smiled. "Is that right, Harlan? You're fully on board with her talk of ghosts?"

"Just tell him, Roz," Harlan said as he returned to his study of the distant notch on the horizon.

"I'm not the only person ever to suggest that something supernatural might be happening in these woods," Roz said, "and Stuart Lamar isn't either. Lots of folks have had sightings like the one he described—a vision of a red ember floating along the path this way that suddenly turns bright white and big, like the headlight of a train, when it gets close."

"All due respect," Ranger K replied, "but I think those folks are either making it up or imagining it. In fact, scientists who've studied the phenomenon have found the red orb to be nothing but the convergence of the taillights of a northbound car, driving away from this viewing area, on a stretch of highway about five miles off. And the white orb is just the opposite—the convergence of headlights on a southbound vehicle coming this way. So it's physically impossible to see a red orb coming at you from here, or to see an orb of any color— red or white—come up close to this spot because the source is so far away."

As the ranger was speaking, a white orb appeared before Harlan, wafting in the distant notch. "There it is," he said as it began a slow trek along the path, toward the viewing area. The others turned to watch it with him.

"There you go," Ranger K said. "Perfect timing. Now just watch. And for starters, note that this one is white, so it's the converging headlights of a southbound vehicle. And I'll tell you right now, it won't come anywhere near us or appear to get much larger than it is now."

They all watched silently for about two minutes until the orb disappeared.

"What did I tell you?" Ranger K said. "You don't even need scientific evidence to know that what you just saw were the headlights of a car."

"I don't disagree," Roz replied. "I'm sure that 99.9 percent of the time that's exactly what people see out here—lights from passing cars and trucks."

"And the other 0.1 percent of the time?" the ranger asked.

Roz held her gaze on the distant notch, choosing not to respond.

"Is that it?" Ranger K asked, turning to Harlan. "Does she really believe that Stuart Lamar had a one-out-of-a-thousand sighting of a ghost train?"

Harlan shrugged.

"Listen, Harlan," the ranger said, "I truly would like to help you with your case, especially after how you helped me with mine today. But if I'm catching her drift, she wants me to back her up on some cockamamie defense theory that would have Stuart Lamar learning the whereabouts of a dead body not from the guy who the cops say buried it out here—your client—but instead from the ghost of a long-gone train that she thinks was traipsing around these woods on the night it happened."

"That can't be true," Riley said, feigning alarm. "Roz, surely you're not suggesting that a ghost train was an eyewitness to the crime—are you?"

Roz nodded.

Ranger K laughed. "And you thought *you* were just a tad bit off the reservation, Detective Summers. I'll tell you what, if we were to treat her ghost story as even remotely possible, people would think we've gone completely rogue on this case and we'd end up being laughing stocks."

"Roz?" Riley pressed, her level of concern seeming to rise. "Please tell me this isn't so. In your defense of George Viola, you haven't gotten this desperate—have you?"

"I don't see it as desperate… or cockamamie. I just don't think what folks see out here is necessarily coming from motor vehicles all the time. Maybe once in a while they're seeing something else… like…"

"Okay," Ranger K chimed back in, his tone wary. "Let's just say for the moment that there is such a thing as ghosts, including train ghosts. Your theory still doesn't make sense because there have never been any train tracks out here. The path traveled by the Mystery Light is the remains of an old military road, not a railway. So you see, there never was a train that once upon a time ran down a railroad brakeman caught on the tracks—not out here anyway—which means there can't be a ghost of any such train out here nowadays."

"According to Lamar," Roz countered, "it's not trying to follow its old tracks. He says it has some other reason for coming here."

"Did he tell you the reason?"

"No. Apparently, the train never told him. But I think it may have something to do with the cars traveling that stretch of road—how their lights could be mistaken for something supernatural, and vice versa."

"Vice versa?" the ranger replied. "What's that supposed to mean?"

"Wait a second," Riley said. "I think I get it. She's saying that the ghost train chose this path *because of the car headlights visible along it*—and how they can serve as camouflage for the ghost train's headlight when it comes here."

"And what are *you* saying, Detective?" the ranger asked. "That you're starting to buy into this crazy idea?"

"No, I'm just saying that I now understand it… maybe."

"You do," Roz said. "Think about it. Suppose you're a supernatural being—or maybe an extraterrestrial one—who likes visiting this world, but you can't do so without manifesting yourself to humans as a floating orb, and you don't want to draw a lot of attention from humans. Where might you visit?"

At that moment there appeared another orb in the notch on the horizon, this one red, drifting into the distance.

"A place where you might be mistaken as something of this world," Riley said as she stepped close to the guardrail, staring down the path at the distant taillights.

"Oh please, Detective," Ranger K said, "don't tell me…"

Riley turned from the orb. "Then you tell me, Ranger K, what else could have compelled Stuart Lamar, half-dressed for winter weather, to hike down the path on the night he found the body? There's not a shred of evidence to suggest how he otherwise suspected something was out there that needed to be found before the spring melt."

"*Un-fucking-believable*," Ranger K replied. "You *are* buying this theory."

Harlan had been waiting for the right moment, and it was now. "So am I."

Ranger K wheeled around to face him. "No way. You too?"

"Why not, Kole? You of all people must admit, this *is* a place where things can be made to appear as something other than what they really are."

"What do you mean, *me of all people*?"

Harlan did not reply.

Ranger K looked back and forth between the red orb and his companions, until his gaze settled on Harlan. "Are you still talking about headlights and floating orbs?"

"You know what I'm talking about."

"I... I'm not sure I do."

"Oh yes you do, Kole. You know damn well I'm talking about the guy who buried Romanelli's body out there in the snow, expecting it not to be found until spring, degraded by the animals and elements, so that it could be mistaken for someone who had a skiing accident last winter."

Ranger K turned back to the horizon in time to see the red orb disappear. "Did you bring me out here tonight because you think that guy was me?"

Chapter 52

Harlan opened his cellphone to a screen that displayed Romanelli's fitness-app recording of the night he died, already cued up to the point where the GPS signal was about to turn onto Robbins Pond Road. He then held the phone between them, tapped play, and studied the ranger as he watched.

"What is this?" the ranger asked.

"I think you know," Harlan replied. "In fact, I think you considered the possibility of Romanelli's cellphone transmitting a signal like this, which is why you destroyed the phone as soon as you discovered it on his person, as we'll soon see when the signal dies right here where we're standing."

When the recording ended, Harlan asked, "Did you notice what *did not* happen after the GPS signal turned onto Robbins Pond Road and continued coming this way?"

The ranger glanced back toward the turnoff but did not answer.

"You told me a little while ago, Kole, that you don't specifically recall blocking the road with your chain that night. I take it you also don't specifically recall later finding your chain to have been damaged or tampered with."

Harlan let the point sink in before adding, "So the chain was removed beforehand by someone able to unlock it without incident."

"But... what makes you think that person was me?" the ranger asked. "My lock is old and simple. Anyone could have picked it."

Riley stepped close to them. "Because the driver called his accomplice in advance to arrange for that assistance," she said, showing the ranger a copy of certain phone records she had obtained with a search warrant issued the day before. She had highlighted the record of a call made on the night of March 12 to a number the ranger no doubt recognized. "He called you," she added.

The ranger gazed back and forth between the phone record and Harlan's cellphone, which still displayed the frozen image of the GPS signal's last transmission. In all likelihood, he was mentally rewinding that transmission, Harlan imagined.

"So, the whole course of the body's movements that night was recorded," the ranger said, "going all the way back to the moment Romanelli was run down by…"

The ranger looked up from Harlan's cellphone. "And that's how you pinned it on Rayden Jude… and why she pulled his phone records from that night."

"Truth is," Harlan replied, "I don't know what I've pinned on Jude. I just know he did it, and you helped him hide it. But just what it was—an accident or murder—I honestly don't know."

"So that's your real reason for bringing me out here tonight. To see if I might answer that question."

"Yes, it is."

"Why should I, assuming I could?"

"Because like I said back at the tavern, Kole, you still owe me. And because I think I know you, the kind of person you are. You made a mistake, a big one, and I think you've been wanting to come clean on it for a long time, especially after it led to George Viola's arrest for a murder he never committed. Why else would you have already helped me on his case as much as you have?"

Another white orb appeared in the distant notch on the horizon and began its slow, undulating journey toward them along the power line right-of-way. Ranger K seemed mesmerized by it as he spoke.

"Jude was panicked when he called that night. He said he got into an accident. Ran over a guy who came out of nowhere, he said, right in front of his truck, and he was sure he was dead. Of course, I knew he should have called the authorities, and I told him so. But he said no way. He'd get fired from the county road crew, he said, and he was not about to let this guy cost him another job. That's when he told me who the guy was—Zach Romanelli, the shyster lawyer whose tax loophole decimated the county budget and cost him and me our jobs as deputies. And that's what started changing my mind. I'm thinking, the son of a bitch is already dead, and it was an accident. What difference would it make if we made it look like a different kind of accident?"

"So that's it," Harlan said. "You just decided, why not? Jude was your friend and former partner, and the dead guy had already messed up his life enough."

Ranger K continued staring ahead at the orb as it floated toward them along the path. "I get it, Harlan. It's like you said, I made a big mistake. I realized that as soon as Jude dropped the body here and I got a look at Romanelli's face. I remember thinking, even this schmuck must have family somewhere who will wonder where he is and will need closure."

"Is that why you buried him close to the path, just beneath the snowpack, rather than further into the woods and underground?"

The ranger nodded. "The plan was also just like you said. I thought he might be discovered by someone using the path, maybe a hiker or cyclist, but not until after the spring melt, when the forensics would be compromised and the best explanation would be that he died in the woods from a skiing accident or ATV hit and run."

"And, of course, that explanation would have been especially forthcoming," Harlan said, "from the ranger who'd likely be the first responder here in the forest's Watersmeet District. But you couldn't explain things that way when you were called out here prematurely as a result of Stuart Lamar's strangely motivated search, which turned up a body still packed in snow and freshly stained with beet juice that had been sprayed on roads miles away."

The orb disappeared but Ranger K's stare remained fixed on the distant horizon. "Believe it or not, I didn't even realize there was beet juice all over the body when I buried it that night. The high winds must have reduced its usual stench, and in the dark, the stains looked like blood. Thing is, those stains have staying power, so I'm not sure my plan would have worked even if the body hadn't been discovered until spring."

"What are you saying, Kole? That you and Jude would have been found out if George Viola hadn't confessed to stalking Romanelli the same night?"

"Maybe. Who knows?"

"So, George Viola may have done you a huge favor."

"I don't see it that way. If anything, he made things a lot worse for me."

"How so?"

"What do you think, Harlan? That I want to see an innocent man convicted of murder because of my cover-up?"

"If you feel so bad about it, why the hell haven't you said anything until now? The man's been in county lockup for two weeks, tormented first by not knowing if he was innocent, and then by not knowing how to prove he is. You could have stopped his prosecution in its tracks."

"You have no idea how badly I wanted to do that. I was tormented, too, from the moment I found out about Viola's arrest. I met with Rayden Jude straightaway and told him what we needed to do... how we needed to, you know, come clean about..."

Ranger K stared at the blank horizon, unable or unwilling to complete his thought.

"Come clean about what?" Harlan asked.

"You know, about the... accident."

"And what did Jude say?"

Ranger K's breathing shifted from his nose to his mouth, emitting a greater volume of steam into the chilly evening air. This heavier breathing, Harlan imagined, probably coincided with an increasing heart rate. There was more to the story of this alleged *accident*, Harlan could tell.

"Tell me, Kole. What did Jude say?"

***

"Is that what you still think, partner? That it was just an accident?"

It was the day after George Viola's arrest for murder, and Rayden Jude had come to the Ottawa National Forest Visitor Center at the behest of Ranger K, who had learned about the arrest only an hour ago from another visitor, Sheriff Jake Mills. The sheriff had dropped in earlier, unannounced, to ask some follow-up questions in light of Viola's seeming confession the night before. The questions, which focused on Stuart Lamar's demeanor on the night he reported his discovery of the body to the ranger, were based on an errant assumption that if Lamar did not learn of the body's location from a ghost, he must have learned of it from the supposed killer, Viola.

Ranger K had kept the visitor center closed since his meeting with the sheriff, and he and Jude were now inside alone, standing on opposite sides of the circular information counter, Jude on the outside and the ranger enclosed within.

"I'll be damned," Jude said as he rested his elbows on the counter. "Look at you. You really do still believe that I just happened to accidentally run down the son of a bitch who blew up our careers."

Ranger K could feel his heart pounding harder and faster. "Wh-what are you... s-saying, Rayden? That you were stalking him too? And ran him down in cold blood?"

"There you go, partner. It's about time you woke up and smelled the denial you've been wallowing in."

"But... but—"

"But nothing, man. Just look at us right now: you, locked inside your little information booth in your Boy Scout uniform; and me, shoveling asphalt into potholes and cleaning up roadside litter—like some fucking convict on the chain gang. You're damn right I stalked and killed the bastard who did this to us. So what? Doesn't change anything *you* did."

"Like hell, Rayden. You made me an accessory after the fact to murder."

Jude laughed. "You must've forgotten our Crim Law class back at the academy, partner. You can't be an accessory after the fact to a crime unless you know about the crime, and apparently you don't—or didn't at the time you accessorized it. Of course, you'd have to convince the jury of your naiveté, Mr. Ranger K."

"What are you talking about. What jury?"

"I'm just yanking your chain, Kole. This thing's never coming back on us, not if it's true what you're saying about this jealous, gun-toting husband stalking Romanelli that same night. Talk about a break. Man, that dude gave us a huge one."

"That wasn't supposed to be *good* news, Rayden. He's an innocent man who now stands falsely accused because of us. We can't let him go down for a murder he didn't commit."

"Really? You say that like there's something we can do about it."

"Well… there is."

"Oh, I see. Now you want to come clean about what we did and try to prove to the jury that you're not an accessory to murder after the fact."

"No, Rayden, that's not what I'm suggesting. Nobody has to know you murdered Romanelli. We can still say it was an accident… and still get Viola off the hook."

Jude shook his head. "What's happened to the smart deputy I once thought you were? At this point, I'm not even sure you could convince anyone that we did it, by accident or otherwise, not with what this Viola dude confessed to doing that night. And even if we could prove ourselves guilty of concealing an accident, that's still a felony—obstruction of justice—which would still land us in the joint, locked down with other felons who hate ex-cops. No, that's not for me. I won't admit anything. And I swear, if you do, I'll bury you a hell of a lot deeper than you buried that fucking lawyer."

"What are you threatening?"

"Use your imagination, Kole. Who had it all worked out to look like something it wasn't—an accident—in *your* forest, off *your* access road, where *you'd* be the first responder? And then *you're* going to tell the sheriff what? That some other dude ran the guy down accidentally? How will that work out for you if the other dude has no idea what you're talking about?"

"Maybe not so well."

"And maybe that's putting it mildly, especially if it were to come back on *me* as what it actually was. Because in that case, I'll most definitely be pointing at you, saying the whole thing was your idea. You were the brains of the criminal enterprise, and I was your pawn. I swear, Kole, if this thing ever goes south, I will become your worst nightmare."

***

As Ranger K wrapped up the account, he turned his back on the biggest and brightest display of the Mystery Light thus far that evening, produced apparently by the high beams of an oversized vehicle. "It's like Jude set me up from the beginning. Nobody will ever believe me now if I say I didn't know he stalked and killed Romanelli."

"I do," Harlan said, "but only because I think I know you. The way you put your life on the line for me, knowing that I was closing in on the truth… and the way you've worked with me, including the shot you gave me at Rayden Jude that day at that moose mineral lick. It's like you wanted me to find out and tell the world."

"I appreciate what you're saying, for whatever good it might do me to have a mobster PI on my side."

"You don't need anyone on your side, Kole. What you need is evidence to back your story—proof that as between you and Rayden Jude, he's the real bad guy."

"How am I supposed to get that at this point?"

Harlan smiled. "Well, geez, haven't I taught you anything?"

Chapter 53

Roz, Riley, Harlan, and Ranger K were still at the Mystery Light viewing area, the ranger now wearing handcuffs that Riley had applied.

"Let me see your cellphone," Harlan said.

The ranger raised his cuffed hands. "It's in my back pocket. The password is 'lone ranger,' all caps with no space."

Harlan raised his eyebrows.

The ranger shrugged. "What can I say?"

After unlocking the device, Harlan continued tapping on the screen, first to initiate its audio recorder and then to place a phone call. As the call went through, he put the phone on speaker and held it in front of the ranger.

"Kole Koerber! To what do I owe the pleasure, man?"

"Hi Rayden. How you doing?"

"Me? Same ole, same ole. How about you—Mr. Defender of Bears?"

"Oh, you heard about that."

"Heard about it? Are you kidding? Everyone in town's talking about you taking down those big-game poachers in the wee hours of the morning. Makes me proud to have been your partner back in the day."

"Why thanks, Rayden. I appreciate you saying that."

"And I get a kick out of who's become your new partner."

"You mean Harlan Holmes?"

"Of course I do. Be honest, you must see some irony in him teaming up with you on your poacher case, given the reason he struggles with his own case, if you know what I mean."

"I guess I do." The ranger laughed briefly before adding, "Just following the old advice to keep your friends close and your enemies closer."

"Hah! Listen to you. It's about time I hear you say something like that, Kole, after the way you set me up to meet that nosey PI. Gives me some assurance about whose side you're on."

"Well, don't start getting too comfortable. I'm not calling with good news."

Jude sighed. "All right, what's wrong now?"

"My new friend may still become a problem for us. He's been pestering me again to arrange another meeting with you for more questioning about his case."

"Why? What questions?"

"The kind that make me nervous. Like how you took to being laid off by the sheriff. And what your thoughts were about the tax attorney who made that happen."

"Why the hell would he be asking questions like that? What have you told him?"

"I haven't told him shit. But he's obviously gotten suspicious of you."

"How?"

"I don't know. But I have a hunch."

Harlan raised his hand, directing the ranger to pause for a moment.

"Well?" Jude said. "What do you think he's up to?"

Harlan waited a little longer before lowering his hand.

"You don't really want to talk about this right now, Rayden, do you? Over the phone like this?"

"Just tell me, dammit."

"Well, okay. Do you remember me telling you about the thing I found that night after you left, when I searched... you know... the guy?"

"Are you talking about the cellphone you found on Romanelli's body?"

"Shit, Rayden, we're on fucking cellphones ourselves right now. Watch what you say."

"Just tell me. What about his cellphone?"

"The dude was a fanatic about cross-country skiing. So when I saw his phone, it got me to thinking about how he might have one of those GPS programs going on it—you know, one of those fitness apps that tracks you when you're hiking, or running, or whatever. I told you about it later—how I destroyed the phone and ditched it, but that I was still worried about it. Don't you remember?"

"All I remember is you telling me about the cellphone. Not this thing about a possible GPS app. Do you think your PI friend found something like that?"

"He was asking specifically about one of your road crew's routes—Route Two he called it—and if you ever drove any of the plow trucks yourself while supervising the crew."

The sound of a deep breath came through the phone's speaker. "So he's learned a little about my job. That doesn't mean he has a case against me. Shit, he's still working for a client who's all but convicted himself of the murder. He's just casting around for whatever he can stir up, I'm sure."

"Maybe so. But I've worked with this guy. He's nobody's fool. I think we should meet with him again and see if we can get a line on what he thinks he's got."

"Meet with him again? Are you fucking out of your mind, Kole? Making that mistake once was enough. Don't even think about doing it again."

"It was no mistake then, Rayden. And it's not now. There *is* something to keeping your enemies close. Maybe he'll say something to tip his hand."

"He's got no hand, man. If he did, so would the sheriff, and I haven't heard nothing from him but a few questions he had about the beet-juice program. No, Holmes doesn't have shit. The guy's still fishing, I'm telling you. Same as he was when he came at me before for the names of my crew to check if any of them might have seen something that night. What a crock. He's desperate, that's all. Grasping at straws."

"I'm telling you, Rayden, don't underestimate this guy. He's got you or someone on your crew in his sights. I can tell. And I don't like it."

"You worry too much, Kole."

"And maybe you don't worry enough."

When Jude did not respond, Harlan raised his hand again, signaling for the ranger to prolong the pause. The lull continued. Jude *was* worrying about it, Harlan thought. And that might help provoke a strong reaction to what Ranger K would propose next.

Harlan lowered his hand.

"You know," Ranger K continued, "if we're not going to meet with Holmes about this, maybe we should give some thought to another way to get out in front of him."

"What do you have in mind?"

"I think you know, Rayden. We've talked about it before."

"What? Are you back to what I think you are?"

"Yes, I am. We still have time to confess to it being an accident and beat Holmes to the punch before he comes out with whatever he might have."

"No way, Kole. You already know what I think of that lame idea. And you're a damn fool if you think I'll ever change my mind about it. Twice the fool."

"What do you mean, *twice*?"

A derisive snort came through the cellphone speaker. Following it, Jude said, "Do you really need to be reminded of the first time, when I called you in the middle of the night, in the middle of my route, and told you about my *accident*, and how the guy I ran down *just happened to be* the same guy who ruined our lives?"

"No, Rayden, you don't have to remind me. I remember it all too well. Thing is, I believed what you said."

"I'm sure you did. That's why I called you—the *Boy Scout* that you are. I knew you'd buy it."

There was another pause, this one initiated by the ranger without a prompt. He had just gotten the admission he needed from the mark and was considering whether to tell him, Harlan imagined.

"You know, Rayden, you're right. I *am* a Boy Scout. Or at least I was one *that* night. But I'm not one tonight."

"What's that supposed to mean?"

"Just something I've learned from my dealings with Detective Holmes."

"Oh yeah, and what would that be?"

Ranger K smiled at Harlan before replying, "How to become the poacher."

Chapter 54

The next morning, Harlan returned Riley and Phoenix to the Gateway Lodge's grass airstrip for a flight back to their respective hometowns of Traverse City and Chicago. Roz had joined them and rode shotgun in the Jeep.

Waiting when they arrived was a twin-engine prop plane and a teenaged kid in a polo shirt and khakis who stood by a set of stairs extending from the plane's fuselage. The kid directed Harlan to pull his Jeep up close. "Allow me to get your bag, sir," he said when Phoenix opened his door.

Phoenix paused before stepping out. "Well, Pops, I guess this is goodbye."

Harlan thought better than to reply with something like, *see you later*, knowing how Roz would feel about even a hint of any future adventures with him. "You take care, Son," he said instead. "And please, when you get back to Chicago, try not to embellish too much the story of our dealings with those poachers."

"Who, me? John Barron Junior? The chip off the old block? What could possibly make you think that I might tell the guys back home anything but the unadulterated truth?"

"I'm just saying, if you make it sound like too much fun, you're bound to upset the guy who was supposed to play your role."

"You mean Tank Lochner? Listen, man, if I could stand my ground when that seven-hundred-pound black bear decided it was time to come down outta that tree, I can deal with him."

"I doubt even that bear could deal with him when he's pissed off."

Riley seemed to be hanging back, waiting for Phoenix to leave, before sharing her parting thoughts. She caught Harlan's eye in the rearview mirror. "I spoke with the captain this morning, Harlan. He wanted a full account of what happened here in advance of my written report."

"What'd you tell him?"

"Why, the unadulterated truth, of course."

"How did he respond?"

"He was impressed, but not surprised. You're good at what you do, Harlan. Always have been. In fact, he was so impressed, he intends to recommend that MSP offer you a job."

Harlan and Roz both spun around in their seats to face Riley directly. "Did I hear you right?" Harlan asked. "The captain wants me back on the force?"

"Harlan!" Roz shouted. "Don't get so excited. You and I have a conversation to finish before you start exploring the possibility of taking on any more detective work. That was the deal we made before taking Viola's case. Remember?"

"But Roz, if MSP thinks I still have what it takes…"

Roz's stare cut him short.

"Actually," Riley continued, "MSP does *not* think you have what it takes anymore."

This confused him. "But you just said…"

"What I said was that I told the captain the truth—all of it, Harlan—including what I saw when you prepped yourself for the operation in the field. I was right there with you in your camper, remember? I watched what you and Roz did to make your body barely functional for fieldwork. All the pain pills you had to take. The topical gel and knee braces you had to use. I saw all of that. And I told the captain about it, in addition to how you saved an innocent black bear, brought down those poachers, and then used the leverage provided by that bust to get a confession out of Ranger K in connection with the Romanelli murder case."

Harlan was still confused. "Then, what kind of offer does the captain have in mind?"

Riley looked at Roz. "Is it okay if I tell him? I promise not to accept any decision he makes until after your conversation."

Roz nodded. "I appreciate that."

"The idea," Riley said, "is to have MSP retain you as an independent consultant for homicide investigations. It's not a field position, Harlan. You'd provide consulting services to detectives like me, throughout the state, who are in the field. Most of your work would be done behind a desk at state headquarters in Lansing. And of course you'd have to give up your PI practice to avoid conflicts of interest."

Harlan could see Roz's expression ease at Riley's last remark. "What about my partner?" he asked. "Would she be on retainer too?"

"I imagine that could be worked out," Riley answered. "I could certainly get behind that after seeing her work."

The plane's propellers began turning, and the kid approached the Jeep, shouting over the rising roar of the twin engines, "Whoever else is coming needs to board now!"

As they watched the plane depart, Roz reached over and took Harlan's hand. "I appreciate you asking her if the MSP job offer included me."

"Well, we're partners. Whatever the decision may be about our next chapter, we're writing it together."

"Then you should know that I'm not too keen on the offer."

"Why?"

"Because Lansing is five hundred miles from where I've decided I want to live."

"Are you saying what I think you are? That you want to stay here? In the western UP?"

Roz glanced around at their surroundings. "What can I say? It feels like home to me... again."

"But what would we do way the heck up here in the middle of nowhere?"

"Well, I guess we'd make ourselves a new home, and do as the Yoopers do."

"You mean spend our twilight years traipsing around the woods hunting, fishing, and the like?"

"Sounds perfect to me."

"But I can't spend the rest of my life just messing around. You know me, Roz. I need to have a job—something productive to do."

"I know you do, and I have a thought about a job that would fit nicely with our new outdoorsy lifestyle. It came to me when we turned Ranger K over to the sheriff last night."

"What did?"

"That the US Forest Service is going to need a new ranger for the Watersmeet District, and that their ideal candidate would be someone with law enforcement background that includes policing the northern woods—someone like you, Harlan, an ex-cop who just saved countless animals from the threat posed by a ruthless band of poachers operating in the district."

"Seriously, Roz? That's how you'd have me finish my career in law enforcement? As a forest ranger?"

"Why not?"

"Because I saw what that job entails while working with Ranger K. The guy spent most of his time at the visitor center talking to tourists and handing out maps. Hell, he was more of a helpdesk employee than a cop."

"I think your focus is too narrow, Harlan."

"What do you mean?"

"All you see right now is a guy stuck behind an information counter in a green shirt and cargo shorts, dealing with tourists. But there's a bigger picture. Much bigger. There's a million-acre forest surrounding that visitor center, and he's the sole law enforcement officer for over a third of it—the entire Watersmeet District. That makes him a lot more than just a helpdesk employee. And considering the unique circumstances in that district, he's more than just a forest ranger."

"What circumstances?"

"You know, those created by the local budgetary crisis, which has left Watersmeet devoid of local law-enforcement resources, and which, in turn, makes the town more reliant on outside agencies, including the United States Forest Service."

Harlan smiled. "You make it sound like Kole Koerber's cellphone password actually described the man's situation—a 'lone ranger' patrolling the lawless frontier."

"That's not quite how I'd describe it."

"Then what are you trying to say?"

Roz returned a smile. "Do you remember the sign at the Watersmeet Plaza, Harlan? I think it best describes what you would be if you took on the job of policing these remote northern woods."

He thought for a moment before responding.

"A Nimrod?"

About the Author

John Marks is an attorney in mid-Michigan who serves as legal counsel to lawmakers at the state capitol. When not on his day job, John writes murder mysteries set in some of his favorite places in Michigan. John's stories draw on his extensive travels throughout the state and the many lessons he has learned as a practicing attorney and professor of law at Western Michigan University.

Note from the Author

Word-of-mouth is crucial for any author to succeed. If you enjoyed *Rail Against Injustice*, please leave a review online—anywhere you are able. Even if it's just a sentence or two. It would make all the difference and would be very much appreciated.

Thanks!
John Marks

We hope you enjoyed reading this title from:

www.blackrosewriting.com

Subscribe to our mailing list – *The Rosevine* – and receive **FREE** books, daily deals, and stay current with news about upcoming releases and our hottest authors.
Scan the QR code below to sign up.

Already a subscriber? Please accept a sincere thank you for being a fan of Black Rose Writing authors.

View other Black Rose Writing titles at
www.blackrosewriting.com/books and use promo code
PRINT to receive a **20% discount** when purchasing.

www.ingramcontent.com/pod-product-compliance
Lightning Source LLC
Chambersburg PA
CBHW010727100726
47899CB00009B/2951